Robert Louis Stevenson
Interviews and Recollections

MACMILLAN INTERVIEWS AND RECOLLECTIONS

Morton N. Cohen (*editor*)
LEWIS CARROLL

Philip Collins (*editor*)
DICKENS (2 vols)
THACKERAY (2 vols)

A. M. Gibbs (*editor*)
SHAW

J. R. Hammond (*editor*)
H. G. WELLS

David McLellan (*editor*)
KARL MARX

E. H. Mikhail (*editor*)
THE ABBEY THEATRE
BRENDAN BEHAN (2 vols)
JAMES JOYCE
SHERIDAN
GOLDSMITH

Harold Orel (*editor*)
KIPLING (2 vols)
SIR ARTHUR CONAN DOYLE
GILBERT AND SULLIVAN

Norman Page (*editor*)
BYRON
HENRY JAMES
DR JOHNSON
D. H. LAWRENCE (2 vols)
TENNYSON

Martin Ray (*editor*)
JOSEPH CONRAD

J. H. Stape (*editor*)
E. M. FORSTER
VIRGINIA WOOLF

R. C. Terry (*editor*)
TROLLOPE
ROBERT LOUIS STEVENSON

ROBERT LOUIS STEVENSON

Interviews and Recollections

Edited by

R. C. TERRY

MACMILLAN

ISBN 978-0-333-65099-8   ISBN 978-1-349-24355-6 (eBook)
DOI 10.1007/978-1-349-24355-6

Selection and editorial matter © R. C. Terry 1996
Reprint of the original edition 1996

All rights reserved. No reproduction, copy or transmission of
this publication may be made without written permission.

No paragraph of this publication may be reproduced, copied or
transmitted save with written permission or in accordance with
the provisions of the Copyright, Designs and Patents Act 1988,
or under the terms of any licence permitting limited copying
issued by the Copyright Licensing Agency, 90 Tottenham Court
Road, London W1P 9HE.

Any person who does any unauthorised act in relation to this
publication may be liable to criminal prosecution and civil
claims for damages.

First published 1996 by
MACMILLAN PRESS LTD
Houndmills, Basingstoke, Hampshire RG21 6XS
and London
Companies and representatives
throughout the world

ISBN 978-0-333-52394-0 hardcover
ISBN 978-0-333-65099-8 paperback

A catalogue record for this book is available
from the British Library.

10 9   8   7   6   5   4   3   2   1
05 04 03 02 01 00 99 98 97 96

For Roger and in memory of Ailsa

He lived to the topmost pulse... he never fails of the thing that we most love letters for, the full expression of the moment and the mood, the actual good or bad or middling, the thing in his head, his heart or his house.

Henry James, *Notes on Novelists*, 1914

Contents

List of Plates	ix
Acknowledgements	x
List of Abbreviations	xi
Introduction	xii
A Stevenson Chronology	xxx

INTERVIEWS AND RECOLLECTIONS

Smout's Favourite Occupation	*Margaret Stevenson*	1
A Taste for Adventurous Tales	*E. Blantyre Simpson*	6
'Cummy, I Was Just Telling Myself a Story!'		
Charles J. Guthrie		10
A Playmate beyond Compare	*Various*	14
Quick and Bright but Somewhat Desultory Scholar		
H. B. Baildon		20
I Have Seen a Young Poet	*E. M. Sellar*	24
A *Poseur*, Prone to Exaggerate Himself, Even to Himself		
Rosaline Masson		27
The Very Worst Ten Minutes I Ever Experienced		
Flora Masson		32
Delightfully and Fearlessly Boyish	*Margaret Black*	38
Edinburgh Ale and Cold Meat Pies	*Charles Lowe*	42
A Wonderful Talker	*George Lisle*	45
I Do Not Remember an Ill-natured Remark		
Charles J. Guthrie		49
As Restless and Questing as a Spaniel	*Edmund Gosse*	52
Sealed of the Tribe of Louis	*Andrew Lang*	57
A Touch of the Elfin and Unearthly	*Sidney Colvin*	62
The Best of All Good Times at Grez	*Isobel Field*	67
Industrious Idleness	*Will Low*	72

Study the Masters *Birge Harrison*	76
The Scotch Literary Mediocrity *Lloyd Osbourne*	81
The Silent and, Truth to Tell, Rather Dejected Youth *Alice Gordon*	85
Submerged in Billows of Bedclothes *Charles Warren Stoddard*	88
The Look as of the Ancient Mariner *Alexander Japp*	92
A Rather Odd, Exotic, Theatrical Kind of Man *Harold Vallings*	96
'You Must Never, Never Write Like That Again' *Adelaide Boodle*	100
Visiting Skerryvore *William and Charles Archer*	104
'Looks Like a Sooercide, Don't He, Sir?' *William Sharp*	111
Beside Himself with Anger *Lloyd Osbourne*	115
A Most Affectionate Observer *M. G. van Rensselaer and Jeanette L. Gilder*	118
Inventing One Project After Another *S. S. McClure*	122
Buffalo Coat and Indian Moccasins *Stephen Chalmers*	128
The Mannerly Stevenson *Charlotte Eaton*	134
As Good a Listener as He was a Talker *Sir Edmund Radcliffe Pears*	138
Always Eager for Excitement *T. M. MacCallum*	143
Everybody Felt Thoroughly at Home *H. J. Moors*	147
Writings as Pure as Possible *Sydney Press*	152
Queer Birds – Mighty Queer Ones Too *Henry Adams*	157
The Misspent Sunday *W. E. Clarke*	164
The Soul of a Peasant *Fanny Stevenson*	169
A Feast at Vailima *Marie Fraser*	174
Patriarchal Relations *Various*	178
Working Away Every Morning Like Steam-engines *Isobel Field*	185
Barley-sugar Effigy of a Real Man *W. E. Henley*	192
Whatever He Did He Did with His Whole Heart *Graham Balfour*	197
Called Home *Margaret Stevenson*	202
Suggestions for Further Reading	208
Index	210

List of Plates

1 Margaret Isabella Balfour Stevenson (*The Stevenson Museum, Edinburgh*)
2 Thomas Stevenson (*The Writers' Museum, Edinburgh*)
3 Alison Cunningham, Louis's nurse (*The Writers' Museum, Edinburgh*)
4 Louis and his father (*The Mansell Collection*)
5 Fanny Stevenson in the mid 1880s at Bournemouth (*The Mansell Collection*)
6 Mrs Isobel Strong (Belle) (*The Writers' Museum, Edinburgh*)
7 Lloyd Osbourne in 1888 at San Francisco (*The Writers' Museum, Edinburgh*)
8 RLS on board the Casco with King Kalakaua, Fanny, Lloyd and Margaret Stevenson (*The Writers' Museum, Edinburgh*)
9 Vailima, the Stevenson home, Samoa (*The Mansell Collection*)
10 Stevenson's family and household at Vailima in 1892, including his wife, mother, Belle and Lloyd (*The Mansell Collection*)
11 Fanny, Louis, Belle and Margaret Stevenson in 1893 at Sydney, Australia (*The Mansell Collection*)
12 RLS in Samoa (*The Mansell Collection*)

Acknowledgements

The editor and publisher wish to thank the following for permission to reproduce copyright-material:

Houghton Mifflin Co., New York, for the extracts from *Henry Adams and his Friends*, edited by Harold Dean Cater, copyright 1947, © renewed 1974 by Harold Dean Cater; all rights reserved.

Charles Neider, for the extracts from *Our Samoan Adventure by Fanny Van de Grift and Robert Louis Stevenson*, edited by Charles Neider (New York: Harper, 1955).

List of Abbreviations

Balfour, *Life*	Sir Graham Balfour, *The Life of Robert Louis Stevenson*, 2 vols (1901).
Baxter Letters	*RLS: Stevenson's Letters to Charles Baxter*, ed. DeLancey Ferguson and Marshall Waingrow (New Haven, Conn., 1956).
Bell	Ian Bell, *Robert Louis Stevenson: Dreams of Exile* (1992).
Calder	Jenni Calder, *RLS: A Life Study* (1980).
Furnas	J. C. Furnas, *Voyage to Windward: The Life of Robert Louis Stevenson* (1951).
Knight, *Treasury*	Alanna Knight, *The Robert Louis Stevenson Treasury* (1985).
Letters	Sidney Colvin, *The Letters of Robert Louis Stevenson to His Family and Friends*, 2 vols (1900).
McLynn	Frank McLynn, *Robert Louis Stevenson: A Biography* (1993).
Swearingen	Roger C. Swearingen, *The Prose Writings of Robert Louis Stevenson: A Guide* (1980).

Introduction

In the early summer of 1875, William Seed, a 48-year-old New Zealander collecting information for the development of more efficient lighthouses along his country's rugged coasts, went to Edinburgh to consult the most distinguished lighthouse engineer of his time, Thomas Stevenson, whose family had pioneered lighthouse construction for many generations.[1] They met several times to discuss winds, tides, currents and fine points of marine engineering, on one occasion at the Stevensons' comfortable Georgian house in Heriot Row. When the conversation turned to travel, Seed revealed that he had been to Samoa five years earlier, to report on trade in the islands for the New Zealand government. Robert Louis Stevenson, then 25, about to sit final Bar examinations at Edinburgh University, listened entranced to his father's guest. Well into the night he questioned Seed about native customs and traders in the Pacific, reporting to his soul-mate, Mrs Frances Sitwell:

> Awfully nice man here to-night. Public servant – New Zealand. Telling us all about the South Sea Islands till I was sick with desire to go there... Navigator's Island [sic] is the place; absolute balm for the weary. (*Letters*, I, 95)

That summer, anxious about the future, guilty about having abandoned the engineering career his father had planned for him – and more than half in love with Mrs Sitwell – Louis fled to France, to the artists' community at Barbizon and Grez-sur-Loing, where, one year later, he would meet another married woman, Fanny Vandegrift Osbourne, who was to become his wife.

These years, 1875 and 1876, were a time of crisis for Louis. Depression at wounding his parents by his loss of faith alternated with rage at their desire to turn him into a sober, respectable Edinburgh lawyer. Dedicated to letters, he longed for the bohemian life, another climate entirely, as he shows in a letter from Edinburgh in January 1876:

> the sun is gone out utterly; and the breath of the people of this

city lies about as a sort of damp, unwholesome fog, in which we go walking with bowed hearts... this damned weather weighs on me like a curse. (*Letters*, I, 113)

Mr Seed's visit so haunted him that he began to write a novel the following year to get it out of his system. *The Hair Trunk or The Ideal Commonwealth* would be about Cambridge friends who found a community in Navigators' Islands. It was unfinished.

Some 15 years later, Louis wrote from Sydney to a friend that Seed had told him he had no business staying in Europe, that he would find all that was good for him in the Navigators' Islands:

And I resisted: I refused to go so far from my father and mother. O, it was virtuous, and O, wasn't it silly! But my father, who was always my dearest, got to his grave without that pang; and now in 1890, I (or what is left of me) go at last to the Navigators' Islands. God go with us! It is but a Pisgah sight when all is said; I go there only to grow old and die; but when you come, you will see it is a fair place for the purpose. (*Letters*, II, 201)

The Seed story provides a central theme of these reminiscences: the struggles of an exile from his homeland and the burdens of an artist's isolation. John Fowles has drawn parallels between the artist's role and the quest among reef, rock and uncharted shore: 'the only answer to the mysteries of life lies in the voyage to the islands'. The Homeric archetype fits Stevenson's life story. As one contemporary noted:

Stevenson is by native instinct and temperament a rover – a lover of adventure, of strange bye-ways, errant tracts... He would fain, like Ulysses, be at home in foreign lands, making acquaintance with outlying races.[2]

The condition though remains as in Tennyson's poem, one of eternal restlessness and exile. Commentators have seized upon the *topoi* of open seas and landfalls to explain Louis's quest for health and wholeness in mind, body and art (as is reflected in the titles of biographies such as J. C. Furnas's *Voyage to Windward*, and, more recently, Ian Bell's *Robert Louis Stevenson: Dreams of Exile*).

Stevenson's adventuring embodies the voyage archetype. The potential dismasting of the yacht *Casco* and his sailing into places of storm and shipwreck, like the treacherous Moorea channel off Tahiti – not the only time the Stevensons came close to drowning – evoke a latter-day *Odyssey*. Louis constantly draws on nautical imagery to describe his drained and puny frame after the recurrent haemorrhages which plagued his life: 'The wreck was towed into port yesterday', he wrote to his mother in October 1882, and in February 1884 he senses 'the creak of Caron's rowlocks and the miasma of the Styx'. The well-known lines of 'Requiem' express calm and home-coming, but also evoke disturbance and point to another journey. Such unrest and ambiguity, the contrary state to home-coming, is sounded in *Songs of Travel*, especially in the lines written at Tahiti in November 1888:

> Home no more home to me, whither shall I wander?
> Hunger my driver, I go where I must...

At the time of his death Stevenson journeyed once more in mind and spirit to Scotland for his novel *Weir of Hermiston*, which, though incomplete, is judged by some to be his masterpiece. Stevenson's cultural situation finally becomes that condition described by Edward Said in *Culture and Imperialism*:

> Exile is predicated on the existence of, love for, and a real bond with one's native place; the universal truth of exile is not that one has lost that love of home, but that inherent in each is an unexpected, unwelcome loss.

Another vital factor is his phthisic separateness and consciousness of the body's exile. This is what enabled him (again Said's words come to mind) 'to regard experiences... as if they were about to disappear'.[3]

Stevenson's life revolves around the ambiguities of exile. Psychic disruptions and realignments common to late adolescence hit Louis hard, producing the rebellious antics described in early sections of this book. Thomas Stevenson, 'brooding over the waves, counting them, noting their least deflection' on one of their forlorn summer trips on the northern coasts in 1871, accepted that whatever Louis did he would not continue the family tradition of maritime engineering. Later in a poem Louis pondered this defection:

> Say not of me that weakly I declined
> The labours of my sires and fled the sea,
> The towers we founded and the lamps we lit,
> To play at home with paper like a child.
> (*Underwoods*, 1887)

His law studies, a sop to family pride, were even more perfunctory and the split in Louis's psyche more decisive. He threw himself into that other life of Edinburgh, its wynds, howffs and harlots. The soubriquet 'Velvet Coat', after his favourite jacket, is said to have been familiar in low-life taverns. 'In the coiled perplexities of youth', with his cousin Bob Stevenson and other free spirits, Baxter, Ferrier, Simpson, he caroused and debated at their tavern club, the LJR (Liberty, Justice, Reverence), formed 'to disregard everything our parents have taught us'. It was, after all, only what Coleridge and friends had done as students, writing revolutionary slogans in gunpowder on the lawns of Trinity, but to Thomas Stevenson reading the constitution of the LJR, it was anathema – blasphemy, indeed – and he was deeply grieved that Louis had lost his faith. Louis wrote:

> What a damned curse I am to my parents! As my father said, 'You have rendered my whole life a failure.' As my mother said, 'This is the heaviest affliction that has ever befallen me.'
> (*Baxter Letters*, 24)

It was a decisive moment, marking the beginning of his wandering and self-discovery. For the next few years Louis kept on the move in Britain and Europe, by boat, train, buggy, on foot, donkey and horseback. Then, in 1879, he embarked for America and Fanny Osbourne. Like D. H. Lawrence, a generation or so later, he soon knew the price of emigration and its meaning:

> Emigration has to be done before we climb the vessel; an aim in life is the only fortune worth the finding; and it is not to be found in foreign lands, but in the heart itself. (*The Amateur Emigrant*, 1895)

This of course raises a paradox which Chesterton resolves in his delightful way by seeing Louis's wanderings, temporary domiciles and wanderings anew, as a double process of risk and protection, of health, self and artistic freedom. It hardly needed the strong colours of the tropics to bring out the sharp outline of word and image in *Treasure Island*, but on the other hand, Stevenson's own leaky vessel needed the white coral shores and the velvet nights of Samoa, as he was well aware. Friends like James and Meredith were forever begging him to return to London to benefit his art, but Mr Seed from New Zealand had set Louis on the right course. The best of his life and some of his best work came from that point of disequilibrium and ambiguous settlement in the Pacific, as later reminiscences in this volume suggest.

When Louis left Edinburgh for the last time in the summer of 1887 he set his course not only towards health, but towards freedom and new art. His departure was witnessed by Flora Masson. As she walked along Princes Street with a friend, an open cab passed on its way to the railway station; a slender, loose-garbed figure stood up and waved a wide-brimmed hat:

'Good-bye!' he called to us – 'Good-bye!'... The cab passed. The grey vista of our Northern Capital, the long line of Princes Street, was at its very best as Louis Stevenson looked back at it and us, over the back of the open cab, still waving his hat and calling 'Good-bye!'[4]

On 22 August the Stevensons boarded the *Ludgate Hill* for New York, and onward to islands from Hawaii to Samoa. The change in Louis's health was remarkable from the time the Silver Ship (*Casco*), sailed out of San Francisco harbour; and the wanderings through the South Sea Islands produce some of his best letters, in which consciousness of exile and new promise are key elements. From Honolulu, to Henry James, he writes: 'to draw near to a new island, I cannot say how much I like' (*Letters*, II, 141); to Colvin: 'we have all a taste for this wandering and dangerous life' (ibid., 143); and to Adelaide Boodle: 'I own we are deserters, but we have excuses. You cannot conceive how these climates agree with the wretched house-plant of Skerryvore.... the interest of the islands is endless; and the sea, though I own it is a fearsome place, is very delightful' (ibid., 147). Regrets and nostalgia accompany his pleasure, and may well have deepened his artistic sensibility. To James Payn he insists:

This climate; these voyagings; these landfalls at dawn; new islands peaking from the morning bank; new forested harbours; new passing alarms of squalls and surf; new interests of gentle natives, – the whole tale of my life is better to me than any poem. (*Letters*, II, 160)

To Colvin once more he vows: 'I will never leave the sea... Life is far better fun than people dream who fall asleep among the chimney stacks and telegraph wires' (ibid., 162–3). Samoa finally captured him. By 1890 he was confirmed in his role of 'a wandering voice... from recondite islands', he and Fanny surrendering to 'their outlandish destinies' (ibid., 198), the promise of more intense work to come. To Henry James he explains:

These last two years I have been much at sea, and I have *never wearied*; sometimes I have indeed grown impatient for some destination; more often I was sorry that the voyage drew so early to an end; and never once did I lose my fidelity to blue water and a ship. It is plain then, that for me my exile to the place of schooners and islands can be in no sense regarded as a calamity. (*Letters*, II, 196)

In such manner did Louis chart the future course of his life.

The divisions and contradictions of Louis's youth might suggest an unstable person wracked by psychic strains, but in fact Stevenson struck his contemporaries as wonderfully whole despite his ravaged body. Consistent throughout these recollections is a man at ease with himself and the world, agreeable, tolerant, boyishly enthusiastic, delightful to be with, a strong-souled individual with great zest for living. It is an agreeable irony that such an integrated personality gave the world the ultimate symbol of fissured human nature in *Dr Jekyll and Mr Hyde*. Biographers have speculated on the sources of this artistic sense of divided souls found in other novels, such as *The Master of Ballantrae*, and have found them in the Scots experience and Edinburgh itself, a city of old and new, progressive and conservative, Calvinist and Jacobite. His parents' mutual content also produced in the cosseted child a curious sense of insecurity and displacement. Louis wrote to Frances Sitwell: 'the children of lovers are orphans'. Despite the attention of his loving nurse, Alison Cunningham, the 'Cummy' to whom he dedicated *A Child's Garden of Verses*, the 'small sickly prince', as Colvin called him, could not, it appears, get enough attention and love.

The relationship with his father, that trojan of a man, forever shelling out and being rebuffed, was strange and painful. Alexander Japp gave a sensitive account of Thomas Stevenson, and few recollections of father and son squaring up before an audience are more eloquent than Flora Masson's. Louis accused himself many times of disloyalty and ingratitude towards his father and he had a dream about him, striking enough to be reported to Adelaide Boodle a few months before he died:

> He now haunts me, strangely enough, in two guises; as a man of fifty, lying on a hillside and carving mottoes on a stick, strong and well; and as a younger man running down the sands into the sea near North Berwick, myself – *aetat* 11 – somewhat horrified at finding him so beautiful when stripped!
> (*Letters*, II, 343)

Consistency in accounts of Louis's figure and personality is striking. Most people wondered how the walking skeleton kept such life in him, and invariably spoke of his attenuated frame (he was 5 feet 10 inches tall) and spectral aspect (he weighed about 120 pounds). When C. W. Stoddard visited him in Monterey prior to his marriage, he found him 'submerged in billows of bedclothes ... of the frailest physique, though most unaccountably tenacious of life ... unfleshly to the verge of emaciation'. According to Lloyd Osbourne, his hair was light brown; he was the blond northern type in Birge Harrison's opinion. The long hair in so many pictures, sometimes described as 'lank locks', was thought to give some protection from colds and hacking coughs which inevitably brought on haemorrhages. After a visit from 'Bluidy Jack' his face was gaunt and sallow, but at sea and in Samoa he could be 'ruddy-complexioned' and sun-burned. A picture from the last year of his life shows him with well-trimmed hair and moustache.

Everyone was drawn to his eyes, variously described as luminous, blazing, brilliant, flashing, clear, glorious, wistful and impish. His eyes, said Harry Moors, 'seemed to penetrate you like the eyes of a mesmerist'; Andrew Lang saw 'a sort of uncommon celerity in changing expression'; 'I have seldom seen eyes further apart', wrote Jeannette Gilder, a view others confirm. The effect was of radiance and animation, enhanced by rapid gesture and movement. His long, tapered fingers are often mentioned. Charlotte Eaton noted their 'marble whiteness', except for the nicotine-stained first finger and thumb of his right hand. Eve Blantyre Simpson said that he talked with his hands, 'shrugging his shoulders absurdly like some typical stage Frenchman'. Meeting him for the first time M. G. van Rensselaer was struck by the 'quick cordiality of his greeting'. At Manasquan, New Jersey, Charlotte Eaton watched him move through the room amidst 'repartee that was contagious, putting everyone on his mettle'.

Restlessness and movement were characteristic. Edmund Gosse said he was 'eminently peripatetic', perching on sofas and throwing his legs over the sides. Lord Guthrie noted that he went in for 'more standing than sitting', and when sitting chose anywhere but the seat of a chair. Then an idea would cause him to spring up and move deftly around obstacles 'as restless and questing as a spaniel'. Sargent's famous portrait shows him bent slightly forward, nervously picking at his moustache, striding out of the left of the picture. His nervous irritability, frenetic activity, wild outbursts of laughter (and tears) may in part be traced to the psychology of pulmonary subjects, but were also characteristic. No part of the writer was not visibly present in the man, declared Graham Balfour.

Louis's charm and graciousness captivated almost everybody. Many point out that he was a good listener, with a knack of putting people at ease and drawing stories out of them, a gift he himself acknowledged. Women were particularly susceptible to the 'mannerly Stevenson', and he responded to female company, sometimes to his wife's irritation. Lady Shelley in Bournemouth swore he was the reincarnation of the dead poet. Charlotte Eaton found that he looked at her directly, and spoke without trace of a Scots accent. Adelaide Boodle, on the other hand, maintained he spoke broad Scots and rolled his 'r's splendidly. Louis was fairly adaptable in speech, it seems, so long as – 'delightful egoist' that he was – he could hold the floor. His high spirits 'bubbling with quips and jests', as Gosse put it, would burst out, but he was not conceitedly looking for the spotlight. It was just that 'he had no patience with half-hearted people', claimed Isobel Strong. What he actually *said* that was so witty is in strangely short supply. Of the many speeches Lord Guthrie heard him give at meetings of the Speculative Society in the University, he could not remember a word, and of conversational gems that fell from the lips of this 'king of speakers' Eve Simpson likewise gives no examples.

Men were generally a little more suspicious of Louis at first. Both Andrew Lang and Henry James were wary, but soon came round. Leslie Stephen never did care for him, although he recognised his talent and welcomed him to the *Cornhill Magazine* circle. In Edinburgh society he was labelled rebel and bohemian; fellow students at university branded him a lightweight and something of a *poseur*. A reminiscence by that Boston Brahmin, Henry Adams, is a good example of how initial wariness and condescension gradually evaporated in the face of Louis's warmth. With few exceptions people quickly appreciated his courage, loyalty and appetite for life. He carried the burdens of greed, jealousy and, materialism lightly, because he had faced death and lived each day as though it were the last. This provided the aura about him, not just his fame and wealth (both of which he dismissed); he was a genuinely lovable man, so much so, Lang declared, that 'some men were jealous of other men's place in his liking'.

As regards his clothes, all witnesses agree. Bohemian or buccaneer, in Edinburgh or the Pacific Islands, he dressed to please himself. It was part of an outlook on life 'boyishly genial and free', said Alexander Japp. His usual garb as a student was a battered straw hat, duck trousers, black shirt with loose collar, a tie that might have been a strip from a cast-off carpet and a jacket of black velvet. He looked, said Eve Simpson, like some 'starveling play actor'. On one occasion, after much teasing, he wound himself in his cloak, bowed low, 'and with a tragic droop of his somberly shrouded form' made an exit. At this time Louis was a member of Fleeming Jenkin's amateur theatrical group, and seems to have enjoyed dressing-up as much as performing. Although by most accounts an indifferent actor, he read well, and had a knack with accents. The imprint of his personality was so strong on Captain Otis of the yacht *Casco* that on arrival in Honolulu, after months at sea with Louis, the skipper sounded just like him and even reproduced some of his gestures.

Sometimes Louis dressed oddly as a practical joke. His favourite aunt, his mother and another relative, driving in Edinburgh High Street, passed a rag-and-bone man one day. Auntie looked hard at him and sighed: 'Oh, Louis, Louis! What will you do next!' Margaret Black recalled Louis and cousin Bob appearing in Princes Street in an open carriage with beribboned sailor hats and striped cricket jackets. At Sidney Colvin's house in the London suburbs, he appeared early one morning in a tattered waistcoat over a black flannel shirt. He had slept rough in an outhouse after prowling the streets; his object, he said, had been to prove, by rousing a policeman's suspicion, that justice fell harder on the ragged than the respectable. Later, he proved the point in Southern France by actually being arrested as a foreign agent. Most of Louis's friends have a story concerning his disreputable get-up. One is Lang's who, being hailed from a distance, waved him away saying:

> No, no; go away, Louis, go away! My character will stand a great deal, but it won't stand being seen talking to a 'thing' like you in Bond Street.

Flamboyance was the rule: an Italian embroidered smoking cap with gold lace and frayed tassels, or a Tyrolean hat; a red and black scarf around his waist instead of suspenders. In Samoa, Sidney Lysaght was fascinated to see Louis attired for dinner in heavily embroidered Indian costume. The cigarette was an accessory that became an addiction. He rolled his own, incredibly thin, and sometimes affected a pipe.

His self-description to J. M. Barrie at the end of his life points to the exuberance and playfulness of his dressing up:

> Exceedingly lean... general appearance of a blasted boy or blighted youth... Past eccentric – obscure and oh no we never mention it – present industrious, respectable and fatuously contented... Name in family, The Tame Celebrity. Cigarettes without intermission except when coughing or kissing. Hopelessly entangled in apron strings. Drinks plenty. Curses some. Temper unstable. Manners purple in an emergency, but liable to trances... Given to explaining the Universe – Scotch, sir, Scotch. (Knight, *Treasury*, 11).

Andrew Lang said that if you want to know Robert Louis Stevenson you had better sit down and read his books. No Victorian writer is so powerfully present in his work. Like Wordsworth or Whitman, about whom he published an essay (American writers, particularly Hawthorne, strongly influenced him), subjectivity was uppermost, modifying, filtering, shaping place and people. Essays, travel books and letters reveal him as self-aware, an egoist and meliorist.

Stevenson's personal imprint presents problems to a biographer, initially from the amount of reflection he left behind in books like *An Inland Voyage*, *Travels with a Donkey*, *Across the Plains*, or *In the South Seas* and *Vailima Letters*. To these must be added a huge correspondence, *belles-lettres* and poetry. Of even greater significance is the family involvement both during his lifetime and after his death. Collaborations with Fanny and with Lloyd are obvious examples, but his mother Margaret also left two volumes of travel and reminiscence, *From Saranac to the Marquesas and Beyond, 1887–88* and *Letters from Samoa: 1891–95*. Another Balfour, cousin Graham, wrote the first biography, with Fanny an ever-present censoring voice. Isobel Field, Lloyd Osbourne, Nellie Sanchez, the disaffected Katharine Osbourne, the compliant Sidney Colvin, editor of the first edition of the *Letters*, constituted a Stevenson clan. They gave the impetus to Stevenson hagiography by friends such as Gosse, Lang, Eve Simpson, Rosaline Masson and others who are represented in the following pages.

Clearly their versions, only a little this side of idolatry, must be interpreted with caution. Scores of friends and acquaintances contributed to the creation of the Stevenson myth in Masson's *I Can Remember Robert Louis Stevenson*, J. A. Hammerton's *Stevensoniana* and the *Bookman* special number of 1913. As a response to the charge of adding yet one more stone to the cairn, I have made sparing references to existing anthologies. Reminiscences of those family members closest to Stevenson have also been kept to a minimum: where Fanny, Belle or Lloyd appear, it is in the context of central episodes, such as the writing of *Dr Jekyll and Mr Hyde*. Despite the fulsomeness, however, many of these contributions are useful: stories passed within a family circle, retold at Vailima to visitors from the old country, and then written down in a memoir, undoubtedly contain kernels of truth. In any case, such views are modified by the recollections of other casual acquaintances and journalists. Many items have been discarded for reasons of space, since geographical sources are world-wide, and Stevenson's personality seems to have inspired much hero-worship. If one consistent element is to be found in what follows it is admiration of his courage.

Lady Jersey observed that 'Stevenson was not only a writer of romance but a hero of romance'. Following Fanny across the Atlantic to marry her and almost expiring in the process certainly fits him for the part, and his ultimate role of Tusitala, plantation owner and lord of the isles, bears out Chesterton's comment that he deliberately turned his life into a romance. Louis came round to that way of thinking, claiming to Colvin in May 1892: 'I wish to die in my boots' (*Vailima Letters*, 178). His greatest heroism, however, was courage in the face of chronic sickness.

Louis's legacy of bronchial infections causing fever and weakness turned to haemorrhages in March 1880, in Oakland, California, on the eve of his wedding. After six weeks of devoted nursing by Fanny he recovered. This became the red skein of his life. At Hyères during the first six months of 1884 he haemorrhaged frequently, his mouth filling with so much blood he could not speak. Every biography marks Louis's stoicism at this time. Forced to lie with his right arm strapped to his side, temporarily blinded by ophthalmia, and with a bandage over his eyes, he communicated by scribbling notes on paper or slate. When the blood gushed at one crisis, he comforted Fanny: 'Don't be frightened. If this is death, it is an easy one' (Balfour, *Life*, I, 213). There were many more frightful attacks until he found relief in sea voyages and hot climates. A fellow patient in the Davos clinic during 1881, Harold Vallings, recalls him making light of his infirmities and playing a frenetic game of billiards. 'His courage was a strong rock', said Lang. The theme of most recollections is of a man who sought adventure and whose spirit served him well in lieu of physical strength. Among the men he sailed with, Captain Otis of the *Casco* began by dreading the first voyage, but ended by respecting Louis's powers of endurance. A reporter in New York in August or September 1887 found him 'as lively and full of spirits as though he had never known what it was to have an ill day'. Another said: 'his body was in evil case, but his spirit more bright, more eager, more ardently and healthily alive than that of any other mortal' (Knight, *Treasury*, 136).

No one knew more of his courage than Fanny. As he wrote to Philip Hamerton in the summer of 1881:

> If I am where I am, it is thanks to the care of that lady who married me when I was a mere complication of cough and bones, much fitter for an emblem of mortality than a bridegroom.[5]

Like Louis, she too was an exile and a fighter, with a troubled past, having lost a beloved son and been abandoned by a feckless husband, Sam Osbourne. Both had passionate natures and liked having their own way, and fierce quarrels flared up throughout their lives, but she was equal to his great needs although obliged to submerge her own in the process. What she did after his death in attempting to perpetuate a Stevenson myth as favourable to herself as to him was less admirable, and has cost her dear: although attempts have been made to tell Fanny's story, she has been treated harshly by modern biographers.[6] She may have separated Louis from his earliest supporters; but then, those supporters were members of the London literary male establishment which resented her as an intruder. Fanny's obsession with guarding Louis's health, and his own acknowledged dependency, became increasingly a symbol of his escape from that world to interests it could not understand and popular art it looked down upon. For Henley, Gosse, Colvin she was bossy, misguided and certainly no lady. Henry James was notably fairer, and so were other contemporary witnesses of both sexes, who found her character stalwart. Fanny did not have Louis's flair for making friends, and she lacked the address and style of her mother-in-law, but by any standards she was remarkable. Through accounts of the exiles and their wanderings through Scotland, England, France, Switzerland, Hawaii, the United States, Australia and the islands of the Pacific, evidence accumulates of her courage and fortitude. Isobel Field was right to claim that her mother was 'a true pioneer at heart'. From Silverado to Samoa she met every kind of challenge: she fetched and carried; she drew water and carried wood; she brought the furs and tended the stove; she made a home on land or sea. Even aboard the *Casco* she ran the galley, although she of all the company was least able to endure the swells and squalls. Far less drawn to the vagrant life than Louis, she found at last her home in Samoa, but too late, for while his health stabilised, her own declined, mentally as well as physically. One attractive aspect of her character, often overlooked, is her interest in gardening. Wherever they stayed for any length of time – Hyères, Bournemouth or Honolulu – she made a garden. Largely at her bidding, one imagines, they leased extra land for oranges, coconuts and bananas, and she also tended the Vailima vegetable garden: 'As none of us like cabbages, I had not intended to plant them, but every white man who comes to the place asks first how my cabbages are doing.' Louis was roped in for weeding, and Fanny added to her stock by contacting Kew and other centres. There is something poignant in this glimpse of the woman digging in the soil, making things grow, while her own hold on things was breaking down.

The Vailima years produced strains of a different kind – but no less severe – from those of Davos, Hyères, Bournemouth and Waikiki. Living with an artist, as Fanny dryly observed, was not easy. Louis, as demanding as ever, now had fame and all its attendant demands. He had fortune, but the mushrooming bills of plantation and entertaining seemed to dissipate it as soon as each royalty statement came in. There were internal domestic discords involving the Osbourne children, and Samoan politics, in which Louis involved himself, added further anxieties. It is silly to heap the blame on Fanny for these circumstances; they were utterly necessary to each other, and Fanny, as Louis's support and mainstay, had much to bear. The comment, deleted from her private memoranda and subsequently recovered by its editor (see p. 169), says much of her frustration and the basis of her despair.

Louis's four years in Apia, Samoa, were the most intense and fulfilling of his life, a vindication of the exile's choice. With renewed health he seems to have been galvanised by the intensity of colour in jungle, reef and coral. Nature took him by the throat, and the Samoans' customs and beliefs in the *aitu* (spirit world) led him to art of greater enigma and ambiguity. That 'division of identity', as Barry Menikoff has called it, so much a part of his major work, is now potently evident in his life and art.[7] Light and dark, forces of fire, flood and earthquake, lush growth and rapid dissolution made Samoa the crucible of further artistic exploration for Louis in a way that evokes the artistic world of Xanadu. Vailima was equally a place of cruel disturbance, restlessness and unpeaceful co-existence for Fanny and Louis, and symbolises the oppositions in his life of home and exile, father and son, art and life. Fascination and repulsion propel Louis to a deeper texture of experience which approaches Conradian territory.

For Louis, home was in the midst of ambiguity, a kind of equilibrium between forces. Ona or 'Owner' (sometimes 'MacRichie') was the laird of Vailima, and over 300 acres on Mount Vaea high above the roaring surf. The crescent-shaped harbour of Apia lay below, where British and German warships were primed for action. The white community of Apia numbered about 300 and was very mixed. An upper crust was strongly present but had a crumbly edge. Louis spent, perforce, much time among colonial administrators, their wives and military personnel, but he liked the seedier fringe: expatriate Brits and Americans, remittance men, missionaries, traders with stories to tell, other Scots exiles, seamen adventurers. He wrote joyfully to Colvin of Christmas dinner, 1889, at the home of Harry Moors and his Samoan wife:

> I wish you could have seen our party at table . . . and the guests of the evening, Shirley Baker, the defamed and much accused man of Tonga, and his son with the artificial joint to his arm – where the assassins shot him in shooting at his father.
> (*Vailima Letters*, 1906 [1895], 41)

Moors, a flamboyant trader, ran his plantation on low-wage labour brought from Melanesia (a practice known as 'blackbirding').

Vailima itself was the ultimate dual place and locus of ambiguities. In the grounds were waterfalls and a bathing pool; nearer the house a tennis court where naval officers and Samoan members of the household played. The house was painted peacock blue with red roof and verandahs. Inside, the worlds of past and present met: white Samoan mats on the floor, and walls hung with tapa; pictures, ornaments, china, furniture which had been shipped from Skerryvore and Heriot Road. In the large hall or on the verandahs, chiefs and colonial powers met for kava and sumptuous dinners attended by Vailima staff in tartan livery. Fireplaces, installed at great cost, added a final incongruity – they made the place more like home, said Louis. This shadow Abbotsford ate up capital. Margaret Stevenson, erect in widow's weeds and starched cap, read her Bible and attended daily prayers, while primitive rituals were practised outside – even to severed heads – as the Samoan war broke out, at one time threatening Vailima itself. Tropical storms beat on the roof, the house itself shaking in frequent earthquakes. Louis, writing to survive, surviving to write, must have grown ever more conscious that the bottle imp had granted his every wish; with every successful outcome another discontent, another step towards oblivion.

In the poem for Fanny, written as the dedication of *Weir*, images of the journey and the ambiguities of the exile's condition are prominent:

> I saw rain falling and the rainbow drawn
> On Lammermuir. Hearkening I heard again

INTRODUCTION   xxvii

> In my precipitous city beaten bells
> Winnow the keen sea wind. And here afar,
> Intent on my own race and place, I wrote.

She found it pinned to the curtain screening her bed. *Weir* continued to delight him. On the morning of 3 December 1894 he put in his usual stint on the book, dictating to Belle, breaking for lunch and then turning to a pile of letters. Fanny was in low spirits, so they played cards for a while and then, partly to cheer her up, Louis asked her to help make the salad for supper. Salads were a Vailima speciality, with vegetables from Fanny's garden and Louis's own blend of mango, papaya, guava, passion fruit – whatever was in season – spiced with grated apple. Returning from the cellar with a special burgundy, he put his hands to his head and said: 'What's that?' and 'Do I look strange?' before he fell to the floor. Doctors were called but could do nothing. Death was attributed to brain haemorrhage. An account of his burial next day ends this collection in the words of Fanny and Margaret Stevenson – fierce, resolute and brave words, to commemorate a courageous man a century later.

For the reader's convenience the volume, like others in the series, follows a chronological order as far as possible, with reminiscences from each phase of Stevenson's life. Each segment is introduced with relevant details about the contributor and is followed by any necessary explanations or significant additional information. Prefatory material indicates location of excerpts by page numbers of the relevant edition. In all cases extracts are reproduced exactly from their originals. Where the editor has omitted portions of narrative to avoid repetition or to focus on significant matters this is indicated in the text. Spelling has been regularised to English usage, and errors have been silently corrected. Explanatory details concerning foreign expressions, terms, places or dates have been supplied within items. In most cases references to Stevenson's works are accompanied by the date of first publication in book form; most quotations are taken from Chatto and Windus editions. In the case of texts which are hard to come by, sources are given by Tusitala edition numbers. At the time of writing, the long-awaited Yale University Press edition of the *Letters* by Bradford Booth and Ernest Mehew was not available. References to Louis's correspondence in this volume are from Sidney Colvin's very incomplete editions of 1900 and 1911 and the *Letters to Charles Baxter* edited by DeLancey Ferguson and Marshall Waingrow in 1956. Some materials are offered to guide the reader to other sources of information. The Stevenson bibliography is vast, so the 'Suggestions for Further Reading' are confined to works of biographical relevance only. 'A Stevenson Chronology', again very limited, may help to place items in the main text. Books are listed by author, title and date, place of publication being London except where stated otherwise. Book titles are italicised. A 'List of Abbreviations' used in the text is also included.

Compiling this book gave me great pleasure. Stevensonians count themselves fortunate in the exotic places to which inquiries lead them, if not always in person, by letters, inter-library loan and electronic communication. I recall with gratitude generous help from the following: the British Library; Edinburgh Central Library; Edinburgh City Museums; the Huntington Library, San Marino, California; the Beinecke Rare Book and Manuscript Library, Yale University; Maui Public Library, Hawaii; San Francisco Art Institute; St Louis Public Library, Missouri; and nearer home, the University of British Columbia and the University of Victoria. I am deeply grateful to my research assistants, Allan Hyggen, Monika Rydygier Smith and Sheila Burgar, and to friends at home and abroad who answered questions: they include Tracy Davis, Northwestern University; Barry Menikoff, University of Hawaii; Peter Edwards, University of Queensland; Keith Costain, University of Regina. To my wife, Judith, I am especially indebted for critical insights and her meticulous editing. Special thanks go to Colleen Donnelly for her patience and skill in preparing the book for publication.

Every effort has been made to trace copyright-holders, but if any have been inadvertently overlooked the publishers will be pleased to make the necessary arrangements at the first opportunity.

Victoria R.C.T.

NOTES

1. The engineering dynasty was founded by Robert Stevenson (1772–1850), who was responsible for 23 lighthouses along the Scottish coast, including the famous Bell Rock lighthouse, and who invented the intermittent and flashing light systems. His three sons, including Louis's father, carried on the tradition. See *Records of a Family of Engineers* (1896); Balfour, *Life*, I, 3–10. William Seed (1827–90), senior civil servant in New Zealand government, first in the Customs department at Wellington; later Secretary and Inspector of Customs and Marine.

2. John Fowles and Fay Goodwin, *Islands* (1978), 73; Alexander Japp, 'A Master of Romance', *Atlanta*, 6 (1892), 304. Stevenson was well aware of the Ulysses parallel. In his poem 'Youth and Love – I' he wrote:

> Hail and farewell: I must arise,
> Leave here the fatted cattle.
> And paint on foreign lands and skies
> My Odyssey of battle.
> 'Song of Travel', in Janet Adam Smith (ed.),
> *Robert Louis Stevenson Collected Poems*, 1971
> (1950) 246.

3. Edward Said, *Culture and Imperialism* (1993), 407. Jenni Calder has called Louis an 'explorer of alienation and isolation' (*RLS: A Life Study* (1980) 316–17).

4. Flora Masson, *Victorians All* (1931), 107.

5. *Philip Gilbert Hamerton: An Autobiography 1834–1858 and a Memoir by his Wife 1858–1894* (1897), 488.

6. See Margaret Mackay, *The Violent Friend: The Story of Mrs Robert Louis Stevenson* (New York, 1968). Balanced estimates of her character may be found in J. C. Furnas, *Voyage to Windward* (New York, 1951), and J. Calder, *RLS* (1980).

7. Barry Menikoff, *Robert Louis Stevenson and The Beach of Falesà* (Edinburgh, 1984) 9.

A Stevenson Chronology

1850	Born 13 November at 8 Howard Place, Edinburgh.
1852	Alison Cunningham ('Cummy') becomes his nurse.
1857–67	Educated at various schools, including Edinburgh Academy.
1867	Enters Edinburgh University and takes up engineering studies.
1871	Gives up engineering for law.
1873	First article, 'Roads', published.
1874	Elected to Savile Club. Cruises Inner Hebrides with Walter Simpson.
1875	Admitted to Scottish bar. Travels in France. Meets Mrs Fanny Vandegrift Osbourne at Grez-sur-Loing.
1876	Canoe excursion in Europe with Simpson.
1877	First short story, 'A Lodging for the Night', published in *Temple Bar*.
1878	First book, *An Inland Voyage*, published. Secretary to Professor Fleeming Jenkin at Paris Exposition. Fanny Osbourne leaves for California. Walking tour of Cèvennes.
1879	Collaborates with W. E. Henley on first play, *Deacon Brodie*. *Travels with a Donkey*. Sails for America. Joins Fanny Osbourne and family at Monterey, California.
1880	Marries Fanny in San Francisco. Honeymoon at Silverado, Napa County.
1881	Davos, Switzerland, for health. *Virginibus Puerisque*.
1882	Travels in Scotland and south of France.
1883	Chalet La Solitude, Hyères. *Treasure Island*.
1884	Leaves Hyères for Bournemouth.
1885	*A Child's Garden of Verses*. Lives at Skerryvore, Bournemouth.
1886	*Dr Jekyll and Mr Hyde*. *Kidnapped*.
1887	Death of father, Thomas Stevenson. Sails for New York with mother, Fanny and Lloyd.
1888	First voyage aboard the *Casco* to South Seas.
1889	Honolulu. Collaboration with Lloyd Osbourne, *The Wrong Box*. Second voyage, on the *Equator*, to Gilbert Islands. *The Master of Ballantrae*. Buys 'Vailima' in Upolu, Samoa.

1890	Sydney. Third voyage, aboard the *Janet Nicholl*, to Gilbert Islands and others. Another call in Sydney. Decides to make Samoa his home.
1891	To Sydney for meeting with Margaret Stevenson, newly arrived from Scotland.
1892	*Across the Plains: A Footnote to History.*
1893	Last visit to Sydney. Samoan war. *Catriona* (first issued as *David Balfour*). *Island Nights' Entertainments.*
1894	*The Ebb-Tide* (with Lloyd Osbourne). Writing *St Ives* and *Weir of Hermiston*. Samoan chiefs make 'Road of the Loving Heart'. Dies 3 December of cerebral haemorrhage.

Smout's Favourite Occupation

MARGARET STEVENSON

From Margaret Isabella Balfour Stevenson, *Stevenson's Baby Book* (1922). The Balfours of Pilrig were of ancient Scots lineage; the portrayal of the Laird of Pilrig in *Catriona* (1893) draws on this ancestry. Margaret Isabella Balfour (1829–97), daughter of the Reverend Dr Lewis Balfour (1777–1860), minister of Colinton, was, like her husband, one of 13 children, and grew up with her brothers, sisters and many cousins in the manse on the Water of Leith outside Edinburgh. Lively, spirited, outgoing, she was the ideal partner for Thomas Stevenson (1818–87), the engineer whom she married in 1848. Louis was their only child and pride of their lives. Inheriting a weak chest from her own father, she suffered ill health during Louis's infancy, and much of his nursery care was undertaken by the adored Alison Cunningham, his 'second mother'. Husband and wife were much absorbed in each other, her buoyancy of temperament compensating for his increasing melancholy. Yet the impression of Thomas Stevenson as a stern workaholic with a strong religious fixation must be balanced by his good nature and sense of humour. Balfour tells us how he solaced many of his son's troubled nights with talks of robbers, sailors, ships and roadside inns (*Life*, I, 24). The eminently practical man had his romantic side, and the diehard Tory held some progressive views: he believed, for example, in easy divorce for women. In a note to *Kidnapped* (1880), Louis states that almost to the end his father had a great gift of pleasing. Louis's mother was to figure more prominently in his later life. Margaret Stevenson ('Maggie'), at 58, voyaged with her son to America and became an integral part of the Samoa household. After his death she returned to Edinburgh.

Mrs Sayers was sent for about 2 a.m. on the 10th of December. Tom and I had seen baby washed for the first time on the evening before and Tom had remarked 'I trust it may never fall to my lot to wash a baby.' When I was told that Mrs S. was sent for I began to cry saying 'I have never even washed him yet' to which Tom replied 'Toots, such nonsense, I'll wash the child myself' which made me laugh when I remembered his solemn speech made a few hours before. Mrs Alan Stevenson's nurse Guest came twice a day to wash him till we got a Mrs Thomson, a widow, as nurse. She stayed three months and was very unsatisfactory, and at last we found out that she drank, so we sent her away and got a very lively active woman called Mackenzie, a capital worker. She stayed until he was 18 months old and then 'Alison Cunningham' to whom the 'Child's Garden of Verse' is dedicated, came.

Place of Birth: 8 Howard Place, Edinburgh.
Time of Birth: Wednesday 13th, November 1850 at 1:30 p.m.
Color of Eyes: Blue at first turning to hazel.
Color of Hair: Very fair almost none at first.
Nurse's Name: Mrs Sayers.
Doctor's Name: Dr Malcolm.
Surname: Stevenson.
Christian Names: Robert Louis Balfour.
Pet Names: Boulihasker, Smoutie, Baron Broadnose, Signor Sprucki, otherwise, Maister Sprook and many others, but Smoutie stuck to him until he was about 15.

November 13, 1851: Our darling boy a whole year old to-day. He is running about famously, calls Tom 'Mama' and warms his hands at the fire, blows out lights and talks a great deal in an unknown tongue besides numerous other accomplishments of a like nature.

September 1852: Smout begins to be fond of stories and sometimes asks to be told about 'the big stick' meaning Cain and Abel, that, and Daniel among the 'growlers' are his favourites.

January 25, 1853: Smout at the Zoological Gardens – highly pleased and very courageous – he went close to the 'Eelinfault' and even in the tiger house said 'My not fightened.'

February 17, 1853: Smout begins to say a prayer as well as his hymn. After Smout went out he expressed great distress because he had not made 'an *elegant* bow to Mama'.

March 10, 1853: Dear little Smout very ill with an attack of croup. He had on a mustard plaster on his chest and two leeches on his dear little foot – when he saw the blood he said 'Cover it up, cover it up.' The bites had to be burned with caustic. He was very patient, dear little man, but accused Cummy of hurting him.

March 17, 1853: Better but pallid.

March 20, 1853: Cummy fears Smout's *affliction has not done him good* as he is much averse to prayers, hymns and all good things.

July 24, 1853: Smout's favourite occupation is 'making a Church'. He makes a pulpit with a chair and stool and reads sitting and then stands up and sings by turns.[1]

March 30, 1854: Smout was distressed to hear that sheep and horses did not know about God and said 'I think somebody might read the Bible to them.'

July 7, 1855: Smout was asked 'What would you do if you were left on a desert island?' S. 'I could come away.' 'But if there was water all round?' S. 'I would come away in a ship.' 'But if there was no ship?' S. 'I would send a letter by the post.' 'If there was none?' S. 'I would sit down and take a hearty greet' [cry].

January 18, 1856: Lewie takes scarlatina to-day, a mild case.

February 5, 1856: Dear wee Lou prayed among other things 'that God would be very near every person that was not very well'.

February 17, 1856: When I asked Lou what he had been doing, he said 'I've been playing all day – at least I've been *making myself cheerful.*'

October 7, 1856: Bob Stevenson comes to stay with us.[2]

November 13, 1856: Lou's *6th birthday*. Aunt Warden gives him a toy theatre and he and Bobbie set to work to paint the scenes with great eagerness.[3]

November 23, 1856: Smout begins to-day to dictate a history of Moses to try for a prize which Uncle David is to give for the best.

November 26, 1856: Lou has inflammation of the cheek. It is terribly swelled and he suffers so much that he tells me perhaps he may never be better.

December 21, 1856: Lou finished his history of Moses to-day. He dictated every word himself on the Sunday evenings.[4]

December 25, 1856: Lou gets a Bible picture as a prize for his Moses and is greatly charmed. When he got it he said 'But I don't deserve it.'

February 6, 1857: Lou is still so feverish that we are alarmed & Tom gets Christison to see him. He says it is nothing but bronchitis, that he should soon be better, but this house [1 Inverleith Terrace] is bad for him it is so cold from being an end house.[5]

February 20, 1857: Took Lou to Colinton to-day for change, he complained of pain in his head and was very sick and ill all night. We sent for the doctor who says it is caused by milk, which he had been ordered – disagreeing with him.

April 10, 1857: Take Lou to Bridge of Allan. Take Mrs Haldane's lodgings where Lou is very happy with his gun. When Mrs Warden saw him crouching behind a bush in the garden and asked what he was doing, he said 'I'm hunting blawbacks.' Auntie had been reading Mayne Reid's books to him.[6]

In May we leave Inverleith Terrace and come to 17 Heriot Row.

May 11, 1857: At Aberdown. Smout is improving very much here. He is getting very wild and like a boy.

September 30, 1857: Dear Lewie goes to Mr Henderson's School in India St from 10 till 12 o'clock.

October 6, 1857: Smout says 'Mr. Henderson is the most nicest man that ever was.'

November 13, 1857: Dear Lewie spents his 7th birthday in bed having taken bronchitis but he is much comforted by the companionship of his Skye terrier dog called 'Coolin' which arrived lately from the West Coast.

NOTES

1. On one occasion the devotions went too far. Playing at church with a friend, W. B. Blaikie (1847–1928), later to become a well-known historian, Louis made paper clerical bands, much to the anger of the other boy's mother who tore them from his neck, enraged at the sacrilege (Masson, *I Can Remember*, 1–2).
2. Robert Alan Mowbray Stevenson (1847–1900). From this time the cousins grew very close, Bob becoming something of a role model. They created (like the Brontë children) their own play-kingdoms of 'Nosingtonia' and 'Encyclopedia', played with tin soldiers and Louis's treasured toy-theatre. His insights into child behaviour derive in part from this early phase. See 'Child's Play' in *Virginibus Puerisque* (1881), source of the well-known porridge anecdote: 'He ate his with sugar, and explained it to be a country continually buried under snow. I took mine with milk, and explained it to be a country suffering gradual inundation' (237). The game was still much a part of my generation's childhood.
3. Skelt's Juvenile Drama, recalled fondly in 'A Penny Plain' and acknowledged by Stevenson to have profoundly influenced his imagination (*Memories and Portraits* (1887, 213–27).
4. David Stevenson (1815–86), middle son of Robert, who with his brothers, Alan (1807–65) and Thomas (1818–87), ran the family engineering business. Louis was six and this was his first literary effort. Splendid illustrations accompanied vivid narrative like this example of the plague-stricken Egyptians: 'After that he sent swarms of flies which buzzed about in the most horrible manner' (Masson, *I Can Remember*, 31). According to his first biographer, an extra prize was even more significant. It was *The Happy Sunday Book of Painted Pictures with Verses to Each for Good Children* (1856). 'From that time forward', the fond mother concluded, 'it was the desire of his heart to be an author' (Balfour, *Life*, I, 39).
5. The Stevensons were unlucky in their first two houses. 8 Howard Place occupied a low-lying area by the heavily polluted Water of Leith. Two and a half years later they moved to 1 Inverleith Terrace, a corner house perpetually cold and damp. At this time Louis's chest problems began. In 1857 the family settled in the New Town at 17 Heriot Row, the Stevenson home for the next 30 years.
6. Captain Thomas Mayne Reid (1818–83) writer of adventure stories such as *The Rifle Rangers* (1850), *The Scalp-Hunters* (1851), *The Headless Horseman* (1866), a prototypical wild-west story, which enjoyed great popular success. Another favourite at this time was *The Coral Island* (1858) by R. M. Ballantyne (1825–94), who visited the Stevensons while they were at Colinton in the mid-1860s. Louis was captivated; later, in verses to *Treasure Island*, he hailed 'Ballantyne the brave'. Reaction set in by the time Louis was 30, and he recoiled from the sadism in *The Coral Island* (McLynn, 28). In the last year of his life Louis groused to Charles Baxter, his lifelong friend, about being dunned for a donation to the Ballantyne memorial (*Baxter Letters*, 353).

A Taste for Adventurous Tales

E. BLANTYRE SIMPSON

From: E. Blantyre Simpson, *Robert Louis Stevenson's Edinburgh Days* (1898), 13–19, 27–31, 33–4. Evelyn Blantyre Simpson (1856–1920) was the daughter of Sir James Young Simpson (1811–70), the pioneer obstetrician who discovered chloroform and battled for its general use. He received the first baronetcy given to a doctor practising in Scotland, and a bust in Westminster Abbey commemorates his achievement. His son, Walter, became one of Louis's close friends. Evelyn Simpson wrote a biography of her father (1906) and several books on Stevenson, including *Robert Louis Stevenson* (1906) and *The Robert Louis Stevenson Originals* (1912). Inaccurate in details, she was particularly sensitive to the bond between father and son. Her account mentions several people involved in Louis's early life, many of whom appear more fully in later extracts, where appropriate references and commentary may be found.

There can be no doubt whence Louis imbibed his love of adventure and of the sea. Ships bulk largely in Tusitala's tales. A ship very appropriately appeared on his monument at San Francisco, a fine old-world galley of the build those Vikings used in their sea-raidings. There hung in the house of Louis's boyish great-grandfather, Alan Stevenson, 'and,' he says, 'successively in those of my grandfather and father, an oil painting of a ship of many tons burthen. The picture was preserved through years of hardship, and remains to this day in the possession of the family, the only memorial of my great-grandsire Alan. It was on this ship that he sailed on his last adventure, summoned to the West Indies by Hugh.'[1] In his *Memories* Louis relates how a frigate in a window took his eyes, and 'when upon any Saturday we made a party to behold the ships we passed that corner, and since in those days I loved a ship as a man loves Burgundy or daybreak, this of itself was enough to hallow it'.[2]

If engineering in 1870 had been as much on the rough as it was some eighty years before, Thomas Stevenson would not have had any difficulty in persuading his son to follow in the footsteps of his sires. Louis, speaking sympathetically, yet enviously, of the difficulties and dangers his grandfather, Robert Stevenson, had to face when trying to light our dark coasts, says: 'It must not be forgotten that these voyages in the tender were the particular pleasure and reward of his existence; that he had in him a reserve of romance which carried him delightedly over these hardships and perils, that to him it was "a great gain" to be eight nights and seven days in the savage Bay of Levensurck – to read a book in the much-agitated cabin, to go on deck and hear the gale scream in his ears and see the landscape dark with rain and the ship plunge at her two anchors, and to turn in at night and wake again at morning in his narrow berth to the clamorous and continued voices of the gale.' This near relative bequeathed some of his characteristics with a bountiful plenitude to his descendant, for from him Louis inherited his 'anxious exactitude about details, an interesting flow of conversation, a taste for sea and adventure, and lastly that *reserve* of *romance*'. Louis, remarking on his grandfather's letters to his small sons, says that besides all these he had 'a fine scent of all that was romantic to a boy'.[3]

From his mother's side Louis, like David Balfour, came of the Balfours of Pilrig. His grandfather was what he called 'a herd of men'. In *Memories and Portraits* he gives us a well-executed sketch of Mrs Stevenson's old home, and of her father, the Rev. Lewis Balfour, in his manse at Colinton. The minister we see grey of locks, handsome of feature, upright of carriage, smacking his lips over a 'barley-sugar kiss', a sweetmeat administered to Louis as a reward after a dose of medicine. Louis's last recollection of his grandfather was of an old gentleman sternly forbidding his daughter, Miss Balfour, to give a lollipop to her expectant nephew, for the boy had had no horrid gregory to swallow. From the Balfours the author took his name, except the Robert, which came to him from the Stevensons. His mother disliked the names Thomas and Robert, and wished the latter excluded. Mr Stevenson, however, had the old-fashioned belief in a grandson bearing the name of his father's father, though he said he might drop it for everyday use. He promised his wife her boy would be spoken of as Lewis, unless she had another son, when, according to hereditary rule, she had the naming of him after her father. Robert Lewis Balfour our hero was baptised. Perhaps he thought there was a superabundance of letters in R. L. B. S. The Balfour soon dropped out of his name, and early he became R. L. S., which initials, says Mr Barrie, 'are, I suppose, the best beloved in recent literature; certainly they are the sweetest to me'.[4]

He also, like his grandsire, started in life with his name spelt Lewis. The story of the change to Louis is remarkable. Mr Stevenson was a strong Conservative. Now in Robert Louis Stevenson's youthful years there was a Radical town councillor yclept Lewis. So strong was Mr Stevenson's aversion to the man that he ordered that in future his son's name should be spelt differently, even with a Frenchified turn in it, for fear the two families should be thought in any way connected. So the boy's patronymic was in a manner severed from the minister of Colinton, and his mother often regretted he had dropped her father's honoured surname....[5]

Louis's mother was a slim, active woman, and no one seeing her in her latter years, with her erect figure and fresh face, would have believed her the mother of a son who had died aged forty-five. Mrs Stevenson was a cultured and clever woman. Luckily Louis inherited her bright, vivacious disposition; but he tells us the Balfours were unemotional, hating the display of what they felt. Their descendant was the reverse of this, and his original unconventionality, historical temperament, and his foreign appearance, cannot be traced to any of his progenitors....

It vexed Mrs Stevenson in her latter years to hear or see it stated that Louis and his father were antagonistic, and had waged a bitter civil war. People, she said, assumed that types of unhappy youths such as Archie Weir and examples of rebellion against parental authority were drawn from the author's own personal experience. There was, it is true, a deal of diversity between Thomas Stevenson's nature and that of his only child, but underlying the engineer's reserved decorum and sombreness there were many points of resemblance and sympathy between father and son. No one enjoyed Thomas Stevenson's talk more than Louis, who says it was 'compounded of so much sterling sense and so much freakish humour, and clothed in language so apt, droll, and emphatic, that it was a perpetual delight to all that knew him. His use of language was both just and picturesque. Love, anger, and indignation shone through him and broke forth in imagery, like what we read of in Southern races.' Louis gloried in his father's whimsical fancies, his 'blended sternness and softness that was wholly Scottish, and at first somewhat bewildering; with a profound essential melancholy of disposition, and (what often accompanies it) the most humorous geniality in company'. No one, I think, appreciated his father's good qualities, his humour, his quips and fads, even his dogged theological views, more than the son who drew so just and masterly a portrait of Thomas Stevenson, Civil Engineer.

'Smout' Mr Stevenson rechristened his small boy, a name he was long known by in his home circle. Smout was simply worshipped by his two mothers. On the brief days of winter, when his mother and Cummy were partakers of a gorgeous banquet, while he, the dispenser of the feast, sat in a paper crown and presided over the mimic tea-set (which still lives on Cummy's table), the small boy, hearing the gate click, and his father's key in the latch, would fly downstairs to greet the master of the house and invite him to the 'party'. No caressing and adoration that had been lavished upon this sole monarch of the nursery was half so appreciated by his majesty as the kindly glance he saw beam on him from out of his father's deep-set eyes, and the strong hand held out to him, and the grave, interrogative greeting, 'Well, Smout?' The open-hearted, manifestly affectionate boy quite understood his apparently undemonstrative father; and though they bickered in words when the son grew up, and argued and discussed with much warmth, a good fellowship always existed between them. Louis always warred in words with his friends, and neither filial affection nor fear of his father's displeasure ever rendered him dumb or submissive. The two fought many a duel which, to outsiders, seemed irreverent rebellion on the son's part, but the father liked his boy's fearless thrusts. He could, truly, from his heart, dedicate a volume 'in love and gratitude' to the father 'by whose devices the great sea-lights in every quarter of the world now shine more brightly'....[6]

Mr Stevenson not only gave his little Tusitala a taste for adventurous tales, but his peculiar theories on education were the theories which best suited his son. To look at Thomas Stevenson a hasty observer would have thought he had been one of those that uphold a rigid course of study, and rigidly apply the tawse if need be. But he himself in his learning time had been a consistent idler, and he held he acquired more by idling than he did on the school bench. He would stop schoolboys in the street, look at their burden of books, shake his head over such trash, and advise them with earnestness to pay no heed to the rubbish which was being crammed into them. He begged them to look about them, play to their heart's content, but to read or study only what their inclination dictated. The schoolboys would, open-mouthed, gaze at the firm-faced man who seriously propounded such palatable views. They keenly suspected he was making fun of them, and went on their way puzzled.

NOTES

1. *Records of a Family of Engineers* (1893). Louis cherished a romantic pedigree based on adventure at sea. His tale of two brothers involves business interests in the West Indies, an agent's skulduggery, flight, pursuit, an open boat, and sudden death. Both forebears, Hugh Stevenson (1749–74) and Alan Stevenson (1752–74), died in their twenties and in the same year. Tragedy, Louis solemnly declared, 'shadowed the cradle of Robert Stevenson', his grandfather (*Engineers*, 15).
2. 'A Penny Plain and Twopence Coloured' (*Memories*, 214).
3. *Engineers*, 53, 45.
4. Sir James Matthew Barrie (1860–1937), dramatist famed for *Peter Pan* (1904). The two never met, but Barrie invented a pub jaunt together as Edinburgh students. See *Letters of J. M. Barrie*, ed. Viola Meynell (1947), 250–2.
5. The account of Thomas's petulance over local rivalries has been queried by modern biographers, but was accepted without hesitation by Colvin, Japp and Gosse. The change from 'Lewis' to 'Louis' occurred when he was about 18, but the pronunciation stayed the same (Balfour, *Life*, I, 30). In the spring of 1872 he wrote to Baxter that he loathed his third initial and had decided to drop it (*Baxter Letters*, 6). Possibly he wished to avoid the three initial pattern of his cousin, R. A. M. Stevenson.
6. Dedication to *Familiar Studies of Men and Books* (1882). Elsewhere Louis quotes the phrase 'the Nestor of lighthouse illumination', referring to his father's work on optics and meteorology regarding wave movements: 'Storms were his sworn adversaries' (*Memories*, 136).

'Cummy, I Was Just Telling Myself a Story!'

CHARLES J. GUTHRIE

From '*Cummy' the Nurse of R. L. S.: A Tribute to the Memory of Alison Cunningham* (1913) pp. 8–23. Charles John Guthrie (1849–1920), later Lord Guthrie, jurist, historian, antiquarian, was a fellow member of the Speculative Society at Edinburgh University. Admitted to the Scottish bar in 1875, Guthrie held many legal and civil posts: Sheriff of Ross,

Cromarty and Sutherland (1900–7), Chairman of the Early Scottish Text Society (1910), President of the Royal Scottish and Geographical Society (1917–19). He published works on John Knox and *Robert Louis Stevenson: Some Personal Recollections by the late Lord Guthrie* (1920). In 1908 he took the tenancy of Swanston Cottage in the Pentland Hills, the Stevensons' country retreat from 1867 to 1881.

Her eyes never lost their gleam, and she had a hearty laugh; her voice was strong, and her memory wonderfully accurate; her wits remained as nimble and her manner as vivacious as in the days, some sixty years ago, when she stored 'Tusitala's' child mind with Scripture passages, tales of Bible heroes, stories of Scots Reformers and Covenanters, and legends of pirates and smugglers, witches and fairies.[1] She used to tell, with a twinkle in her eye, how shocked she was, or tried to be, when Louis asserted that she, a strong Calvinist and a strict Free Church Presbyterian, was responsible for his love of the theatre! '"You know quite well, Cummy, how you acted all these stories, as if you had seen them yourself!" Think of Lou saying that to me, when I was never in a theatre all my days!' After his death his widow wrote to Cummy, 'Louis once said to me: – "They may talk about heredity; but, if I inherited any literary talent, it was from Cummy! It was she who gave me the first feeling for literature." Then he told me how you used to recite poems and tell stories to him till you seemed better than any book he could read. Once at Bonaly Burn, he got you started telling stories, that I might judge whether or not you were a person of real genius. I agreed with him that you were, and that you must have had much to do with the bent of his mind'....

His mother's delicate health threw the main care of him on Cummy.[2] The charge was no light one. He was a small, delicate child when he was put into her strong, skilful and tender hands. Miss Cunningham told me that, when his father first saw the infant, he said he had 'never seen such a wee thing. He's just a *smout*.' And 'Smout', or 'Smoutie', his parents often called him.[3] The reason why she read so much to him, and told him so many tales and legends, was thus explained: – 'You see, he was more than seven years old before he could read. He began to read after a bad attack of gastric fever. They thought he would die. He lay for days unconscious. I was in the next room when I heard him cry, "Cummy, I want some bread." Oh, I was thankful!'...

What Louis owed to her was lavishly acknowledged by him,

as boy and man, in word and deed, in public and private, and by his parents. While his name was still unknown beyond the family circle, he wrote to her: – 'Do not suppose, Cummy, that I shall ever forget those long, bitter nights, when I coughed and coughed and was so unhappy, and you were so patient and loving with a poor, sick child. Indeed, Cummy, I wish I might become a man worth talking of, if it were only that you should not have thrown away your pains. . . .

'My dear old nurse (and you know there is nothing a man can say nearer his heart, except his mother or his wife), next time when the spring comes round, and everything is beginning once again, if you should happen to think that you might have had a child of your own, and that it was hard you should have spent so many years taking care of someone else's prodigal, just you think this: you have made much that there is in me, just as surely as if you had conceived me, and there are sons that are more ungrateful to their own mothers than I am to you. . . .'

Sir Sidney Colvin, printing this letter, refers to Cummy as 'the admirable nurse whose care, during his ailing childhood, had done so much both to preserve Stevenson's life and awaken his love of tales and poetry, and of whom, until his death, he thought with the utmost constancy of affection'.[4]

The passages quoted on the previous page occur in the earliest of the series of letters given by Miss Cunningham to me some years ago, unique human documents which will, I hope, be permanently preserved in Swanston Cottage. The last of the series, dated from Samoa, full of gay spirits, was written two months before his death. Here is a bit of it: – 'My dear Cummy, so I hear you are ailing. Think shame to yourself! Do you think there is nothing better to be done with time than that? Be sure we can all do much ourselves to decide whether we are to be well or ill. I kept myself alive for years by an effort, like a man on the gymnastic bars. As for me, there is nothing the matter with me in the world, beyond the disgusting circumstance that I am not so young as once I was!

'. . . We have had a very interesting business here. I helped the chiefs, who were in prison; and when they were set free, what should they do but offer to make a part of my road for me out of gratitude! Well, I was ashamed to refuse; and the trumps dug my road for me, and put up this inscription: – "Considering the great love of His Excellency Tusitala, in his loving care of us in our tribulation in the prison, we have made this great gift. It shall never be muddy; it shall go on forever, – this road that we have dug!"'

'Weel, guid-bye to ye, and joy be wi' ye! I hae nae time to say mair. They say I'm gettin' *fat*, – a fact! – Your laddie, with all love,
'ROBERT LOUIS STEVENSON'[5] . . .

Mr Stevenson, senior, liked her buoyant spirits and her dry humour, and shared her national love of and aptitude for theological disputation. He was a very kind as well as a very able man; and he was much entertained by her ardent but ineffectual attempts to argue and coax him, a Tory and an Established Churchman, into the creed, if not the fold, of the Free Church of Scotland. For the memory of Louis's mother, Cummy had profound reverence. Examining a portrait of Mrs Stevenson one day, she said to me: – 'A lady looked at that picture once, and she said – "A beautiful woman that!" "If you please, mum," I answered, "she had a beautiful soul!"' When Mrs Stevenson died, her sister, Miss Balfour, wrote a long letter to Cummy, dated 16 May 1897: – 'About midnight I was told I might see her. Her dear hand was pushed out to clasp mine for the last time.[6] Suddenly she said, "Louis, I must go," and tried to get up. She then became unconscious, and knew nothing after.' . . .

I could never quite make out whether, in the early days, with all her admiration and devotion, she had anticipated great things for Louis. Perhaps she may have doubted, as did others better able to judge, whether, with all the sparkle of thought and expression which we, his companions and friends, acknowledged and admired, he was not too casual, too shy, too ill for supreme achievement. Yet, even in her early experiences, coming events cast some shadows before. 'Once when I put him in the corner,' she told me, 'he never came out. I asked him why he stayed, when the time was up, and more than up; and he said, "Cummy, I was just telling myself a story!" He was great on stories, his own stories, and other folk's stories forbye. Long before he could write himself, he used to get me to put things down to what he called his dictation. So I would write a bit, and then I would say, "Lou, that's plenty! What you're making me write is perfect nonsense!" "Never you heed, Cummy," says he, "just you write away." Aye, I wish I had kept some of those funny stories. But they were all burnt or lost.'

NOTES

1. Alison Cunningham (1822–1913), known as 'Cummy' (sometimes 'Cummie'), was the daughter of a Fife fisherman and strict in Free Church doctrine. Despite her religious severity she was 'full of life and merriment' (Balfour, *Life*, I, 37) and Louis adored her to the end of his life. He dedicated *A Child's Garden of Verses* (1885) to her. In old age she added to the Stevenson myth, as eager pilgrims beat a path to her door, playing the role of Nurse to Genius to the hilt. See, for example, Clayton Hamilton, *On the Trail of Stevenson* (1916).
2. Both mother and father were inclined to be valetudinarian. Their frequent recuperative trips to France or Italy seeking refuge from Edinburgh's icy blasts, however, gave Louis a taste for foreign travel and culture, and turned him into a sophisticated teenager.
3. Cummy did not much care for the pet name, but his father used it constantly; when asked his name 'the little rascal would look up with mischief in his face and answer "Smoutie"' (Simpson, *Edinburgh Days*, 100). After 'Smout' he became 'little Lou'.
4. Sir Sidney Colvin (1845–1927), Slade Professor of Fine Art at Cambridge (1873–85), Keeper of Prints at the British Museum (1884–1912). He edited the Edinburgh edition of Stevenson's works (1894–7) and the *Letters*, 2 vols (1900).
5. *Letters*, II, 360–1. He refers to the title Samoans conferred on him – 'Teller of Tales' – and, of course, the Road of the Loving Heart made under their leader Mataafa, whose cause Louis had approved during turbulent political and economic struggles in 1893. The road from the main route across the island to the Stevenson estate of Vailima was completed in October 1894.
6. Jane Whyte Balfour (1817?–1907), 'Chief of our aunts' in *Child's Garden*. She bought him the toy soldiers which fostered a lifelong interest in war games. Aunt Balfour, injured as a girl while riding, had kept house for her father, the Reverend Louis Balfour, at Colinton.

A Playmate beyond Compare

VARIOUS

(1) from 'Robert Louis Stevenson', by two of his cousins, *English Illustrated Magazine*, XXI, April–Sep 1899, 121–31. There were plenty of children to play with – around 50 cousins according to his first biographer. Visits to Cramond, some five miles out of Edinburgh, and especially Colinton Manse were one remedy for Louis's ailments. Here he could enjoy a normal childhood. About Colinton Manse he wrote with great fondness, a place of incomparable adventure and freedom (see 'Reminiscences

of Colinton Manse', in Balfour, *Life*, I, 40–7, and 'The Manse', *Memories and Portraits*). The cousins, Mrs Marie Clothilde Balfour and her husband, Dr J. Craig Balfour of Edinburgh, are full of sentimental rhapsody, but there is plenty of evidence of his telling stories, partly to withstand the boredom of long periods of convalescence; (2) from 'R. L. S. as Playmate', by 'Lantern-Bearer', *Chambers's Journal*, n.s. 96, Aug 1919, 583–6. This glamourised memorial by an unknown contributor draws on the kind of material in 'The Lantern Bearers', *Across the Plains* (1892), in which Stevenson records his delight in exploring, climbing, picnicking, angling, exploring tidal pools, braving the icy water for a bathe, and learning to smoke. The events described here occurred on the North Berwick coast. The writer's soubriquet draws on what was central to the experience, setting out at night, with a bull's eye lantern under his topcoat: 'The essence of this bliss was to walk by yourself in the black night; the slide shut, the top-coat buttoned; not a ray escaping, whether to conduct your footsteps or to make your glory public: a mere pillar of darkness in the dark; and all the while, deep down in the privacy of your fool's heart, to know you had a bull's eye at your belt, and to exult and sing over the knowledge' (215–16).

(1) He was a very delicate child, as has been said, and not always fit for play with other children; but he had a delightful and untirable companion always at hand – himself. He never was lonely, even in the 'land of counterpane'.[1] He told himself stories, of which instalments were told sometimes to other people also: they were generally tales of adventure so complicated that it was a marvel how he ever found his way through them; and yet he never made a mistake – or, at least, never let himself be found out in one. He was once telling such a tale when his hearer noticed, as she thought, a discrepancy. Some shipwrecked sailors (it was a tale of savages and tropical seas and all the delightful glamour of unfamiliar things, untried things, which charmed him, child, as it entranced him, man) had plunged into a river, and, after having left everything on the further side, suddenly were repossessed of their guns.

'But you forget, Louis,' she put in, 'they have left them behind.'

'You wait,' was his reply; 'just you wait, and you'll see.'

He went on and on, till she thought he had altogether forgotten the thing; but at length, so cleverly worked in that it seemed to come in its natural place and inevitably, the explanation turned up. What it was is not of much consequence now; but his hearer could not help wondering then, and does not know yet, whether it was put in only because she had called his attention to it, or whether it had all been planned out and arranged in his mind from the beginning. She wondered over it so much and so often that at last, in the days when he had made his home in Samoa, she recalled the story to him and begged him to try and remember, but he could not. And for that matter it was odd enough either way; for that a child of five could have so kept the thing in mind and worked in the explanation as to make it *seem*, at least, as if he had foreseen it from the beginning, shows an amount of intuitive literary skill that many practised writers might envy.

With his cousins 'Smout' was always a favourite. 'Even when it was at his own expense, he had a way of telling a story that made it seem the funniest thing in the world,' one of them says of him. 'I've heard him repeating old tales against me, and he made us laugh over them consumedly – I as much as anyone.' . . .

Louis Stevenson not only had a 'museum' himself, but he was a great purveyor to the others, by way of exchange; for in wintering abroad with his mother he had special opportunities, and was able to bring back from the Riviera bits of Roman pottery, tear-bottles, plaited palms from Bordighera, and so on.[2] But his manner of exchange with his cousins was so peculiar: he 'sold' the things at the rate of so many 'whacks' on the hand given with a strap or cane, to be taken without flinching. If the 'buyer' so much as winced, it had all to be begun over again. One of the cousins, who was not very old then, remembers having hard work sometimes to stand it when the object was a very enviable one, and the price of it, in 'whacks', was high. It must be remembered that it was then a common thing that the entry into boys' societies was made conditional on bearing pain without complaint. I do not know whether it still is so.

Frequently, too, the cousins went bird-nesting together. There is certainly nothing very remarkable in that, except that now the town covers much of the ground that then was garden, field, or park; where they happily trespassed is become a wilderness of villas. Then there were old houses set about with trees and thick shrubberies and lawns, and shut in with high walls: when the elder cousins went a-nesting – generally where they had no business to go – the younger ones, 'big' and 'little' Jamie, were left perched on the top of these same walls to keep a look-out and give warning in case of danger, and then to get down therefrom and save themselves as best they might. Not always very easy when the boy was very small, and the wall very high; but that was an unconsidered detail to the elders. Louis Stevenson did not lose his love for such things; and there is a certain tree in the garden of Swanston Cottage where later, a long-legged lad of twenty-one or thereabouts, he climbed to rifle a magpie's nest; and coming down with a run, the eggs in his mouth, found them, by personal assay, to be addled.[3] ...

In the library [at Heriot Row] he shared with his cousins a world of adventure, amid pirates and savages, in unknown seas and strange waters; a long folding arm-chair or lounge was usually chosen for the boat, being conveniently on castors, and was pushed about by the bar-bells, which he was ordered to use to develop his chest. He was apt to remember their existence more often for other, and less improving, purposes, such as the above. It was here, upstairs, that he undertook to make his younger cousins 'see ghosts'; they were shut, each in his turn and alone, in a dark room, where the spectres were produced by means of a magic-lantern worked by threads passing out under the door. Louis, upon the landing outside, vastly enjoyed the fun; the small boy within submitted to it – with a difference. One of them is even willing to admit that he may have been a *little* bit frightened ... Still, Louis had the knack of making anything in which he shared delightful, though it might be, and generally was, 'creepy'. It is only fair to allow also that he frightened himself quite as much as he ever frightened anyone else. Later, indeed, when he was abroad and alone, having read some old books on magic, it came into his head that he, too, would like to 'raise the devil', and with great pains he copied the circles, the double pentagon, and the mystic symbols, drawing them about himself upon the floor, and making all his preparations carefully according to instruction. It was at night, and he was alone: 'And I got into the very biggest fright you can just imagine,' he afterwards told his cousin, one of the writers of this article, 'lest the devil should take me at my word, and really appear. I wondered how on earth I was going to get rid of him. I tell you, even now when I think of it I get hot all over.'[4] ...

Once, when he was about twelve years old, a little cousin was born in a neighbouring street, a little further down the hill; and Louis took a mild interest in the baby, as he managed to do in most things. He arrived one day and made himself vastly agreeable, as he always knew how to do; and after a great flow of conversation, he remarked that he had bought a rattle for the baby. 'But I've lost it on the way down,' he added vaguely; 'I'll go and get her another.'

Later in the day he reappeared, and continued the conversation as if it had never been interrupted. It was only when he got up, at last, to go away, that the rattle was recalled to him.

'Oh ... yes,' he said; 'I did get another. But ... I lost that on the way down, too!'

The baby, who is one of the present writers, never looks at the penny-plain-and-twopence-coloured window when she passes it to-day without thinking of the rattle she never got.[5]

Indeed; all the most vivid memories of Louis Stevenson – or, at least, so it seems to some of his cousins and playmates – are whimsical odds and ends such as this: mere trifles that live in one's thoughts because they were 'so like him', or else because they were told by him with that inimitable freshness and charm which is not to be forgotten. We cannot recall any details of work that he may – that he must – have done when, to begin with, he was preparing to follow the profession of his family, but we remember that he and his father took levels of nights in the drawing-room at Heriot Row, and built beacons with a complicate pyramid of chairs. We do not know whether, in his trips on the *Pharos*, he ever gained any practical experience, but we shall always remember his own story of climbing a narrow ledge along a precipitous cliff-face.[6] When at its narrowest, he met with a large and opinionated gull. He carefully reached out a foot – it was a spot where movement had to be calculated – to shove it off, but the gull only opened a huge beak and looked unfriendly. Same manoeuvre with the other foot: same result. The gull remained in possession, and Louis crawled back ignominiously into safety, to tell with delight the story against himself. ... Louis was not 'important' to his cousins; he was just the best of companions, a playmate beyond compare, an incarnate delight of youth. And it is as such they like best to think of him still, young – never grown old; one of themselves – not yet become famous. To others he may be celebrated; to them he is just 'Louis' – and that is more.

(2) I was a mere child when I first made the acquaintance of Robert Louis Stevenson, and in a sufficiently unusual and dramatic manner. His father and mine were friends of a lifetime, drawn together by some likeness of character and the same profession, and interested in one another by the dissimilarity that frequently ce-

ments a friendship. I had in my quiet, guarded childhood, passed in a lovely and all-sufficing old garden, smaller occasion and less liberty for adventure than the wild spirit of R. L. S. He was spoken of as a 'curious boy', unlike others; and perhaps the mothers of my generation had an unacknowledged distrust of the thin, elfin lad with the brilliant eyes. In any case, we had not met save at those terrible entertainments called 'children's parties', and had eyed one another with the reserved and clear-sighted silence that in thoughtful children is the substitute for older diplomacy.

Our family had in the 'sixties settled for August and September at North Berwick, then a small, unfashionable seaside place, with an East Bay, and a very nebulous West, that had about half-a-dozen villas.[7] The East Bay was to us then a real Elysium – rocks, sea, a safe beach called 'the sands', on which we had any amount of unusual liberty; and, under the eyes of tenants of the line of villas, little danger could come to the boys and girls who played and dreamed there. The Black Rock was an Alp to be climbed, and I had, with another playfellow, a dear cousin now long dead, begun the ascent. The rock was very hot and dry, and polished in places by the many feet that had gripped in its few niches. Just at the top I found I had the wrong foot foremost, nothing to hold to, and a sensation of fear. My head barely reached the top, but my hand did. To my relief, a thin, brown hand with long fingers came over the edge of the rock, and a thin, brown face, with very keen, interested, gray-brown eyes, looked over. 'Take my hand,' said a boy's voice, and the fingers curved for the grip. I looked at the very thin, very long wrist that reached out of a pepper-and-salt shabby coat, and hesitated to trust to it, it looked so very unequal to any efficient help, then up to the eager grey eyes bent on me, and felt that I might trust to the owner's willingness. 'All right,' I said, and put a sandy paw in the thin one. 'Hold tight and change your foot'; then, 'One, two, three', and a good pull landed me on the top. 'I am Louis Stevenson,' the boy said. 'I was lying up here in the sun, on the warm rock. Isn't it fine?' I still think of him as 'Louis', French fashion, without an 's', as his surname obliterated the final consonant, and it was many years before I realised that it was the English Louis.

NOTES

1. *A Child's Garden*. An absurdly sentimental view, of course, about poems which reveal a disquieting subtext of fear, pain and loneliness:

'What have I done, and what do I fear,
And why are you crying, mother dear?'
('The Sick Child', *Underwoods*, 1887, 56-7)

2. A contemporary practice of making up collections of curios, seashells, ornaments, into 'museums' and exchanging items with friends.
3. On another occasion he marked a kestrel to its nest high on a cliff, a dangerous climb, but Louis got to the top with an egg in his cap (Masson, *I Can Remember*, 20).
4. The kind of game lasted quite up to the outbreak of the Second World War. Another, 'Mesmerism', called for Louis, then about eight, to copy a 'mesmerist' who would touch the underside of a 'magic' plate and then make signs on his face. Louis's plate was smeared with lamp black and when he was shown the results in a mirror he was mortified (Masson, *I Can Remember*, 6-7).
5. A reference to the well-known essay in *Memories and Portraits*, recalling 'the face of what was once myself' (prefatory note).
6. *Pharos* was the steamer of the Commissioners of Northern Lights in which Louis journeyed with his father in a vain attempt to become interested in the family career. See 'The Education of an Engineer' (*Across the Plains*). Sir Walter Scott had accompanied his grandfather around the Scottish coasts and found him agreeable company. See 'Scott's Voyage in the Lighthouse Yacht', by R.L.S. in *Scribner's Magazine*, XIV (Oct 1893) 492-4.
7. Possibly in 1862, although the Stevensons visited the Berwick coast on several occasions.

Quick and Bright but Somewhat Desultory Scholar

H. B. BAILDON

From *Robert Louis Stevenson: A Life Study in Criticism* (1901) 18-23. Henry Bellyse Baildon (1849-1907) met Louis at Robert Thompson's day school in Frederick Street, Edinburgh, in 1864 and they collaborated in the school magazine until Baildon left for the University in the autumn of 1865, where their friendship later resumed. He remained one of those friends to whom Louis in Samoa could indulge his nostalgic longings for Scotland. Baildon was the author of *Rosamund, a Tragic Drama* (1875) and several books of poems. He contributed the Stevenson entry to

Homes and Haunts of Famous Authors (1906). In *Temple Bar*, 104 (March 1895) 325–33, he paid tribute to Stevenson as the enemy of moral pedantry and the most genuinely modest of men, revolted by the grim severity of Calvinism, yet with 'his own rather exacting standards for human behaviour' (331).

It was at Mr Thomson's [sic] school that I first saw Robert Louis Stevenson in the flesh – to use a somewhat inappropriate phrase. I do not think there were at this little seminary more than a dozen boys, ranging in ages from nine or ten to fourteen or fifteen, and our intellectual calibre varied fully as much as our years.[1] For some of us were sent there for reasons of health, and others because they had not made that progress with their studies which their fond parents had hoped. Others were there, I fancy, merely because the scheme of education upon which the proprietor, Mr Robert Thomson, proceeded, fell in with the views of our parents. One feature of this system was that we had no home lessons, but learned, in the two or three hours of afternoon school, what we were expected to remember next day. My impression is, either that Stevenson joined the school later than I did, or that he was absent on one of his frequent health pilgrimages, when I first made the acquaintance of my schoolmates. However, when he did come, being older and somewhat more advanced than the others, we were naturally drawn much together, and whatever I may have done for him, he certainly played a leading *rôle* for me among this juvenile 'cast'.[2] Our freedom from home tasks gave us leisure for literary activities, which would otherwise have been tabooed as a waste of time. Perhaps with some of us they were, but not with Stevenson. For even then he had – to the grief of his father, if not of both his parents – a fixed idea that literature was his calling, and a marvellously mature conception of the course of self-education through which he required to put himself in order to succeed. Among other things, we were encouraged to make verse-translations, and, for some reasons or other, I specially well remember a passage of Ovid, which he rendered in Scott-like octosyllabics, and I in heroic couplets, which I probably thought commendably like those of Mr Pope. But, even then, Stevenson showed impatience of the trammels of verse, and longed for the compass and ductility of prose.

At school Stevenson was a quick and bright but somewhat

desultory scholar, and never – being encouraged in this position by his father – strove after distinction in his class. Nor was he wanting in liking or ability for his tasks, and at any rate French, Latin, and Geometry were interesting and congenial studies to him. In Greek I doubt if he ever got very far, certainly never the length of reading the original with ease and pleasure. In French he had the advantage of having been a good deal in the country, and already appreciated some of the beauties of French prose. Latin he enjoyed also from a literary and stylistic point of view, and some of the care and finish of his style and its frequent felicities may be traced back to his early love for Cicero and Horace, Ovid and Virgil. But he was already full of his own literary projects and activities, and we took, I fancy, a keener interest in the school magazine (beginning modestly and dubiously under the title of 'The Trial', to blossom forth later into the avowedly romantic 'Jack o' Lantern') than in our more regular and legitimate studies. That we were rather ambitious is witnessed by the fact that we must need run *two* serial stories abreast. One of these Stevenson wrote himself, while he and I collaborated over the other.[3] He suggested and discussed with me the plot, which was of true Stevensonian type, and was laid in the tropical island of Jamaica, and I wrote up the details (including a monstrous Negro of colossal villainy, with his headquarters in an appropriately horrible and inaccessible Cavern) with such unfortunate vividness and effect that the story was speedily proscribed by my parents as *sensational*, and either remained a *torso*, to use a fine phrase, or was finished single-handed by Stevenson himself.

Stevenson calls himself 'ugly' in his student days, but I think that is a term that never at any time fitted him.[4] Certainly to him as a boy about fourteen (with the creed which he propounded to me, that at sixteen one was a man) it would not apply. In body Stevenson was assuredly badly set up. His limbs were long and lean and spidery, and his chest flat, so as almost to suggest some malnutrition, such sharp angles and corners did his joints make under his clothes. But in his face this was belied. His brow was oval and full, over soft brown eyes, that seemed already to have drunk the sunlight under southern vines. The whole face had a tendency to an oval Madonna-like type. But about the mouth and in the mirthful, mocking light of the eyes, there lingered ever a ready Autolycus roguery, that rather suggested the sly god Hermes masquerading as a mortal. Yet the eyes were always genial, however gaily the lights danced in them; but about the mouth there was something tricksy and mocking, as of a spirit that had already peeped behind the scenes of Life's pageant and more than guessed its unrealities.

I would now give much to possess but one of Stevenson's gifts – namely, that extraordinary vividness of recollection by which he could so astonishingly recall, not only the doings, but the very thoughts and emotions of his youth.[5] For, often as we must have communed together, with all the shameless candour of boys, hardly any remark of his has stuck to me except the opinion already alluded to, which struck me – his elder by some fifteen months – as very amusing, that 'at sixteen we should be men.' He of all mortals, who was, in a sense, always still a boy!... He and my other schoolmates were, I fancy, pretty often at my house, which, being in the country, was more attractive on holidays than their town houses. I was not very often in 17 Heriot Row, and I had a notion then, of which I have never been disabused, that I was not a *persona grata* to Stevenson *père* on account of my being an art-and-part accomplice in his son's literary schemes and ambitions. Mrs Stevenson was always kind and gracious, but, in spite of that, I always felt rather like a bale of contraband goods, as I passed in at the door of No. 17, and followed Stevenson to his den in the attic story. One of these occasions I do distinctly remember, on which Stevenson was brimful of the story of 'Deacon Brodie', and I believe he then read to me, probably in 1864, portions of a proposed drama on the subject.[6]

On the other hand, our house, Duncliffe, Murrayfield, seemed to have taken his romantic fancy, and in one of his short stories, 'The Misadventures of John Nicholson', it is powerfully and, in the main, accurately described, in its very gloomiest aspect, as the scene of a murder, so vividly portrayed that I cannot think of it without seeing the dead body lying in a certain position on the dining-room floor.[7]

NOTES

1. Robert Thompson's school in Frederick Street, Edinburgh, had fewer than 20 pupils and seems to have been run on progressive lines. At least it enabled Louis to indulge his growing urge to write, while grounding him in Greek and Latin.

2. Louis was about 13 years old. Since his entire schooling was interrupted by convalescent breaks and his parents' holiday plans, his early education was a patchwork. He attended Cannonmills School briefly in 1857, then Henderson's Preparatory, India Street, intermittently (1857–9), from whence he proceeded to the famous Edinburgh Academy (1861). A boarding-school in Isleworth, Middlesex, was tried in 1862, but did not suit. Some private tuition went on in Torquay. His last school was Mr Thompson's (1864–7), after which he went to university.

3. Their collaboration in the *Trial Magazine* in 1865 produced 'The Count's Secret' and 'The Convicts', both MSS now in the Beinecke Collection at Yale.

4. Stevenson's self-portrait in his student days: 'a certain, lean ugly, idle, unpopular student, of changing humours, fine occasional purposes of good, flinching [sic] acceptance of evil, shiverings on wet, east-windy morning journeys up to class, infinite yawnings during lecture and unquestionable gusto in the delights of truantry made up the sunshine and shadow of my college life' ('Some College Memories', *The New Amphion* (1886), repr. in *Memories and Portraits*).

5. Baildon may be unconsciously parroting Stevenson's claim: 'I am one of the few people in the world who do not forget their childhood' (*Letters*, II, 107).

6. *Deacon Brodie*, eventually the play written with W. E. Henley, privately printed by T. & A. Constable, Edinburgh, 1880, and several times performed. Brodie was an eighteenth-century cabinet-maker by day and burglar by night, plundering with his gang the homes of Edinburgh citizens. He was tried and hanged in 1788. The story had particular frisson for Louis since one of Brodie's cabinets had stood in his nursery. Several commentators have drawn attention to its *doppelgänger* motif as one of several tributaries to *Dr Jekyll and Mr Hyde*.

7. 'The Misadventures of John Nicholson', a Christmas story published in *Yule-Tide*, Cassell's Christmas Annual, 1887. Critics have drawn attention to the painful father–son relationship at its centre.

I Have Seen a Young Poet

E. M. SELLAR

From *Recollections and Impressions* (1907) 195–9. Eleanor Mary Sellar (b.1829), *née* Dennistoun, was the wife of William Young Sellar (1825–90), Professor of Latin at Edinburgh University from 1863 until his death. They had a family of highly intelligent children, and entertained frequently at their house in Buckingham Terrace. Her husband's writings include *The Roman Poets of the Republic* (1863) and *The Roman Poets of the Augustan Age* (1892). Professor Sellar was one of several bewildered academics who found themselves called upon for testimonials when Louis applied for the Chair of Constitutional Law at the University in 1881.

It would be strange to write about Edinburgh and take no notice of one of her most remarkable sons – R. L. Stevenson. I had been his mother's bridesmaid, and I stayed with Mr and Mrs Stevenson in 1851, a year after they were married, in the house their baby was born in, 8 Howard Place, and a fractious little fellow he was! though decidedly pretty with his dark eyes and fair hair. This uncommon combination he inherited from his mother, – from her also his light heart, which carried him bravely through the many years of delicacy that would have depressed most people into thorough invalidism. This was almost my first visit from home, and it was an intense interest to me to watch the development of my girl friend into a wife and mother, and to study the character of her grave scientific husband. He delighted in her livelier spirits, for, left to himself, life was 'full of sairiousness' to him; and had it not been for his strong sense of humour, which was a striking trait in his character, the Calvinism in which he had been brought up would have left its gloomy mark upon him.

Among the pictures on the wall there was a fine engraving of David Hume, whose writings, in spite of his opinions, he greatly admired; 'but,' he said, 'I shall take that down when the boy is old enough to notice it, for I should not like him to think Hume was one of my heroes.' He could not guess how far his son was to travel from the orthodox paths, and yet always to bear about him the indelible mark of the Shorter Catechism![1]

The Stevensons took me to dine one evening with his brother, Alan Stevenson, to meet the daughter of Thomas de Quincey. I thought Florence de Quincey a lovely girl. She was dressed in a pale-pink muslin, and had long black velvet ribbons hanging from the back of her head. This may not now sound very elegant, but it was, and so was she, and 'the mind, the music breathing from her face', made her a creature that once seen could never be forgotten. Mr Alan Stevenson made a great impression on me, and I thought I had never met a more interesting man.[2] He was one of those men who, as has been well said, 'pass beyond the facts of science to the truths of science'. He was rather sad-looking, as if the weight of this unintelligible world hung heavily on his spirit, which was of a highly imaginative order. Science was his forte, but poetry was his passion. Both powers came into play in the perpetual warfare he waged with the awful forces of nature while building lighthouses on almost impossible and inaccessible rocks all round the coast of Scotland – a work which culminated in the splendid triumph of the Skerryvore Lighthouse, so graphically described by the late Duke of Argyle in his most interesting autobiography published this year (1906)....

Of Louis himself, when we came to Edinburgh and later, we did not see much. Our children were, I think I may say, clever and lively, but their ways were not his ways, and to a youth so eccentric no doubt they appeared shallow and conventional, as he – with his long hair and black shirt, a freak of his – appeared to them affected, not to say intolerable! I think I ought to mention here that later, when they became acquainted with his works, he had no warmer admirers than every member of our family. I remember his mother telling me when he was a lad that he would sometimes go off for two days at a time – no one knew where; and in extenuation of this conduct he would tell his mother that she must pay the penalty of having given birth to a tramp!

He must have been about eighteen when Professor Fleeming Jenkin came to Edinburgh as Professor of Engineering.[3] Mrs Jenkin gave me once an interesting account of the beginning of her friendship with Louis, – one of the happiest influences in his life. She had been returning her first calls, – a weary business to one who used to say that nothing tired her but the conventionalities of life. Dusk was falling, and one name, Mrs Thomas Stevenson, Heriot Row, remained on her list. She hesitated: the thought of home was very alluring, but she resolved to finish all her calls at once. She found her hostess sitting in a room lit only by the firelight. Mrs Stevenson would have rung for lights, but Mrs Jenkin assured her that she preferred the cosiness of the dusk. Into the conversation suddenly broke a young voice, and Mrs Jenkin became aware of the figure of a youth, half-hidden in the window recess. So interesting did the conversation become that Mrs Jenkin lingered under the charm of this unseen interlocutor till she suddenly realised that she would be late for dinner. The young man accompanied her to the door, and under the gaslight in the hall she saw the slender figure, long hair, and brown eyes with which we are all familiar. 'I hope you will come and see me,' she said, shaking hands. 'When shall I come?' 'Tomorrow,' was the flattering response. When her husband remonstrated with her on being late, 'Never mind,' she said; 'I have seen a young poet.'[4]

NOTES

1. An integral part of Louis's religious indoctrination, along with Foxe's *Book of Martyrs*, Cummy's constant readings from the Bible and her fund of hell-fire and damnation stories. The Catechism, derived from the Psalms in easily assimilated doggerel, became something of a label hung around Stevenson's neck. See Henley's poem (p. 197).
2. Alan Stevenson (1807–1865), one of Robert Stevenson's three sons involved in the family firm. He was famed for designing the Skerryvore lighthouse, built in 1844, which Louis commemorated by renaming his home in Bournemouth. Alan is important among Louis's forebears. He was cultured, artistic, a linguist, who had conformed to the expected professional calling. At 45 he suffered a 'sudden shattering of his nervous system' (*Stevensoniana*, 5) and died young. Significantly, his son, Robert Alan Mowbray (Bob) Stevenson, rejected the family career to become an artist and Louis's bosom friend.
3. Anne Fleeming Jenkin, wife of Henry Charles Fleeming Jenkin (1833–85) was in her mid-thirties, an accomplished amateur actress and a charming hostess. She encouraged her husband to run an amateur dramatic society and set up a room in their house for regular shows. Mrs Jenkin's salon was a desirable meeting place for young professionals and students in Edinburgh.
4. This story is also recounted by Rosaline Masson, with some embellishment: 'Who was this son who talked as Charles Lamb wrote? this young Heine with a Scottish accent' (*Stevenson*, 34).

A *Poseur*, Prone to Exaggerate Himself, Even to Himself

ROSALINE MASSON

From *The Life of Robert Louis Stevenson* (1923) 60–85. Rosaline Orme Masson (d.1949) was the youngest daughter of David Masson (1822–1907), Professor of Rhetoric and English Literature at Edinburgh University (1865–95), greatly respected teacher and leader in higher education for women; first editor of *Macmillan's Magazine*; editor of works of Goldsmith, de Quincey, Milton and others, including the six-volume *Literary History of His Time* (1859–80); historiographer-royal for Scotland (1893). Rosaline Masson, anthologist, biographer and amateur historian, is best known for *I Can Remember Robert Louis Stevenson* (1922), a collection of reminiscences.

He was not a worker, and was therefore not among the workers. And he made his own friends. He wilfully selected, sought out, and went about with companions of habits and characters that made him appear unsuited for the society in homes where he might otherwise have found sympathy and inspiration. In Edinburgh today we have still among us, and we had among us until yesterday, eminent citizens, men high in their professions and universally liked and respected, who were fellow-students of Stevenson, who knew his people and his companions, and whose testimony of that time in his life, given kindly but honestly, is of more value from the point of view of truth than the criticisms of those who knew him only when their judgments were coloured by knowledge of what he had become. One of these fellow-students, speaking of Stevenson, related: 'Once, in later years, Dr Whyte said to me, "But why, man, did you not see more of Louis Stevenson when you were at the University with him?" I told him in reply that I was not at all keen to see much of him, still less of the friends who surrounded him[1] ... That R.L.S. neglected his classes at the University was not indeed a serious matter for him. He was an only child, and need never want, though he had idled through life ... The mass of students knew very well that we should have to earn our own living by the sweat of our brows, that our course at the University was the highest privilege we were ever likely to enjoy before buckling to life's work ... for the most part we could not afford to mix ourselves up with apparent idlers.'

Here is the evidence of another who knew him well in his college days, and read with him in Classics and Philosophy later on, when Stevenson was studying for the Bar, – the late Rev. Archibald Bisset of Ratho:

'The truth is that Stevenson never was a University student in the usual sense of the word. Not only was his attendance at classes intermittent, but he followed no regular curriculum. Then he took very little part in the work of the classes which he did attend. He used to sit on a far-back bench, pencil in hand, and with a notebook before him, and looking as if he were taking notes of the lectures. But in reality he took no notes, and seldom listened to the lectures. "I prefer," he used to say, "to spend the time in writing original nonsense of my own." He always carried in his pocket a notebook, which he sometimes called his "Book of Original Nonsense", and not only during the class hour, but at all odd times, he jotted down thoughts and fancies in prose and verse. Of course he generally gave class exams the go-by. And thus it came to pass that, excepting among his intimates, he was regarded as an idler.'[2] . . .

These days of the very early 'seventies, however, were certainly the days of revolt and of the 'hot fits of youth'. Hot fits of youth are not unusual in a temperamental boy emerging into manhood: hot fits and cold fits also, – aggressive outbreaks of revolt, and equally aggressive times of depressed and morbid egoism. With a nature so complex and so finely wrought as Stevenson's, both the hot fits and the cold fits were accentuated. And Stevenson liked to study all his moods, and to present them as of interest; and, as he was Stevenson, they were of interest, especially as presented by him. Moreover, it should be taken into account that he was a *poseur*, prone to exaggerate himself, even to himself. When he went into the grim Calton Cemetery 'to be unhappy' in the shade of the prison walls and by the grave of David Hume, he really did feel miserable, but it was what another poet has called 'congenial woe'.[3] He distorted his misery and cherished it. When he saw a housemaid signalling to him from a window of the grimy hotel that overlooks the cemetery and the prison, she was to him 'beautiful' and a 'wise Eugenia' and 'kept my wild heart flying'. But he recognises the *poseur* in himself, for he presently confesses 'And yet in soberness I cared as little for the housemaid as for David Hume.'

It was probably in these early days of revolt and, in the modern phrase, of 'self determination', when his circle 'was continually changed by the action of the police magistrate' – or he liked to think it was – that one day Miss Balfour – 'Auntie' as she was always known in the family, – and her youngest sister, Mrs Stevenson, Louis's mother, were driving, with another relative, down the High Street of Edinburgh. Mrs Stevenson was lamenting the escapades of her son, and telling her troubles to 'Auntie' when suddenly the eyes of the other relative were attracted by a queer-looking ragamuffin walking along the pavement with a bag of bones over his shoulder.

'Do look at that queer old-bones-man!' she cried. Auntie looked, and heaved a sigh. 'Oh, Louis, Louis! What will you do next!' was all she said....

By the winter of 1870-71 Louis Stevenson had become more popular with several of his old school classmates who were his fellow-students at the University, and from whose fraternity he had hitherto held somewhat aloof, as 'they and he looked upon various matters of importance from different points of view'.

This growing popularity was furthered by his taking a leading part in the formation of a club among them, a club destined to become well known – the D'Arcy Thompson Class Club.[4] Several meetings of old members of D'Arcy Thompson's Academy class were held, generally at 'Rutherford's' [a public house, and a well-known resort of students before the luxurious 'Union' was founded in 1886], and then the Club was formally constituted, on the fourth of December, 1870, in the more sober quarters of one of the halls at 5 St Andrew Square. Thus the winter, Louis's fourth year in Arts at the University, ostensibly spent in non-attendance of the classes of second Mathematics, Natural Philosophy, Engineering, and Mechanical Drawing, was enlivened by more congenial occupations....

Two incidents, both in March, 1871, must have given Louis's much-tried father sympathetic pride. One was that Louis stood true to his Conservative principles, and voted in the Speculative Debate want of confidence in Gladstone's Ministry. Thomas Stevenson was a Tory, and ever denounced Gladstone and all his works; and in this father and son were at one. Louis remained a Conservative in politics all his life. His cousin and biographer, Sir Graham Balfour, says he 'probably throughout life would, if compelled to vote, have always supported the Conservative candidate'.

The other flame of pride and hope to Thomas Stevenson was kindled when Louis (only twenty years and four months old) read a paper on March 27 to the Royal Scottish Academy of Arts on 'A New Form of Intermittent Light for Lighthouses', which was adjudged 'well worthy of the favourable consideration of the Society and highly creditable to so young an author', and won him a £5 medal from the Society of Arts.[5] Poor Thomas Stevenson! It may well at that moment have seemed to him as if the wayward son had really inherited some of the family form of genius, and that his feet were to follow in the family footsteps.

NOTES

1. Dr Alexander Whyte (1836–1921), Principal of New College, Edinburgh (1909–18), published a commentary on the *Shorter Catechism* (1882) and other works on religious subjects. The source of this comment is Patrick W. Campbell (Masson, *I Can Remember*, 14). Campbell also noted how Whyte, a serious young clergyman, astonished Thomas Stevenson with enthusiastic praise of his son.

2. Bisset makes it clear that, rather than idling, Louis was assiduously reading French and English classics. He records that, when first introduced as 'son and successor of Thomas Stevenson, the well-known lighthouse engineer', Louis responded '"Son, certainly"... "but not successor if I can help it."' Bisset describes him as 'a fragile-looking youth of about eighteen with a very noticeable stoop of the shoulders... long hair, which made his face look emaciated'. Like several witnesses he was drawn to the eyes: 'quick-glancing and observant and brimful of humour, or, I should rather say, of banter' (Masson, *I Can Remember*, 49).

3. Stevenson cultivated the image of the doomed poet, based on his idol, Robert Fergusson (1750–74), a Scots poet who died insane from the effects of a fall. To his dying day Louis saw himself as one of a trio with Fergusson and Burns – 'Scotland's three puir Rabbies'.

4. D'Arcy Wentworth Thompson (1829–1902), classical master of Edinburgh Academy (1852–63), was noted for progressive educational views. He became Professor of Greek at Queen's College, Galway, in 1863. In *Day-Dreams of a Schoolmaster* (1864–5), he argued the case for the study of ancient languages and the further education of women. He made many translations from the Greek, notably *Ancient Leaves* (1862), and also wrote children's books, popular in their day.

5. Thomas Stevenson's moment of glory was brief. The following month Louis gave up engineering for law. At the time his mother wrote in her diary: 'On the 16th of October we hear that Louis is to get a £3 prize for his improvement on lights; ... and he says: "No one can say that I give up engineering because I can't succeed in it, as I leave the profession with flying colours"' (quoted in *Baxter Letters*, 1). According to J. A. Hammerton, the award was the Society's silver medal, value three sovereigns. The pamphlet of four leaves was the author's first 'book' with his name on the title-page (*Stevensoniana*, 31).

The Very Worst Ten Minutes I Ever Experienced

FLORA MASSON

From: Flora Masson, 'Louis Stevenson in Edinburgh', in *I Can Remember Robert Louis Stevenson*, ed. Rosalie Masson (1922) pp. 125–32. Flora Masson (d.1937), eldest daughter of David Masson, devoted herself to editing and arranging her father's work. Her books include *Florence Nightingale By One Who Knew Her* (1910), *The Brontës* (1912), *Charles Lamb* (1913) and *Robert Boyle* (1914). One of her earliest literary efforts was a contribution to *Edinburgh Past and Present*, ed. James B. Gillies (1886). She wrote articles for *Cornhill* and *Chambers's* during 1910–11. Her recollection gives a valuable impression of the thrust and parry of conversation between father and son in the early 1870s when critical decisions were about to be taken that would cause such pain to both.

My first recollection of Louis Stevenson is a hazy one, dating back to a bitterly cold winter in the early 'seventies, when all Edinburgh was skating on Duddingston Loch. My brother, Orme Masson, and I were skating there one day, more or less with the Fleeming Jenkins; but Professor and Mrs Jenkin almost always skated together on a little well-swept oval of ice which seemed to have become their special property.[1] Mrs Jenkin, easily tired, used to kneel in the centre of this, looking, in her close-fitting winter garb, the outline of profile against the white banks and jagged, frozen reeds, the hands held in front of her in the small muff, rather like an effigy against the wall of an old church. And the Professor described wonderful figures round about his kneeling wife, circling and pirouetting by himself till she seemed to be rested, when they took hands again. Louis Stevenson came and went about them, skating alone; a slender, dark figure with a muffler about his neck; darting in and out among the crowd, and disappearing and reappearing like a melancholy minnow among the tall reeds that fringe the Loch. I remember that we walked home, several of us together – but not Professor and Mrs Jenkin

– by the Queen's Park and Arthur Seat, all white with snow. And Louis Stevenson came part of the way with us, walking a little separately from us – it was a case, with us all, of heads down against a biting north-east wind – and then turned off by himself across the snow, somewhere about St Leonards, towards the Old Town.

My next recollection is a much more vivid one, of a dinner-party at the house of Louis Stevenson's parents, in Heriot Row; one of the 'young dinners' that were rather prevalent in Edinburgh at that time. It was a pleasant little dinner of twelve or fourteen. One or two sisters and brothers had come together; all were young members of Edinburgh families, and some were more or less intimates in the house in Heriot Row. It was my first visit there, and the first grown-up dinner-party at which I can remember being present.

Diagonally opposite, across the flowers and silver of the dinner-table, I could see Sir Walter Simpson on Mrs Stevenson's right hand; and I have still in my memory the picture of the pretty mother sitting at the head of her table, gently vivacious; and of the young Sir Walter, somewhat languidly attentive to her all dinner-time.[2]

Our end of the table was, to me, almost uncomfortably brilliant. Mr Stevenson had taken me in, and Louis Stevenson was on my other side. Father and son both talked, taking diametrically opposite points of view on all things under the sun. Mr Stevenson seemed to me, on that evening, to be the type of the kindly, orthodox Edinburgh father. We chatted of nice, concrete, comfortable things, such as the Scottish Highlands in autumn; and in a moment of Scottish fervour he quoted – I believe *sotto voce* – a bit of a versified psalm. But Louis Stevenson, on my other side, was that evening in one of his most recklessly brilliant moods. His talk was almost incessant. I felt quite dazed at the mount of intellection he expended on each subject, however trivial in itself, that we touched upon. He worried it as a dog might worry a rat, and then threw it off lightly, as some chance word or allusion set him thinking, and talking, of something else. The father's face at certain moments was a study; an indescribable mixture of vexation, fatherly pride and admiration, and sheer bewilderment at his son's brilliant flippancies and the quick young thrusts of his wit and criticism.[3]

Our talk turned on realism as a duty of the novelist. Louis

Stevenson had been reading Balzac. He was fascinated by Balzac; steeped in Balzac. It was as if he had left Balzac and all his books locked up in some room upstairs – had turned the key on him, with a 'Stay there, my dear fellow, and I'll come back as soon as I can get away from this dinner!'

I knew nothing about Balzac, and I believe I said so. I remember feeling sorry and rather ashamed that I did not know; and Louis Stevenson began telling me about Balzac, and about his style and vocabulary; and I felt grateful to the father for at least appearing to know as little about Balzac as I did, and to care even less. It may have been Balzac's vocabulary that set us talking about the English language; the father and son debated, with some heat, the subject of word-coinage and the use of modern slang. Mr Stevenson upheld the doctrine of a 'well of English undefiled', which of course made Louis Stevenson rattle off with extraordinary ingenuity whole sentences composed of words of foreign origin taken into our language from all parts of the world – words of the East, of classical Europe, of the West Indies, and modern American slang. By a string of sentences he proved the absurdity of such a doctrine, and indeed its practical impossibility. It was a real feat in the handling of language, and I can see to this day his look of pale triumph. The father was silenced; but for a moment he had been almost tearfully in earnest. One could see it was not a matter of mere vocabulary with him. . . .

In the drawing-room upstairs, after dinner, there was a change in the atmospheric conditions. I sat with Mrs Stevenson on a sofa on one side of the fire, and when the men came in there was no more argument, nor, indeed, any brilliant talk. Louis Stevenson stood, facing us, listening to the talk and laughter of others, a slight, boyish figure with a very pale face and luminous eyes, one of a little group of men in the centre of the room. And certainly on that occasion Louis Stevenson wore ordinary conventional evening dress, 'but not exprest in fancy'.

Mr Charles Baxter brought a small chair and sat down on it in front of the sofa where Mrs Stevenson and I were sitting; and, tilting the chair backwards, he broke off a piece of the wood, and instead of seeming sorry or apologetic, handed it with mock gravity to Mrs Stevenson: 'My dear Mrs Stevenson,' he said, 'this is what comes of having cheap furniture!'[4]

Louis Stevenson, from where he stood, watched this performance, but took no notice of it; and Mrs Stevenson, with a glance round her drawing-room, laughed a contented little laugh and laid the offending bit of walnut wood on the arm of the sofa beside her....

As everybody knows, Louis Stevenson was only intermittently in Edinburgh during the years that followed; its 'icy winds and conventions' always drove him away. He never looked really well or happy there, and I believe he owned some of his lightest-hearted hours to the friendship of Professor and Mrs Jenkin. One can scarcely imagine what he would have done or been without them. Certainly it is impossible to recall the Louis Stevenson of the seventies except as one — a favoured one — of that delightful Jenkin *coterie*.

Edinburgh has greatly changed since those days. When people launch on amateur theatricals now, they do it on a large scale, taking one of the theatres. But I doubt if these performances are as much an event, in the Edinburgh of to-day, as those dear old 'private theatricals' were, to which we were so hospitably invited in Professor and Mrs Jenkin's own house; where the audiences went packed, night after night, into the dining-room, and the wall between the dining-room and the room behind it was made to 'let down' in some mysterious way to form a stage, with a real curtain and footlights, and what not. And each successive winter, there was the same pleasant secrecy as to 'what it was going to be this year'; if it were to be 'something of Shakespeare's', or 'from the Greek', or 'something new'. The members of the little company were always very loyal in keeping up the mystery to the last possible moment, and then, when it leaked out, there was always the important question, 'Which night are you asked for?' And afterwards there were all sorts of comments and criticisms, and the theatricals continued to be talked about till a fresh fall of snow heralded the approach of our Edinburgh summer. And with all this, I fear we were not always grateful enough for the immense amount of trouble that was taken to teach us what dramatic art might be under the domestic roof.

Louis Stevenson was not one of the chief actors in that company. Yet there are people who remember his Orsino in *Twelfth Night* – the slender figure in the 'splendid Francis I. clothes, heavy with gold and stage jewellery' and the satisfied languor of his opening words:

> 'If Music be the food of love, play on.
> Give me excess of it, that, surfeiting,

The appetite may sicken, and so die.
That strain again! it had a dying fall. . . .'

But it was not so much the play that Louis Stevenson enjoyed, nor even the 'thrill of admiration' in successive audiences, as to 'sup afterwards with those clothes on', amid all the Shakespearian wit and raillery and badinage that circulated about the supper-table: 'That,' he wrote, 'is something to live for.'[5]

At the end of one of those performances of *Twelfth Night*, when the audience was thronging into the hall, and the carriages were being called at the front door in stentorian tones, we saw Louis Stevenson's mother making her way out alone, her pretty face still radiant with maternal pride. Louis Stevenson, one of a little group of the performers who were waiting, I suppose, 'to sup afterwards with those clothes on', was looking down over the balustrade, half-way up the staircase. But in a moment he was down among the departing guests; wrapped his mother's cloak with an infinite tenderness about her, and then, escaping from the crowd's admiring eyes, fled up the staircase again. I can still see the upward look of adoration his mother gave him, as she went on her way among the departing guests, triumphant.

There are some humorous recollections of Louis Stevenson in the green-room. On one occasion I saw him walking up and down a little bit of the big drawing-room, looking, in a dreamy, detached way each time he passed, into a mirror that was hung on the line of sight. It was as if he were acting to himself being an actor; and then he brought carmine and powder, and began making himself up, peering gravely close into the little glass.

Another time he fell to disputing with a bigger and altogether more muscular member of the company as to which of the two could claim to have *the larger girth of calf*. Louis Stevenson was under the impression his own was the larger; and so in earnest was he, and so anxious to prove his case, that he actually fetched an inch-tape, and inveigled his muscular friend into kneeling on the drawing-room carpet, while each, with much solemnity, took the exact measurements of the other's calf!

But once Louis Stevenson surpassed himself. It was in Greek tragedy. The curtain had fallen on a powerful and moving scene, amid the applause of the audience, and the stage was left in the possession of two of the young actors – Mr Hole and my brother – both in Greek garb. In a momentary reaction after so much unrelieved tragedy, these two, oblivious of their classic draperies, threw themselves into one another's arms, performed a rapid war-dance, and then flung themselves on to opposite ends of a couch at the back of the stage, with their feet meeting in a kind of triumphal arch in the centre. Louis Stevenson, who had been officiating at the curtain, took one look at them. He touched a spring, and up went the curtain again.

The audience, scarcely recovered from the tragic scene on which the curtain had fallen, gave one gasp of amazement, and then broke into a roar of applause. That roar was the first thing that showed the two luckless acrobats that something had happened. They leapt to their feet, only to see the curtain fall once more. Professor Jenkin, who was host and stage-manager in one, had been watching this particular portion of the play from the front. Without a word, he left his seat and went behind the scenes. 'Mr Stevenson,' he said, with icy distinctness, 'I shall ask you to give me a few minutes in my own room.'

Anybody who ever saw Louis Stevenson can imagine the little enigmatic flutter of a smile, the deprecatory bend of the head, with which he followed the Professor. What happened in that stage-manager's room? There was some trepidation among the members of the company; and a furtive whisper circulated among them: *'Can it be corporal punishment?'* And there was a general feeling of relief when Louis Stevenson sauntered into the drawing-room with a look of absolute unconcern.

But one of the little company – the brilliant, charming, irrepressible Leila Scot-Skirving (afterwards Mrs Maturin), had been interested enough to linger behind the others, and to waylay Louis Stevenson as he left the Professor's room. I am indebted to her brother, A. A. Scot-Skirving, for the end of this anecdote.

'What happened?' she whispered; and Louis whispered back: 'The very worst ten minutes I ever experienced in the whole course of my life!'

NOTES

1. The loch was a favourite winter skating rendezvous. 'If you had seen the moon rising, a perfect sphere of smoky gold, in the dark air above the trees, and the white loch thick with skaters, and the great hill, snow-sprinkled, overhead! It was a sight for a king' (to Mrs Sitwell,

23 Dec. 1874, *Letters*, I, 83). Cousin Bob, a better figure-skater than Louis, would perform wearing a crimson sash around his waist, a fashion Louis adopted. Henry Charles Fleeming Jenkin, Professor of Engineering at Edinburgh University (1868–85), pioneer of electrical application in transportation, contributor to the technology of submarine cable-laying.

2. Sir Walter Grindlay Simpson (d.1898), one of Stevenson's best friends since Edinburgh University days. Son of Sir James Young Simpson (1811–90), obstetrician who pioneered the use of chloroform, he succeeded to the baronetcy in 1870. Known to Louis as 'the Bart' or 'Simp', he appears as Athelred in 'Talk and Talkers'. They travelled to Germany in 1872, cruised the Inner Hebrides in 1874, and, more notably, canoed in north-eastern France in 1876, an expedition which became the subject of *An Inland Voyage* (1878).

3. Several witnesses refer to this rivalry, and the mixed emotions in both parties. Eve Blantyre Simpson's report of the badinage reveals some of the psychological strains. See *R. L. Stevenson's Edinburgh Days*, 34–6.

4. Charles Baxter (1848–1919), life-long friend and custodian of Louis's publishing business affairs after 1887. Prior to that time W.E. Henley had acted for him: 'He is my unpaid agent – an admirable arrangement for me, and one that has rather than doubled my income on the spot', Louis wrote in 1883 (*Letters*, I, 268). Fellow-students at Edinburgh, they maintained a correspondence in which they indulged in burlesques, playing the roles of Thomson and Johnson, ex-elders of the Scottish kirk. See *R.L.S.: Stevenson's Letters to Charles Baxter*, ed. DeLancey Ferguson and Marshall Waingrow (1956).

5. 'I play Orsino every day, in all the pomp of Solomon, splendid Francis the First clothes, heavy with gold and stage jewellery. I play it ill enough, I believe; but me and the clothes, and the wedding wherewith the clothes and me are reconciled, produce every night a thrill of admiration' (*Letters*, I, 93–4).

Delightfully and Fearlessly Boyish

MARGARET BLACK

From *Robert Louis Stevenson* (1898) 39–64. Margaret Moyes Black grew up with many of the Balfours, especially the family of Dr John Balfour (d.1887), who had treated cholera victims during the Indian Mutiny. He returned to Scotland in 1849 and found himself again dealing with outbreaks of cholera in the parish of Cramond. During another epidemic in 1866 he practised at Leven, Fife, and built his house, 'The

Turret', where Louis was often a visitor. Margaret Black was to become a friend of Louis's mother in the 1870s and attended some of the dinner parties at Heriot Row where, depending on the company assembled, Louis commanded attention by his 'buoyant freshness of mind and outlook' (quoted in Masson, *I Can Remember*, 39–42). Margaret Black won success with several Scottish novels such as *A Woman and Pitiful: A Deeside Story* (1893), *The Ghost of Gairn, A Tale of 'the Forty Five'* (1894) and *The House of Cargill, A Tale of the Smuggling Days* (1895).

It was a stirring time at the University, and the students who warred manfully against the innovation of Dr Sophia Jex-Blake and the pioneers of the Lady Doctors' movement, were, it would seem on looking back, scarcely so mildly mannered, so peacefully inclined as those who now sit placidly beside 'the sweet girl graduates' of our day, on the class-room benches, and acknowledge the reign of the lady doctor as an accomplished fact.[1] A torchlight procession of modern times is apparently a cheerful and picturesque function, smiled on by the authorities, and welcomed as a rather unique means of doing honour to a new Lord Rector or some famous guest of the city or the University. In Mr Stevenson's time, a torchlight procession had all the joys of 'forbidden fruit' to the merry lads who braved the police and the professors for the pleasure of marching through the streets to the final bonfire on the Calton Hill, from the scrimmage round which they emerged with clothes well oiled and singed, and faces and hands as black as much besmearing could make them; while anxious friends at home trembled lest a night in the police cells should be the reward of the ringleaders. . . .

Another old-time enjoyment of that date was a snowball fight. Whether snow is less plentiful, or students are too cultured and too refined for these rough pastimes it is impossible to say, but certain it is that a really *great* snowball fight is also a thing of the past. In those days they were Homeric combats, and a source of keen enjoyment to Robert Louis Stevenson, a very funny account of whom, on one of these occasions, was given me at the time by his cousin, Lewis Balfour, from Leven, himself a jovial medical student enjoying an active part in the melée. On the occasion of a great battle in the winter of 1869 – or 1870 – Mr Stevenson and one or two men, now well known in various professions, had seated themselves on a ledge in the quadrangle to watch the fight. From this vantage ground they encouraged the combatants, but took no active part in the fray. Within swarmed the students armed with snowballs, without, the lads of the town, equally active, stormed the gates. All were too intent on the battle to notice the advent of the police, who rushed into the college quadrangle and made prisoners where they could. Craning his neck too much, in his keen enjoyment, Mr Stevenson overbalanced himself, slipped from his perch and was promptly captured by 'a bobby', and, in spite of gallant efforts for his rescue, was ignominiously marched off to the Police Office at the very moment that his blandly unconscious mother was driving up the Bridges. It was useless for his attendant friends to assert that he had been a non-combatant. Was he not taken in the very thick of the fight? The police had him and they meant to keep him for he could not produce sufficient bail from his somewhat empty pockets. His cousin and his friends, by leaving all their stray coins, their watches and other valuables, managed to secure his release so that he had not the experience – which it is possible he might have enjoyed – of passing a night in the police cells of his native city....

Stories of all sorts were handed about in our little clique of the wondrous Robert Louis whose sayings and doings were already precious to an appreciative circle of relatives and friends. But it was not till sometime in the autumn of 1869 that he first became personally known to me.

The introduction took place on a September afternoon in the drawing-room of 'The Turret', and he inspired a great deal of awe in a youthful admirer who even then had literary aspirations, and who therefore looked up to him with much respect as someone who already wrote. From that time he was regarded as one of the quaintest, the most original and the most charming personalities among one's acquaintances. There was about him, in those days, a whimsical affectation, a touch of purely delightful vanity that never wholly left him in later life, and that far from repelling, as it would have done in any one more commonplace, was so intrinsically a part of his artistic nature that it was rather attractive than otherwise. Full of delightful humour, his idlest sayings – when he took the trouble to say anything which he frequently did not! – were teeming with the elements not only of laughter but of thought, and you wondered, long after you had talked with him, why it was that you saw new lights on things, and found food for mirth and matter for reflection where neither had suggested itself before.

In those days he was not only original himself, but he had to a great degree that rare faculty of bringing to the surface in others the very smallest spark of originality, and of remembering it and appreciating it in a way that was stimulating and helpful to those who had the pleasure of knowing him. When the little seaside town was empty of visitors, and it was not time to pay Edinburgh visits for the season, in February and March, one kindness of his was very greatly prized by some of us who beguiled the tedium of the winter months by writing for and conducting an amateur magazine, called *Ours*. For this, in 1872 and 1873, Mr Stevenson gave us a short contribution, *The Nun of Aberhuern*, a trifle in his own graceful style, which, as he was even then beginning to be known in the world of letters, we valued much.[2] Moreover, he took a friendly interest in the sheets of blue MS. paper so closely written over with our somewhat juvenile productions, and made here a criticism, there a prediction, which has not been without its effect on the future work of some of us. . . .

Except at a wedding, or some such solemn function, whereat he probably looked misery personified, one cannot remember him so conventionally apparelled as in the frock-coat and the tall hat. Possibly it was before this access of propriety temporarily had him in its grasp that one day we saw him in Princes Street 'taking the air' in an open cab with a Stevenson cousin, attired in like manner with himself.[3] In those days fashionable people often walked in Princes Street in the afternoon, so what was our dismay, in the midst of quite a crowd of the gay world, to see that open cab, at a word of command from Robert Louis, draw near the pavement as we approached, when two battered straw hats were lifted to us with quite a Parisian grace. Both young men wore sailor hats with brilliant ribbon bands, both were attired in flannel cricketing jackets with broad bright stripes, and round Louis's neck was knotted a huge yellow silk handkerchief, while over both their heads one of them held an open umbrella. In days when the wearing of cricketing clothes, except in the playing fields, was in Scotland still so uncommon that it is on authentic record that an elderly unmarried lady in an east coast watering place, on meeting on its high street a young man in boating flannels, was so shocked at the innovation that she promptly went home, leaving all her shopping undone and her tea-drinking and friendly gossip forgotten, such an apparition as that in the open cab required more courage to face than people accustomed to the present-day use of gay tennis garb can easily imagine. It was fortunate that nerve to return the salutation smilingly was not wanting, or Mr Stevenson would certainly have pitilessly chaffed the timid victims of conventionality afterwards.

Having borne the ordeal with such courage as we possessed, we hastened to have tea with Mrs Stevenson, whose first question was, 'Have you seen Lou?'

And when we described that startling vision that was slowly creeping along Princes Street in the open cab, she laughed till her tears fell. In half an hour or so her son came in cool and unconcerned, and as punctiliously polite as if his attire had been the orthodox apparel for an afternoon tea-party.

NOTES

1. Sophia Jex-Blake (1840–1912), pioneer in medicine as a career for women and author of *Medical Women: A Thesis and a History* (1886). Throughout the 1870s she battled the medical establishment at Edinburgh University; the University admitted women to graduation in medicine in 1894. She founded the London School of Medicine (1874), and a women's hospital in Edinburgh (1883).
2. Vincent Starrett identified the work as 'The Inn of Aberhuern'. The MS. was restored to Stevenson in 1894 and probably destroyed. See *Letters*, II, 351; Starrett, *Bookman's Holiday* (1942).
3. Probably his boon companion, R. A. M. (Bob) Stevenson.

Edinburgh Ale and Cold Meat Pies

CHARLES LOWE

From 'Robert Louis Stevenson: a Reminiscence', *Bookman*, I, (Nov 1891), 60–1. Charles Lowe (1848–1931) was a fellow student at Edinburgh who went on to become Berlin correspondent of *The Times* for 13 years (see *The Tale of a Times Correspondent*, 1928); his publications include *Prince Bismarck: An Historical Biography* (1885), *Alexander III of Russia* (1894), *The German Emperor, William II* (1895), and *The Life Story of Edward VII* (1910).

Curiously enough, it was in what might be called an arena of abstract science that I first made the acquaintance of a young man who is now one of the most distinguished *littérateurs* of the age. On a sunny spring morning, now, alas! a score of years ago – sunny, though the huge stove was still roaring away in the corner with a rumbling sound like the rush of an express train through a tunnel – we were sitting in the mathematical class-room of the University of Edinburgh awaiting the incoming of our dear old Professor (Kelland),[1] I being then deep in the *Daily News* description of the German entry into Paris, when I felt a hand gently laid on my shoulder, and, turning round, beheld a young man with whose face I was quite familiar, though not yet cognisant of his name. Having always had a sharp and roving eye for varieties of type and character among my fellow-students, this particular youth had already arrested my attention by the possession of exterior qualities which marked him off strongly from the rest of his comrades – a certain grace and refinement of manner and person not very common among the academic communities of Scotland, and withal a free and unconventional air with which a black velvet jacket and flowing flaxen locks were well matched. His whole appearance was much more indicative of the poet or the aesthete than of the scientist, and yet here was this attractive youth tapping my shoulder in one of the front benches of the mathematical class. Was not my name so and so, and was not I the fellow who had sent in a poem to the editors of the *University Magazine*, of whom, he added, he was one.[2] His co-editor, who was sitting near him engaged in the perusal of a love sonnet instead of a treatise on logarithms, was another young man of equally fascinating exterior and charming manners – Walter Ferrier, son of a St Andrews professor and grandson of Christopher North – a young man of high aspirations and great promise too soon blasted by death;[3] and nothing would content these *Arcades ambo* but that they should at once launch out into the literary career and try their 'prentice hand on a monthly venture entitled the *Edinburgh University Magazine* – a venture which did not last very long, and probably, indeed, received its death blow from the verses, monopolising about a third of one number, which the editors were indiscreet enough to accept from me and insert in their otherwise sparkling enough pages. It was a cantata, partly in the Lowland Scots dialect, written in imitation of one of Burns's larger pieces; and though I would give my worst enemy a very considerable *douceur* rather than that he should now rake this effusion up against me, I am at the same time pleased and proud to think that it was the means of bringing me into personal contact with Robert Louis Stevenson, for that was the name of the young man who had tapped me on the shoulder. Stevenson was, on the whole, well pleased with my poem, though he insisted on making certain editorial emendations, some of which, however, I am bound to say, did more credit to the delicacy of his taste than to the accuracy of that sense of rhythm, of which he subsequently became so great a master. From the mathematical class-room we hastened to repair to the privacy of a snug house of entertainment close by, called 'The Pump', there to continue our discussion over Edinburgh ale and cold meat pies; and I cannot remember that ever I spent a more pleasant, or, indeed, a more inspiring, hour in Auld Reekie than the first one I thus passed with Robert Stevenson. From that single hour's conversation with the embryo author of 'Treasure Island' I certainly derived more intellectual and personal stimulus than ever was imparted to me by any six months' course of lectures within the walls of 'good King James's College'. He was so perfectly frank and ingenuous, so ebullient and open-hearted, so sunny, so sparkling, so confiding, so vaulting in his literary ambitions, and withal so widely read and well-informed – notwithstanding his youth, for he could scarcely have been out of his teens then – that I could not help saying to myself that here was a young man who had commended himself more to my approval and emulation than any other of my fellow-students.

NOTES

1. Philip Kelland (1808–79), Professor of Mathematics, University of Edinburgh (1838–79), of whom Stevenson wrote 'No man's education is complete or truly liberal who knew not Kelland' (*Memories and Portraits*, 30).

2. The magazine, Stevenson records, ran 'four months in undisturbed obscurity, and died without a gasp' (*Memories and Portraits*, 73). His contributions included 'An Old Scotch Gardener', 'Edinburgh Students in 1824', 'The Modern Student Considered Generally', 'The Philosophy of Umbrellas' (with J. W. Ferrier), 'Debating Societies', and 'The Philosophy of Nomenclature'.

3. James Walter Ferrier (d.1883) was the son of James Frederick Ferrier

(1808–64), the distinguished philosopher, whose works appeared in three volumes in 1875. Afflicted by tuberculosis, the son became an alcoholic and died young, his mother blaming Stevenson for contributing to his dissipation. Deeply moved by his death, Stevenson wrote to Henley: 'I think of him as one who was good, though sometimes clouded. He was the only gentle one of all my friends, save perhaps the other Walter [Simpson].' Interestingly, he sees Ferrier in terms of dual selves: 'the good, true Ferrier obliterates the memory of the other, who was only his 'lunatic brother' (*Letters*, I, 280–1). See also the tribute in 'Old Mortality' (*Memories and Portraits*, 50–5).

A Wonderful Talker

GEORGE LISLE

From 'R.L.S. and Some Savages on an Island', *Cornhill*, 51 (Dec 1921), 706–12. The contributor had been a pupil at Henderson's School, some 15 years later than Stevenson. He dates this recollection as after 1875, when the novelist would have been in his mid-twenties. Cramond had been a favorite spot for Stevenson and his Balfour cousins, one of whom had been given the identifying nickname from the locality. See 'The Lantern Bearers', first published in *Scribner's Magazine*, Feb 1888, or a similar celebration of childhood haunts in 'Memoirs of an Islet', *Memories and Portraits* (1887).

At the top of the island there are the remains of a cairn which was, no doubt, built by the Picts or other aborigines and improved by the Romans, but of which very little now remains. Near this there was a favourite outlook tower, and one lovely afternoon of brilliant sunshine and strong west wind two canoes were seen by many anxious eyes from this vantage ground, struggling up the Forth from Granton in the teeth of the wind. There was a very good telescope on the island, and this was at once brought to bear on the canoes, which certainly seemed to be in difficulties. The sea was washing over the tiny craft, but the occupants were very persevering, and instead of running before the wind for Granton Harbour, seemed determined to come to the island for shelter, although they were evidently getting exhausted. At one time they appeared to be in such distress that two flags were run up the flag-staff on the cairn to let the boatman at Cramond know that he was urgently required.¹ Soon, however, it was seen that the canoeists were in calm water and the SOS signal was withdrawn. The whole available population of the island were not long in running down to the rocky south-east shore of the island to give the ship-wrecked mariners a welcome. The first canoe to land was occupied by a lanky, cadaverous, black-haired, black-eyed man, apparently six feet in height but very slim, in a velveteen coat.² His canoe was built of mahogany, with a deck of either cedar or mahogany; the other was a canvas canoe of a somewhat nondescript appearance; had it got upon the rocks it would not have lasted long. As I was the biggest of the lot of wreckers who had come to welcome them, the canoeists asked me if I would help them up with their canoes above high-water mark, as they had had enough sailing for one day and were badly in need of a rest. I was delighted at the job, and as I was accustomed to climb among the rocks and over slippery seaweed, and did not mind getting myself wet, it was not long before the two canoes were safely above high-water mark. He of the canvas canoe immediately lay down to rest in the sunshine, but the other before doing so thanked me in the nicest way possible for my stalwart assistance, and presented me with a shilling, which I, of course, with some diffidence and much internal joy accepted.³ The canoeists rested for some time, but were not long before they completely recovered from their exhaustion, and then he of the wooden canoe proved to be a wonderful talker, a very easy 'speirer', and sometimes a very difficult one to answer.³ Among other questions he asked of the half-dozen of us, who were all about the age of twelve –

'What other savages live upon the island?'

I felt somewhat nettled at being called a savage, and replied:

'You must have forgotten your "Robinson Crusoe" or you would know that it was the savages who came to the island in canoes. There were no savages till you came.'

Both voyagers laughed heartily, and he of the canvas canoe said to the other:

'You're fairly caught this time, Louis!'

In thinking over the matter I rather imagine that it was after this remark that I got my famous shilling and not before it. However, they insisted upon seeing the text of 'Robinson Crusoe', where the two canoes and the savages are mentioned. I was too keen in examining their own boats, as I had never seen such things before, to go up to the house to get my 'Robinson Crusoe'; but Annie Reid, she of the long pig-tail and blue eyes, was always anxious to be the slave of anyone who would employ her, volunteered to go and fetch the book, which she did, and handed it over to the unbelieving savages.[5] I thought the beautiful book, with its brightly coloured frontispiece of Robinson Crusoe in a red cowl and blue jacket reading a huge Bible, and many other illustrations, both in colour and in black and white, would impress the savages, but its effect upon them was far beyond my expectations. Stevenson gave a war-whoop like a genuine savage, and exclaimed:

'Oh shades of Cocky Henderson and the companions of my palmy days! I too was at this school in the days of my misspent youth.' And then burst out with great gusto into song, –

> 'Here we suffer grief and pain
> Under Mr. Hendie's cane,
> If you don't obey his laws
> He will punish with his tawse.'

This parody was current in the school in my time quite recently completed, and had evidently been in vogue in Stevenson's day at least fifteen years prior. In fact, Stevenson may have been the author of it. The awful doggerel may have been part of his merry muses – a preliminary canter to 'A Child's Garden of Verses'. He talked much of 'Cocky' Henderson, as he irreverently was called by some of his pupils. We both agreed in our estimate of Henderson, which did not coincide with that of our parents. There were other poets at the school, but none ever gave Henderson the credit for their development in that direction. . . .[6]

It was a beautiful Sunday afternoon when Stevenson took me to Inchmickery. Sunday must have been the only day available, because we had both been brought up very strictly to reverence the Sabbath day, and I have no doubt we justified the matter by putting it in as a work of necessity, as it was a necessity that the sea should be absolutely calm when we took such an adventurous voyage in a cockle shell of a boat. Inchmickery is fully a mile from Cramond Island, and in one of the deepest channels of the Firth of Forth, which perhaps from the slim deck of a canoe looked even deeper than it really was. Stevenson talked about every subject under the sun, but I remember he specially enlarged on Sunday observance, for I told him that a few Sundays before I had been nearly drowned, early in the morning, off the north side of Cramond Island, and that the orthodox vision of his whole life, which the drowning man sees, had not been vouchsafed to me; that what disturbed me was that there would be a paragraph in the papers about a Sabbath-breaker having met his just punishment. Stevenson laughed heartily at my disappointment in not having the whole of my uneventful life flash before me (for I thought I was drowning), and at my positive objection to being made an awful warning to all Sunday-school scholars. I also told him how my cousin and I had got so tired of the Shorter Catechism on Sundays that one Sunday we hid it.[7] But it was of no avail, because my mother knew by heart and in their order, not only the Answers but the Questions. His comment on that was:

'Boy, you have a mother!'

NOTES

1. Cramond Island in the Firth of Forth, about three-quarters of a mile from the village of Cramond, was a favourite haunt. Stevenson describes the area as 'a little hamlet on a little river, embowered in woods, and looking forth over a great flat of quicksand to where a little islet stood planted in the sea' (*St Ives*, ch. xxx). On a walk to Cramond on 8 April 1871, Louis broke the news to his father that he could not go into engineering.

2. 'Velvet coat' was one of the soubriquets applied frequently and relished by the young bohemian.

3. The other canoeist was probably 'Cramond' Lewis Balfour. The numerous Balfour progeny were given nicknames according to where they were born.

4. A diligent questioner.

5. The book, a school prize, establishes the date as post-1875. The Reids were long-time residents of the island.

6. This was the preparatory school in India Street that Louis attended for a short time in 1857 and again in 1859.

7. Stevenson returned several times to the island and took the boy out in his canoe. The Shorter Catechism had exercised a strong influence on his formative years, as W. E. Henley's well-known poem suggests. 'Sabbath observance', Louis wrote, 'makes a series of grim, and perhaps serviceable, pauses in the tenor of Scotch boyhood – days of great stillness and solitude for the rebellious mind, when in the dearth of books and play, and in the intervals of studying the Shorter Catechism, the intellect and senses prey upon and test each other'. See 'The

Foreigner at Home' (*Memories and Portraits*). Something of the Shorter Catechist stuck to Louis all his life. See *Letters*, II, 304.

I Do Not Remember an Ill-natured Remark

CHARLES J. GUTHRIE

From *Robert Louis Stevenson: Some Personal Recollections* (1920) 30–41. Guthrie's memories, frank, shrewd and fair-minded, arise from genuine affection governed by a lawyer's detachment. Both were contemporaries at University and studied for the Bar, being called in the same year, 1875 (see p. 10). As far as questions of legal right were concerned, Guthrie noted, there were many men he would have sought out before Stevenson, 'but on a nice point of personal honour, or on a question of generous treatment, I would unhesitatingly have placed myself without reserve in his hands'. Like Andrew Lang and several others who became Louis's friends, Guthrie was initially inclined to write off the flamboyant youth as something of a dilettante: 'a light horseman, lacking two essentials for success – diligence and health' (Simpson, *Robert Louis Stevenson*, 35).

Stevenson was a student in the University of Edinburgh during two separate periods, first, preparatory to his entrance on the life of a civil engineer, and, second, on the abandonment of that career, as a student of law qualifying for the Scottish Bar.[1] I often rubbed shoulders with him during the first period; I knew him intimately in the second.

There is a characteristic incident connected with the first period. In 1866, Thomas Carlyle and Benjamin Disraeli were the rival candidates for the Lord Rectorship of the University of Edinburgh. The contest was a keen one. Louis, thick and thin Tory, voted for Disraeli; I, detached radical, for Carlyle. Carlyle was elected; and, when he rose to address the University as Lord Rector, the Music Hall was packed with the usual noisy, excited mob of students. Loyal to tradition, the supporters of the defeated candidate, Louis Stevenson prominent among them, were there in a compact crowd, bent on making a disturbance, which they duly did during the preliminary proceedings.[2] But when the old man, throwing off his gorgeous Rectorial robe stood forward, no longer the victorious candidate but an old Edinburgh student, who had risen to the highest place as a man of letters, not by birth or favour, but by his own genius and industry, to speak to us as a father would to his sons, it was too much for the lads. They and we sprang to our feet together, and cheered and cheered, and cheered again. The late Sir Andrew Fraser, Lieutenant-Governor of Bengal, told me that he met Stevenson leaving the Hall, and chaffed him on the palpable inconsistency between his politics and his conduct.[3] 'Inconsistency! Politics!' quoth Stevenson. 'Don't talk blazing nonsense, Fraser! What have politics to do with that glorious old Scot?' . . .

At the Tuesday night meetings [of the Speculative Society] he was a regular attender and a frequent speaker, and he used the rooms of the Society during the week to lounge in.[4] He read in the well-furnished library, and delighted, above all, to discuss and discourse with any specimen of that genus, rare in a Scots university, a loafer. There were cliques even in that little company, limited to thirty members, and admitted by a drastic ballot. But Louis' catholic camaraderie made him the friend of all. In repartee he could take as well as give, and I do not remember an ill-natured remark of his to anybody or of anybody. Never once did we see him depressed. He would be absent, down with haemorrhage from the lungs, and within a few days he would return, the liveliest of the lively, the gayest of the gay.

On one occasion I proposed that a bust of Lord Jeffrey, one of the Society's most distinguished members, should be brought from its obscurity in the lobby to a conspicuous place in the Inner Hall. The proposal was unanimously negatived, the opposition being led by Stevenson, who professed to doubt my identification of the bust, and reminded the Society, as was the fact, that it had lain in the lobby from time immemorial, with a large ticket on it bearing the scornful legend, 'Who the devil is this?' Just before the next meeting, I, the secretary of the Society, bound to obey all its orders, had the bust removed from the lobby and placed in the Inner Hall, between the portraits of two former members, Sir Walter Scott by Sir John Watson Gordon, and Francis Horner by Sir Henry Raeburn. I well remember Stevenson's entry, his start of amazement, his shouts of laughter at my 'superb audacity,' and his motion of condonation and approval, which was carried with acclamation! . . .

Of the many score speeches, smart rather than serious, I heard him make, I do not remember a word. But a favourite subject of study has impressed on my memory his remarkable paper on 'John Knox and his Relations to Women', now included in his *Familiar Studies of Man and Books*, and his valedictory address in 1873 as president [of the Speculative Society]. . . .

I doubt whether Stevenson ever seriously meant business at the Bar. I do indeed remember one morning in the Parliament House, when he came dancing up to me waving a bundle of legal papers in great glee: 'Guthrie, that simpleton So-and-So has actually sent me a case! Now I have tasted blood, idle fellows like you will see what I can do!' No doubt he was pleased with the four complimentary pieces of employment he is said to have received, the fees for which did not run into two figures; but he must have known that his feeble frame and uncertain health could never weather the long sittings and the late sittings, and the nervous strain of the daily conflict, in over-heated, badly ventilated courts, with obtuse judges, dull juries, deaf witnesses, exacting solicitors, and unreasonable clients. He had no natural taste for law. He lacked what is perhaps the prime requisite for success at the Bar, namely, that love of the business which makes easy the sacrifice of time and strength, of leisure and amusement, that would be intolerable in the interests of almost any other profession. Stevenson had not even the love for the curiosities of legal history and legal lore which fascinated Sir Walter Scott. Nor had he the comprehensive insight into human nature, the balance of mind and sobriety of judgment, which, with his industry and his predilection for law, might have made Sir Walter a great judge, if not a great advocate.

NOTES

1. Louis entered Edinburgh University in 1866. His engineering studies proceeded in lackadaisical fashion, except for field trips (1868–70), notably in 1868 to Wick, when he made a descent in a diving suit. In the spring of 1871, Fleeming Jenkin was approached for a certificate of attendance, which he declined to give. Louis passed the preliminary examination for the Scottish Bar in 1872, and his finals in July 1875. Throughout this period he travelled extensively, suffering the usual bouts of ill-health, indulging in bohemian pursuits, reading voraciously and

practising his future calling. For comment on his Edinburgh University professors see 'Some College Memories' (*Memories and Portraits*).

2. Thomas Carlyle (1795–1881) was elected Rector in April 1866. Carlyle anticipated the occasion with mounting dread, but when the moment came he 'spoke to the students as if the celebrities were accidental onlookers', addressing 'Young Scotland' directly rather than from a prepared paper. After tumultuous applause, 'students surging forward to touch him', he was pursued into the street amidst 'vivats and vociferations' (Fred Kaplan, *Thomas Carlyle: A Biography* (1983) 466–9).

3. Sir Andrew Henderson Leith Fraser (1848–1919), civil servant, served 27 years in the Central Provinces of India. He wrote *Report on the Famine in the Central Provinces in 1899–1900*, 3 vols (1901), and was appointed Lieutenant Governor of Bengal, receiving the KCSI (1903). Towards politics Louis at this time was indifferent, but he joined the Conservative Club, at the same time professing himself 'a red-hot Socialist'. See 'Crabbed Age and Youth' (*Virginibus Puerisque*, 1881).

4. Louis was elected in February, 1869 to this exclusive debating society. He made a dismal maiden speech, but went on to become one of its five presidents by 1872. He gave eight papers on topics including the Covenanters, American Literature, Law and Free Will, and Knox (two papers). In his valedictory address he noted that 'some of the happiest hours of my life' had been in the Spec. See 'A College Magazine' (*Memories and Portraits*).

As Restless and Questing as a Spaniel

EDMUND GOSSE

From *Critical Kit-Kats* (1896) 276–82. Sir Edmund William Gosse (1849–1928), poet, scholar and critic, is now best known for *Father and Son* (1907), an account of life with his Plymouth Brethren father, but also wrote on Gray, Congreve, Donne, Patmore and Swinburne, and – an expert in Scandinavian language – a life of Ibsen (1908). His *Collected Poems* appeared in 1911. In 1865 Gosse joined the cataloguing section of the British Museum; in 1875 became translator to the Board of Trade; in 1910 librarian to the House of Lords, a post he held for ten years. Stevenson portrayed him as Purcel in 'Talk and Talkers' (*Memories and Portraits*, 1887). His friendship with Stevenson began on a boat off the Hebrides in the summer of 1869 and he contributed biographical notes to the *Pentland Edition of the Works of Robert Louis Stevenson* (1906–7), and wrote the Stevenson entry for the *Encyclopaedia Britannica*, 10th edition. This recollection has been acknowledged by several biographers as a fine rendering of Stevenson's mercurial nature in the early years. Gosse was not in the closest circle: he was too much the strait-laced conservative – too English in a sense – for intimacy of the kind Louis shared with Simpson, Baxter or Henley. However, Gosse showed great concern for his career, and they corresponded regularly, Louis addressing him by a nickname drawn from his initials 'WEG', the name of Dickens's disreputable ballad-seller in *Our Mutual Friend*. Like Colvin and others, he was unhappy about Stevenson's departure for America and uncomfortable with his choice of a wife. 'He took this last made journey to America', he wrote in December 1879, 'in despite of all his friends' (Evan Charteris, *The Life and Letters of Sir Edmund Gosse* (1931) 128). Fanny, a shrewd judge of character, described Gosse in 1884 as 'smooth, silken, like a purring cat, very witty, rather maliciously so, but vain beyond belief' (Ann Thwaite, *Edmund Gosse: A Literary Landscape 1847–1928* (1984) 219). Two days before he died, Stevenson wrote to thank Gosse for dedicating his latest poems, *In Russet and Silver*, 'To Tusitala', and called to mind their first meeting almost a quarter of a century before.

At the tail of this chatty, jesting little crowd of invaders came a youth of about my own age, whose appearance, for some mysterious reason, instantly attracted me. He was tall, preternaturally lean, with longish hair, and as restless and questing as a spaniel. The party from Portree fairly took possession of us; at meals they crowded around the captain, and we common tourists sat silent, below the salt. The stories of Blackie and Sam Bough were resonant.[1] Meanwhile, I knew not why, I watched the plain, pale lad who took the lowest place in this privileged company.

The summer of 1870 remains in the memory of western Scotland as one of incomparable splendour. Our voyage, especially as evening drew on, was like an emperor's progress. We stayed on deck till the latest moment possible, and I occasionally watched the lean youth, busy and serviceable, with some of the little tricks with which we were later on to grow familiar – the advance with hand on hip, the sidewise bending of the head to listen. Meanwhile darkness overtook us, a wonderful halo of moonlight swam up over Glenelg, the indigo of the peaks of the Cuchullins faded into the general blue night. I went below, but was presently aware of some change of course, and then of an unexpected stoppage. I tore on deck, and found that we had left our track among the islands, and had steamed up a narrow and unvisited fiord of the mainland – I think Loch Nevis. The sight was curious and bewildering. We lay in a gorge of blackness, with only a strip of the blue moonlit sky overhead; in the dark a few lanterns jumped about the shore, carried by agitated but unseen and soundless persons. As I leaned over the bulwarks, Stevenson was at my side, and he explained to me that we had come up this loch to take away to Glasgow a large party of emigrants driven from their homes in the interests of a deer-forest. As he spoke, a black mass became visible entering the vessel. Then, as we slipped off shore, the fact of their hopeless exile came home to these poor fugitives, and suddenly, through the absolute silence, there rose from them a wild kerning and wailing, reverberated by the cliffs of the loch, and at that strange place and hour infinitely poignant. When I came on deck next morning, my unnamed friend was gone. He had put off with the engineers to visit some remote lighthouse of the Hebrides.[2] . . .

It was in 1877, or late in 1876, that I was presented to Stevenson, at the old Savile Club, by Mr Sidney Colvin, who thereupon left us to our devices. We went downstairs and lunched together, and then we adjourned to the smoking-room. As twilight came on I tore myself away, but Stevenson walked with me across Hyde Park, and nearly to my house. He had an engagement, and so had I, but I walked a mile or two back with him. The fountains of talk had been unsealed, and they drowned the conventions. I came home dazzled with my new friend, saying, as Constance does of Arthur, 'Was ever such a gracious creature born?' That impression of ineffable mental charm was formed at the first moment of acquaintance, and it never lessened or became modified. Stevenson's rapidity in the sympathetic interchange of ideas was, doubtless, the source of it. He has been described as an 'egotist', but I challenge the description. If ever there was an altruist, it was Louis Stevenson; he seemed to feign an interest in himself merely to stimulate you to be liberal in your confidences.[3]

Those who have written about him from later impressions than those of which I speak seem to me to give insufficient prominence to the gaiety of Stevenson. It was his cardinal quality in those early days. A childlike mirth leaped and danced in him; he seemed to skip upon the hills of life. He was simply bubbling with quips and jests; his inherent earnestness or passion about abstract things was incessantly relieved by jocosity; and when he had built one of his intellectual castles in the sand, a wave of humour was certain to sweep in and destroy it. I cannot, for the life of me, recall any of his jokes; and written down in cold blood, they might not be funny if I did. They were not wit so much as humanity, the many-sided outlook upon life. I am anxious that his laughter-loving mood should not be forgotten, because later on it was partly, but I think never wholly, quenched by ill health, responsibility, and the advance of years. He was often, in the old days, excessively and delightfully silly – silly with the silliness of an inspired schoolboy; and I am afraid that our laughter sometimes sounded ill in the ears of age. . . .

My experience of Stevenson during these first years was confined to London, upon which he would make sudden piratical descents, staying a few days or weeks, and melting into air again. He was much at my house; and it must be told that my wife and I, as young married people, had possessed ourselves of a house too large for our slender means immediately to furnish. The one person who thoroughly approved of our great, bare, absurd drawing-room was Louis, who very earnestly dealt with us on the immorality of chairs and tables, and desired us to sit always, as he delighted to sit, upon hassocks on the floor. Nevertheless, as arm-chairs and settees straggled into existence, he handsomely consented to use them, although never in the usual way, but with his legs thrown sidewise over the arms of them, or the head of a sofa treated as a perch. In particular, a certain shelf, with cupboards below, attached to a bookcase, is worn with the person of Stevenson, who would spend half an evening while passionately discussing some great question of morality or literature, leaping sidewise in a seated posture to the length of this shelf, and then back again. He was eminently peripatetic, too, and never better company than walking in the street, this exercise seeming to inflame his fancy. But his most habitual dwelling-place in the London of those days was the Savile Club, then lodged in an inconvenient but very friendly house in Savile Row.[4] Louis pervaded the club; he was its most affable and chatty member; and he lifted it, by the ingenuity of his incessant dialectic, to the level of a sort of humorous Academe or Mouseion.

At this time he must not be thought of as a successful author. A very few of us were convinced of his genius; but with the exception of Mr Leslie Stephen, nobody of editorial status was sure of it. I remember the publication of *An Inland Voyage* in 1878, and the inability of the critics and the public to see anything unusual in it.

Stevenson was not without a good deal of innocent oddity in

his dress. When I try to conjure up his figure, I can see only a slight, lean lad, in a suit of blue sea-cloth, a black shirt, and a wisp of yellow carpet that did duty for a necktie. This was long his attire, persevered in to the anguish of his more conventional acquaintances.[5] I have a ludicrous memory of going, in 1878, to buy him a new hat, in company with Mr Lang, the thing then upon his head having lost the semblance of a human article of dress. Aided by a very civil shopman, we suggested several hats and caps, and Louis at first seemed interested; but having presently hit upon one which appeared to us pleasing and decorous, we turned for a moment to inquire the price. We turned back, and found that Louis had fled, the idea of parting with the shapeless object having proved too painful to be entertained.

NOTES

1. Samuel Bough (1822–78), self-taught Scottish landscape painter who became a member of the Royal Scottish Academy (1875) and specialised in watercolours. On meeting Bough for the first time, Louis wrote home of his delight: 'He and I have read the same books, and discuss Chaucer, Shakespeare, Marlowe, Fletcher, Webster, and all the old authors . . . I was very much surprised with him, and he with me. "When the devil did you read all these books?" says he; and in my heart I echo the question' (quoted in Masson, *Life*, 75–6).
2. Although Stevenson's mind was more on literature than engineering, he worked at the profession between 1868 and 1870, travelling extensively around the coasts. In the far north at Wick, Caithness (1868), he got to know the fishermen and went down in a diving-suit to inspect an unfinished breakwater. His response is a literary man's rather than a technologist's: 'I had a fine, dizzy, muddle-headed joy in my surroundings, and longed, and tried, and always failed, to lay hands on the fish that darted here and there about me, swift as hummingbirds' ('Random Memories, II, The Education of an Engineer', *Across the Plains*, 1892). He spent three weeks on the Isle of Earraid during construction by his father's firm of the Dhu Heartach lighthouse offshore. Earraid was recalled for settings in *Kidnapped* (1886) and *The Merry Men* (1887). See his essay 'Memoirs of an Islet' (*Memories and Portraits*, 1887).
3. Gosse adds in a note that to the end of his life Stevenson used the stratagem of telling some of his own escapades first to draw confidences from the person he was addressing.
4. The Savile Club moved to 15 Savile Row in 1871. It operated on the principle of admitting a 'mixture of men of different professions and opinions' and stressing informality and good conversation. Some

of its values are embodied in Stevenson's double essay 'Talk and Talkers' (*Memories and Portraits*). Gosse noted that two of the best among the talkers in the 1880s were 'R.L.S. and his wonderful cousin R.A.M.S.' ('The Savile Club', *Silhouettes* (1925) 375–80).

5. Charles Brookfield, the actor (1857–1913), also recalled his bizarre get-up: 'His hair was smooth and parted in the middle and fell beneath the collar of his coat; he wore a black flannel shirt, with a curious, knitted tie twisted in a knot; he had Wellington boots, rather tight, dark trousers, a pea-jacket and a white sombrero hat (in imitation, perhaps, of his eminent literary friend, Mr W. E. Henley). But the most astounding item of all in his costume was a lady's sealskin cape, which he wore about his shoulders, fastened at the neck by a fancy brooch, which also held together a bunch of half a dozen daffodils' (*Random Reminiscences* (1902) 30–1).

Sealed of the Tribe of Louis

ANDREW LANG

From *Adventures among Books* (1905) 42–52. Andrew Lang (1844–1912), poet, essayist, historian, came from an old Border family at Selkirk, where his father was sheriff-clerk. From his earliest days he was fascinated by myth and balladry. His education, referred to briefly here, was at Edinburgh Academy, prior to Stevenson's arrival, followed by St Andrews and Oxford, where he became a fellow of Merton College (1868). His prolific output included works on folklore, such as *Myth, Ritual and Religion* (1899), on Greek literature, several books of verse, anecdotal memoirs, and contributions to Scottish history; among his biographies the best known is *Life and Letters of J. G. Lockhart* (1896). He was one of the founders of the Psychical Research Society and its President (1911). Lang's initial response to Stevenson was lukewarm, but friendship grew, and Lang paid tribute on his death. (See 'The Late Mr. R. L. Stevenson', *Illustrated London News*, 5 Jan 1895; 'Robert Louis Stevenson', *Longman's Magazine*, Feb 1895, and 'Recollections of Robert Louis Stevenson', *North American Review*, Feb 1895). Stevenson was similarly wary of Lang: 'too good-looking, delicate, Oxfordish ... a la-de-dady Oxford kind of Scot' (quoted in Knight, *Treasury*, 104). They were friendly enough by the summer of 1881, however, for Stevenson to solicit a testimonial from him in support of his bizarre attempt to gain the chair of History and Constitutional Law at Edinburgh University. Two days before his death, Stevenson wrote thanking Lang for a picture of Lord Braxfield (1722–99) needed for his portrayal of Lord Adam Weir in *Weir of Hermiston* (1896).

Like Keats and Shelley, he was, and he looked, of the immortally young. He and I were at school together, but I was an elderly boy of seventeen, when he was lost in the crowd of 'gytes', as the members of the lowest form are called. Like all Scotch people, we had a vague family connection; a great-uncle of his, I fancy, married an aunt of my own, called for her beauty, 'The Flower of Ettrick'. So we had both heard; but these things were before our day. A lady of my kindred remembers carrying Stevenson about when he was 'a rather peevish baby', and I have seen a beautiful photograph of him, like one of Raffael's children, taken when his years were three or four. But I never had heard of his existence till, in 1873, I think, I was at Mentone, in the interests of my health. Here I met Mr Sidney Colvin, now of the British Museum, and, with Mr Colvin, Stevenson. He looked as, in my eyes, he always did look, more like a lass than a lad, with a rather long, smooth oval face, brown hair worn at greater length than is common, large lucid eyes, but whether blue or brown I cannot remember, if brown, certainly light brown. On appealing to the authority of a lady, I learn that brown *was* the hue. His colour was a trifle hectic, as is not unusual at Mentone, but he seemed, under his big blue cloak, to be of slender, yet agile frame. He was like nobody else whom I ever met. There was a sort of uncommon celerity in changing expression, in thought and speech. His cloak and Tyrolese hat (he would admit the innocent impeachment) were decidedly dear to him. On the frontier of Italy, why should he not do as the Italians do? It would have been well for me if I could have imitated the wearing of the cloak!

I shall not deny that my first impression was not wholly favourable.[1] 'Here,' I thought, 'is one of your aesthetic young men, though a very clever one.' What the talk was about, I do not remember; probably of books. Mr Stevenson afterwards told me that I had spoken of Monsieur Paul de St Victor, as a fine writer, but added that 'he was not a British sportsman'. Mr Stevenson himself, to my surprise, was unable to walk beyond a very short distance, and, as it soon appeared, he thought his thread of life was nearly spun. He had just written his essay, 'Ordered South', the first of his published works, for his 'Pentland Rising' pamphlet was unknown, a boy's performance.[2] On reading 'Ordered South', I saw, at once, that here was a new writer, a writer indeed; one who could do what none of us, *nous autres*, could rival, or approach. I was instantly 'sealed of the Tribe of Louis', an admirer, a devotee, a fanatic, if you please....

Mr Stevenson was in town, now and again, at the old Savile Club, in Savile Row, which had the tiniest and blackest of smoking-rooms. Here, or somewhere, he spoke to me of an idea of a tale, a Man who was Two Men. I said '"William Wilson" by Edgar Poe', and declared that it would never do. But his 'Brownies', in a vision of the night, showed him a central scene, and he wrote 'Jekyll and Hyde'. My 'friend of these days and of all days', Mr Charles Longman, sent me the manuscript.[3] In a very commonplace London drawing-room, at 10:30 p.m., I began to read it. Arriving at the place where Utterson the lawyer, and the butler wait outside the Doctor's room, I threw down the manuscript and fled in a hurry. I had no taste for solitude any more. The story won its great success, partly by dint of the moral (whatever that may be), more by its terrible, lucid, visionary power. I remember Mr Stevenson telling me, at this time, that he was doing some 'regular crawlers', for this purist had a boyish habit of slang, and I *think* it was he who called Julius Caesar 'the howlingest cheese who ever lived'. One of the 'crawlers' was 'Thrawn Janet'; after 'Wandering Willie's Tale' (but certainly *after* it), to my taste, it seems the most wonderful story of the 'supernatural' in our language....

It is a trivial reminiscence that we once plotted a Boisgobesque story together.[4] There was a prisoner in a Muscovite dungeon.

'We'll extract information from him,' I said.

'How?'

'With corkscrews.'

But the mere suggestion of such a process was terribly distasteful to him; not that I really meant to go to these extreme lengths. We never, of course, could really have worked together; and, his maladies increasing, he became more and more a wanderer, living at Bournemouth, at Davos, in the Grisons, finally, as all know, in Samoa. Thus, though we corresponded, not infrequently, I never was of the inner circle of his friends. Among men there were school or college companions, or companions of Paris or Fontainebleau, cousins, like Mr R. A. M. Stevenson, or a stray senior, like Mr Sidney Colvin. From some of them, or from Mr Stevenson himself, I have heard tales of 'the wild Prince and Poins'. That he and a friend travelled utterly without baggage, buying a shirt where a shirt was needed, is a fact, and the incident is used in 'The Wrecker.' Legend says that once he and a friend *did* possess a bag, and also, nobody ever knew why, a large bottle of scent. But there was no room for the bottle in the bag, so Mr Stevenson spilled the whole contents over the other man's head, taking him unawares, that nothing might be wasted. I think the tale of the endless staircase, in 'The Wrecker,' is founded on fact, so are the stories of the *atelier*, which I have heard Mr Stevenson narrate at the Oxford and Cambridge Club. For a nocturnal adventure, in the manner of the 'New Arabian Nights', a learned critic already spoken of must be consulted. It is not my story. In Paris, at a café, I remember that Mr Stevenson heard a Frenchman say the English were cowards. He got up and slapped the man's face.

'Monsieur, vous m'avez frappé!' said the Gaul.

'A ce qu'il parait,' said the Scot, and there it ended. He also told me that years ago he was present at a play, I forget what play, in Paris, where the moral hero exposes a woman 'with a history'. He got up and went out, saying to himself:

'What a play! what a people!'

'Ah, Monsieur, vous êtes bien jeune!' said an old French gentleman.

Like a right Scot, Mr Stevenson was fond of 'our auld ally of France,' to whom our country and our exiled kings owed so much.

I rather vaguely remember another anecdote. He missed his train from Edinburgh to London, and his sole portable property was a return ticket, a meerschaum pipe, and a volume of Mr Swinburne's poems. The last he found unmarketable; the pipe, I think, he made merchandise of, but somehow his provender for the day's journey consisted in one bath bun, which he could not finish....

Mr Stevenson possessed, more than any man I ever met, the power of making other men fall in love with him. I mean that he excited a passionate admiration and affection, so much so that I verily believe some men were jealous of other men's place in his liking. I once met a stranger who, having become acquainted with him, spoke of him with a touching fondness and pride, his fancy reposing, as it seemed, in a fond contemplation of so much genius and charm. What was so taking in him? and how is one to analyse that dazzling surface of pleasantry, that changeful shining humour, wit, wisdom, recklessness; beneath which beat the most kind and tolerant of hearts?[5]

People were fond of him, and people were proud of him: his achievements, as it were, sensibly raised their pleasure in the world, and, to them, became parts of themselves. They warmed their hands at that centre of light and heat. It is not every success which has these beneficent results. We see the successful sneered at, decried, insulted, even when success is deserved. Very little of all this, hardly aught of all this, I think, came in Mr Stevenson's way. After the beginning (when the praises of his earliest admirers were irritating to dull scribes) he found the critics fairly kind, I believe, and often enthusiastic. He was so much his own severest critic that he probably paid little heed to professional reviewers. In addition to his 'Rathillet', and other MSS which he destroyed, he once, in the Highlands, long ago, lost a portmanteau with a batch of his writings.[6] Alas, that he should have lost or burned anything! 'King's chaff,' says our country proverb, 'is better than other folk's corn.'

NOTES

1. First meetings of artists are often a let-down, and Stevenson may have been tempted to parade his oddities. His first meeting with J. A. Symonds was hardly a success. Leslie Stephen did not take to him at all. Henry James was also initially wary: 'a pleasant fellow, but a shirt-collarless Bohemian and a great deal (in an inoffensive way) of a *poseur*' (Leon Edel, *Henry James: The Middle Years* (1963) 61–2).

2. Louis was 16 when he took the historical events of the Pentland Rising of 1666 and fictionalised them, somewhat to his father's dismay. His 'novel' was destroyed, but 100 copies of a pamphlet, *The Pentland Rising: A Page of History, 1666* were published anonymously at his father's expense by Andrew Elliott in Edinburgh in 1866. Subsequently Thomas Stevenson bought in as many copies as he could trace (Balfour, *Life*, I, 67–8). 'Ordered South' appeared in *Macmillan's Magazine*, May 1874 (*Virginibus Puerisque*, 1881). His first published essay was 'Roads' in the *Portfolio*, December 1873.

3. Stevenson claimed that 'Brownies' or 'Little People' would come to him, mostly at night, and give him ideas for stories; when these were nightmarish or gruesome he called them 'crawlies'. Charles Longman (1852–1934) of the publishing house, Longmans, Green & Co.

4. One collaboration, proposed by Lang during the spring of 1882, was a story called 'Where is Rose?', a sensation novel of Wilkie Collins cast. Stevenson responded by sending Lang some notes, but the project was abandoned. See Lang, *Adventures*, 252–4; Swearingen, 79.

5. In various attempts at defining Stevenson's psychological make-up some biographers have drawn attention to the 'homoerotic' aspect of his appeal. Frank McLynn concludes that he aroused sexual responses in both men and women (*Robert Louis Stevenson*, 94).

6. Before he was 15, Stevenson began a novel on Hackston of Rathillet. The MS was presumably destroyed (Swearingen, 3).

A Touch of the Elfin and Unearthly

SIDNEY COLVIN

From *Memories and Notes of Persons and Places, 1852–1912* (1921) 99–109, 121–3. Sir Sidney Colvin (1845–1927) became Slade Professor of Fine Arts at Cambridge (1873–85), Director of the Fitzwilliam Museum (1876–84), and Keeper of Prints at the British Museum (1884–1912), adding considerably to the collection, particularly of Far Eastern art. He was knighted in 1911. His literary interests centred on Landor and Keats, and he produced *John Keats, His Life and Poetry* (1917). Colvin first met Stevenson in the summer of 1873 at the home of his cousin, Maud Balfour Babington, at Cockfield Rectory, Surrey, and they became life-long friends. In June 1874, supported by Andrew Lang, he nominated Stevenson for membership of the Savile Club. Hereafter they kept up their friendship with letters and meetings whenever Louis was in London at the 'Monument', his name for Colvin's residence in the east wing of the British Museum. Although Colvin's judgements on the author's writings were suspect, he had a keen understanding of his character. He edited the *Letters*, 2 vols (1900) and the Edinburgh edition, 28 vols (1894–8). See also 'The Death of Mr R. L. Stevenson', *Pall Mall Gazette*, 19 Dec 1894. A perceptive appreciation introduces the *Letters*.

And first, to wipe away some false impressions which seem to be current: – I lately found one writer, because Stevenson was thin, speaking of him as having been a 'shadowy' figure; another, because he was an invalid, describing him as 'anaemic', and a third as 'thin-blooded'. Shadowy! he was indeed all his life a bag of bones, a very lath for leanness; as lean as Shakespeare's Master Slender, or let us say as Don Quixote.[1] Nevertheless when he was in the room it was the other people, and not he, who seemed the shadows. The most robust of ordinary men seemed to turn dim and null in presence of the vitality that glowed in the steadfast, penetrating fire of the lean man's eyes, the rich, compelling charm of his smile, the lissom swiftness of his movements and lively expressiveness of his gestures, above all in the irresistible sympathetic play and abundance of his talk. Anaemic! thin-blooded!

the main physical fact about him, according to those of his doctors whom I have questioned, was that his heart was too big and its blood supply too full for his body. There was failure of nutrition, in the sense that he could never make flesh; there was weakness of the throat and lungs, weakness above all of the arteries, never of the heart itself; nor did his looks, even in mortal illness and exhaustion, ever give the impression of bloodlessness. More than one of his early friends, in describing him as habitually pale, have let their memory be betrayed by knowledge of what might have been expected in one so frail in health. To add, as some have done, that his hair was black is to misdescribe him still farther. As a matter of fact his face, forehead and all, was throughout the years when I knew him of an even, rather high, colour varying little whether he was ill or well; and his hair, of a lightish brown in youth, although the brown grew darker with years, and darker still, I believe, in the tropics, can never have approached black.

If you want to realize the kind of effect he made, at least in the early years when I knew him best, imagine this attenuated but extraordinarily vivid and vital presence, with something about it that at first struck you as freakish, rare, fantastic, a touch of the elfin and unearthly, a sprite, an Ariel. And imagine that, as you got to know him, this sprite, this visitant from another sphere, turned out to differ from mankind in general not by being less human but by being a great deal more human than they; richer-blooded, greater-hearted; more human in all senses of the word, for he comprised within himself, and would flash on you in the course of a single afternoon, all the different ages and half the different characters of man, the unfaded freshness of a child, the ardent outlook and adventurous day-dreams of a boy, the steadfast courage of manhood, the quick sympathetic tenderness of a woman, and already, as early as the mid-twenties of his life, an almost uncanny share of the ripe life-wisdom of old age. He was a fellow of infinite and unrestrained jest and yet of infinite earnest, the one very often a mask for the other; a poet, an artist, an adventurer; a man beset with fleshly frailties, and despite his infirm health of strong appetites and unchecked curiosities; and yet a profoundly sincere moralist and preacher and son of the Covenanters after his fashion, deeply conscious of the war within his members, and deeply bent on acting up to the best he knew.[2] ...

I first saw him at the beginning of August, 1873, that is all but forty-eight years ago, when he was twenty-three and I twenty-eight. I had landed from a Great-Eastern train at a little country station in Suffolk, and was met on the platform by a stripling in a velvet jacket and straw hat, who walked up with me to the country rectory where he was staying and where I had come to stay.[3] ... The first shyness over I realized in the course of that short walk how well I had done to follow the advice of a fellow-guest who had preceded me in the house – to wit Mrs Sitwell, my wife as she came later on to be. She had written to me about this youth, declaring that I should find him a real young genius and urging me to come if I could before he went away. I could not wonder at what I presently learnt – how within an hour of his first appearance at the rectory, knapsack on back, a few days earlier, he had captivated the whole household. To his cousin the hostess, a woman of a fine sympathetic nature and quick, humorous intelligence, he was of course well known beforehand, though she had never seen him in so charming a light as now. With her husband the Professor, a clergyman of solid antiquarian and ecclesiastical knowledge and an almost Pickwickian simplicity of character corresponding to his lovable rotund visage and innocently beaming spectacles – with the Professor, 'Stivvy', as he called his wife's young cousin, was already something of a favourite. Of their guests, I found one, a boy of ten, watching for every moment when he could monopolize the newcomer's attention, either to show off to him the scenes of his toy theatre or to conduct him confidentially by the hand about the garden or beside the moat; while between him and the boy's mother, Mrs Sitwell, there had sprung up an instantaneous understanding.[4] Not only the lights and brilliancies of his nature, but the strengths and glooms that underlay them, were from the first apparent to her, so that in the trying season of his life which followed he was moved to throw himself upon her sympathies with the unlimited confidence and devotion to which his letters of the time bear witness. He sped those summer nights and days for us all as I have scarce known any sped before or since....

At the Suffolk rectory he had been neatly enough clad: most of the images of him that rise next before me present him in the slovenly, nondescript Bohemian garments and untrimmed hair which it was in those days his custom to wear. I could somehow never feel this to be an affectation in Stevenson, or dislike it as I should have been apt to dislike and perhaps despise it in anybody else. We agree to give the name of affectation to anything markedly different from common usage in little, every-day outward things – unconcerning things, as the poet Donne calls them. But affectation is affectation indeed only when a person does or says that which is false to his or her nature. And given a nature differing sufficiently from the average, perhaps the real affectation would be that it should force itself to preserve an average outside to the world. Stevenson's uncut hair came originally from the fear of catching cold. His shabby clothes came partly from lack of cash, partly from lack of care, partly, as I think I have said elsewhere, from a hankering after social experiment and adventure, and a dislike of being identified with any special class or caste. . . .

More characteristic of his ordinary ways was his appearance one very early morning from London at the Norwood cottage. He presented himself to my astonished servant, on her opening the shutters, wearing a worn-out sleeved waistcoat over a black flannel shirt, and weary and dirty from a night's walking followed by a couple of hours' slumber in a garden outhouse he had found open. He had spent the night on the pad through the southern slums and suburbs, trying to arouse the suspicions of one policeman after another till he should succeed in getting takeup as a rogue and vagabond and thereby gaining proof for his fixed belief that justice, at least in the hands of its subordinate officers, has one pair of scales for the ragged and another for the respectable. But one and all saw through him, and refused to take him seriously as a member of the criminal classes. Though surprised at their penetration, and rather crestfallen at the failure of his attempt, he had had his reward in a number of friendly and entertaining conversations with the members of the force, ending generally in confidential disclosures as to their private affairs and feelings. . . .

But to turn from such social memories, which will be shared by a dwindling band of survivors from the middle and later seventies, to those private to myself: – it was in the early summer of 1874, soon after the appearance of his second, published paper, *Ordered South*, that he spent a fortnight with me in my quarters on Hampstead Hill. One morning, while I was attending to my own affairs, I was aware of Stevenson craning intently out of a side window and watching something. Presently he turned with a radiant countenance and the thrill of happiness in his voice to bid me come and watch too. A group of girl children were playing with the skipping-rope a few yards down the lane. 'Was there ever such heavenly sport? Had I ever seen anything so beautiful? Kids and a skipping-rope – most of all that blessed youngest kid with the broken nose who didn't know how to skip – nothing in the whole wide world had ever made him half so happy in his life before.' ... Did anything in life or literature please him, it was for the moment inimitably and incomparably the most splendid and wonderful thing in the whole world, and he must absolutely have you think so too – unless, indeed, you chose to direct his sense of humour against his own exaggerations, in which case he would generally receive your criticism with ready assenting laughter. But not quite always, if the current of feeling was too strong. My wife reminds me of an incident in point, from the youthful time when he used to make her the chief confidante of his troubles and touchstone of his tastes. One day he came to her with an early, I think the earliest, volume of poems by Mr Robert Bridges, the present poet-laureate, in his hand; declared here was the most wonderful new genius, and enthusiastically read out to her some of the contents in evidence; till becoming aware that they were being coolly received, he leapt up crying, 'My God! I believe you don't like them,' and flung the book across the room and himself out of the house in a paroxysm of disappointment – to return a few hours later and beg pardon humbly for his misbehaviour. But for some time afterwards, whenever he desired her judgment on work of his own or others, he would begin by bargaining: 'You won't *Bridges* me this time, will you?'

NOTES

1. When Colvin first met him he weighed under 120 lb (*Letters*, I, 53).
2. 'Jekyll is a dreadful thing, I own; but the only thing I feel dreadful about is that damned old business of the war in the members' (to J. A. Symonds, *Letters*, II, 20).
3. Cockfield Rectory, Suffolk, near Bury St Edmunds, was the Georgian house owned by the Reverend Churchill Babington, husband of Stevenson's cousin, Maud Balfour.
4. Mrs Frances Sitwell (b.1841), estranged from her husband, the Reverend Albert Sitwell, was at Cockfield with her son, Bertie. She married Colvin in 1903 after many years' devoted companionship. Her importance in Stevenson's young manhood can be seen in his corre-

spondence. On 31 Jan 1873 Louis had faced his father with his loss of faith (see *Letters*, I, 40) and home life had become intolerable. Desperately lonely and guilt-ridden, he found in this charming woman, nine years his senior, an outlet for emotion and confession. Acknowledging that Colvin suppressed many of his letters to Fanny, and that he burned most of hers, modern biographers assume an intense relationship, in due course transposed so that she became 'Madonna' and 'Consuelo' – a 'mother' figure. Alanna Knight notes similarities of feature and nature between her and the Fanny who became Stevenson's wife (*Treasury*, 183). See E. V. Lucas, *The Colvins and their Friends* (1928).

The Best of All Good Times at Grez

ISOBEL FIELD

From *This Life I've Loved* (1937) 102–11. Isobel (Belle) Osbourne (1858–1953), daughter of Fanny Osbourne (1840–1914), studied art at the School of Design, San Francisco, as did her mother, and could take her place on equal terms in the male community at Grez, where she caused quite a stir. Bob Stevenson fell for her, as did Frank O'Meara. She married the painter Joe Strong, in 1880, at much the same time as her mother married Louis, whom at that period she did not much like. Her son, Austin, who went on to become a playwright, was born in 1882. Both she and her husband were a constant anxiety and drain on Louis's resources, especially when they joined the household in Vailima in 1891. After her divorce (1893) she came to appreciate Louis more, and helped him considerably as his amanuensis, before her attachment to Graham Balfour caused another disquieting episode. She married Edward (Ned) Salisbury Field (1914) when she was 56, and ended her life a millionairess, as a result of the discovery of oil on land acquired by her late husband. Her writing included *Memories of Vailima* (as Isobel Strong and with Lloyd Osbourne, 1902) and *Robert Louis Stevenson* (1911).

Then, when we were beginning to feel as though the place belonged to us, a stranger appeared; an artist evidently, from his velvet jacket and flowing tie. He was slim and dark and so odd and foreign-looking that we thought he was a Pole, or a sort of gentleman gipsy, and were surprised when he greeted us somewhat formally in English.

R. A. M. Stevenson, for it was he, has been described by Henley, Gosse, Henry James, and by his cousin, R.L.S. as the most brilliant talker of his time. Will H. Low, in his *Chronicle of Friendship*, regrets that 'no one of the many who listened spellbound to this rare genius has adequately recorded his conversation'. It is not surprising that we found him very entertaining. He had never met Americans before, and was much interested in us. Lloyd, a little boy of eight, rather shy, with very nice manners, had a wit of his own that surprised and delighted him. I wish I had recorded some of their conversations.

A few days later Sir Walter Simpson arrived, not to paint, but to meet his friend Louis Stevenson, who would be at Grez in a few days. He was fair, ruddy, and decidedly Scotch. He and Louis had just finished their 'inland voyage' in canoes, and he told us some of their adventures, usually with his companion as the hero. That started Bob off, and he used his 'genius for talk' in describing his cousin. It was like a scene from an old melodrama, the way R.L.S. was praised by his admirers and heralded with enthusiasm before he appeared on the scene.

Frank O'Meara, an Irish boy of twenty, was the next arrival at the Hotel Chévillon.[1] He, too, praised Louis to the skies. This handsome youth, in his rough country tweeds, knitted stockings, and stout brogues, with a blue béret on his curly head and a blackthorn shillelagh in his hand, distracted me somewhat from the talk about a stranger's arrival. Added to his fine figure and Irish blue eyes, he had a voice that melted the heart. 'The Harp that Once through Tara's Halls', 'The Minstrel Boy', and 'The Exile of Erin', are songs that to this day bring back memories of my first love.

O'Meara – as all the men called each other by their last names, we fell into the habit, too – promptly tied himself to my apronstrings, or rather, took me under his wing, explaining the universe to me and correcting my speech.

He told me that the most important men in the United States at that time were Irishmen, and named them. The North would never have won the war against the South if it hadn't been for several more Irishmen, and as for Art, Literature, and the Drama in any country, Ireland led them all. I listened admiringly and believed every word. Like many Americans, I called dew 'doo' and duke 'dook'. O'Meara was much upset by this. 'Use the English language correctly,' he implored. 'Say "jew" and "juke."'

One night we were at dinner; though the lamps were lit, it was not yet dark. We had finished our meal, and were talking idly and pleasantly over our coffee. Happening to glance at my mother, I saw that she was looking towards the window with an odd, intent gaze. It was not exactly a window, but a half-door, and standing in the opening, the lights from the hanging lamps showing up his figure like a portrait painted against a black background, stood a young man, slender, dark, with a high colour and yellow hair worn rather long. He was leaning forward staring, with a sort of surprised admiration at Fanny Osbourne. Years afterwards, he told me he had fallen in love with her then and there.

Amid sudden cries of 'There he is!' 'It's Stevenson!' 'Louis!' the stranger vaulted lightly into the room, his friends greeting him noisily. There were explanations, introductions, laughter. He'd had his dinner, he said, but would join us with coffee, and took his seat on my mother's right, which was his place at table all the time we were at Grez.

That was the first time I noticed the extraordinary effect that Louis Stevenson made on any company he joined, bringing out the best in everyone, and arousing enthusiasm and admiration. That I am not exaggerating, that my memory is clear on this point, I can prove from E. F. Benson's book, *As We Were*.[2] In it the author states that Edmund Gosse, the poet, who 'had been intimate with R.L.S. in the gallant days of his youth', considered him 'the most entrancing personality he had ever come across'. He goes on to say, '"The Gods had come down in the likeness of men" and he was to Gosse the most radiant of all his memories.'

We, at Grez, felt something of this from the very first, for Louis brought into our lives a sort of joyousness hard to describe. On sunny days we played on the river, our new friend leading the games with the gaiety and zest he put into everything he did. We all had canoes, the small narrow kind that capsize if you wink. If there were enough of us to have several on a side the rule was to paddle into the middle of the river and try to upset one of the enemy; if you succeeded, he had to join the winner's side....

On rainy days and evenings we amused ourselves indoors with charades or we played 'Consequences', 'Telegrams', or games that involved the writing of verses, drawing of cartoons, and many that we made up ourselves. But the best of all our good times at Grez were the talks, either in the big bare dining-room, or out in the arbour by the river, the white tablecloth flecked with the shadows of vine leaves, and the air heavy with the scent of roses, mingled occasionally with whiffs of freshly roasted coffee, or loaves just out of the oven. Our fare was simple, but marvellously well cooked; *pot-au-feu*, served in a heavy yellow bowl, yard-long loaves of bread, cheese made in the village, lettuce salad flavoured with garlic and tarragon, chicken roasted on a spit before the open fire, all accompanied by bottles of good red wine. We finished off with tall glasses of black coffee and often sat talking for hours.

And such talk – gay, inspiring, electric. Everyone joined in; we discussed art, fashions, religion, history; any subject that came up was pounced upon, tossed back and forth, ridiculed or lauded; each brilliant sally or *bon mot* applauded to the echo. Or it might be a book we had all read. The story would be commented on, as it was, as it might have been, what variations could be made in the plot, whether it could be improved by adding or leaving out a character. We argued, we beat the table, we shouted to be heard; the two Stevensons and Sir Walter in Scotch accents that grew stronger with excitement; Palmer in a Yankee twang, O'Meara in a brogue that was music to my ears, and Will Low in straight American.[3] Fanny Osbourne's voice was low in tone, and she spoke with very little modulation. Louis described it as sounding like 'water running under ice.' Mine, I am afraid, was high and sharp for I was often corrected by my mother with a downward wave of the hand and the repeated quotation: 'A low sweet voice in woman.'

The painters scorned sunlight, and endless time was wasted waiting for a grey day. Then we would all be off; O'Meara and I in one direction, my mother in another, with Louis carrying her painting outfit. Bob might join one couple or the other, or go by himself. In the late afternoon we would come trailing home, range our wet canvases in a row along the wall in the dining-room, and criticize each other's work, which we did with more wit, I am afraid, than kindness.

We spent two summers at Grez and part of a third, returning to town in the autumn when the studios reopened.

I found Paris much pleasanter now that we had a few friends. Mrs Wright took a flat in the same building with us at number 8 Rue de Douai, up in the Montmartre quarter. Marian and I worked side by side at Julien's, and Charley Wright, about Lloyd's age, went with him to a private school in the neighbourhood where they were the only foreigners, all the other scholars being French.

One or both of the Stevensons made flying visits to Paris for a week or a month; O'Meara who roomed on the other side of the river often joined us and we made a very pleasant congenial party....

We had two rather unusual visitors that summer [1879] – strolling players who gave an entertainment in the big *salle à manger* that was most enthusiastically received. There happened to be a good many at the inn that evening including a French count who drove over from Menours in a smart dogcart. Lloyd, who had been allowed to stay up for the evening, and his two friends Paul and Kiki, had a hilarious time. Monsieur did sleight of hand tricks, and Mademoiselle sang sentimental French songs. We all bought tickets for a *tombola*, winning a number of trifles that we gave to the children. The last lottery was for a *grande surprise*. Everybody competed and it was run up to a high figure amid great excitement. Sir Walter Simpson's shy brother Willie happened to be there, and of course he won the prize – the privilege of kissing Mademoiselle. Later, Louis had a long talk with the players and it was through his efforts that they were invited to spend a week at Grez, the artists contributing to pay their board.

It was pathetic to see how much they enjoyed it – the rest, the good food and the friendliness after a very cruel experience. Louis told us about it after they left. They had walked from one village, where they had not made more than enough to pay for their lodging, for many weary miles carrying their bags. When they arrived at the next inn, tired and hungry, they were turned away as they could not pay in advance. They begged to be allowed to give a performance which they were sure would bring in enough to pay for the night's lodging. But that was refused and they slept that night in a haystack. Fortunately for them Madame Chévillon not only let them in, but gave them a good dinner before the performance. While at Grez they took their meals in the taproom and I saw very little of them, but it was from these people Louis got his story of *Providence and the Guitar*.[4] They had a little girl at school in Paris and it was their constant anxiety to get money enough to keep her there. When the story was published Louis sent the cheque he received for it to the players and the grateful letter they sent in reply was very touching.

NOTES

1. Frank O'Meara (1853–88), Irish figure and landscape painter, who studied at Barbizon and Grez-sur-Loing.
2. Edward Frederic Benson (1867–1940), playwright, biographer, novelist and author of several books of reminiscence, notably *As We Were* (1930), which includes a tepid appreciation of R.L.S.: 'A charming essayist of chaste and hammered style, and a writer of books of rollicking and brave adventure' (276).
3. The artist with a Yankee twang was Walter Launt Palmer (1854–1932), genre and still-life painter who studied in Paris; he exhibited widely in America, winning several awards for his winter landscapes, some of them painted at Grez.
4. 'Providence and the Guitar' appeared in *London* (2–23 Nov 1878), (*New Arabian Nights*, 1882).

Industrious Idleness

WILL LOW

From *A Chronicle of Friendships* (1908) 51–5, 59–60, 151–3. Will Hicok Low (1853–1932), American figure and genre painter, studied in Paris (1873–7) and later kept a studio in New York. He was a prolific illustrator, notably of Keats and Shakespeare. See also *Stevenson and Margarita* (1922). Low got to know Louis when he joined his cousin, Bob, in Paris in April 1875. That first meeting is recorded here, together with other memories of the late 1870s, particularly of Montigny-sur-Loine where the Lows had their home. The Stevensons visited Low in Paris in 1886 and a year later he welcomed them again, with Louis's widowed mother and Fanny's son, Lloyd, when they disembarked from the cargo ship *Ludgate Hill* together with a cargo of monkeys and about a hundred horses. Low introduced Louis to Augustus Saint-Gaudens (1848–1907), who made the famous bas-relief of the novelist in bed. Louis wrote a poem 'To Will H. Low' and also dedicated the epilogue of *The Wrecker* (1892) to him. Early chapters of that novel recall the Latin Quarter and student life, and Loudon Dodd perhaps contains elements of Low. The Stennis *frères*, 'the pair of hare-brained Scots' with 'no baggage but a greatcoat and a toothbrush', are Louis and Bob. What makes this account of the Barbizon days so interesting is the presentation of Louis in that mode of living which he and others termed 'idling', in which sensations, sounds, thoughts, fragments of conversation, were allowed to ripen in the novelist's mind for future essay and story. Lloyd Osbourne was to claim that Low's book conveyed more of Stevenson's personal attractiveness and high spirits than any other.

Descending to the courtyard I joined him, and in passing we paused at the porter's lodge to inquire for letters. There was one for Bob which he tore open, and after scanning it passed to me, saying, 'Louis is coming over.' I read the brief note; it was the first time I saw the handwriting which was to become so familiar to me and by whose medium the world was to gain so greatly. I fancy I can see it yet, the blue-grey paper with the imprint of the Savile Club in London, the few scrawled words to the effect that the writer was 'seedy', that the weather was bad in London, and that he would arrive the next morning in Paris to seek sunshine and rest, and at the end the three initials R.L.S. which now are known the world over.

I had heard much of this cousin, of the life which Bob and he had led in Edinburgh, where their revolt against the overstrict conventionality of that famous town had been flavoured with the zest of forbidden fruit. I had heard in detail of escapades innocent enough, the outcome of boyish spirits, in which both had shared, and of which Bob, philosophically enough, had borne the blame of leading the younger cousin into mischief.[1] I had also heard that Louis was 'going in' for literature, but this had not interested me particularly, for in those days we were all 'going in' for one thing or the other; and so long as it was not banking, commerce, politics, or other unworthy or material pursuits it merely seemed the normal and proper function of life. I had heard enough, however, aided by my hearty affection for my friend Bob, to be keenly interested in the advent of the cousin, and I awaited the morrow with some impatience, for it was at once decided that we would meet the newcomer on his arrival at the St Lazare station. . . .

At the appointed hour there descended from the Calais train a youth 'unspeakably slight', with the face now familiar to us, the eyes widely spaced, a nose slightly aquiline and delicately modelled, the high cheek bones of the Scot; a face which in repose was not, I fancy, unlike that of many of his former comrades in his native town. It was not a handsome face until he spoke, and then I can hardly imagine that any could deny the appeal of the vivacious eyes, the humour or pathos of the mobile mouth, with its lurking suggestion of the great god Pan at times, or fail to realize that here was one so evidently touched with genius that the higher beauty of the soul was his. . . .

One other detail of personal appearance I mention, for we hear much in his latter life of his long black hair. His hair never was black, though it grew darker with advancing years and became brown of the deepest hue, but at the time of our first meeting and for some years later it was very light, almost of the sandy tint we are wont to associate with his countrymen. In proof of this I have a little colour-sketch, painted in the autumn of '75, which shows him with his flaxen locks; 'all that we have', as his wife once said sadly, 'that will make people believe that Louis' hair was ever light'.

Of his dress my memory is less vivid. He may have worn a velvet coat or a knit jersey in guise of waistcoat; I have known him to do both at later periods, unconscious that for the boulevards at least his costume was less than suitable; but I aver nothing. Later he laughingly recalled that I appeared to him that morning in a frock coat and a smoking-cap; and if his recollection was correct – if I had, knowing that I was to meet one free from Gallic prejudice, temporarily resurrected my sealskin *toque*, which in any case was not a smoking-cap – it will be seen that my taste in dress was sufficiently eclectic to condone any lapse from strict conventionality on his part.

The formalities of introduction were soon over. The formalities of intercourse never weighed heavily upon us in those days, nor indeed with Louis in aftertime; his luggage was despatched to Lavenue's hotel, contiguous to the restaurant, and consequently near our studios, and light-handed and light-hearted we proceeded to retrace our steps across Paris....

Knowing him as intimately as I did, it was not until a much later time that I realized that his early sojourns in the South of France were in the quest of health. At Barbizon he was among the foremost in our long walks over the plains or in the forest of Fontainebleau, and in the summers of 1876–77 at Grez, where he led a semi-amphibious life, on and in the river Loing, he never seemed ill, and as youth is not solicitous on questions of health, it never occurred to us that his slender frame encased a less robust constitution than that of others. 'My illness is an incident outside of my life' was his watchword later, and I need not enlarge on his brave attitude in that respect....

There were few drones in this busy hive of art, but of these Louis was apparently the most consistent. We have learned since how many impressions of scenes and manners were garnered from this apparent idleness, and through what a formative period in his work he was passing at the time. But I never remember him withdrawing to the seclusion of his room on the plea of work to be done, or in the long afternoons spent in his company, while I was industriously 'spoiling canvas', as with more truth than I imagined we were wont to say with facetious intent, can I recall him as busy with paper and pencil. Even the book, which was his frequent companion, was more than likely left unopened. On the other hand, it is with gratifying frequency that I find in his published works ideas and reflections born of that time, and in many instances phrases and incidents that bring back some special place in the forest, or the life that we lived at Barbizon, Grez, or Montigny-sur-Loing. Industrious idleness it was to him; for his mind was a treasure-house, where every addition to its store was carefully guarded against the day of need. Many incidents of our common experience, long forgotten by me, I have thus met in fresh guise in after years; and in most cases I imagine that it was his memory and not his notes that served him – at least of these last there was no visible evidence at the time. Despite our intimacy we lived so much in the present, each day bringing its quota of fresh experience, that it was long after in interchange of reminiscent talk that I learned of his earlier life, of the days when he was 'ordered South', and of the storm and stress of his adolescent years.[2] . . .

The charm of his presence was both appealing and imperative, and though for other friends – for Bob especially – the ties that bind young men together and lay the foundations for lifelong friendships were quite as strong, Louis, quite unconsciously, exercised a species of fascination whenever we were together. Fascination and charm are not qualities which Anglo-Saxon youths are prone to acknowledge, in manly avoidance of their supposedly feminizing effect, but it was undoubtedly this attractive power which R.L.S. held so strongly through life; and which, gentle though it may have been, held no trace of dependence or weakness, that led Edmund Gosse to exclaim, when I chanced to meet him at a crowded reception in New York long before Stevenson had attained a trans-Atlantic reputation: 'I am told that you are a friend of Louis Stevenson. Do you know any one in the world that you would better like to have walk in on us at the present moment?'

NOTES

1. Early biographers drew a veil over these escapades, which were far from 'innocent'. Louis needed little encouragement in sampling the drinking dens and whorehouses of Edinburgh during his student days; such outlets were by no means uncommon for young men of his class, and, in any case for the reckless, anti-establishment, would-be artist were an essential phase of development. A suggestion that Louis was passionately involved with a prostitute named Kate Drummond was quashed by J. C. Furnas, but, as one biographer puts it, 'he certainly had affectionate as well as sexual relationships with Edinburgh prostitutes' (Calder, 54).

2. The essay came about when a London specialist, Dr Andrew Clark (1826–93), specialising in lung disease, advised sea air and a more benevolent climate. Louis went to Menton in Nov 1873 without his parents. As he wrote to Baxter: 'I am away in my own beautiful Riviera, and I am free now from the horrible worry and misery that was playing the devil with me at home' (*Baxter Letters*, 31). 'Ordered South' was published in *Macmillan's Magazine* in May 1874 (*Virginibus Puerisque*, 1881).

Study the Masters

BIRGE HARRISON

From 'With Stevenson at Grez', *Century Magazine*, 93 (Dec 1916) 306–14. Lowell Birge Harrison (1854–1929), the American artist, studied at the *Ecole des Beaux Arts* in Paris and first exhibited his work in 1881; returning to America the following year, he painted in New Mexico. He became an authority on landscapes, and his book, *Landscape Painting* (1909), went to eight editions. Harrison gives a charming picture of the Grez community in which the new arrival played second fiddle to his cousin.

I shall not forget Stevenson's joy at the manner in which Robinson once put an end to a rather tiresome rainy-day discussion on the subject of genealogy, during which he had been treated to more or less colorful accounts of the distinguished lineage of most of those present.[1]

Robinson had remained silent throughout the discussion, with only an occasional subterranean chuckle to indicate that he was listening to the conversation. Finally some one called out:

'Bobbie, we have not yet heard from you. Who were your noble ancestors, anyway?'

With a subdued twinkle he replied:

'Well, if you really wish to know, I will tell you. My father was a farmer, and my grandparents were both very respectable and deserving domestic servants. I have never carried my investigation any further up the family-tree.'

There was a short, somewhat embarrassed silence, and then Stevenson threw his arms about Robinson's shoulders with a shout of joy.

'Tu es vilain, Robinson,' he cried; 'mais je t'aime.'

Another member of our little colony who has left an indelible mark upon my memory is Robert Mowbray Stevenson, Louis's cousin, the *Bob* of the 'Vailima Letters', who came down from Paris shortly after Stevenson's own arrival.[2] . . . If it comes to a mere question of genius [in discourse and conversation] pure and simple, no one who knew the two cousins intimately would have hesitated for an instant to award the primacy to Bob, and Louis himself would have been the first to concur in the justice of this decision. When the after-dinner coffee was on the table in the old *salle à manger*, it was Louis's custom to stir up a discussion upon some subject connected with ethics or morals or the general conduct of life, and then, if he succeeded in getting Bob started, to sit back and enjoy the intellectual feast which was sure to follow, just dropping in a word of dissent now and then in order to keep the stream flowing.

On these occasions Bob's flights of imagination were not only brilliant to a degree, but they were often humorous and most entertaining. Not infrequently they took the form of a story, with a complicated plot evolved on the spur of the moment, and with characters who by their acts and words gave living form to the abstraction which he had set out to ride to earth. Louis, being the artist that he was, made notes, and several of the stories which later appeared in the 'New Arabian Nights' and are there duly accredited to 'my cousin Robert Mowbray Stevenson', were thrown off by the latter during one of these impromptu symposia. First among these was the famous 'Suicide Club', to which, however, Stevenson himself added what was perhaps the most original and telling touch – the incident of the young man with the cream tarts.[3] The gruesome idea of the main story grew out of an indignant protest on the part of Bob to an opinion set forth by his cousin to the effect that in the domain of morals men were in no sense free agents, and that no man had the right to dispose of his own life any more than he had the right to dispose of the life of his friend or neighbor . . . contending hotly that inasmuch as we had not been consulted when we were thus rudely and without our own consent dumped into life, the option was surely ours as to the time and the manner of leaving it. . . .

I have a vivid recollection of a most interesting shop-talk with him about this time which occurred during a long walk to Fontainebleau.[4] As we tramped along under the shade of the tall poplars, he outlined to me the writer's *credo* as he knew it, and explained his own methods of work.

'You painter-chaps make lots of studies, don't you?' he exclaimed. 'And you don't frame them all and send them to the Salon, do you? You just stick them up on the studio wall for a bit, and presently you tear them up and make more. And you copy Velasquez and Rembrandt and Vandyke and Corot; and from each you learn some little trick of the brush, some obscure little point in technic. And you know damn well that it is the knowledge thus acquired that will enable you later on to deliver your own message with a fine and confident bravado. You are simply learning your *métier*; and believe me, *mon cher*, an artist in any line without the *métier* is just a blind man with a stick. Now, in the literary line I am simply doing what you painter-men are doing in the pictorial line – learning the *métier*.'

'Yes, but how do you work the game?' I inquired. 'We artists use paint and canvas and brushes precisely as the masters did.'

'Well, I use pen and ink and paper precisely as did the masters of the pen,' laughed Stevenson, 'only a pencil is quite good enough for me at present. Just now I am making a story *à la* Balzac, with a French plot, French local color, and every little touch and detail as close to the old boy as I can possibly make it. And *isn't* he a wizard! Look at "Cousine Bette" and "Peau de chagrin" and the "Médecin de campagne". Aren't they just marvels of literary perfection![5] Really, I believe that Balzac held up to nature a more wonderful mirror than even the great W.S. himself. And dear old *Père Goriot*, don't you just *know* him better even than if you had met him right here on the *grande route* and had an hour's chat with him? I like to swallow a great master whole as it were, to read everything he's written at one go, and then have a try myself at something in his manner. The only way to become a master is to study the masters, take my word for it. It's all one whether it's in paint or clay or words. And then, if you are humble enough and keep an open mind *and* have something of your own to say, you may one of these long days learn how to say it. I have at various periods thus sat at the feet of Sir Walter Scott and Smollett and Fielding and Dickens and Poe and Baudelaire, and the number of things which I have written in the style of each would fill a clothes-basket.' . . .

But I would not give the impression that the artist colony of Grez during that memorable summer was wholly masculine in its make-up, for this was far indeed from being the case, and most of the unforgettable dramatic quality of the place and the time would have been lacking but for the presence of a very fair proportion of the female element. There was a certain return to primitive standards in the relation between the sexes, but primitive standards, nevertheless, in which honor and a regard for the square deal held a high place. In matters of morals Stevenson himself was the least censorious of judges, providing there was no infringement of the law of nature or the law of friendship; though perhaps it would be truer to say that he entered no judgment either for or against the accused, preferring to leave the decision in such matters to the Maker of all laws.

But if he heard of anything mean or underhand, any tricky blow beneath the belt, he was a very firebrand, flaming with a fury which nothing could quell. I remember one case in which he forced two very unwilling opponents to accept a duel as the only possible solution of an entanglement involving an unmanly act on the part of one of the pair. Fortunately the duel was never fought, the chief offender considering discretion the better part of valor and deciding that the woods about Barbizon at that particular season of the year offered better material for the painter than the river at Grez.

I would not, however, by any means have it understood that there was in the colony no sense of decency or morality in the ordinary acceptance of those terms, for that would be a misstatement as manifestly unfair and untrue as to claim a standard of rigid puritanism for the whole region. If there was a fair sprinkling of the grisette and the model element, which had followed the painters down from Paris, there were also a certain number of very serious women-painters who were studying hard, and some of whom were destined to make an enviable place for themselves later on. Among these I may mention Mlles Loestadt and Lilienthal, Swedish painters of genuine talent, and more particularly the lady 'Trusty, dusky, vivid, [and] true' to whom Robert Louis Stevenson inscribed the most beautiful love-song of our time, and who later on was destined to become his wife.[6] Mrs Osbourne could not at the time have been more than thirty-five years of age, a grave and remarkable type of womanhood, with eyes of a depth and a somber beauty which I have never seen equaled – eyes, nevertheless, that upon occasion could sparkle with humor and brim over with laughter. Yet upon the whole Mrs Osbourne impressed me as first of all a woman of profound character and serious judgment, who could, if occasion called, have been the leader in some great movement. But she belonged to the quattrocento rather than to the end of the nineteenth century. Had she been born a Medici, she would have held rank as one of the remarkable women of all time.

NOTES

1. Theodore Robinson (1852–96), American artist, who also wrote on Corot and Manet in *Modern French Masters* (1896). Stevenson took to this semi-invalid who would not talk about his chronic asthma or allow it to dominate his life.
2. At this period R. A. M. Stevenson was striving to become a landscape painter but showing greater aptitude for the art of conversation. Although never a great artist, he exhibited at the Royal Academy, published essays in the *Portfolio*, and held the Chair of Fine Arts at Liverpool University College (1889–93), after which he became art critic for the *Pall Mall Gazette*. His best-known work was *The Art of Velasquez* (1895).
3. 'The Suicide Club', first published *London*, 8 June–26 Oct 1878 (*New Arabian Nights*, 1882). The Young Man with the Cream Tarts was very much a portrayal of Bob. Birge describes how Bob's monologue developed two plots for the story, one of which, abandoned by Louis, made each character seeking death board a luxury train, which would plunge over the cliffs of Dover. Lloyd Osbourne, however, attributes the train plot entirely to Louis (*Intimate Portrait*, 10–11).
4. An essay, 'Fontainebleau: Village Communities of Painters', appeared in the *Magazine of Art*, May 1884, later in *Across the Plains* (1891).
5. In 'Reflections and Remarks on Human Life' he calls *Cousine Bette* 'a pretty bad book', but about Balzac he was generally enthusiastic.
6. The opening lines of the much quoted poem 'To my Wife' (*Songs of Travel*, 1896). See also his dedication to her in *Weir of Hermiston*, which many readers prefer to the better known poem.

The Scotch Literary Mediocrity

LLOYD OSBOURNE

From *An Intimate Portrait of R.L.S.* (1924) 2–13. Samuel Lloyd Osbourne (1868–1947) was born in San Francisco, son of a scapegrace ex-Civil War officer, prospector and pioneer. He had one sister, Isobel, and a brother, Hervey, who died in childhood. Dazzled by his step-father's example, he took to writing, collaborating with Louis in *The Wrong Box* (1889) and also, though less substantially, in *The Wrecker* (1892) and *The Ebb Tide* (1894). At Vailima he functioned inadequately as estate manager, and at one time became involved with a Samoan girl. As a beneficiary of the Stevenson estate, Lloyd spent his last years in comparative ease, but continued to write, producing such pot-boilers as *Love the Fiddler* (1903), *Baby Bullet* (1905), *The Motor Maniacs* (1906) and *The Adventurer* (1907). Lloyd's book on his step-father was probably his best work, despite some creative recollection regarding the collaborations and life at Vailima. Lloyd was a man of limited talent and something of a loafer, perhaps taking after his father, Samuel Osbourne, who drifted in and out of Fanny's life until he finally disappeared without trace, having walked out on his second wife. Lloyd's unseemly wrangling with his mother over estate and copyrights shows him in a bad light, but his childhood trials, his mother's possessiveness and the difficulties of having a genius for a step-father must elicit sympathy. Louis adored him, and he Louis. Lloyd also edited *The Stevenson Reader* (1898) and collaborated with Isobel Field (Strong) in *Memories of Vailima* (1902).

While the others talked I appraised him silently. He was tall and slight, with light-brown hair, a small golden moustache, and a beautiful ruddy complexion; and was so gay and buoyant that he kept every one in fits of laughter. He wore a funny-looking little round cap, such as schoolboys used to have in England; a white flannel shirt, dark trousers, and very neat shoes. Stevenson had very shapely feet; they were long and narrow with a high arch and instep, and he was proud of them. However shabbily he might be dressed, he was always smartly shod. I remember being much impressed by his costume, which was in such contrast to that of his cousin, 'Bob', who had preceded him to Grez, and whom I already knew quite well. Bob was attired in a tattered blue jersey such as fishermen wore, trousers that needed no Sherlock

Holmes to decide that he was a landscape-painter, and wooden *sabots* of the slightly superior order....

It was the custom of them all to rail at the respectable and well-to-do; R.L.S.'s favorite expression was 'a common banker', used as one might refer to a common labourer. 'Why, even a common banker would renig at a thing like that' – 'renig' being another favorite word. I got the impression that people with good clothes, and money in their pockets, and pleasant, big houses were somehow odious, and should be heartily despised. They belonged to a strange race called Philistines, and were sternly to be kept in their place. If any had dared install themselves in the Hotel Chevillon they would have found it a nest of hornets.

R.L.S. always said he hoped to die in a ditch. He must have dwelt on it at great length, and with all his matchless humor, for, while I have forgotten the details, the picture of him as a white-haired and expiring wanderer is ineffaceably fixed in my mind. It cost me many a pang that such was to be his end while common bankers jingled by in shining equipages, oblivious and scornful. But the tragedy that hung over Bob was even worse. Bob had divided his modest patrimony into ten equal parts, and after spending one of these every year was to commit suicide at the end. I never saw him lay out a few coppers for tobacco without a quivery feeling that he had shortened his life.[1]

Young as I was I could not help noticing that R.L.S. and my mother were greatly attracted to each other; or rather how they would sit and talk interminably on either side of the dining-room stove while everybody else was out and busy.[2] I grew to associate them as always together, and in a queer, childish way I think it made me very happy. I had grown to love Luly Stevenson, as I called him; he used to read the 'Pilgrim's Progress' and the 'Tales of a Grandfather' to me, and tell me stories 'out of his head'; he gave me a sense of protection and warmth, and though I was far too shy ever to have said it aloud, he seemed so much like *Greatheart* in the book that this was my secret name for him.

When autumn merged into early winter and it was time for us to return to Paris, I was overjoyed when my mother said to me: 'Luly is coming, too.' [In August 1878 Fanny Osbourne and Lloyd sailed for America. Prior to their departure, Louis joined them briefly in London.]

When R.L.S. finally came I was conscious of a subtle change in him; even to childish eyes he was more assured, more mature and responsible. I was quite awed by his beautiful blue suit with its double-breasted coat, and the new stiff felt hat he threw on one side; and there was much in his eager talk about 'going to press', and 'closing the forms', and Henley 'wanted a middle' about such and such a subject. He was now connected with a new weekly, called *London*, and evidently found the work very congenial and amusing.[3] He was constantly dashing up in cabs, and dashing away again with the impressive prodigality that apparently journalism required. Indeed, he seemed extraordinarily happy in his new occupation, and was full of zest and high spirits. . . .

One evening, with a kind of shyness he never outgrew, he produced a manuscript from his pocket, and read aloud 'Will o' the Mill'.[4] Though I understood very little of it, its melodious cadence affected me profoundly, and I remember being so pleased with my mother's enthusiasm. R.L.S. beamed with pleasure; he loved to have his work praised; and he put several questions, as he was always wont to do, for the sheer delight of prolonging such precious moments. Unlike most authors, he read aloud incomparably well, endowing words and phrases with a haunting quality that lingered in one's ears afterward. I have never heard any one to equal him: the glamour he could give, the stir of romance, the indescribable emotion from which one awoke as though from a dream.

At Grez a young Irish painter had once presented a new arrival to the assembled company after dinner, and in doing so had mockingly labelled the various *habitués*. R.L.S. he had described as 'Louis Stevenson – Scotch literary mediocrity.' The phrase had stung R.L.S. to the quick; it was one of the very few slights he kept alive in his memory. I remember that after he had finished 'Will o' the Mill' and was still in the glow of my mother's praise, he murmured something about its not being so bad for 'Scotch literary mediocrity'. . . .

Meanwhile the hour of parting was drawing near. I had not the slightest perception of the quandary my mother and R.L.S. were in, nor what agonies of mind their approaching separation was bringing; and doubtless I prattled endlessly about 'going home', and enjoyed all our preparations, while to them that imminent August spelled the knell of everything that made life worth living. But when the time came I had my own tragedy of parting, and the picture lives with me as clearly as though it were yesterday.

We were standing in front of our compartment, and the moment to say good-bye had come. It was terribly short and sudden and final, and before I could realize it R.L.S. was walking away down the long length of the platform, a diminishing figure in a brown ulster. My eyes followed him, hoping that he would look back. But he never turned, and finally disappeared in the crowd. Words cannot express the sense of bereavement, of desolation that suddenly struck at my heart. I knew I would never see him again.

NOTES

1. Clearly in this kind of talk, however much may have been worked up from hindsight, is the germ of Louis's story 'The Suicide Club'. Lloyd insists he heard his step-father outline the plot (*Intimate Portrait*, 11–12).
2. In these passages he is attempting to convey the memories of a child from the age of eight to ten. The visitors had just moored their canoes, the *Cigarette* and the *Arethusa*, which figured in *An Inland Voyage* (1878) at the riverside in Grez-sur-Loing. Another version is recorded in his contribution to A. St J. Adcock (ed.), *Robert Louis Stevenson: His Work and Personality* (1924).
3. W. E. Henley was the editor of *London*, with which Louis became involved in 1877. The journal lasted under two years, folding after its 114th issue. Louis's contributions included 'The Suicide Club', 'The Rajah's Diamonds', 'A Plea for Gas Lamps', 'Pan's Pipes', and other occasional pieces. He confessed to Baxter early in 1878: '*London* is rapidly hustling me into the abhorred tomb; I do write such damned rubbish in it, that's a fac', and I hate doing it so inconceivably' (*Baxter Letters*, 51).
4. 'Will o' the Mill' earned him £20 and was published by Leslie Stephen in *Cornhill*, Jan 1878, later in *The Merry Men* (1887). A curious story, it resonates uncomfortably, with its protagonist convinced that moving beyond his happy valley is fruitless, finally confronted by and welcoming Death. To my mind, Stevenson is far closer to Hawthorne here, as elsewhere in his writing, than critics have allowed. Contemporaries were unmoved, except for L. Cope Cornford. George E. Brown declared it 'as perfect as any short work of Stevenson's' (*A Book of R.L.S.* (1919) 282).

The Silent and, Truth to Tell, Rather Dejected Youth

ALICE GORDON

From 'The first meeting between George Meredith and Robert Louis Stevenson', *Bookman*, VI (Jan 1895) 111–12. 'Alice Gordon' was Lady Alice Mary (Brandreth) Butcher, wife of J. G. Butcher QC, Tory MP for York. She is best known for *Memories of George Meredith* (1919), which came out of her friendship with the novelist over 41 years. Her first marriage, to her cousin James Edward Henry Gordon, an expert in the field of electricity, resulted in her book *Decorative Electricity* (1889). She also wrote one novel, *Anscombe* (1892). The meeting described here gave a timely boost to Stevenson's confidence. Friendship was established from this, their second meeting, at Box Hill in the spring of 1879, and an amiable correspondence continued, except when Meredith joined other tiresome voices urging Louis to leave Samoa and re-enter the literary mainstream. R.L.S. retorted that human nature was much the same in Samoa as in London, and that his art was the better for standing away from the crowd (McLynn, 484). Critics have tended to deplore Meredith's influence on Stevenson's writing, seeing *Prince Otto* (1885), for example, as a bad case of Meredithian preciosity. Gower Woodseer, in *The Amazing Marriage* (1895), shows touches of the young Stevenson, as Louis himself recognised (*Letters*, II, 324).

Sometime in the seventies Robert Louis Stevenson came with his mother and took up his abode for a summer at the romantic little inn at the foot of Box Hill known as the Burford Arms. At that time we were living about ten minutes' walk from the little hostel, and among our most honoured and best beloved friends was the sage of Box Hill, George Meredith.[1] A publisher friend wrote to us from London and begged my mother to make the acquaintance of Mr Louis Stevenson, requesting her if possible to invite him to meet George Meredith. Thus it came to pass that Robert Louis Stevenson, then entirely unknown to fame, would occasionally drop into our garden and sit at the feet of the philosopher and listen with rapt attention and appreciative smiles to his conversation.

I well remember the eager listening face of the student Stevenson, and remember his frank avowal that from henceforth he should enrol himself 'a true blue Meredith man'. He was an inspiring listener, and had the art of drawing out the best of Mr Meredith's brilliant powers of conversation, so that those were halcyon days.[2] Though preferring to listen, Mr Stevenson would speak of Dumas, Hazlitt, Defoe, Congreve, and a host of other writers and creators of fiction with enthusiasm and with that artistic appreciation of their various and differing qualities which is only possible to a workman in the same craft. Everyone knows how Stevenson taught himself to write, in the literary sense of that word, by loving and constant search for the apt word, the artistic and appropriate phrase with which to clothe his thought so that the adjectives and nouns, original and effective though they might be in their application, should yet slip into their right places in the narrative, and seemingly without effort, for simplicity is the soul of a good style.[3]

Mr Stevenson had by this time given up all thought of following his father's profession, and likewise of making a career at the Scottish bar. He had already written and published a good many of his delightful essays; but his name was unknown, and his success far from assured when we knew him in the seventies. I never met him after fame and glory had crowned his efforts.

My sister, I remember, was much interested in Stevenson, and even in those early days, expected great things from him in the future. And I well remember her satisfaction, one afternoon when after he had taken his departure from our circle, and one of us was idly wondering why our friend, the publisher, was so hopeful about young Stevenson's future, Mr Meredith trumpeted down our feeble utterances by informing us that some day he felt sure we should all be proud to have known him, and prophesied success and fame for him in the future. I was not so discriminating, and remember when 'Treasure Island', 'Virginibus Puerisque', and his other masterpieces appeared, feeling surprised that they should be the work of the silent and, truth to tell, rather dejected-looking youth who had lodged with his mother in our neighbourhood for a short space of time, and whose highest merit in my eyes had been his enthusiastic appreciation of George Meredith's writings and conversation.[4]

Yet I can remember two of Mr Stevenson's sayings that struck me at the time, and have in consequence remained in my memory ever since. One day he wandered in, and with a desolate expression of countenance, remarked that he was having a bad time with his heroine. He said, 'She is turning ugly on my hands. It is no use my saying she is beautiful and charming and fascinating, and that everybody in the book is falling in love with her – it is unconvincing, and I feel the reader won't believe it, and I don't know what to do.' The exact words, I fear, I do not accurately remember, but that, at any rate, was the substance of his observation. And I remember how delighted he was when his confession drew from George Meredith a treatise on heroines in general, and his own in particular. I understand that Mr Stevenson always felt that he had not the gift of describing women characters with vitality, and when 'Catriona', his greatest achievement in that difficult task, was published, his keenest anxiety was to know what was thought of her and Barbara Grant by the critics and literary judges in England.[5]

One other day I remember we were talking of our dislike to prigs as heroes in books, and Mr Stevenson said, 'An aspirant novelist should always comprehend that if in the first two or three chapters of books readers are convinced that the hero cannot by any possibility do or think anything wrong, or commit even the smallest indiscretion, the authors have given themselves away, and by no possibility can readers be any more interested in the adventures and fortunes of such immaculate but unattractive characters.'

NOTES

1. George Meredith (1828–1909) author of *The Ordeal of Richard Feverel* (1859), *Harry Richmond* (1871), *The Egoist* (1879) and other novels, as well as the powerful poems *Modern Love* (1862). Stevenson told Henley in April, 1882: 'I see more and more that Meredith is built for immortality' (*Letters*, I, 239).

2. The writer amplifies this a little elsewhere, saying that mutual conversational powers brought them close: 'In his turn Mr Meredith would break staves of wit on the head of the younger man, which he sturdily parried, returning with vigour the elder man's hits' (Lady Butcher, *Memories of George Meredith*, OM (1919) 58).

3. No writer on Stevenson's mastery of style fails to quote the passage in 'A College Magazine' in which he says he played 'the sedulous ape to Hazlitt, to Lamb, to Wordsworth, to Sir Thomas Browne, to Defoe, to Hawthorne, to Montaigne, to Baudelaire and to Obermann' (*Memories*, 59).

4. At one point Louis exclaimed that he saw himself as Sir Willoughby Patterne of *The Egoist*, to which Meredith blandly responded, 'No, my dear fellow, he is all of us' (quoted in Bell, 167).
5. Always a sore point with Louis, who endured some needling from Fanny on the subject. Perhaps because he had done the two heroines so well in *Catriona*, he told Meredith he thought that it was his best book (McLynn, 436).

Submerged in Billows of Bedclothes

CHARLES WARREN STODDARD

From *Exits and Entrances* (1903) 14–18, 34–5. Charles Warren Stoddard (1843–1909), prolific travel writer and poet, whose books included *South Sea Idyls* (1873), published in Britain as *Summer Cruising in the South Seas* (1874), *The Lepers of Molokai* (1899) and *Over the Rocky Mountains to Alaska* (1899). Louis got to know him in Monterey where he was one of its artistic colony. In San Francisco in 1880 Stoddard started him reading Melville. Fascinated by his home, Louis used the location in the 'Faces on the city front' chapter of *The Wrecker*. From Bournemouth in February 1886, he recalled Stoddard's 'strange den upon a hill in San Francisco; and one of the most San Francisco-y parts' (*Letters*, II, 19). See also the description in *The Silverado Squatters* (1883). In his customary oleaginous style, Stoddard wrote of his friend in 'Stevenson's Monterey', *National Magazine*, Dec 1906; 'Stevenson in the South Seas', *Kate Field's Washington*, XI, 26 Jan and 2 Feb 1895.

Soon after Stevenson's arrival in California, we met. The happy hour brought us together in the studio of an artist friend; there, with a confusion of canvases for a background, and an audience as clever as limited, all things were possible save only the commonplace, and in the prevailing atmosphere – an atmosphere not unpleasantly tinged with Bohemianism – the situation became spectacular.[1]

There I heard him discourse; there I saw him literally *rise* to the occasion, and striding to and fro with leonine tread, toss back his lank locks and soliloquise with the fine frenzy of an Italian *improvisatore*. We were all on our mettle. I am inclined to think that every one was at his best – I mean that he was keyed up to concert pitch – while in the presence of that inspiring man. He was so entirely master of himself and of the situation that each listener was on the alert and thus unconsciously assumed his pleasantest expression. It is not unlikely that the exceptional brilliancy of the rhetorical Stevenson dared his guest to unaccustomed efforts and that in consequence he achieved an intellectual spurt that, though brief, was brave enough, and astonished no one so much as himself, when he came to weigh it complacently in comfortable recollection. I wonder how many entirely harmless people have been led to think very pleasantly of themselves after an interview with such a man as Robert Louis Stevenson? I don't believe that he ever belittled any one who didn't richly deserve it – no, not even in an irritable moment. Let us hope for all our sakes that he was tempted alike as we are.

At the time I first knew him, Stevenson's itinerary was extremely limited; he usually travelled from his couch to his lounge, possibly touching at the armchair on the way. Those who are acquainted with 'A Child's Garden of Verses' will see the delightful possibilities of this prescribed journey in such company. For a long time his tours were not greatly varied; with him it was nearly the same daily routine with an occasional change of horizon. His familiars grew to think of him and to look upon him as being but a disembodied intellect; his was the rare kind of personality that inspires in the susceptible heart a deep though passionless love. I take him to have been the last man in the world to awaken or invite passion.

In his own select circle, necessarily a very limited one, he was reverenced, and it does not seem in the least surprising that there should have been found those who were glad to gather at his knee in worshipful silence, while he, in an exalted state of spirituality, read and expounded the Scriptures with rabbinical gravity.

I have visited him in a lonely lodging – it was previous to his happy marriage – and found him submerged in billows of bedclothes; about him floated the scattered volumes of a complete set of Thoreau; he was preparing an essay on that worthy, and he looked at the moment like a half-drowned man – yet he was not cast down.[2] His work, an endless task, was better than a straw to him. It was to become his life-preserver and to prolong his years. I feel convinced that without it he must have surrendered long before he did.

I found Stevenson a man of frailest physique, though most unaccountably tenacious of life; a man whose pen was indefatigable, whose brain was never at rest; who as far as I am able to judge, looked upon everybody and everything from a supremely intellectual point of view. His was a superior organisation that seems never to have been tainted by things common or unclean; one more likely to be revolted than appealed to by carnality in any form. A man unfleshly to the verge of emaciation, and, in this connection, I am not unmindful of a market in fleshpots not beneath the consideration of sanctimonious speculators; but here was a man whose sympathies were literary and artistic; whose intimacies were born and bred above the ears.

After a phenomenal success in letters which had made him the idol of the reading world, a world from which he had vainly striven to banish himself, he suddenly weighed anchor and descended into the abysmal waters of the sea. Now, for a time at least, he was lost to us all; we could not follow him with any assurance of finding him, or of gaining any very definite knowledge of him until he reappeared from the underworld, richer for an experience that is rare enough even in these days of general peregrination, and which is daily growing more rare through the fatal evolutions of the age.

It seems that the distinguished author of 'Treasure Island' was about to set forth in search of new island worlds.[3] Absent from California at this time, I received a letter from an old comrade in San Francisco revealing to me something of the mystery of the romancer's sudden and rather unceremonious taking off. This intelligence I had been watching for with no little anxiety, inasmuch as I had been aware that for months a sea voyage, and a very long one, had been in contemplation. Later Mr Stevenson, now a benedict, arrived in California, and the preparations for departure were entrusted to the willing and experienced hands of our common friend, the writer of the letter above referred to.

I wondered at Stevenson's temerity. Though better than when we first met, he was far from well. He was obliged to deny himself to most of his friends, and to quite forswear the curious who had persistently tracked him ever since he startled the world with that appalling psychological study, that vivisection of a soul – 'The Strange Case of Dr Jekyll and Mr Hyde'. But the voice of the siren was in his ears and go he must....

He left in search of those islands where the anthropophagi still flourish, or are supposed to flourish, and the remote seas held few secrets that the adventurous voyager did not wrest from them before he came to shore in Samoa and made his final home. He took with him a wealth of trinkets, for these does the gentle savage most delight in; glowing calicoes, and such light kitchen utensils as may be clustered about the neck or glisten upon the unabashed bosom of dusky maidenhood. His enchanting cargo comprised a hand-organ to beguile the ear of sable majesty, and a magic-lantern – the slides thereof were destined to work latter-day miracles among the unregenerated. Thus astonishingly equipped, I assured myself that Stevenson must appear in the eyes of the islanders but little less than a god; and if he were not dowered with kingdoms, principalities, and powers, because of his preternatural accomplishments – then the heathen will have forgotten their simplicity and the voyager will have opened his heart and his purse in vain.

It was my conviction that when the true story of this romantic expedition – it was but one of several – was given to the world, we should have a record of adventure set forth in a fashion so exquisite that all the log-books of all the mariners that ever sailed the seas, and at last got into port or print, must pale before it. I believed it must surely be a picture of the Antipodes so brilliant in colouring and so unique in treatment that the pages of 'Treasure Island' would seem grey by comparison; or that the world of readers would realise that they had never before been taken so close to the heart of its author – for they would feel the strength and power of its pulsation for the first time.

NOTES

1. In Aug 1878, Fanny had returned to the United States for a showdown with her husband, Sam. One year later, Louis had sailed for New York on the *Devonia*, from which voyage came *The Amateur Emigrant* (1894). Guilt-ridden at leaving his parents without a word, weakened by the voyage, he arrived in Monterey at death's door. The artist here is Virgil Williams and his wife, Dora, old friends of Fanny, to whom Louis dedicated *The Silverado Squatters* (1883). Virgil Macey Williams (1830–86), formerly teacher of drawing at Harvard College, was the first director of the School of Design, San Francisco, when it opened in 1874. The majority of students were women, among them Belle and her mother, who won a silver medal for one of her drawings. From Grez

Fanny brought a water-colour scene of the village, which she gave to her lawyer friend, Timothy Henry Rearden (1839–92), in lieu of a fee when he negotiated her divorce from Sam Osbourne. After their marriage, the Stevensons, on Williams's advice, found inexpensive lodgings in the Napa Valley for the summer (1880).

2. 'Henry David Thoreau: his Character and Opinions', *Cornhill*, June 1880, XLI, 665–82 (*Familiar Studies*, 1882).

3. The circumstances alluded to are the Stevensons' scheme to hire the schooner-yacht *Casco* and sail to the Galapagos. Belle and Dora Williams were on hand to wave goodbye on 28 June 1888.

The Look as of the Ancient Mariner

ALEXANDER JAPP

From *Robert Louis Stevenson: A Record, an Estimate and a Memorial* (1905) 7–12, and 'Robert Louis Stevenson', *Argosy*, LIX (Feb 1895) 232. Alexander Hay Japp (1839–1905), a prolific journalist, wrote under several pseudonyms on topics from cuckoos to labour relations; his literary studies centred on de Quincey; his work on Stevenson included five articles and one full-length study. They became acquainted through a common interest in Thoreau, and Stevenson invited him to Braemar in August 1881. Japp's signal contribution to the Stevenson story is that he urged James Henderson of *Young Folks' Paper* to publish *The Sea-Cook*. Henderson requested the change of title to *Treasure Island or the Mutiny of the Hispaniola* and serialisation began, from 1 October 1881 until 28 January 1882. It was issued under the pen-name 'Captain George North'. At first the serial was not a success, although it was to become the book most commonly associated with the famous initials R.L.S. Despite condescension from old friends such as Henley, the book was a turning point in Louis's career. (See 'My First Book: *Treasure Island*', *McClure's Magazine*, 3 (Sep 1894) 283–93; Hammerton, *Stevensoniana*, 53–61; Swearingen, 63–70.)

Mr Stevenson's is, indeed, a very picturesque and striking figure. Not so tall probably as he seems at first sight from his extreme thinness, but the pose and air could not be otherwise described than as distinguished. Head of fine type, carried well on the shoulders and in walking with the impression of being a little thrown back; long brown hair, falling from under a broadish-brimmed Spanish form of soft felt hat, Rembrandtesque; loose kind of Inverness cape when walking, and invariable velvet jacket inside the house. You would say at first sight, wherever you saw him, that he was a man of intellect, artistic and individual, wholly out of the common. His face is sensitive, full of expression, though it could not be called strictly beautiful. It is longish, especially seen in profile, and features a little irregular; the brow at once high and broad. A hint of vagary, and just a hint in the expression, is qualified by the eyes, which are set rather far apart from each other as seems, and with a most wistful, and at the same time possibly a merry impish expression arising over that, yet frank and clear, piercing, but at the same time steady, and fall on you with a gentle radiance and animation as he speaks. Romance, if with an indescribable *soupçon* of whimsicality, is marked upon him; sometimes he has the look as of the Ancient Mariner, and could fix you with his glittering e'e, an he would, as he points his sentences with a movement of his thin white forefinger, when this is not monopolised with the almost incessant cigarette. There is a faint suggestion of a hair-brained [sic] sentimental trace on his countenance, but controlled, after all, by good Scotch sense and shrewdness. In conversation he is very animated, and likes to ask questions. A favourite and characteristic attitude with him was to put his foot on a chair or stool and rest his elbow on his knee, with his chin on his hand; or to sit, or rather to half sit, half lean, on the corner of a table or desk, one of his legs swinging freely, and when anything that tickled him was said he would laugh in the heartiest manner, even at the risk of bringing on his cough, which at that time was troublesome. Often when he got animated he rose and walked about as he spoke, as if movement aided thought and expression. Though he loved Edinburgh, which was full of associations for him, he had no good word for its east winds, which to him were as death. Yet he passed one winter as a 'Silverado squatter', the story of which he has inimitably told in the volume titled *The Silverado Squatters*; and he afterwards spent several winters at Davos Platz, where, as he said to me, he not only breathed good air, but learned to know with closest intimacy John Addington Symonds, who 'though his books were good, was far finer and more interesting than any of his books'. He needed a good deal of nursely attentions, but his invalidism was never obtrusively brought before one in any sympathy-seeking way by himself; on the contrary, a very manly, self-sustaining spirit was evident; and the amount of work which he managed to turn out even when at his worst was truly surprising.[1]

His wife, an American lady, is highly cultured, and is herself an author. In her speech there is just the slightest suggestion of the American accent, which only made it the more pleasing to my ear. She is heart and soul devoted to her husband, proud of his achievements, and her delight is the consciousness of substantially aiding him in his enterprises.

They then had with them a boy of eleven or twelve, Samuel Lloyd Osbourne, to be much referred to later (a son of Mrs Stevenson by a former marriage), whose delight was to draw the oddest, but perhaps half intentional or unintentional caricatures, funny, in some cases, beyond expression. His room was designated the picture-gallery, and on entering I could scarce refrain from bursting into laughter, even at the general effect, and, noticing this, and that I was putting some restraint on myself out of respect for the host's feelings, Stevenson said to me with a sly wink and a gentle dig in the ribs, 'It's laugh and be thankful here.' On Lloyd's account simple engraving materials, types, and a small printing-press had been procured; and it was Stevenson's delight to make funny poems, stories, and morals for the engravings executed, and all would be duly printed together.[2] Stevenson's thorough enjoyment of the picture-gallery, and his goodness to Lloyd, becoming himself a very boy for the nonce, were delightful to witness and in degree to share. Wherever they were – at Braemar, in Edinburgh, at Davos Platz, or even at Silverado – the engraving and printing went on. The mention of the picture-gallery suggests that it was out of his interest in the colour-drawing and the picture-gallery that his first published story, *Treasure Island*, grew, as we shall see.

I have seen copies of the rude printing-press productions, inexpressibly quaint, grotesque, a kind of literary horse-play, yet with a certain squint-eyed, sprawling genius in it, and innocent childish Rabelaisian mirth of a sort. At all events I cannot look at the slight memorials of that time, which I still possess, without laughing afresh till my eyes are dewy. Stevenson, as I understood, began *Treasure Island* more to entertain Lloyd Osbourne than anything else; the chapters being regularly read to the family circle as they were written, and with scarcely a purpose beyond. The lad became Stevenson's trusted companion and collaborator – clearly with a touch of genius.[3]

I have before me as I write some of these funny mementoes of that time, carefully kept, often looked at. One of them is 'The Black Canyon; or, Wild Adventures in the Far West: a Tale of Instruction and Amusement for the Young, by Samuel L. Osbourne, printed by the author; Davos Platz', with the most remarkable cuts. It would not do some of the sensationalists anything but good to read it even at this day, since many points in their art are absurdly caricatured. Another is 'Moral Emblems; a Collection of Cuts and Verses, by R. L. Stevenson, author of the Blue Scalper, etc., etc. Printers, S. L. Osbourne and Company, Davos Platz'. . . .

Delightfully suggestive and highly enjoyable were the meetings in the little drawing-room after dinner, when the contrasted traits of father and son came fully into play, when Louis would sometimes draw out a new view of things by bold, half-paradoxical assertion, or compel advance on the point from a new quarter by a question casuistically couched, or reveal his own latent conviction finally by a few sentences as neatly-rounded as though they had been written, while he rose and gently moved about as his habit was in the course of these more extended remarks. The greatest treat of all was the reading of the 'Sea-Cook'. It is one thing to read the printed page; it was quite another to hear Stevenson as he stood reading it aloud, with his hand stretched out, and his body gently swaying as a kind of rhythmical commentary.[4]

NOTES

1. Despite chronic catarrh and lung problems, this was a productive time for Louis. At Pitlochry (June–July 1880) he had written the powerful 'Thrawn Janet' and 'The Merry Men', worked on 'The Body Snatcher' and made a start on The Sea-Cook.

2. These early collaborative efforts bonded Lloyd and his step-father. Lloyd had a printing press, acquired in California, which was brought to Davos and to Scotland. Many items, now much coveted by Stevensonians, were jointly produced with engravings and illustrations. From Davos in April, 1882, he sent one of Lloyd's efforts with the comment: 'this is *simply the first time he has ever given one away*. I have to buy my own works, I can tell you' (Letters, I, 236–7).

3. Japp overestimates Lloyd's talent. Much speculation has surrounded the inspiration and implementing of Treasure Island. Lloyd took much of the credit, talking especially with regard to the map, but critics now

acknowledge the role of Thomas Stevenson in its genesis, recalling the stories he made up to calm Louis's disturbed nights. Certainly his encouragement is not to be overlooked. Fanny recalled him as entranced when a chapter was read: 'Every incident of the story could be read in his changing countenance' (quoted in Calder, 167).

4. Writing *Treasure Island* at Braemar went on at full speed, with 15 chapters in as many days. Early receipts were a meagre £30; in book form (1883) it realised £100; by 1901 it had earned only £2000 for the estate, due to widespread pirated editions. Much fruitless speculation has been devoted to establishing the island's location: the Shetlands, the Pentland Hills, the Isle of Pines near Cuba, and parts of California have all been canvassed. See also 'Writings as Pure as Possible' (p. 152).

A Rather Odd, Exotic, Theatrical Kind of Man

HAROLD VALLINGS

From 'Stevenson among the Philistines', *Temple Bar*, 122 (Feb 1901) 205–9. Following the Stevensons' return to Scotland in October 1880, and the ordeal of meeting Louis's parents and friends, which Fanny managed successfully, the couple spent two periods in Davos, where Louis was treated by Dr Karl Ruedi at his clinic for consumptives. Stevenson dedicated *Underwoods* to Ruedi – 'the good genius of the English in his frosty mountains'. Stevenson wrote little in his first stay, although *Virginibus Puerisque* was seen through the press. In the second period, however, he wrote *The Silverado Squatters* (1883), finished *Treasure Island* (1883), and managed 90 pages for the *Cornhill*. He wrote to Alexander Japp: 'My wicked carcase, as John Knox calls it, holds together wonderfully ... I begin to hope I may, if not outlive this wolverine upon my shoulders, at least carry him bravely like Symonds and Alexander Pope' (*Letters*, I, 237). Vallings, who later wrote popular novels, was fairly representative of the stolid, middle-class types Stevenson was most anxious to keep away from, but the merit of this recollection during March 1881 was precisely in its commonplace perspective. For further detail on this period see W. G. Lockett, *Robert Louis Stevenson at Davos* (1934).

How did he impress us, the simple Philistines among whom he was sojourning for a space?

I believe he struck us, to begin with – for it is as well to confess one's sins openly and at once – as a rather odd, exotic, theatrical kind of man; a man framed somewhat on the model of one of Du Maurier's aesthetes. His personality had a tinge of that picturesqueness and Bohemianism which seldom fail to sharply impinge upon the prejudices of a true-born Briton.[1] It is possible, too, that even his un-British courtesy of manner may have caused some misgivings. A want of bluntness on the part of one who addresses us for the first time, if he speaks our own tongue, is apt to cause qualms; a tendency to put any suavity into the curt commonplaces that we bark out half resentfully at each other, with a view to promoting acquaintanceship, is to many of us an alarming symptom.

Nevertheless, when our first natural alarm has passed, the phenomenon of courteous speech has a charm proportioned to its rarity; and I can answer for its effect in this case at any rate upon one young Philistine – then just invalided from the army, and doubtless redolent of Aldershot. Upon him, at least, the phenomenon acted promptly and beneficently; it was an emollient to all insular prejudices, a soother of all British apprehensions. In brief, the very first impression recorded by one memory of 'the Mr Stevenson' who was understood to have 'written something' is that of his courteous willingness to please.

And close beside that first entry upon one's mental tablets, a brief search discloses a second, and not less marked, impression – that of his pluck.

One knew at once that he was, in Davosian parlance, 'lungy'– more 'lungy' even than the majority; but, though so obviously a member of the crock-company, he would, whenever he had an ounce of strength to spare, insist upon a place with the robust brigade.[2] The latter were doing their tobogganing, the season being already far advanced, in the early morning, down slopes perfected by the action of a hard night frost upon the sun-thaw of the previous day, and with them, often enough, went Stevenson. To the detriment of his feeble health, I fear, for I have a most vivid recollection of a first view of him homeward bound from one of those before-breakfast expeditions. He was dragging himself wearily along, towing a toboggan at his heels, his narrow hunched-up figure cut clear against the surpassing brilliance of the white Davosian world. With that pathetic, half-broken figure making so dominant a note in one's recollection, one marvels indeed at the fortitude that made possible his later achievements.

Through the closing weeks of that winter season it was my hap, through sheer good luck, fostered in some measure by a nascent enthusiasm for Art – to foregather pretty frequently with the courageous invalid, and only once do I remember his uttering a despondent word. 'I can't work,' he said to me one day. 'Yet now that I've fallen sick I've lost all my capacity for idleness.'

That one brief plaint of a chained genius has echoed long and sadly in one's memory.

The man was an artist to the marrow; it is a satisfaction to know that one appreciated so much at least at the first touch. His outlook all round was that of an artist, an ingrained Bohemian.

As he sat on the verandah of a morning in the sunshine of early March, with Hamley's 'Operations of War', his study of the moment, on his knees, he would talk paint-and-canvas to one's heart's content; commenting vividly upon his Bohemian experiences in France, touching regretfully more than once upon that idyllic barge excursion which he had planned – abortively as it turned out – in conjunction with half-a-dozen ardent brothers of the brush.[3] Upon art questions, as upon any other, he was a delightful opponent; always keenly enthusiastic, always hotly eloquent, yet unfailingly tolerant and good-tempered. Between the friendly wrangles, the jargonings and anecdotes, he would stop to flatter a mere youngster, deprived by Fate of a beloved profession, by asking for his eminent judgment upon one of Hamley's maps or some technical point in the text....

Failing the hotel verandah, one could often chance upon Stevenson in the billiard-room, though not often with a cue in his hand. Once only do I remember seeing him play a game, and a truly remarkable performance it was. He played with all the fire and dramatic intensity that he was apt to put into things. The balls flew wildly about, on or off the table as the case might be; but seldom indeed even threatened a pocket or got within a hand's breadth of a cannon. 'What a fine thing a game of billiards is,' he remarked to the astonished on-lookers, – 'once a year or so!'

But the after-dinner hour when the menkind got together in the same room was the right one for Stevenson. A crowd would always kindle him; and one man in particular, whom I will call the Professor, had an especial knack of stirring his mettle.

The Professor was jovial, loud-voiced, and as vehement as Stevenson himself. The rallies between those two were full of life and entertainment. On a certain evening, I remember, the Professor, with one hand clutching his long straw-coloured beard, was holding forth in his violent knock-me-down fashion upon the subject of Englishwomen.

'I don't care a rap for them,' he ejaculated. 'They are a poor tame-spirited lot, not worth conquering. Your milk-and-water Englishwoman falls in love with you before you've had time to say ten words to her,' and so on and so forth. 'Now German women,' he continued, after thus demolishing those of his own country, 'are very different – '

'What!' cried Stevenson, with a theatrical outfling of both hands. 'Do you talk of German women? I tell you, this neck is wet with the tears of German women!'

'Well, all I can say is,' the Professor grunted sulkily, 'I haven't found them like that myself.'

'Haven't you?' shouted Stevenson, whose opponent was far from being a beauty-man. 'Then, by Jupiter Ammon, it only shows how heavily handicapped you are in the race!' And, with that, he fell back into a corner and clasping his lean body in both arms literally hugged himself; the Professor meanwhile glaring sullenly at him through a mist of unparliamentary mono-syllables.

How many are there left, I wonder, of those who egged on the combatants that night? Few, very few most likely; for Davos was then a veritable haunt of the much-stricken, rather than, as now, a rendezvous for winter pleasure-seekers.

In scenes like the above one got a glimpse of the real Stevenson, the high-strung, fervid, excitable artist. The weak invalid frame, so pathetic in its first impression, was forgotten; the inner fires of the man burst forth; the sparkle and vividness of his talk were amazing, and even to some of us benighted Philistines the thought must have occurred that this man was born to be famous.

NOTES

1. Louis's first impressions of the Davos clientele were committed in verse to his friend A. G. Dew Smith:

> The company? Alas the day
> That I should dwell with such a crew,
> With devil anything to say
> Nor any one to say it to!
> (*Letters*, I, 185)

One consolation was getting to know John Addington Symonds (1840–93), himself consumptive, then living with his wife and daughters in a nearby chalet. Symonds, his reputation established as essayist, poet and man of letters was kindly but prickly; Lloyd Osbourne said that he had detected 'veiled condescension' (*Intimate Portrait*, 33). He dedicated 'Wine, Women and Song' (1884) to his younger colleague. Stevenson represented him as Opalstein in 'Talk and Talkers', which irritated Symonds. Their meetings had the advantage of stirring Louis to write again in a dry period, and he produced some essays on the Alps for the *Pall Mall Gazette*, Feb–March 1881.

2. Louis's lung problems had flared up badly in California. He bled so severely that his mouth filled with blood. 'Bluidy Jack' was now a constant threat, alleviated for a while by Dr Karl Ruedi's regimen of milk, meat and red wine and a limit on cigarettes.

3. Sir Edward Bruce Hamley (1824–93), *The Operations of War* (1866) and other books on military matters, notably his *War in the Crimea* (1891) which ran to ten editions. The book had been presented to him by an old general in Oct 1880: 'I am drowned in it a thousand fathom deep', wrote Louis (*Letters*, I, 196–7). Toy soldiers had fascinated him as a child. Now he developed an elaborate *kriegspiel* with Lloyd which could go on for weeks. (See Lloyd Osbourne, *Intimate Portrait*, 36–9.)

'You Must Never, Never Write Like That Again'

ADELAIDE BOODLE

From: *R.L.S. and his Sine Qua Non: Flashlights from Skerryvore by the Gamekeeper* (1926) 7–9, 16–17, 57–61, 88–9. Despite its unpromising title and gushing enthusiasm, Adelaide Anne Boodle's reminiscence has vitality. Adelaide called on the Stevensons in 1884, as they were moving into Skerryvore, the Bournemouth house Thomas Stevenson bought as a wedding gift for his daughter-in-law. Lloyd was already at boarding school in the seaside resort, where they would stay for three years. Louis suffered regular calls from 'Bluidy Jack', and was a target for nuisances, whom Fanny despatched in short order; Miss Boodle, however, got on her right side and was soon having free writing lessons. At intervals she would look after the family pets and thus acquired the name of 'Gamekeeper'. Louis grew fond of her and sent her Christmas boxes until his death.

Valentine (by some inspired mistake, as we afterwards learnt, for she had been charged to admit no living creature that afternoon) ushered us into a carpetless room, bestrewn with packing-cases and straw.[1] There R.L.S. and his wife, in happy security, were overhauling buried treasures to furnish the new home.

Both were curiously clad. He, I remember, had on the velvet coat and dark red tie that were afterwards to become to so many of us almost like a part of his actual personality; her garment was a mysterious-looking over-all (really, I believe, a painting-apron) admirably adapted to her needs at the moment.

There was, if I remember rightly, but one chair in the room: this was told off for the use of my mother; my first resting-place in Skerryvore was a packing-case.

How clearly it all comes back; the radiant cordiality of their welcome! Had we been friends of long standing we should have been fully satisfied; as it was, we were almost bewildered by a reception so far beyond all that we had looked for. Shy as my mother was up to a certain point, no one ever thawed more rapidly in the sunshine of kindness; her heart made one leap to this curious and delightful pair, and in a very few moments she was, to my amazement, in full flow, absolutely at her ease and radiant with pleasure.

Tea was called for, and we drank it like nectar, in a sort of intoxication of delight.

R.L.S. at his very best. How many pictures that will call up in the memories of those who knew him. As a host, in those surprising circumstances he surpassed himself. Lightly perched on his packing-case, and emphasising his words with a brandished teaspoon, he flowed from one anecdote to another with a brilliance that only those who have listened to him in his inspired moments can imagine. It was chiefly nonsense that he talked that day, the gay, enchanting nonsense of a perfectly happy child! Our brains, at this first meeting, received no very special edification; but as for our hearts, from that day forth he had them in possession. . . .

At Skerryvore, for after-experience of their battlefields of conscience taught me that R.L.S. was wholly at one with her in this, there was no such thing as moral indolence: that was a vice for which neither had the least toleration. 'A professional repenter' was, in the eyes of R.L.S., 'the meanest creature on God's earth.' To realise that a thing was wrong meant that the thing had to be abandoned for good and all; to indulge it in driblets and then make weak apologies and weaker promises of amendment was no less than criminal folly.

This doctrine held good also in literature: there was to be no second-best in work. A luckless disciple who once, in an exercise written for his criticism, ventured to defend the careless use of the word 'however', on the ground that it was a valuable refuge from dead monotony in a poor sentence, was rebuked in these words: 'Your favourite refuge! – For-r-r-sake it, woman! For-r-r-sake it for ever! It is a r-r-refuge of lies!' His Scotch r's in moments of excitement suggested rumbles of stage thunder....

R.L.S. welcomed me as usual in the Blue Room; but, for the first time since my adoption as his pupil, we were not alone for the lesson. The *Sine qua non*, to all appearances sound asleep, was lying on the divan. With a red silk pillow as her background, she looked so superbly beautiful that, for a moment, my attention wandered.

Suddenly there was a low (but crescendo) rumble of thunder: 'Oh, but this work is disgracefully bad! It could hardly be worse. What induced you to bring me stuff like this?' My answer was rather wildly given.

'You told me to describe some place, and when I said I couldn't do it, you just repeated that I must. I knew I couldn't do it.'

'Well, as yet you most certainly can't,' came the withering reply. 'I never in my life read a worse description, and I hope I may never read another half so bad!'

What answer could I make? There was nothing to be said. Weep I would not. Before the lessons began I had told him in all good faith that I could bear any amount of criticism without flinching. And here I was in te———. No! Ten thousand times No! Whatever happened, not one tear should overflow. If it did, he would just write me down as another of those 'Pilates', and disinherit me on the spot. So I choked pretty badly instead and strove (in vain) to make an airy apology without a tremor.

But the words died on my tongue.

The *Sine qua non*, like a couching lioness bereaved of her whelps, sprang to the rescue. All in a moment she reared her glorious head, and from the divan at the far end of the room rang out this scorching denunciation: 'Louis! You are a brute! I told you it would kill the child – and it *will*.'

'No, it won't,' gasped the (somewhat elderly) child. 'I want him to say just whatever he thinks. I don't mind a bit. I *will* learn to write. *I'm going* to do it or die.'

'Of course you are!' he cried triumphantly.

In a moment, all his anger gone, he was on his knees beside me on the hearth-rug, my trembling hand firmly clasped in his own.

'*Of course* you are!'

Then in a tone which, even in memory, still sends a glow to my heart, he went on eagerly:

'And *I'm going* to teach you. Fanny is right. I really am a brute. But I did not mean to be so cruel. Oh, but the work *is* bad, you know – very bad, and you must never, never write like that again. It really is intolerable that you should have done it.'

When he smiled suddenly into my eyes like that, what was there to weep about?

'Oh, it's all right,' I faltered. 'Please, please go on: tell me the very worst. I want to know why it is so horribly wrong. Of course, I ought to understand by this time, but I don't. What was it that made you so furiously angry?'

Here I had touched the right chord to awaken instant response.

'That's just what I want to explain,' he said eagerly. 'You must once for all see for yourself what is wrong. Otherwise, you may be doing something else of the sort one fine day, and then...! As a first step in the right direction we will do a sum together. Count the adjectives in that exercise.'

I did so.

'Now then, see how many times that will go into the number of words allowed for the whole description.'

The result proved that my modest percentage of adjectives was $17\frac{1}{2}$.

'And mostly weak ones at that!' remarked the Master with a queer little grimace at the culprit.

'But how ought it to have been done?'

The voice that made this appeal for light and leading was no longer in the least lachrymose: it was now, I flattered myself, that of a vigorous and determined student.

'You should have used fewer adjectives and many more descriptive verbs,' came the swift reply. 'If you want me to see your garden, don't, for pity's sake, talk about "climbing roses" or "green, mossy lawns". Tell me, if you like that roses twined themselves round the apple trees and fell in showers from the branches. Never dare to tell me again anything about "green grass". Tell me how the lawn was flecked with shadows. I know perfectly well that grass is green. So does everybody else in England. What you have to learn is something different from that. Make me see what it was that made your garden distinct from a thousand others. And, by the way, while we are about it, remember once for all that *green* is a word I flatly forbid you to utter in a description more than, perhaps, once in a lifetime.'

Well, it was a strenuous time enough that we wrestled through that afternoon; but, like everything else that befell me at Skerryvore, it was well worth suffering for; and when we came to talk it over afterwards, we found ourselves nearer friends than we had ever been before. From that day forward the *Sine qua non* laid aside her fears for me. We all knew that, having lived through that phase of criticism, I might thenceforth be warranted invulnerable. After all, R.L.S. *'was going* to teach me to write'. What on earth did anything else matter?[2]

NOTES

1. Valentine Roch, a Swiss-born servant who came to the Stevensons when they were at Hyères in 1883. Stevenson called her 'Joe' and she was part of the household for six years. When she was ill Fanny nursed her. At Bournemouth when Louis was in a haemorrhage phase, she slept by the fire in his room. She sailed with the Stevensons on the *Casco* but left them abruptly. Louis commented: it was 'the usual tale of the maid on board the yacht' (*Baxter Letters*, 240). Some biographers suggest she was discharged for theft.

2. Despite the lessons, Adelaide Boodle produced only one story, *The Children's Guest* (1888).

Visiting Skerryvore

WILLIAM AND CHARLES ARCHER

(1) from William Archer, 'Robert Louis Stevenson at "Skerryvore"', *Critic*, 5 Nov 1887, 225–7. William Archer (1856–1924), critic, journalist, dramatist, was educated at the University of Edinburgh and called to the Bar (1883) but never practised law; he became drama critic of *London Figaro* (1879–81) and other journals; he produced the *Collected Works of Ibsen*, 11 vols

(1906–7) whose plays he promoted in England, as well as those of Pinero and Wilde. He became a friend of Stevenson's after reviewing *A Child's Garden of Verses* (*Time*, March and Nov 1885) and was a welcome visitor to Skerryvore thereafter. See *Letters*, I, 358–9; (2) from Charles Archer, *William Archer: Life, Works and Friendships* (1931) 137–60. In the biography of his brother, Charles Archer expands on the relationship, especially during the period prior to the Stevensons' departure for America in August 1887. At Stevenson's death William Archer wrote a warm tribute: 'In Memoriam R.L.S.', *New Review*, Jan 1895. He also contributed reminiscences to Rosaline Masson (*I Can Remember*, 219–21).

(1) From the principal railway-station in London to Skerryvore is a Sabbath-day's journey, and if you have fixed things so as to arrive at dinner-time, the South Western Railway Company, haughtily regardless of time-piece tyranny, will take care to bring you in just too late. On a summer evening, however, it is still light enough for you to see, in the little porch-veranda enclosed with wire-netting, the model in Skerryvore granite of Skerryvore light, designed to serve as a lamp to this vestibule, though I confess I never saw it in operation.[1] Behind it is a panelled wall, the divisions of which are in time to be filled up with mural paintings by the artists who are among the most frequent guests at Skerryvore. Some of the panels are already occupied – two, at least, by the pleasant landscape-work of Mr H. R. Bloomer, the American painter, one of Mr Stevenson's oldest friends; but many spaces still await contributions.[2] The door is now opened, and you are greeted in the narrow entrance-hall either by your host or by his stepson, who hales you forthwith into the dining-room, assuring you that, though too late for the feast, you shall not fail of some sufficient aftermath. Accordingly you soon find yourself seated at the dinner-table, not precisely a 'groaning board', but an eminently well-appointed one, for Mr Stevenson, student though he be of Thoreau, is no despiser of creature comforts. Has he not had the frankness to place 'Books, *and my food*, and summer rain' among his chiefest allies in his 'great task of happiness'?

He now sits at the foot of the table rolling a limp cigarette in his long, limp fingers, and talking eagerly the while, with just enough trace of Scottish intonation to remind one that he is the author of 'Thrawn Janet' and the creator of Alan Breck Stewart. He has still the air and manner of a young man, for illness has neither tamed his mind, nor aged his body.[3] It has left its mark, however, in the pallor of his long oval face, with its wide set eyes, straight nose and thin-lipped sensitive mouth, scarcely shaded by a light moustache, the jest and scorn of his more ribald intimates. His long dark hair straggles with an irregular wave down to his neck, a wisp of it occasionally falling over his ear, and having to be replaced with a light gesture of the hand. He is dressed in a black velvet jacket, showing at the throat the loose rolling collar of a white flannel shirt; and if it is at all cold, he has probably thrown over his shoulders an ancient maroon-coloured shawl, draped something after the fashion of a Mexican poncho. When he stands up you see that he is well above the middle height, and of a naturally lithe and agile figure. He still moves with freedom and grace, but the stoop of his shoulders tells a tale of suffering.

Opposite to him sits Mrs Stevenson, the tutelary genius of Skerryvore, a woman of small physical stature but surely of heroic mould. Her features are clear-cut and delicate, but marked by unmistakable strength of character; her hair of an unglossy black, and her complexion darker than one would expect in a woman of Dutch-American race. I have heard her speak of a Moorish strain in her ancestry, whether seriously or in jest I know not. Beneath a placid though always alert and vivacious exterior, Mrs Stevenson conceals much personal suffering, and continual anxieties under which many a stronger woman might well break down. Her personality, no less than her husband's, impresses itself potently on all who have the good fortune to be welcomed at Skerryvore.

We are in the 'blue room' known to readers of 'Underwoods,' where hangs the Venetian mirror presented to the poet by that 'Prince of Men, Henry James'.[4] It is an ordinary English dining-room of post-morrisian yet not ultra-aesthetic decoration, the work of the previous tenant, the Sheraton furniture, however, being introduced by the present owner. Over the fireplace is an engraving of Turner's 'Bell Rock Lighthouse', built by Mr Stevenson's grandfather. Another wall is adorned by two of Piranesi's great Roman etchings, between which hangs the conventional portrait of Shelley (a gift from his son, Sir Percy Shelley, who lives near Bournemouth), with under it a small portrait of Mary Wollstonecraft.[5] A small armoury of buccaneering weapons is grouped under the Venetian mirror, some of which were presented to Mr Stevenson as having belonged to Pew and Long John Silver – for the blind pirate of 'Treasure Island', and he of the wooden leg, are (more or less) historic personages. Photographs of Mr Sidney Colvin and of the late Sir Henry Taylor, author of 'Philip van Artevelde', an etching by Mr Will H. Low, the American artist; a water-colour from the New Forest, by Mr A. W. Henley; and a few specimens of blue china, in which Mr Stevenson greatly delights, complete the decoration of the room.

The adjoining drawing-room, to which we soon make a move, is stamped much more thoroughly than the dining-room with the Stevensonian individuality. It is not encumbered with superfluous furniture, tables heaped with 'drawing-room books', or whatnots burdened with Japaneseries. Half-way along one side of the room runs a low divan formed of a series of oak boxes covered with yellow silk cushions. Lounging chairs, mainly of light wicker-work, are scattered about, and a large oaken cabinet stands beside the door. It is surmounted by a beautiful group in plaster executed as an illustration to one of Victor Hugo's poems by the French sculptor Rodin, for whom Mr Stevenson has the warmest admiration, having publicly defended him from the charge (if charge it can be called) of being 'the Zola of sculpture'. This group is flanked by a couple of grinning Burmese gods; and, perhaps to counteract the influence of these uncanny deities, a Catholic devotional image of ancient date stands in an opposite corner. Over the cabinet, again, hangs a beautiful 'Landscape with Horses' by Mr Arthur Lemon, with a photograph of the late Prof. Fleeming Jenkin to the right of it and one of Mr W. E. Henley to the left, both being, like the photograph of Mr Colvin in the dining-room, the work of a private friend. From another wall, Mr John E. Sargent's half-grotesque yet speaking portrait of Mr Stevenson himself looks out at us livingly. It represents him pacing noiselessly up and down this very room in the ardour of conversation, stroking his moustache and turning his head with eager interest to look his unseen interlocutor full in the eyes. A close examination will discover Mrs Stevenson as well, reclining in fantastic costume upon the divan; but this is a joke of the artist's rather than a piece of serious portraiture.[6] Underneath this quaint little picture hangs a copy by Miss Una Taylor (a daughter of Sir Henry) of what purports to be an authentic portrait of Chatterton, with hard by it an imposing piece of flower-embroidery, framed and glazed, by the same accomplished lady. Over the divan some curious little wood-cuts, done in strict accordance with the rules of the 'white line,' are pinned to the wall. They illustrate a certain moral ballad of a converted pirate, and are the work of Mr Stevenson himself. It was at Davos, I believe, that he took to wood-engraving, to while away the tedium of the 'Land of Counterpane'. Later, in London, I remember finding him one day sitting up in bed industriously modelling medallions in clay; but I am not aware that any of these works of art have been made permanent. The piano is another of his resources, his performances with one finger being truly surprising....

He relates some anecdotes of his experience as an amateur actor on the boards of Prof. Jenkin's private theatre, and hence the conversation turns to the drama at large. Messrs Pinero, Jones and Grundy, Mr Irving, Miss Mary Anderson and Mrs Kendal, are canvassed in turns, Mr Stevenson asking questions rather than expressing opinions, for his health has long forced him to do his play-going in imagination, which is perhaps not the least satisfactory plan. Mr E. J. Henley's striking impersonation of the title part in 'Deacon Brodie' is then described; and the question is raised of an ideal cast for 'Beau Austin', another of the dramatic works of Mr W. E. Henley and Mr Stevenson.[7] Soon the conversation flits across the Channel, and Mr Stevenson redoubles his vivacity as he enlarges on the delightful humour of Labiche, or denounces the didactics of Dumas *fils*, for whose literary talent, however, as shown in such a play as 'Monsieur Alphonse', he entertains a great admiration.

(2) Other meetings followed, both in London during Stevenson's rare visits, and at Bournemouth, to confirm the impression – other disputatious *Noctes Skerryvorianae*, when, as Archer wrote: 'You would pace the long drawing-room up and down, a cigarette between your fingers and your arm in its (I hope long-disused) sling; I, meanwhile, quiescent in body on the low divan, and revelling in the intellectual gymnastic of coursing, so to speak, your nimbler wit.' The appearance of *Underwoods* completed the conquest. The cool, clear-cut grace and noble feeling of the poems filled Archer with delight, and, while in his public utterances he strove with some success to maintain the critical integrity which was in him both first and second nature, in his heart, as his letters show, he was 'sealed of the tribe of Louis' from that time forth.

Then came the parting. The story of the last meeting, late of a

Saturday night, in a bedroom of that City hotel 'called Todgers's for short,' is told in the letter here printed, with some details naturally omitted from Archer's published account of it. The next day but one the Stevensons sailed, and henceforth occasional letters had to serve, in place of those eager encounters of wits (somewhat, one fancies, of the Spanish galleon and English man-of-war type) which illuminated the visits to Skerryvore....

[In a letter to his son dated 19 August 1887 he writes:] Having just finished a short and stupid letter to the *Pioneer* (there will be blasphemy in Allahabad) I must find time to give you a scart o' the pen. Scotch is running in my head, thanks to Stevenson's *Underwoods*, which I was reviewing all yesterday.... He's really a great being, is R.L.S., and I feel jolly remorseful for ever having written anything that gave him a moment's – not pain, but dissatisfaction. I went down to Bournemouth for a day last week and had a long yarn with him. He was up to his eyes in old papers which he was destroying in preparation for a start to America. I wish I could remember a tithe of our talk. I had it out with him about *The Egoist*, but without coming to any very definite result.[8] By the by, he is one of the heretics who depreciate George Eliot. Of course it is natural that the leader of the narrative-at-any-price school should have a certain down on her methods, and I knew already that he had; but I was rather taken aback to hear him say that, if Mrs Oliphant[9] had only husbanded her strength, he thought she had more genius than George Eliot. He found far more 'geniality' in Mrs O. than in George Eliot. He says he knows as a literal fact that Mrs Oliphant writes at her meals – but for my part I shouldn't be surprised to learn that she wrote in her sleep....

I see the *Times* in a long article echoes my *P.M.G.* [*Pall Mall Gazette*] review [of *Underwoods*], which gratifies me a good deal; not that I had any doubt of the merit of the book, but because I was rather afraid that a glowing notice in the *Gutter Gazette* would set the other papers against it. I forget whether I told you of my last interview with R.L.S. at an hotel in South Place, Finsbury ('I call it Todgers's for short,' he said), and how I tore half over London at 10 p.m. one Saturday night to find a lawyer to help him to draft a codicil to his will, at which operation I subsequently assisted. On reflection, I don't think I can have told you this. He was in bed when I went, being much exhausted with his journey from Bournemouth; but my *P.M.G.* notice of *Underwoods* had just appeared that day, and he insisted on seeing me to tell me that he was delighted with the review, for, as in the case of the *Child's Garden*, I had accurately hit his intention, which was to react against the hysterical school of poetry. He agreed with me that it might possibly do the book harm with other reviewers, but he said he didn't care – he naturally would say so, but I believe he thought so too. He said, too, that he shared my opinion as to the blank verse being the best [thing] in the book, and was also very glad that I had said a word for the 'Requiem', which a lot of people had told him was nonsense and advised him not to print.

NOTES

1. When they took possession of 'Sea View', the Stevensons renamed it 'Skerryvore', commemorating the lighthouse in the Inner Hebrides built by Louis's uncle, Alan Stevenson.
2. Hiram Reynolds Bloomer (1845–1910), landscape artist, studied in New York and Paris; he exhibited in Paris and Philadelphia.
3. Desperately ill a good deal of the time, Louis none the less wrote an astonishing amount. In the Bournemouth years there appeared: *A Child's Garden of Verses* (1885), *More New Arabian Nights* (1885), *Prince Otto* (1885), *Dr Jekyll and Mr Hyde* (1886), *Kidnapped* (1886), *Underwoods* (1887), *The Merry Men and Other Tales* (1887), as well as several essays.
4. Consolations of living in such a backwater of Victorian gentility were the coming and going of friends like Colvin, Henley and James, the latter on his first visit being mistaken for a tradesman and kept waiting at the door. See Margaret Mackay, *The Violent Friend* (1968) 203.
5. Social prestige, rather highly prized by Fanny, accrued from contacts with Sir Percy and Lady Shelley, who saw Louis as the poet reincarnated. Sir Henry Taylor, then in his mid-eighties, author of *Philip van Artevelde* (1834), and Lady Taylor were also friends. See Una Taylor, *Guests and Memories: Annals of a Seaside Villa* (1924).
6. John Singer Sargent (1856–1925) was introduced to Stevenson by Mr and Mrs Charles Fairchild of Boston. The Fairchilds provided hospitality on the Stevensons' arrival in the United States in summer 1887. Sargent painted two portraits, the first not a success; the second caused Louis to comment to Will Low: 'It is, I think, excellent, but is too eccentric to be exhibited' (*Letters*, I, 362–3).
7. The unfortunate collaboration in plays with Henley, encouraged by Fanny, produced, besides *Deacon Brodie* (1880), *Beau Austin* (1884), *Admiral Guinea* (1884) and *Macaire* (1885). Archer was one of the few who saw merit in them.
8. Louis considered *The Egoist* (1879) the masterpiece of Victorian fiction.
9. Mrs Margaret Oliphant (1828–97), prolific novelist in the Trollopian mode, best known for *Chronicles of Carlingford* (1863–76).

1. Margaret Isabella Balfour Stevenson

2. Thomas Stevenson

3. Alison Cunningham, Louis's nurse

4. Louis and his father

5. Fanny Stevenson in the mid 1880s at Bournemouth

6. Mrs Isobel Strong (Belle)

7. Lloyd Osbourne in 1888 at San Francisco

8. RLS on board the *Casco* with King Kalakaua, Fanny, Lloyd and Margaret Stevenson

9. Vailima, the Stevenson home, Samoa

10. Stevenson's family and household at Vailima in 1892, including his wife, mother, Belle and Lloyd

11. Fanny, Louis, Belle and Margaret Stevenson in 1893 at Sydney, Australia

12. RLS in Samoa

'Looks Like a Sooercide, Don't He, Sir?'

WILLIAM SHARP

From *Literary Geography* (1907) 20–33. William Sharp ('Fiona Macleod', 1855–1905) was born in Paisley and brought up in the Highlands. After attending Glasgow University, he was put to work as a lawyer's clerk at his father's wishes, and escaped to Australia (1876) with suspected consumption. Returning to London he associated with the Rossetti circle and wrote several biographical studies, of Rossetti (1882), Shelley (1888) and Browning (1890). Under his own name he wrote poetry and fiction. As 'Fiona Macleod' he produced novels of Celtic nostalgia, including *Pharais, A Romance of the Isles* (1894), *The Mountain Lover* (1895), *The Sin Eater* (1895) and *Green Fire* (1896). Others have commented on Stevenson's sartorial oddities, but none with such brio as Sharp.

The first time I saw Robert Louis Stevenson was at Waterloo Station. I did not at that time know him even by sight, and there was no speculation as to identity in my mind when my attention was attracted by a passenger, of a strangeness of appearance almost grotesque, emerging from a compartment in the Bournemouth train which had just arrived.[1] I was at the station to meet a French friend coming by the Southampton route, but as I did not expect his arrival till by the express due some twenty minutes later, I allowed myself an idle and amused interest in the traveller who had just stepped on to the platform close by me. He was tall, thin, spare – indeed, he struck me as almost fantastically spare: I remember thinking that the station draught caught him like a torn leaf flowing at the end of a branch. His clothes hung about him, as the clothes of a convalescent who has lost bulk and weight after long fever. He had on a jacket of black velveteen – I cannot swear to the colour, but that detail always comes back in the recalled picture – a flannel shirt with a loose necktie negligently bundled into a sailor's-knot, somewhat fantastical trousers, though no doubt this effect was due in part to their limp amplitude about what seemed rather the thin green poles familiar in dahlia-pots than the legs of a human creature. He wore a straw hat, that in its rear rim suggested forgetfulness on the part of its wearer, who had apparently, in sleep or heedlessness, treated it as a cloth cap. These, however, were details in themselves trivial, and were not consciously noted till later. The long, narrow face, then almost sallow, with somewhat long, loose, dark hair, that draggled from beneath the yellow straw hat well over the ears, along the dusky hollows of temple and cheek, was what immediately attracted attention. But the extraordinariness of the impression was of a man who had just been rescued from the sea or a river. Except for the fact that his clothes did not drip, that the long black locks hung limp but not moist, and that the short velveteen jacket was disreputable but not damp, this impression of a man just come or taken from the water was overwhelming. That it was not merely an impression of my own was proved by the exclamation of a cabman, who was standing beside me expectant of a 'fare' who had gone to look after his luggage: 'Looks like a sooercide, don't he, sir? one o' them chaps as takes their down-on-their-luck 'eaders inter the Thimes!' And, truth to tell, my fancy was somewhat to the same measure. I looked again, seriously wondering if the unknown had really suffered a recent submersion, voluntary or involuntary.

Meanwhile he had stepped back into the compartment, and was now emerging again with a travelling rug and a book he had obviously forgotten. Our eyes met. I was struck by their dark luminousness below the peculiar eyebrows; and, if not startled, which is perhaps too exaggerated a term, was certainly impressed by their sombre melancholy. Some poor fellow, I thought, on the last coasts of consumption, with Shadow-Ferry almost within hail.

The next moment another and more pleasant variant of the Dr Jekyll and Mr Hyde mystery was enacted. The stranger, who had been standing as if bewildered, certainly irresolute, had dropped his book, and with long, white, nervous fingers was with one hand crumpling and twisting the loose ends of his plaid or rug. Suddenly the friend whom he was expecting came forward. The whole man seemed to change. The impression of emaciation faded; the 'drowned' look passed; even the damaged straw hat and the short velveteen jacket and the shank-inhabited wilderness of trouser shared in this unique 'literary renascence'. But the supreme change was in the face. The dark locks apparently receded, like weedy tangle in the ebb; the long sallow oval grew rounder and less wan; the sombre melancholy vanished like cloud-scud on a day of wind and sun, and the dark eyes lightened to a violet-blue and were filled with sunshine and laughter. An extraordinarily winsome smile invaded the face... pervaded the whole man, I was about to say.

The two friends were about to move away when I noticed the fallen book. I lifted and restored it, noticing as I did so that it was *The Tragic Comedians*.

'Oh, a thousand thanks... how good of you!' The manner was of France, the accent North-country, the intonation somewhat strident – that of the Lothians or perhaps of Fife.

Who was this puzzling and interesting personality, I now wondered – this stranger like a consumptive organ-grinder, with such charm of manner, perforce or voluntarily so heedless in apparel, and a lover of George Meredith?

This problem was solved for me by the sudden appearance on the scene of my French friend. After all he had come by this train, but, a traveller in an end carriage, had not seen me on arrival, and, too, had been immersed in that complicated jargon indulged in between foreigners and the British porter which is our Anglo-Franco variety of Pidgeon-English.

We had hardly greeted each other, when he exclaimed, 'Ah!... so you know him?' indicating, as he spoke, the retreating fellow-traveller in the velveteen jacket and straw hat.

'No? why... I thought you would have known... why, it is your *homme-de-lettres vraiment charmant*, Robert Louis Stevenson! I have met him more than once in France, and when he saw me at a station he jumped out and spoke to me – and at Basingstoke he sent me by a porter this French volume, see, with a kind message that he had read it and desired me not to trouble about its return.'

Often, of course, in later years, I recalled that meeting. It was the more strange to encounter Robert Louis Stevenson, and to hear of him thus from a foreigner, at an English railway-station, as only a few days earlier I had received a letter from him, apropos of something on a metrical point which I had written in the *Academy*. How glad I would have been to know to whom it was I handed back the dropped *Tragic Comedians*!...

Was he really 'a changeling', as one of his friends half-seriously averred? No, he was only one of those rare temperaments which gather to themselves the floating drift blowing upon every wind from every quarter; one of those creative natures which, in their own incalculable seasons and upon their own shifting pastures, reveal again, in a new and fascinating texture and pageant of life, the innumerable flowers and weeds come to them in invisible seed from near and far. But, to many people, Stevenson had something of the elfish character. A bookseller's assistant, who knew him well in the early Edinburgh days, told me that 'Mr Stevenson often gave the impression he wasna quite canny' – not in the sense that he was 'wandering', but that 'he had two ways wi' him, an' you never kenned which was Mr Stevenson and which was the man who wasna listening, but was, as ye micht say, thinkin' and talkin' wi' some one else'. Very likely 'R. L. S.' occasionally gave a fillip to any bewildered fancy of the kind. Some will recall how he himself at one time thought that the unfortunate Scottish poet Ferguson was reincarnate in himself. But others also 'felt strangely' to him. There is that singular story, told by a friend of the family, Miss Blantyre Simpson, of how the late Sir Percy and Lady Shelley both believed that Shelley had been re-born in Robert Louis Stevenson, and how Lady Shelley went so far as to bear a deep resentment against Mrs Stevenson as the mother of the child that ought to have been her own![2]

NOTES

1. During three years in Bournemouth (1884–7), Stevenson found it necessary to escape from its balmy breezes and deadly respectability. As Una Taylor put it: 'The people we have here are divided into visitors and residents. The visitors are mostly invalids. Death is a resident' (*Guests and Memories: Annals of a Seaside Villa* (1924) 334). The meeting described may have occurred in Nov 1886, when Stevenson visited Colvin.

2. More than one elderly friend laid claim to Louis. Fanny wrote to her mother-in-law that Lady Taylor had said with a sigh: 'I wish he were mine.' Fanny added, 'You will have to contest your maternal rights with more than Lady Shelley it seems ... It is not often that a wife gets three mothers-in-law at once and three such very delightful ones' (quoted in Pope-Hennessy, *Robert Louis Stevenson*, 178).

Beside Himself with Anger
LLOYD OSBOURNE

From: *An Intimate Portrait of RLS* (1924) 62–7. (See headnote to 'Scotch Literary Mediocrity' (p. 81) for biographical details.) The circumstances by which *The Strange Case of Dr Jekyll and Mr Hyde* came into existence have been much debated, but no account is better than Lloyd's, however it may strike the reader as worked up into a good narrative in its own right. Fanny's account of how she woke Louis from a terrible nightmare to be grumbled at for having interrupted a 'fine bogey tale' is also part of the mythology. Certainly evidence is plentiful for the importance Louis attached to dream-inspiration, and to the 'Brownies' who came to him in the night. His doctor, Thomas Bodley Scott, records that on his morning visit to Skerryvore he was greeted by an exultant Louis with news of a dream and the words: 'I've got my shilling shocker!' (Masson, *Life*, 238). Whatever the true derivation, 'The story catapulted Stevenson to fame' (Bell, 193) after a review in *The Times* (25 Jan 1886), a sermon in St Paul's Cathedral, and a parody in *Punch* (Feb 1886). Balfour estimated that it sold 40,000 copies in Britain in six months and by the end of the century 250,000 copies had sold in the United States. It became, with *Treasure Island*, the tale most associated with Stevenson's name.

One day he came down to luncheon in a very preoccupied frame of mind, hurried through his meal – an unheard-of thing for him to do – and on leaving said he was working with extraordinary success on a new story that had come to him in a dream, and that he was not to be interrupted or disturbed even if the house caught fire.[1]

For three days a sort of hush descended on 'Skerryvore'; we all went about, servants and everybody, in a tiptoeing silence; passing Stevenson's door I would see him sitting up in bed, filling page after page, and apparently never pausing for a moment. At the end of three days the mysterious task was finished, and he read aloud to my mother and myself the first draft of 'Strange Case of Dr Jekyll and Mr Hyde'.

I listened to it spellbound. Stevenson, who had a voice the greatest actor might have envied, read it with an intensity that made shivers run up and down my spine.² When he came to the end, gazing at us in triumphant expectancy and keyed to a pitch of indescribable self-satisfaction – as he waited, and I waited, for my mother's outburst of enthusiasm – I was thunderstruck at her backwardness. Her praise was constrained; the words seemed to come with difficulty; and then all at once she broke out with criticism. He had missed the point, she said; had missed the allegory; had made it merely a story – a magnificent bit of sensationalism – when it should have been a masterpiece.

Stevenson was beside himself with anger. He trembled; his hand shook on the manuscript; he was intolerably chagrined. His voice, bitter and challenging, overrode my mother's in a fury of resentment. Never had I seen him so impassioned, so outraged, and the scene became so painful that I went away, unable to bear it any longer. It was with a sense of tragedy that I listened to their voices from the adjoining room, the words lost but fraught with an emotion that struck at my heart.³

When I came back my mother was alone. She was sitting, pale and desolate before the fire, and staring into it. Neither of us spoke. Had I done so it would have been to reproach her, for I thought she had been cruelly wrong. Then we heard Louis descending the stairs, and we both quailed as he burst in as though to continue the argument even more violently than before. But all he said was: 'You are right! I have absolutely missed the allegory, which, after all, is the whole point of it – the very essence of it.' And with that, as though enjoying my mother's discomfiture and her ineffectual start to prevent him, he threw the manuscript into the fire! Imagine my feelings – my mother's feelings – as we saw it blazing up; as we saw those precious pages wrinkling and blackening and turning into flame!⁴

My first impression was that he had done it out of pique. But it was not. He really had been convinced, and this was his dramatic amend. When my mother and I both cried out at the folly of destroying the manuscript he justified himself vehemently. 'It was all wrong,' he said. 'In trying to save some of it I should have got hopelessly off the track. The only way was to put temptation beyond my reach.'

Then ensued another three days of feverish industry on his part, and of a hushed, anxious, and tiptoeing anticipation on ours; of meals where he scarcely spoke; of evenings unenlivened by his presence; of awed glimpses of him, sitting up in bed, writing,

writing, writing, with the counterpane littered with his sheets. The culmination was the 'Jekyll and Hyde' that every one knows; that, translated into every European tongue and many Oriental, has given a new phrase to the world.

The writing of it was an astounding feat from whatever aspect it may be regarded. Sixty-four thousand words in six days; more than ten thousand words a day. To those who know little of such things I may explain that a thousand words a day is a fair average for any writer of fiction. Anthony Trollope set himself this quota; it was Jack London's; it is – and has been – a sort of standard of daily literary accomplishment.[5] Stevenson multiplied it by ten; and on top of that copied out the whole in another two days, and had it in the post on the third!

It was a stupendous achievement; and the strange thing was that, instead of showing lassitude afterward, he seemed positively refreshed and revitalized; went about with a happy air; was as uplifted as though he had come into a fortune; looked better than he had in months.

NOTES

1. Louis acknowledged the role of his dream: 'I had long been trying to write a story on this subject, to find a body, a vehicle, for that strong sense of man's double being which must at times come in upon and overwhelm the mind of every thinking creature... For two days I went about racking my brains for a plot of any sort; and on the second night I dreamed the scene at the window, and a scene afterward split in two, in which Hyde, pursued for some crime, took the powder and underwent the change in the presence of his pursuers' ('A Chapter on Dreams', *Scribner's*, 3 Jan 1888; *Across the Plains*, 250).

2. His acting abilities were not great. Among Fleeming Jenkin's amateurs in the Edinburgh days he made an adequate showing as Orsino. Mrs Fleeming Jenkin observed: 'he had a fine voice, and read well (tho somewhat artificially); and he was too self-conscious on the stage to sink his own personality into that of any character he might be playing' (Arthur Wing Pinero, *Papers on Play-making* (1914) 17).

3. The genesis and development of the novel is complicated. According to Nellie Sanchez, her sister's objections were put in writing at Louis's request, and, seeing the point of her criticism, he burned the original. 'She was appalled when he burned it, for she had only wanted him to

change it' (*Life*, 18). The best summary of the evidence is to be found in Swearingen (98–102), who concluded that Stevenson wrote and destroyed at least one initial treatment, then produced from Fanny's criticism a fairly complete second draft which he revised substantially over several weeks. See also Balfour, *Life*, 2, 12–14; and Hammerton, *Stevensoniana*, 80–1, 85.

4. It is interesting that Louis's disposal of the manuscript is bracketed with another incendiary act. 'The Travelling Companion' written after *Jekyll and Hyde*, was rejected as 'a work of genius and indecent' (*Across the Plains*, 250) and subsequently burned.

5. Anthony Trollope (1815–82), whose novels Stevenson admired, set himself to produce 250 words every quarter of an hour for at least two hours. He observed that 'three hours a day will produce as much as a man ought to write' (*Autobiography*, xv). Trollope's average was 40 pages a week, i.e. 10,000 words. Stevenson himself told the *San Francisco Examiner* (8 June 1888) that *Jekyll and Hyde* was drafted in three days and written in six weeks.

A Most Affectionate Observer

M. G. VAN RENSSELAER AND JEANETTE L. GILDER

(1) from M. G. van Rensselaer, 'Robert Louis Stevenson, and his Writing', *Century Magazine*, LI: new series XXIX (Nov 1895), 123–9. Mariana Griswold van Rensselaer (1851–1934) was the author of a large number of books on art and architecture such as *English Cathedrals* (1892) and *American Etchers* (1883); she received the American Academy of Arts and Letters gold medal in 1923; (2) from Jeannette L. Gilder, 'Stevenson and After', *Review of Reviews*, XI (Feb 1895), 186–90. Jeanette Leonard Gilder (1849–1916) was one of a family of distinguished journalists. With her brother, Richard Watson Gilder, she worked for *Scribner's Monthly* (later *Century Magazine*); with another brother, Joseph B. Gilder, she started the *Critic* (*Putnam's Magazine*); she wrote several books of memoirs including *Pen Portraits of Literary Women* (1887). Both memories concern the time when the Stevensons were leaving the United States for their South Seas explorations.

(1) He was ill when I saw him in New York in the spring of 1888, after he had come down from the Adirondacks. He was in bed, as he often used to be for days together – so often that the beautiful portrait which, in the previous autumn, St Gaudens had made of him, backed by his pillows and covered by his blankets,

must, I fancy, seem to many American friends the Stevenson whom they knew best. He was in a dismal hotel, in the most dismal possible chamber. Even a very buoyant soul might have been pardoned if, then and there, it had declined upon inactivity and gloom. But these were not the constituents of the atmosphere I found.

There were a great many things on Stevenson's bed – things to eat and to smoke, things to write with and to read. I have seen tidier sick-beds, and also invalids more modishly attired: this one wore over his shoulders an old red cloak with a hole for the head in the middle (a *serape*, I supposed), which, faded and spotted with ink, looked much like a school-room table-cloth. But the untidiness seemed a proof of his desire to make the most of each passing minute; clearly, the littering things had been brought, not in case they might be wanted, but as answers to actual and eager needs. Ill as he was, Stevenson had been reading and writing – and smoking, as St Gaudens shows; and in fact, I call him an invalid chiefly because, as I remember him, the term has such a picturesque unfitness.[1] His body was in evil case, but his spirit was more bright, more eager, more ardently and healthily alive than that of any other mortal. . . .

Despite his mastery of the arts of language, I do not believe that Stevenson ever excelled in the artifice of small talk; he must always have had too many real words to say, and have felt too sure that other folk would like to hear them. This, indeed, was one great secret of his charm: he assumed that you too were alertly alive; he believed that you would understand and share his interest in all interesting things. Therefore one interview was enough to prove him what his friends assert and his books declare him to have been – a philosopher very wise in that most precious kind of lore which gives the soul modesty and poise, cheerfulness, humor, and courage; a student of human nature, not with classifications and categories to fill out, but with a special welcoming niche prepared for the reception of each new human soul; a 'detached intelligence', but a heart, intimately attached to every palpitant fiber in the web of existence, which loved to love, and chose for its hatred only fundamentally hateful and harmful things like hypocrisy, vanity, intolerance, and cowardice in the face of life. He seemed so individual, not because he was more eccentric than others, but because he was more genuine and more broad, more self-expressive, and possessed of a wider and richer self to be explained.

Look at his portrait in profile, and you will see sensitiveness and refinement of a virile sort in the general cast of the face and head, sagacity in the long but not prominent nose, and poetic feeling in the contour of the brow. But in a full view the countenance was still more remarkable. The upper part, extraordinarily broad between the eyes, was deerlike in its gentle serenity, but the lower part, very narrow in comparison, was almost fox-like in its keen alertness; and the mobility of the mouth hardly seemed to fit with the steady intentness of the wide, dark eyes. But if at first this face appeared to contradict itself, the reason lay, I think, in the fact that we seldom see the face of a man who is at once a lover of action and a lover of dreams and of books, an astute and yet a most affectionate observer of life and of men and of the humors of the lives of men, and, besides, an artist of imaginative mold.

I remember how Stevenson's face looked, when he said that, long though he had been tied to sedentary habits, and deeply though he loved the art they permitted him to practise, the one thing in the world that he held to be the best was still the joy of outdoor living: it was a beautiful face just then, because it revealed a soul which could endure without bemoaning itself. And for the same reason it was beautiful again when it turned merry over a little tale of attempts to learn the art of knitting as a solace for hours of wearisome languor – unavailing attempts, although he had persisted in them until he brought himself to the verge – nay, he declared, actually over the verge – of tears. An amusing little story it seemed as he told its details, yet in itself and in the manner of its telling it might have moved a listener to tears in his turn, so unconscious did the teller seem that a lifelong story of smiling conflict with bitter denials and restrictions, when reduced to its very lowest terms, then showed the very sharpest, most tragical edge of its pathos.

I should like to make you understand how Stevenson gave this story, and how he spoke (now with a very conscious pride) about the strategical soldier-games which, in scientific ways, he and his stepson were in the habit of playing; I should like to relate how he pounced upon every Americanism I chanced to utter, not deriding it, but shaking it in the teeth of a pleased curiosity as a bit of treasure-trove, a new fragment of speech with an origin, a history, a utility that must be learned; and in other ways to explain what a zest he had for those myriad little interests, little occupations, discoveries, and acquisitions, which make existence a perpetual joy to a fresh and questing mind, but which most adult minds have grown too stiff and dull to value. And of course I should like to record how he spoke about his own writings, and, with even quicker pleasure, talked about those of others. But to mummify beautiful, vivid speech is to do it deep injustice, and so I will not try to reproduce his words; and if I should try to paraphrase them, I should merely blur their meaning to myself and make it clear to no one else.

(2) I never saw Robert Louis Stevenson but once, but I shall not soon forget the impression made upon me by the singular charm of the man. It was on the occasion of his second, or it may have been his third, visit to the United States and he was staying at the Victoria Hotel with his wife and step-son, Lloyd Osbourne.[2] I was a perfect stranger to him and I wonder now how I ever had the temerity to beard this lion in his den. My only excuse was that we had had some correspondence and that we also had some friends in common. Two of these friends came in soon after I had shaken hands with the romancer. They were Mr and Mrs Will H. Low, the well-known painter and his wife. The Lows and the Stevensons were old and dear friends and they had not seen each other in a long time. It was a delightful meeting. Such handshaking and such embracing you would not expect to see outside of France. The men threw their arms around each other's necks with all the effusion of schoolgirls, but with infinitely more depth to their emotions. It was a great time and rejoicing was general. I did not stay very long, for though they gave me no reason to suspect that they would not like to have me spend the day, I sympathized with their reunion too sincerely to intrude myself upon the scene any longer than ordinary civility permitted.

Mr Stevenson was arrayed then as you see him in most of his pictures, in velvet sack-coat, turned-down collar and loose tie. He was smoking the inevitable cigarette, as was his step-son also. His dress suited his face, which was not that of an ordinary man. I have seldom seen eyes further apart or more striking, as they were coal-black, or, at least, had that appearance in contrast with his pale complexion. He was as lively and full of spirits as though he had never known what it was to have an ill day. His conversation – which was entirely unbookish, as befitted the occasion – bubbled over with fun, and altogether he suggested anything rather than an invalid in the vain search for health.

NOTES

1. Stevenson would have been a godsend to cigarette advertisers. Neither Dr Ruedi in Davos nor Dr Trudeau in Saranac made any headway with their injunctions that he should give up or at least cut down. 'Cigarettes without intermission', he insisted to James Barrie, 'except when coughing or kissing' (Knight, *Treasury*, 11). Barrie, a confirmed smoker himself, also praised the habit in his smoking club stories, 'My Lady Nicotine' (1890).
2. The meeting took place when the Stevenson clan arrived in New York prior to their removal to Saranac.

Inventing One Project After Another

S. S. McCLURE

From *My Autobiography* (1914) 184–7, 188–93, 197–200. Samuel Sidney McClure (1857–1949), ex-patriate Scot, founded *McClure's Magazine* (1893) and established the McClure Syndicate (1884), the first of its kind in the United States. Stevenson indicated something of his restless nature in the character of Pinkerton in *The Wrecker*. When McClure went to London a little later than the period covered here, he astutely assessed the jealousy and irritation of the Stevenson set at the attention he was getting in America. In May 1887 Thomas Stevenson died. Three months later his widow, Louis and Fanny, boarded the *Ludgate Hill* for New York, to be welcomed on 7 September by Will Low and the American press. Louis was a celebrity. The Fairchilds whisked them off to Newport, Rhode Island, and from there they moved to Saranac Lake in the Adirondacks near the Canadian border. The publishers, E. L. Burlingame of Scribner's and Sam McClure, were quick to bid for the now-famous author, offering huge sums for work to come. McClure was willing to pay $10,000 a year for a weekly contribution to the *World* magazine, but Scribner's had been one jump ahead and had signed Louis up for 12 essays of his own choice for $3 500. The Stevensons were now comparatively wealthy; Margaret Stevenson had her own fortune, Louis a legacy of £3 000 from his father, and the prospect of commissioned work. 'O, I am now a salaried person,' he wrote to Henley, 'but the slavery may over-weigh me'; and to Bob Stevenson a month later: 'Wealth is only useful for two things: a yacht and a string quartette' (*Letters*, II, 66–7). The wind was already blowing in a new direction.

Mrs McClure and I called upon Stevenson, accordingly, and were taken to his room, where he received us in bed, very much in the attitude of the St Gaudens medallion, for which he was then posing.[1] We had a pleasant call, but there was nothing very unusual about it. Stevenson, though he was in bed, did not seem ill; he looked frail but not sick. The thing about his appearance that most struck me was the unusual width of his brow, and the fact that his eyes were very far apart. He wore his hair long. Stevenson was already a famous man; the publication of 'Dr Jekyll and Mr Hyde' had made him so.

I did not see him again before he went to the Adirondacks. In October I went up to Saranac to see him, commissioned by Mr Pulitzer of the *World* to offer him $10,000 a year for a short essay every week, to be published in the *World*. He had already such a 'news value' as to be worth that to a paper.

Brander Matthews had told me about three long adventure stories that Stevenson had published in *Henderson's Weekly*, an English paper of about the character of the New York *Ledger* in this country.[2] These stories were 'Treasure Island', 'Kidnapped', and 'The Black Arrow'. He had received only $500 apiece for them. They had not appeared over his own name, but were signed with his pseudonym, 'Captain [George] North'. I believe some of his literary friends in England were very much opposed to his publishing adventure stories, such as 'Kidnapped', under his own name, as they thought it might compromise his future.

'Kidnapped' and 'Treasure Island' had already been republished in book form, but 'The Black Arrow' had never been resurrected, and lay unknown to the world in the back files of *Henderson's Weekly*. When I went up to Saranac for Mr Pulitzer, I told Stevenson that I would publish 'The Black Arrow' serially in my newspaper syndicate, and pay him a good price for it. Mrs Stevenson was not at home then, and Stevenson said he could not decide the matter without consulting her, as she had never liked the story, and he thought she might be unwilling to have it republished under his own name. She never was much in favor of the project, but gave her consent.

Stevenson had no copy of the story, but he sent to England and got the files of *Henderson's Weekly* which contained the story, and sent them to me. I read the story, and told him that I would take it if he would let me omit the first five chapters. He readily consented to this. Like all writers of the first rank, he was perfectly amiable about changes and condensations, and was not handicapped by the superstition that his copy was divine revelation and that his words were sacrosanct. I never knew a really great writer who cherished his phrases or was afraid of losing a few of them. First-rate men always have plenty more.

Stevenson's news value was such that it was a great thing for the syndicate to be able to offer the newspapers a serial of adventure by Robert Louis Stevenson. But we had no copyright law then, and if I published the story under its original title, 'The Black Arrow', any American paper might cut in, get a file of *Henderson's Weekly*, and come out ahead of me. In the hope of keeping possible pirates in the dark, I advertised and published the story under the title 'The Outlaws of Tunstall Forest'. I had it illustrated with line drawings by Will H. Low, an old friend of Stevenson's since their Barbizon days. That was the first illustrated story we ran in the syndicate, and it brought in more money than any other serial novel we ever syndicated.

While it was running in the syndicate under a new title, Stevenson arranged for the book publication of 'The Black Arrow' with Charles Scribner's Sons. His friend William Archer went over the proofs for him in October. It was in April of that year, at Saranac, that he wrote the dedication of the book, inscribing it to Mrs. Stevenson, the 'Critic on the Hearth'. . . .

While the preparations for this were going on, I went up to Saranac several times to see Stevenson. He was living in the Baker cottage, a rented furnished house near an ice-pond with trees around it. I remember once I took up a pair of skates for him and a pair for myself, and we skated. He was then going over Lloyd Osbourne's story, 'The Wrong Box'. Osbourne had written the story throughout, and Stevenson went over it and touched it up. I read it, and thought it a good story for a young man to have written; but I told Stevenson that I doubted the wisdom of his putting his name to it as joint author.[3] This annoyed him, and he afterward wrote me that he couldn't take advice about such matters. He told me, during that visit, that he had two new novels in mind, one of them a sequel to 'Kidnapped'. The other was 'St Ives'. I told him that I would take either story and pay him $8 000 for it. He blushed and looked confused and said that his price was £800 ($4 000), and that he must consult his wife and Will Low before he made any agreement. He went on to say that he didn't think any novel of his was worth as much as $8 000, and that he wouldn't be tempted to take as much money as that for a novel, if it were not for a plan he had in mind. He was always better at sea, he said, than anywhere else, and he wanted to fit up a yacht and take a long cruise and make his home at sea for a while.

When I left Saranac that time, Stevenson had agreed to let me have the serial rights of a novel for $8000. About two weeks later he wrote to his friend Charles Baxter:

'I am offered £1600 [$8000] for the American serial rights on my next story! As you say, times are changed since the Lothian Road. Well, the Lothian Road was grand fun, too; I could take an afternoon of it with great delight. But I'm awfu' grand noo, and long may it last!'

His exultation, however, was short-lived. When he made this agreement with me, he was already under contract with Charles Scribner's Sons to let them handle all his work in this country. Two days after the above letter to Baxter, he wrote to Mr Charles Scribner:

'Heaven help me, I am under a curse just now. I have played fast and loose with what I said to you, and that, I beg you to believe, in the purest innocence of mind. I told you that you should have the power over all my work in this country; and about a fortnight ago, when McClure was here, I calmly signed a bargain for the serial publication of a story. You will scarce believe that I did this in mere oblivion; but I did; and all I can say is that I will do so no more, and ask you to forgive me.' . . .

The evening of the day on which I offered Stevenson an increase in his serial rates was the first time I ever heard him talk of his desire to take a long ocean cruise. He told me again that he didn't think his novels were worth what I had offered him, and that the consideration which most influenced him to accept such a price was his wish to take a yacht and live for a while at sea. I thought at once of 'An Inland Voyage' and 'Travels with a Donkey', and told him that if he would write a series of articles describing his travels, I would syndicate them for enough money to pay the expenses of his trip. I think the South Seas must have been mentioned that evening, for I remember that after I returned to New York I sent him a number of books about the South Seas, including a South Pacific directory. The next time I went to Saranac, we actually planned out the South Pacific cruise, talking about it until late into the night.

That was a night not easily forgotten. Stevenson's imagination was thoroughly aroused. He walked up and down the floor, or stood leaning against the mantel, inventing one project after another. We planned that when he came back he was to make a lecture tour and talk on the South Seas; that he was to take a phonograph along and make records of the sounds of the sea and wind, the songs and speech of the natives, and that these records were to embellish his lectures. We planned the yacht and the provisioning of the yacht, and all possible adventures. We planned a good deal more than a man could ever accomplish, but it was all real that night, and out of that talk came the South Sea cruise. That was just before I went to London to syndicate 'The Outlaws of Tunstall Forest' in England, and I never saw Stevenson again. When I returned to New York from London, he was in San Francisco, fitting out the yacht *Casco* before his departure to the South Pacific, from which he never returned.

His 'South Sea Letters' ran for about a year in the syndicate. They were, on the whole, a disappointment to newspaper editors, for they revealed a side of Stevenson with which the public was as yet not much acquainted.[5] There were two men in Stevenson – the romantic adventurer of the sixteenth century, and the Scotch Covenanter of the nineteenth century. Contrary to our expectation, it was the moralist and not the romancer which his observations in the South Seas awoke in him, and the public found the moralist less interesting than the romancer. And yet, in all his essays, the moralist was uppermost.

Stevenson was the sort of man who commanded every kind of affection; admiration for his gifts, delight in his personal charm, and respect for his uncompromising principles. Underneath his velvet coat, his gaiety and picturesqueness, he was flint. It was probably this unusual combination of qualities in him that made one eager to serve him in every possible way. I remember saying to Mr Phillips once: 'John, I want the syndicate business to be run exactly as if it were being conducted for the benefit of Robert Louis Stevenson.' And that was the way I felt about him. . . .

The more I saw of the Stevensons, the more I became convinced that Mrs Stevenson was the unique woman in the world to be Stevenson's wife.[6] Every one knows the story of their first meeting: how, when Mrs Osbourne was traveling in France with her daughter, Stevenson one afternoon, passing in the street, happened to look into the dining-room window of the little hotel at Grez just as Mrs Osbourne was rising from the table; how he looked into her face for a moment, and said, when he went on up the street, that there was the only woman in the world he would ever marry.

There had been a Spanish ancestor somewhere back in Mrs Stevenson's family, and in every other generation the strain asserted itself. She herself is a very marked Spanish type. When Stevenson met her, her exotic beauty was at its height, and with this beauty she had a wealth of experience, a reach of imagination, a sense of humor, which he had never found in any other woman. Mrs Stevenson had many of the fine qualities that we usually attribute to men rather than to women: a fair-mindedness, a large judgment, a robust, inconsequential philosophy of life, without which she could not have borne, much less shared with a relish equal to his own, his wandering, unsettled life, his vagaries, his gipsy passion for freedom. She had a really creative imagination, which she expressed in living. She always lived with great intensity, had come more into contact with the real world than Stevenson had done at the time when they met, had tried more kinds of life, known more kinds of people. When he married her, he married a woman rich in knowledge of life and the world. Mrs Stevenson's autobiography would be one of the most interesting books in the World.[7]

NOTES

1. Augustus St Gaudens (1848–1907), the eminent sculptor, introduced to Stevenson by Will Low, began work on a medallion at the end of Sep 1887. Stevenson posed in his red poncho, cigarette in hand, which was changed to a pen for the memorial in St Giles' Cathedral, Edinburgh.

2. Stevenson was at last financially secure; ironically, his father was no longer around to savour his son's independence. *Kidnapped* and *Treasure Island* were bringing in substantial royalties. *Dr Jekyll and Mr Hyde* had been a huge success; a stage version opened in New York as the Stevensons arrived. He was soon to embark on *The Master of Ballantrae* for Scribner.

3. *The Wrong Box* (1889), usually cited as the disastrous result of Louis's collaborations. Burlingame, editor of *Scribner's Magazine*, concurred and only published the book on condition that Stevenson's name preceded Lloyd's as co-author. Burlingame paid $5000 for the American rights (Swearingen, 126).

4. Stevenson had no head for business; even the exchange rate on the dollar confused him. For an account of his mix-ups with the publishers, see Roger Burlingame, *Of Making Many Books* (1946).
  5. *The South Seas: A Record of Three Cruises* (1890). The issue is complex. From New York McClure sent Louis several books on the South Seas to get him started. An exclusive deal with the New York *Sun* was supposed to bring in $10,000 for 50 letters, with another $5 000 from sales in Britain. In the event 37 instalments ran in the *Sun*, and Stevenson received just over £1 000 – about one-third of what had been anticipated (Swearingen, 140–2). Fanny grew alarmed at the way the series evolved, polemical and factual rather than picturesque and romantic, and begged Colvin to influence him to her point of view. 'What a thing it is to have "a man of genius" to deal with', she wrote. 'It is like managing an overbred horse' (quoted in McLynn, 344).
  6. Modern biographers treat Fanny severely (none more so than McLynn), so it is worth noting that several contemporary observers found much to admire – her loyalty, courage and humour. It was far from easy living with a genius, as she herself observed.
  7. Fanny Stevenson did, of course, have ample opportunities to give her side of the story, directly and indirectly in Colvin's *Life*. See also *Our Samoan Adventure*, ed. Charles Neider (1956); *The Cruise of the 'Janet Nichol' Among the South Sea Islands: A Diary* (1915); Nellie van de Grift Sanchez, *The Life of Mrs Robert Louis Stevenson* (1920); Margaret Mackay, *The Violent Friend: The Story of Mrs Robert Louis Stevenson, 1840–1914* (1968).

Buffalo Coat and Indian Moccasins

STEPHEN CHALMERS

From *The Penny Piper of Saranac: An Episode in Stevenson's Life* (1916) 12–21, 26–33, 59–64. Stephen Chalmers (1880–1935), writer of mystery stories; he also wrote *The Beloved Physician, Edward Livingstone Trudeau* (1916) and *Enchanted Cigarettes: or Stevenson Stories that Might Have Been* (1917). See also 'The Man in Portsmouth Square', *Overland Monthly*, Jan 1930, concerning an area of San Francisco Louis was fond of and where a monument was placed. Chalmers paints an idealised picture of Louis living in obscurity in the little Adirondack village, skating on the lake behind the cottage, and gossiping with his landlords, the Bakers, and with his physician, Edward L. Trudeau. It was a bitter winter (1887–8), and Fanny loathed the cold. With her customary practicality she kitted the party out with furs from Montreal. Louis withstood the climate well, even when the outside thermometer, dubbed 'the Quarterly Reviewer', dipped to minus 40 degrees (Bell, 206). In the Saranac period he went for 15 months without a haemorrhage (McLynn, 286). He worked well, too, on *The Master of Ballantrae* (1888), the genesis of which is told in *Juvenilia*, and many essays: 'Pulvis et Umbra', 'The Lantern Bearers', 'A Chapter on Dreams', 'Gentlemen' and 'Beggars'.

Dr Trudeau was probably one of the few in the village at that time who appreciated what manner of man had come to it; and it is clear that Stevenson was quick to appreciate the intellectual qualities of the man who came to see him, first with a cold stethoscope, then with the warm hand of friendship.[1]

This friendship was spontaneous. The nature of it may be judged from the fact that, when they did not agree, they did not agree to disagree, – after the manner of the lukewarm, – but quarreled!

But the quarrels! They were of the kind indulged in by brothers who part with black murder in their hearts and burst out laughing next time they meet. They were quarrels of the kind in which one holds it a private, personal privilege to criticize the other, but woe unto the third person who ventures to criticize either to the other!

On the really great things of life they were in perfect accord; so they chose the most trivial matters upon which to differ.

The best illustration of this is, perhaps, the 'check story', which Dr Trudeau used to relate, and always with immense delight. There was no stenographer present, and Dr Trudeau himself did not undertake to repeat the exact dialogue, but from the facts and from a knowledge of the two personalities this is how it was: –

Stevenson: My dear Trudeau! I have the greatest respect for your intelligence. For that reason it distresses me – distresses me! – to hear you utter such fallacy. How *can* the American baggage system be superior to the British luggage system?

Trudeau: But, my dear Stevenson, we are dealing with facts! I know that, as a Britisher, you are naturally prejudiced –

Stevenson (interrupting): I beg your pardon, Dr Trudeau. I would never allow racial prejudice to warp my judgment in the matter of a ten-and-sixpenny trunk. The British system *is* the best. You hire a porter. You look after your own luggage. At your destination you claim it in person. It is not at all necessary to put your head out of the compartment at every stop and cry, like the Irishman: 'Gyard! Is me tronk all right?'

Trudeau (who has been waiting with fortitude for a chance to continue): Of course not. Now, then, – the American system! You are bound, say, from New York to San Francisco. You buy your railway ticket, indicate your baggage to a baggage-master with a pencil stuck in his ear and a bunch of tags in his hands. He gives you a brass check. In a week you are in San Francisco. You haven't seen or heard of your blessed trunk since you left New York; yet there it is, safe and sound. And all that is required of you in San Francisco is that brass check. *Now* what have you to say?

Stevenson (who is cornered, but hates to admit it): We – ell . . . (*He puffs great clouds of cigarette smoke and walks up and down, greatly agitated. Then, with a burst of exasperation*) That is just you Americans all over! Checks! Checks! Checks! You eat on the check system. You hang your hat on the check system. Why, an American can't speak of dying without saying that he 'hands in his checks'!

Trudeau (twenty years later): He had me that time.

After such animated discussion one may picture Dr Trudeau as he tramps down the road to his own house, a muffled figure in coonskin cap and coat, his thick moccasins crunching on the frozen snow under the clear, snapping stars of the Adirondack midwinter, and vowing never to darken the Penny Piper's door again!

But next day Trudeau would remember that Stevenson was a sick man, that he was his physician, and that it was his duty to go and see his patient even if he could never meet him again as a friend. If he didn't go, no doubt the Penny Piper would be sitting in that eight-by-ten room with the piano and the old desk and the penny whistle, and with all the air excluded through the keyhole by cigarette smoke and sideward displacement.[2]

Probably about the same time Stevenson would be blowing from his whistle that mournful Jacobite air to which he fitted 'Sing me a song of a lad that is gone', and wondering whether he ought not to put on his buffalo coat and Indian moccasins and carry the hatchet to the Doctor for burial.

If it happened that he did not go, the Doctor would come sooner or later – professionally, of course! Robert Louis would receive him like a prince. Each would admit that the other was possibly right about the baggage system, except, perhaps, that –

And as like as not they would start in just where they had left off; or, if that subject were exhausted, take up another for argument, such as whether, according to Trudeau's theory, it were not wiser to conserve the health by observing moderation (say in the use of cigarettes), or, according to Stevenson's theory, regard ill health as something altogether outside a man and death merely a possibility of any minute and from any of a number of unexpected causes....

Still aglow with the high thoughts of 'The Lantern-Bearers', Stevenson put on his buffalo coat and hurried away through the snow.[3]

The sight of the grave scientist bending over his work in that strange place of crucibles and tubes stirred the dreamer's enthusiasm afresh. Here was the thought materialized – the man with the bull's-eye, who was thinking less of fame than of the moment's task allotted.

The Penny Piper told his friend of the day's work, talking as only he talked, every muscle and facial expression in action, his eyes aglow, and his long arms gesturing in illustration. But suddenly he remembered why he had come to the laboratory.

'Now, Trudeau,' said he, 'let me see your light!'

Dr Trudeau picked up a tube containing a sickly-looking liquid.

'The scum you see in this tube,' said he, 'is consumption. It is the cause of more human suffering than anything else in the world. We can produce tuberculosis in the guinea-pig with it, and if we could cure tuberculosis in the guinea-pig, this great burden of human suffering might be lifted from the world.'

Then he told of his own experiments upon guinea-pigs with cultures of tubercle bacilli, and produced charts showing results that made similar symptoms in the human case comprehensible, and more combatable. He pointed to a row of large stoppered bottles containing tuberculous organs of guinea-pigs, ghastly evidences of the destroyer's poison. With a bottle in his hand, Trudeau turned to his very silent companion and – found that Robert Louis Stevenson had vanished!

Astonished and puzzled, the medical scientist laid down his charts and went in search of the Penny Piper. He found him in the open air, leaning against a veranda post and looking very pale.

Trudeau (rushing to his side): Stevenson, are you ill?
Stevenson (swallowing hard): N – no.
Trudeau: You don't look well. How do you feel?

Stevenson (with a brave but sickly smile): Trudeau, I know – I know your lamp is very bright, but – to me it smells of oil like the devil!

The Penny Piper was fair above all things, however, and he generously admitted that the fact of an oil smell upsetting a particular stomach did not dim the luster of a particular light....

[From an Appendix by Lloyd Osbourne at the unveiling of a memorial at the Baker Cottage, Saranac Lake, New York, 30 October 1915]

Once in this house Stevenson laid down the copy of 'Don Quixote' he was reading, and said, with a curious poignancy that lingers still in my ears: 'That's what I am – just another Don Quixote.' I think this was the most illuminating thing he ever said about himself. It was the realization that his high-flown ideals, his supersensitive honor, his vehement resentment of wrong and injustice were perhaps hopelessly at discord with the world he lived in – the momentary faltering of a great altruist. It is surprising that in his essay on 'Books that have Influenced Me' I believe he made no mention of 'Don Quixote', yet in conversation I can recall his referring to it often – 'that it was the saddest book he had ever read'; 'that Don Quixote was the greatest gentleman in fiction'; 'that the Duke and Duchess were a pair of detestable cads to make sport of the old fellow, and he their guest'. Moreover, he had even stumbled through the original in his halting, laborious Spanish.[4]

Stevenson had a wonderful reading voice; I have never heard any one who could equal him; in listening to him one was stirred by an indescribable sense of romance, of emotion, – of the heartstrings being played upon. I imagine, from what I have heard, that Charles Dickens possessed the same magic quality of evolving so complete an illusion that the fictive characters seemed alive – that one seemed to see as well as hear them – that the scenes merged imperceptibly from description into poetic fact. In the long winter evenings in Saranac, Stevenson read aloud 'Othello', 'The Tempest', 'Julius Caesar', and 'Macbeth'; read them with mantling face and increasing enthusiasm till the old room seemed to disappear in the glittering pageantry and matchless, swelling periods of Shakespeare.[5]

It is one of the most regrettable things about Stevenson that his long hair and strange attire are always assumed to be an affectation. On the contrary, he was a man absolutely devoid of pose, and hated it and derided it in others. But during his prolonged illnesses, when often for weeks at a time he would be condemned to lie in the same position lest a single movement might bring on a fresh hemorrhage of the lungs, his hair would grow excessively long; as cutting it afterwards often caused him to catch cold (and a cold to him meant a repetition of the frightful illness), it was left much as it was, save for a slight trimming. The shawls, cloaks, etc., so familiar and so fantastic, in his photographs, were only too often seized up hastily and thrown over his nightgown to keep him from the fatigue of dressing. The truth is, that until he went to Samoa, where he enjoyed a sufficiency of health that allowed him to dress and wear his hair in the ordinary manner, every day might have been his last. So far, indeed, from his long hair and singular clothing being a mark of affectation, they are a pathetic reminder of his sickroom, and show how rarely he emerged from it into the light of day.

It is not easy for those who loved him to forgive such tales as his walking down Piccadilly – 'very jauntily', as the book observes – in a lady's fur coat, pilfered from a party, and with a bunch of daffodils at his neck; and similar falsehoods, too often malicious in their origin.[6] I would beg all admirers of Robert Louis Stevenson not to credit such idiocies, which some people, who knew him well, have not been ashamed to put into circulation.

NOTES

1. Edward Livingstone Trudeau (1848–1915), founder of the Adirondack Cottage Sanitarium (1884) at Saranac Lake in the Adirondacks, near the Canadian border. Trudeau, himself consumptive, had found the climate beneficial. He was one of those who believed that Louis's haemorrhages were caused by fibrous growths in the blood vessels, not consumption. Whether or not he was then in remission from tuberculosis is still an open question. Although their relations were stormy, Stevenson gave him a set of his works inscribing the appropriate volume: 'Trudeau was all the winter at my side / I never spied the nose of Mr Hyde.'

2. Louis had taken up the piano in Bournemouth and gone at it pell-mell, as he did with most hobbies. His composing and practising proved a trial to the household, and the penny-whistle (in Samoa the flageolet) were no less nerve-wracking at close quarters. The whistle, he

acknowledged, 'explodes with sharp noises, and has to be patched with a court-plaster like a broken nose' (Balfour, *Life*, II, 35).

3. See 'A playmate beyond Compare' (p. 14).

4. 'Books which have influenced me', *British Weekly*, Aug 1887, 17–19; St J. Adcock (ed.), *Robert Louis Stevenson: His Work and Personality* (1924) 22–32.

5. Opinions differ on this point. Stevenson had a rather high pitch, which rose higher when he grew excited, a feature his father had somewhat tactlessly drawn attention to in company. See Simpson, *Edinburgh Days*, 34–5.

6. The culprit in this case was Charles Brookfield, *Random Reminiscences*, 31.

The Mannerly Stevenson

CHARLOTTE EATON

From *A Last Memory of R.L.S.* (1916) 8–43. Charlotte Eaton was the wife of the Canadian-born artist, Wyatt Eaton (1849–96), a friend of Stevenson's in the Barbizon days. Fanny Stevenson had been in San Francisco since the beginning of April, visiting family and looking out for a suitable craft, while Louis travelled to New York (where he met Mark Twain) and then on to Manasquan, New Jersey, with his mother and stepson. Will Low had taken a summer cottage; another old friendship was renewed also with St Gaudens. The Eatons were staying on the estate of a wealthy Quaker family, the Sanborns. During this month of nostalgia and farewells, evoked in the following recollections, Louis wrote to friends in England of his greatest adventure, now imminent: to Henry James, on 28 May 1888: 'This year, dear James, is a valedictory. On June 15 the schooner yacht "Casco" will (weather and a jealous providence permitting) steam through the Golden Gates for Honolulu, Tahiti, the Galapagos, Guayaquil, and – I hope *not* the bottom of the Pacific. It will contain your obedient, 'umble servant and party. It seems too good to be true, and is a very good way of getting through the greensickness of maturity which, with all its accompanying ills, is now declaring itself in my mind and life. They tell me it is not severe as that of youth; if I (and the Casco) are spared, I shall tell you more exactly, as I am one of the few people in the world who do not forget their own lives' (*Letters*, II, 107).

Now, of all places in the world, the quaint little Sanborn Cottage on the river-bank, where we were stopping, seemed to me the spot best suited for a first meeting with Stevenson.[1] The Sanborns were very little on the estate and the place had a neglected look. Indeed, more than that, one might easily have taken it for a haunted or abandoned place – with its garden choked with weeds, and its window-shutters flaunting old spider-webs to the breeze.

It was, of course, the fanciful, adventure-loving Stevenson that I looked forward to seeing, and I was not disappointed; and while others spoke of the flight of time with its inevitable changes, I felt sure that, to me, he would be just Stevenson who wrote the things over which I had burned the midnight oil.

He came promptly at the hour fixed, appearing on the threshold as frail and distinguished looking as a portrait by Velasquez. He had walked across the mile-long bridge connecting Brielle and Manasquan, ahead of the others, for the bracer he always needed before joining even a small company.

Shall I ever forget the sensation of delight that thrilled me, as he entered the room – tall, emaciated, yet radiant, his straight, glossy hair so long that it lay upon the collar of his coat, throwing into bold relief his long neck and keenly sensitive face?

His hands were of the psychic order, and were of marble whiteness, save the thumb and first finger of the right hand, that were stained from constant cigarette rolling – for he was an inveterate smoker – and had the longest fingers I have ever seen on a human being; they were, in fact, part of his general appearance of lankiness, that would have been uncanny, but for the geniality and sense of *bien être* that he gave off. His voice, low in tone, had an endearing quality in it, that was almost like a caress. He never made use of vernacularisms and was without the slightest Scotch accent; on the contrary, he spoke his English like a world citizen, speaking a universal tongue, and always looked directly at the person spoken to.

I have since heard one who knew him (and they are becoming scarce now) call him the man of good manners, or 'the Mannerly Stevenson', and this is the term needed to complete my first impression, for more than the traveller, the scholar or the author, it was *the Mannerly Stevenson* that appeared in our midst that day. He moved about the room to a ripple of repartée that was contagious, putting every one on his mettle – in fact, his presence was a challenge to a *jeu d'esprit* on every hand. How self-possessed he was, how spiritual! his face glowing with memories of other days. . . .

Stevenson was now seated before the grate, the flickering light from the wood fire illuminating his pale face to transparency. Now and then he relapsed into silence, gazing into the fire with the rapt look of one who sees visions.

'Are you seeing a Salamander,' I asked, 'or do the sparks flying upward make you think of the golden alchemy of Lescaris?'

'A Salamander,' he replied, smiling. 'Yes, a carnivorous fire-dweller that eats up man and his dreams forever.'

'Gracious! But you are going to worse things than Salamanders, the Paua [giant clams], they will get you, if you don't watch out.'

And then, suddenly becoming conscious of my temerity in interrupting the thread of his reflections, to cover my embarrassment, I ran upstairs for my birthday-book.

An autograph!

Of course. And he wrote it, reading out the quotation that filled in part of the space. It was one of Emerson's Kantisms, something about not going abroad, unless you can as readily stay at home (I forget the exact words). It was decidedly malapropos and called out much merriment.

> 'Oh, stay at home, dear heart, and rest;
> Home-keeping hearts are happiest.'

Somebody quoted, to which another replied:

> 'Home-keeping hearts have ever homely wits.'

The autograph has long since disappeared, but how often have I thought with regret of the amused expression in Stevenson's eyes at the Salamander fancy! What tales of witchery might have been spun from those themes worthy of the magic of his pen, the fire-dwelling man-eater, or the discovery of the Greek Shepherd!

Stevenson was amused over our enthusiasm, and the eagerness of some of the younger members of the company to lionize him.

'And what do you consider your brightest failure?' inquired our host.

'*Dr Jekyll and Mr Hyde*,' he replied, without a moment's hesitation, adding, 'that is the worst thing I ever wrote.'

'Yet you owe to it your dream-expedition,' some one reminded him.

'The dream-expedition?' he repeated. 'Yes, that was perhaps a compensation for the bad things.'[2] ...

As he went from reminiscence to reminiscence, we felt that from this period of his vivid obscurity might have been drawn material for some of his most stirring romances, and we were rewarded as good listeners by the discovery of that which he thought his best work, namely, the little story called 'Will o' the Mill'.[3]

'Ah!' exclaimed Mr Sanborn, his eyes beaming, 'if you live to be as old as Methuselah, with all the world's lore at your fingerends, you could never improve on that simple little story.'

We teased Stevenson a good deal on the enormity of his royalties on 'Dr Jekyll and Mr Hyde', which, besides having had what the publishers call a 'run' that means something vastly different from the same term when applied to a bank, was bringing in a second goodly harvest from its dramatization, by which his voyage to the South Seas had become a reality....

I do not now remember whether it was referring to Samoa as Stevenson's 'port o' dreams' that brought up the discussion *of* dreams.[4] To some one who asked him if he believed that dreams came true, he replied, 'Certainly, they are just as real as anything else.'

'Well, it's what one believes that counts, isn't it, and one can form any theory in a world where dreams are as real as other things, and is it the same with ideals?' somebody ventured.

'Ideals,' said Stevenson, 'are apt to stay by you when material things have taken the proverbial wings, and are assets quite as enduring as stone fences.'

'And was it from a want of faith in the durability of stone fences, or ignorance of their dream-assets that accounts for the way that Cato and Demosthenes solved their problems?' was the next question, but as this high strain was interrupted by more frivolity, my thoughts again reverted to the solidity of Stevenson's dreams, that now furnished his inquiring soul with new fields for exploration, as well as a dominant interest to fill up the measure of his earthly span.

He regretted leaving the haunts of man, he told us, particularly the separation from his friends, which was satisfactory, coming, as it did, from the man who coined the truism that the way to have a friend is to *be* one.

NOTES

1. The Sanborns were part of the American dynasty of New England pioneering families, among them the doyen of transcendental interpreters and historians, Franklin Benjamin Sanborn (1813–1917).
2. Dreams had been important since childhood, as has been noted; and dreaming became an integral part of the writer's creative process. See 'A Chapter on Dreams' (1888) (*Across the Plains*, 1892).
3. 'Will o' the Mill' was published in *Cornhill*, Jan 1878 (*The Merry Men*, 1887). L. Cope Cornford, *Robert Louis Stevenson* (1899) judged it 'his highest achievement in literature' (51).
4. Here the witness has been misled into some creative recall, for as yet Samoa was not in the itinerary.

As Good a Listener as He was a Talker

SIR EDMUND RADCLIFFE PEARS

From 'Some Recollections of Robert Louis Stevenson', *Scribner's Magazine*, LXXIII (1) (Jan 1923) 3–8. Edmund Radcliffe Pears (1862–1941), born in Ootacamund, India, was educated in England and entered the Royal Navy in 1875; he saw action in Suez, Nicaragua and Somalia, and rose to the rank of Admiral (1924). At the time of meeting Stevenson he was a lieutenant on HMS Cormorant. The yacht *Casco*, skippered by Captain A. H. Otis (Owen Nares in *The Wrecker*), took Fanny, Louis, Aunt Maggie, their maid Valentine Roch, and Lloyd to the Marquesas, the most easterly islands in Polynesia. They landed at Nuku-Hiva on 22 July 1888, and then headed for Hiva-Oa, which Paul Gauguin was to visit in 1901. On 4 September they sailed to the Tuamoto archipelago, the dangerous waters of the Paumotos, thence to Fakarava, and on to Papeete, the capital of Tahiti. After many adventures they arrived at Hawaii in December 1888; they stayed there until June the following year, when Louis, now addicted to ocean life, sailed aboard the *Equator* to the Gilbert Islands. A second stop at Honolulu came in September to October 1893. Louis's health and spirits improved vastly, and new lands inspired some of his finest writing in both fiction and non-fiction. (See early chapters of *In the South Seas* and *Letters*, II, 114–61.) As he wrote to Henry James: 'I have had more fun and pleasure of my life these past months than ever before, and more health than any time in ten long years' (Honolulu, March 1889, *Letters*, II, 141).

On the day appointed I set forth and walked out, along the beautiful tree-lined roads, to Waikiki, where I found the bungalow I sought, standing amid trees and oleanders, and so close to the beach as almost to overhang the sea.[1] As I approached, a man dressed in flannels came out on the veranda and welcomed me heartily. Him I recognized instantly, from portraits I had seen, as R. L. Stevenson: a tall, thin figure, very quick and graceful in movement; a face of extraordinary character, not to be easily forgotten; dark hair worn rather long; slight mustache; clean-cut features, and the most expressive brown eyes. The charm of his manner struck me instantaneously, and enthralled me throughout our conversation. I had rather expected to find something of an invalid, knowing of his long ill-health, but he looked nothing of the sort. There was, it is true, a certain delicacy in his looks, but it appeared more the delicacy of refinement and culture than of ailment; he had a well-colored, rather bronzed complexion, and a wonderful suggestion of activity and energy in his talk and movements.

He led me into the 'lanai', a large room which was really a roofed veranda overlooking the sea, and which had no side walls, though the sides could be closed by shutters or 'tatties', if required. It made an ideal living-room for such a climate, cool, spacious, and comfortable. Here we sat and talked, and I straightway found myself under the spell of Stevenson's wonderful charm of conversation. I say we sat, but for the most part I sat while he paced up and down as he talked, pausing now and then to fix his dancing brown eyes on me or to roll a new cigarette with his nimble fingers. He professed, by the way, scorn for the ready-made cigarette. 'The true cigarette-smoker,' he said, 'always makes his own'; and a jar of tobacco and packets of cigarette-papers on the table provided his wants. Cigarette followed cigarette, and the time flew while he talked. I wish that, Boswell-like, I had taken notes of that conversation so that I could reproduce it now! He was in the highest spirits, and wit and humor flowed from him without the least suggestion of effort....

While we were talking we were joined by Mrs R. L. Stevenson, known as an authoress by the name of Fanny van de Grift Stevenson, who very soon struck me as a woman of character and intellect, and of marked individuality.[2] Small and dark-haired, she was dressed in a 'holoku' – the invariable dress of the South Sea Island women – a very sensible garment for a warm climate, being a loose gown flowing freely from the shoulders; and her feet were bare. She must have possessed considerable beauty in her youth, still retained a good figure, and had beautifully shaped little hands and feet.

Conversation turned somehow to the stage and the dramatization of 'Dr Jekyll and Mr Hyde', which, of course, none of us had seen. I said that I had heard that in the stage version Dr Jekyll had a wife or a sweetheart – I was not sure which. Stevenson was interested to hear of this, and said: 'I thought of that, but I couldn't do it; it was too horrible.' We went on to speak of Shakespeare, and Stevenson told an amusing story of a performance of 'Macbeth', by Salvini, which he had seen, I think, in Edinburgh, in which, owing to some mismanagement, the ghost of Banquo, rising slowly and solemnly, twice appeared prematurely, and had to be lowered again with ludicrous rapidity; when the proper moment for his appearance arrived the stage-hands, daunted by their previous mistakes, failed to hoist him, and an awkward pause ensued; the manager behind the scenes must have fired out a volcanic order, for with a terrific jerk up shot the ghost of Banquo, so violently that an effect still more comic was produced. Stevenson's description of this incident, in which he vividly imitated the action of the unfortunate ghost, especially the final jerk, which caused his long hair to fly outward, was intensely amusing.

I had intended to pay a short call, not wishing to take up too much of the author's time, but when I rose to go I found I had actually stayed two hours, entranced by the charm of his talk. He made light of my apologies, however, and invited me to dine with him one evening a day or two later.

At that dinner, besides Stevenson and his wife, his mother (the elder Mrs Stevenson), Lloyd Osbourne, and his sister, Mrs Strong, were present. It was an unconventional, but most delightful, affair; the men in flannels, Mrs R. L. Stevenson in her 'holoku', with a brazier burning under the table to keep mosquitoes away from her bare feet, Mrs Strong (whose husband was an artist of San Francisco) similarly attired; the food plain but good; the table undecorated; the conversation unflagging and lively.[3] One felt that both food and formality were not worth troubling one's head about; it was the company and talk that mattered. In this Bohemian atmosphere the elder Mrs Stevenson, a most lovable and charming old lady, neatly, almost primly, dressed in black, with a white muslin cap, looked at first sight out of her proper element; but it was not so in reality; she understood her companions and was entirely sympathetic. The strong affection binding the typical Scotch mother to her strange, brilliant bantling, and him to her, was unmistakable and beautiful.

Stevenson, eager and vivacious, did most of the talking, but entirely without egotism or arrogance. The fact is, it was so delightful to listen to him that no one felt inclined to cut in, unless to prompt or to spur. Dinner over and the plates removed by the attendant Chinaman (who, I was amused to note, seemed to be as devoted to, and fascinated by, his whimsical master as any of us), coffee and tobacco-jar were placed on the table, and as we rolled our cigarettes and smoked we continued to talk and laugh till a fairly late hour.[4] Much of Stevenson's lively conversation was about his South Sea cruise and the *Casco*, but all sorts of things were discussed besides, including experiences with publishers and magazine editors. He was then engaged on 'The Master of Ballantrae', which, although not quite completed, was running in *Scribner's*. I admitted that I was reading it as it appeared monthly in that magazine, an admission for which he strongly reproved me! Somewhat taken aback, I pleaded that I could not restrain my impatience, but he would not accept the excuse. 'What?' I asked, in rather feeble self-defense, 'isn't one supposed to read it in *Scribner's*?' 'Of course not!' he replied. Still more flabbergasted, I inquired why, in that case, was it published in the serial form? 'Simply as an advertisement,' was the answer. I had not, in my simplicity, realized this fact, which, of course, must be well understood in the publishing world, and which Stevenson, being quite aware of the market value of his work, could state without vanity. On the other hand, the work would be useless as an advertisement unless thousands of magazine readers were ready to enjoy it in serial form. But, for the true book-lover, to read a long novel in monthly installments is neither doing justice to the author nor giving complete enjoyment to the reader, and this would naturally be Stevenson's point of view.

Stevenson and Osbourne discussed their jointly written book, 'The Wrong Box', which had not long been published, and which I had not read. Stevenson said it was nothing but 'wild farce', and we laughed over its absurdities. Apparently they had another book on the stocks, for they were anxious to learn something about tidal waves, and questioned me closely as to the localities and effects of these phenomena. I gathered that their intention was to get rid of some of their characters with a tidal wave, but I do not remember if this idea was ever used.[5] . . .

He loved music, of which he had considerable knowledge (as

of most subjects), and finding I was an amateur of the violin asked me to bring my fiddle with me one evening. Although I assured him I was a very poor performer, he insisted, and I brought it accordingly, expecting that Mrs Strong would accompany me on the piano. On that occasion, however, I found Stevenson alone, and to my dismay he asked me to play to him without accompaniment. I did so, feeling that my efforts could not possibly give him any pleasure. He sat by me, leaning forward, head on hand, listening intently, and (to my inward amazement) evidently enjoying it. The secret of this (and it was characteristic of the man) was that his attention was concentrated, not on me or my fiddle, but on the music itself, the beauties of which, however, indifferently rendered, he appreciated and enjoyed.

It was interesting to hear his opinions on contemporary authors. Of then living novelists he held Hardy and Meredith to be the greatest. 'I am an out-and-out Meredith man,' he said, and advised me to make the acquaintance of 'Rhoda Fleming', which I had not read. I asked him whether William Archer was a Socialist. 'Not exactly,' he replied with twinkling eyes, 'but he has aspir-r-ations in that direction' (rolling the r in the slight Scotch accent which never quite deserted him); he spoke of both William Archer and Andrew Lang with much affection. He appeared to regard Rider Haggard as his own chief rival in popular esteem.

NOTES

1. The meeting occurred in March 1889, through an introduction effected by Lloyd, who had met Pears at a reception given by King Kalakaua. Kalakaua was struggling to retain Hawaiian nationalism amidst engulfing Americanisation, and to extend his influence in Polynesian affairs. Stevenson's involvement in Samoan politics reflected something of the king's tuition; he admired Kalakaua's bravura and appetite for life.

2. Fanny's chequered fiction career had included 'Too Many Birthdays', *St. Nicholas Magazine*, July 1878; 'Miss Pringle's Neighbours', *Scribner's*, June 1887; and with Louis, 'The Dynamiter', *More New Arabian Nights* (1885) and 'The Hanging Judge'. Her story 'The Nixie', *Scribner's Magazine*, March 1888, caused a scandal as plagiarisation of work by Katharine de Mattos and led to the final break with Henley. Her last published story was 'Under Sentence of the Law (The Story of a Dog)', *McClure's*, June 1893. Again, biographers give Fanny a hard time on her literary aspirations, failing to take into account sufficiently the psychological burdens of second-fiddle to genius, not to mention

the physical and mental investment of energy Louis demanded. Jenni Calder is fairer to her in this regard: 'It is possible that she might have made something more of her ability if she had persevered' (*RLS*, 194).

3. Fanny adopted the 'Mother Hubbard' at once and wore it constantly. Even Louis's mother at times wore the traditional loose dress over the mumu, although pictures usually show her looking like Queen Victoria in black dress and widow's cap with streamers.

4. Ah Fu was a great acquisition, a resourceful cook, greatly admired for his quaint English. He left the Stevensons in April 1890 to visit his mother in China, and was never heard of again.

5. Active collaboration on *The Wrecker* began when they were in Apemama in the summer of 1889.

Always Eager for Excitement

T. M. MacCALLUM

From *Adrift in the South Seas: Including Adventures with Robert Louis Stevenson* (1934) 227–45. Thomas Murray MacCallum was first deckhand then cook aboard the *Equator*, captained by a highly skilful 23-year-old Scot, Denny Reid. His memories in old age may take 'cautious sifting' (Furnas, 533) but give a first-rate picture of ship-board life, of Louis's spirit, and of his friendship with the captain. In an omitted section, MacCallum describes how Louis and Lloyd thought seriously of going into trading with Reid and buying their own boat, to be called the *Northern Light*. As a company name MacCallum offered the 'Jekyll-Hyde & Company'. From Reid and his crew Louis learned much of trading practices, knowledge put to use in *The Wrecker* and *The Beach of Falesà*. The Hawaiian interlude came to an end with a flurry of activity (May 1889) over Molokai's leper colony and Father Damien, about whose detractor, one Reverend Dr Hyde, Stevenson later wrote scathingly. The Stevenson party, minus Aunt Maggie who had returned briefly to Scotland, sailed south. In the remote Gilbert Islands of Micronesia they made a landfall at Butaritari. At Apemama Louis met the tyrannical King Tembinoka, and typically won over this dangerous figure, who said his farewells in November 1889 with tears coursing down his fat cheeks. On 7 December the *Equator* steamed into Apia harbour, Samoa.

The Stevenson party had been in Honolulu ever since returning from a trip to the Marquesas Islands. Their many friends planned a series of good-bye parties for them, and in return, Stevenson entertained them on the 'Equator'.

The day before we were to sail, the old man called me into the cabin and told me that I would have to spread myself, because Mr Stevenson was going to entertain his Majesty, King Kalakaua, at luncheon the next day, and the reputation of the 'Equator' was at stake.

To say that I was nervous would be putting it mildly.

Captain Reid, Mr and Mrs Stevenson, Ah Fu and I went into a 'Committee of the whole', and planned the luncheon in every detail.

On learning that I had never even seen champagne, let alone served it, Stevenson explained in detail just how I should cool and serve it. The captain made me rehearse the luncheon service several times, till my performance met with the approval of all. We celebrated the achievement by actually opening a bottle of champagne the last time, and there being enough, I was given a glass also, much to the disgust of Anderson, the mate, who witnessed the rehearsal through the skylight.

Stevenson's farewell luncheon was quite a success.

Kalakaua was accompanied by two of his ministers. I was much surprised when His Majesty came aboard. I had read a number of stories of the fierce cannibals who inhabited the Sandwich Islands, and of course had pictured them in my mind. The polished gentleman who sat in our little cabin, engaging R.L.S. in friendly conversation and making gallant speeches to Mrs Stevenson, was a revelation to me. The meal passed off to everyone's entire satisfaction, and I twice refilled the royal glass without dropping the bottle, or spilling any of the sparkling wine on the spotless white of His Majesty's pants.[1] ...

One of the first things that won my admiration for Stevenson was his happy faculty of always seeing the bright side of everything. No matter how disappointing things were, he never seemed to get blue or discouraged. He possessed, to a marvellous degree, the ability to make people like and admire him; whether it was the king of Hawaii or the kanaka [native] sailors, he had a personal magnetism that drew them all.

I think his Chinaman, Ah Fu, would have gladly cut off his right hand if he thought it would help 'Misee Slevens'. R.L.S., as he liked to be called, was often spoken of as the 'Apostle of Sunshine', and I think it fits him better than any of the endearing names that have been given him.

That his optimistic sunniness was blended with humour, was clearly demonstrated on his last cruise in the 'Equator'.

We were lying becalmed one night, when the schooner was struck by a white squall. The lookout must have been asleep, as we were caught with all standing, even to the balloon jib and fore gaff topsail. The schooner was thrown on her beam ends, with the lee rail clear under water. At the first burst of wind the fore topmast went by the board. The noise of the breaking spar and the thrashing of the canvas sounded as though Bedlam had broken loose. All hands were put to work clearing away the wreckage, and as the sheets were eased off and the schooner brought into the wind, she was soon on an even keel again.[2]

Mr and Mrs Stevenson's stateroom was on the starboard side of the cabin and their berths were next to the ship's side, so instead of being thrown out on the floor, they were merely rolled back against the wall; as that was on the lee side of the ship. As soon as order had been brought out of chaos the old man told me to serve coffee to the crew. Hearing me leave the cabin, R.L.S. called me into his stateroom and said:

'Oh Murray, I wish you would present my compliments to Captain Reid, and tell him how much we appreciate his thoughtfulness in having the squall strike us while the schooner was on the starboard tack, and thus saving Fanny and myself the inconvenience of being thrown out of bed.'

I delivered the message to the old man, who was at the wheel himself, swearing beautiful oaths at the sailors, that could be heard above the storm clear to the fo'c'sle.

Stevenson's message brought him up all standing, then he started laughing, and said:

'All right, Murray, give him my love and tell him to go to the devil.' . . .

While on the schooner, Stevenson was engaged in writing 'The Wrecker,' on which he and Osbourne collaborated. Most of his writing was done while lying in his bunk, knees drawn up in front of him, and pillow piled behind his head and shoulders. There was a window at the head of his bunk, opening onto the main deck, and two portholes at the back, with an unobstructed view of sky and sea.

The familiar sight of the 'Frail Warrior', as Carré calls him, propped in his bunk with a writing pad against his knees, either with a pensive far away look in his eyes, or else, feverishly covering page after page with his manuscript, will always linger in my memory.[3] . . .

On our last voyage with the Stevenson party we celebrated the thirty-ninth birthday of R.L.S. It came just about a week after we had lost our fore topmast in the squall. Stevenson and Osbourne got a lot of fun out of kidding the captain about his missing topmast. . . .

Mrs Stevenson and Lloyd planned a surprise for R.L.S., and together wrote a song, congratulating him on his birthday and also kidding the captain about his lost spar. The song, set to the tune of a popular air and lustily rendered in Osbourne's fine baritone, made a wonderful hit at the dinner. I have forgotten the lines of the song, excepting the chorus, which was repeated after each verse and ran:

'Captain Darling, where has your top-mast gone, I pray,
Captain Darling, where has your top-mast gone?'

A few weeks later we arrived at Apia, where Stevenson planned to make his home. As we approached the passage, R.L.S. stood in the bow and surveyed the beautiful background of Apia. The beach was still looking desolate from the hurricane. The wrecks of the 'Trenton' and 'Vandalia' still littered the beach in front; while to the west, the iron hull of the 'Adler' lay stark and rusted on the reef.[4]

The time had come for the happy wanderers to say good-bye to the little schooner that had been a home to them so long. We on the 'Equator' were very sorry to see them go, as they had endeared themselves to each one of us, from the captain to little Muggeree, the cabin boy. I have never forgotten Stevenson's last words to me, as he said good-bye the day before we sailed for Butaritari.

'Remember, Murray; there is always a sunny side, if you look for it. And another thing, don't worry. It does not matter much, what you accomplish. The only thing that really counts is, that you tried.'

Coming to know him as they did, it would have been impossible for the happy hearted Samoans to do other than give him their friendship and love.

Next morning we got under way, and again the 'Equator' headed out through the narrow passage for the blue Pacific.

NOTES

1. King Kalakaua's absorption rate was legendary. As Louis put it to Baxter: 'Kalakaua is a terrible companion: a bottle of fizz is like a glass of sherry to him; he thinks nothing of five or six in an afternoon as a whet for dinner' (*Baxter Letters*, 243).
2. Storms dogged the last stage of the voyage to Samoa. At one point the ship hit a reef, and Reid had to prepare to abandon ship. Fanny sat through the night with a cat in her lap, fearing that it might be forgotten when the order came. Like the *Casco*, this vessel came to an ignominious end, as ballast for a breakwater at Snohomish before being raised and towed to Seattle (McLynn, 352).
3. Jean-Marie Carré, *The Frail Warrior* (1931).
4. The devastating storm of 16 March 1889.

Everybody Felt Thoroughly at Home

H. J. MOORS

From *With Stevenson in Samoa* (1910). When the 'Equator' eased its way into the sheltered anchorage of Apia against a backdrop of bush and the green slopes of Mount Vaea, one of the first to meet the Stevenson party was a voluble Mid-Westerner named Harry Jay Moors, who had a chain of trading posts and numerous contacts in Samoan business, finance and politics. 'No mouse squeaked or plot hatched without his getting some inkling' (Furnas, 360). Delicately placed among American, British and German business interests and indigenous discontents, Moors managed skilfully. At first he provided temporary residence for the new arrivals, while they planned a trip to Australia; but, more significantly, within weeks he had encouraged Louis to buy land and settle in Samoa. Moors's friendship has been thought a mixed blessing (Calder, 284). Plantation economy was precarious, and Stevenson's business sense did not equip him for the role of planter. Fanny loathed Moors from the start, and perhaps with good reason, for he systematically cheated them by overcharging for supplies from his Apia store until Louis found him out and took his business elsewhere. Moors had a Samoan wife and five children, one of whom was educated in the United States. Intrigued by the American trader as a sample of many morally dubious characters who made their livelihoods in the South Seas, Louis came to find in his company a respite from the gathering tensions of his home life. See *Baxter Letters*, 266; Furnas, 360–3.

I needed not to be told that he was in indifferent health, for it was stamped on his face. He appeared to be intensely nervous, highly strung, easily excited. When I first brought him ashore he was looking somewhat weak, but hardly had he got into the street (for Apia is practically a town with but one street) when he began to walk up and down it in a most lively, not to say eccentric manner. He could not stand still. When I took him into my house, he walked about the room, plying me with questions, one after another, darting up and down, talking on all sorts of subjects, with no continuity whatever in his conversation. His wife was just as fidgety as himself; Lloyd Osbourne not much better. The long lonesome trip on the schooner had quite unnerved them, and they were delighted to be on shore again....

Many a day and many a night did Stevenson spend with me.[1] Time and again, when he felt played out and written out, when inertia or despondency seized him, he would come down to be cheered up. Sometimes he was pretty hopeless – 'all done for'. But, as a rule, it was nothing more than brain weariness, and he only required a rest to put him right again, a change of atmosphere and surroundings. After a short trip away he always came back benefited. I fancy the women folk were given to coddling him too much at home, and too much of this is good for neither man nor beast.

Though he would come to me full of all sorts of troubles, he rarely uttered a word of complaint concerning his bodily ailments; indeed, for a man who suffered so much he was one of the most resigned and uncomplaining men I ever met. His fortitude in this respect was one of the distinguishing characteristics of the man. But in other matters he was easily upset, and I have seen him get into a rage over the most trivial thing. I have likewise seen him engrossed in trifling subjects; and I have known him to use his best energies to assist a friend in some small matter in which he had little or no real concern.

When in a rage he was a study. Once excite him, and you had another Stevenson. I have seen him in all moods. I have seen him sitting on my table, dangling his bony legs in the air, chatting away in the calmest manner possible; and I have seen him, becoming suddenly agitated, jump from that table and stalk to and fro across the floor like some wild forest animal, to which he has, indeed, been already compared. His face would glow and his eyes would flash, darkening, lighting, scintillating, hypnotizing you with their brilliance and the burning fires within. In calm they were eyes of strange beauty, with an expression that is almost beyond the power of pen to describe. 'Eyes half alert, half sorrowful', said our common friend, Mr Carruthers once, and I have neither read nor heard anything which seems to approach so near the mark.[2] They carried in them a strange mixture of what seemed to be at once the sorrow and joy of life, and there appeared to be a haunting sadness in their very brightness. . . .

Dr Japp, in his book on Stevenson, errs in stating that Stevenson cleared the whole of the four hundred acres comprising the Vailima property; he cleared only fifteen acres, and part of this was done by myself during the time he was in Sydney. On these fifteen acres he farmed and gardened, and his *Letters* show how the farming life got into his system – so that 'if I go out and make a sixpence bossing my laborers and plying the cutlass or spade, idiot conscience applauds me; if I sit in the house and make twenty pounds, idiot conscience wails over my neglect and the day wasted'. But he would never have made a fortune – I doubt if he ever would have made a living even – as a farmer, for his schemes were always impracticable ones. Starting to grow cocoa, he wanted to do it in a way that nobody else had ever heard of, and very little grist came to his mill.[3] But I have no doubt his improved health was due to some extent to the out-door life he led at Vailima, as well as the natural advantages of the climate itself. It has been said that he took his ill health cheerfully; that is wrong, it was his good health that he took cheerfully. When he was not feeling well, Stevenson was a man who cheerfully damned the whole universe; but such occasions were rare during his life in Samoa, and so well did the place agree with him that he used to say that he would start a sanitorium for consumptives – though I do not think he ever seriously contemplated such a thing.

Stevenson rose as a rule at six o'clock, though he was up, often enough, as early as four, writing by lamp light. He wrote at all hours, and at all times. Oftentimes he would come down town on 'Jack' and tell me he had got 'stuck' in some passage of a story and was out in search of an inspiration.[4] 'The orange is squeezed out,' he would say. He used generally to wear a little white yachting cap worth about twenty-five cents. As he was very thin and boyish in appearance, the cap suited him. I never saw him in a stiff shirt, or a stand-up collar in my life. Up at Vailima they all went about in their bare feet, except when expecting guests, and generally looked about half dressed. When Stevenson came into Apia he still looked only half dressed. He always came down with a soft shirt on and generally white flannel trousers, sometimes with a red sash tied round the waist. He was very careless about his personal adornment, just 'a man of shirt sleeves'; and his clothes invariably had the appearance of being a misfit, because of his extremely slight frame.[5] . . .

Stevenson was a charming host, and it mattered not whether he was receiving Europeans or natives. Everybody felt thoroughly at home at Vailima. There were invariably several dinner parties there when a British or American warship put into port. In him the navy had a great champion, and he used to have a printed list of the warships that had been to Apia fixed up in front of his house, and every succeeding ship that arrived duly had its name printed there. To meet the officers from these ships a number of friends would be invited to Vailima, for the afternoon and evening. While dinner was being prepared the guests would sit on the wide veranda, smoking and talking, and an 'appetizer' would be handed round. Those were happy times. Stevenson the writer, the talker, the charmer, was in his element. He loved to have friends around him. Over the dinner plates he entertained the company with his anecdotes. But he never monopolized the conversation; he was as ready a listener as he was a ready talker. After dinner, music, or more smoking and more talking on the veranda – and coffee par excellence – coffee the sugar in which had first of all been soaked in burnt brandy! . . .

Sometimes he amused me by getting quite excited over matters of the most trivial moment. Some small event among the natives, some small domestic affair, or some amusing scandal, would crop up, and the whole family would discuss it with animation and become, indeed, theatrical over it. Stevenson would take rapid strides and throw his arms about, as if performing a part, and the excitement would flush his face and paint his eyes bright. These were the occasions when the man was eloquent, but it was the eloquence of the actor, shown in the looks as much as in the words. His face carried absolute conviction; and when he was burning with indignation the fire in his eye showed it more clearly than any words could do. Henley was right; he was a born actor; and it seems strange that his efforts as a dramatist should have proved a dismal failure.

While he was staying at my house, we exchanged endless yarns, generally in the evenings, as we sat in our pajamas on the balcony. Some of his phrases were inimitable, many of them quaint. Once he told of 'a fellow who would stay long enough to take soup with the devil, and then leave the table before the other courses came on'. When anything good came his way, he used to tell, it was 'better than a dig in the eye with a sharp stick'.

NOTES

1. If Moors is to be believed, Stevenson would sometimes be so intent on jawing at his house that he would stay to supper, leaving Fanny's dinner to take care of itself. Moors observed: 'never once did I hear a harsh word pass between them', but it seems highly likely that Moors was involved in discussion of Louis's domestic situation, at one point counselling his removal to Nassau Island for the benefit of his work and state of mind (*With Stevenson*, 201–2). However, it is also on record that Fanny herself dreamed of moving to Nassau (*Cruise of the 'Janet Nichol', Among the South Sea Islands, A Diary*, 1915). Moors bought the island himself for $4 000.

2. R. Hetherington Carruthers, an Apia solicitor, acting for Moors. An Englishman with a Samoan wife, he lived about a mile from Vailima. He came to Stevenson's rescue over a libel case by briefing Louis as an advocate in order to prevent him being put in the witness box. Stories circulated about Carruthers' shadowy past (Mackay, 389).

3. Perhaps some special pleading here; Moors has been criticised for encouraging Louis in plantation schemes for which he had little skill. What Moors did provide, however, was reliable knowledge on Samoan politics, which bore fruit in *A Footnote to History: Eight Years of Trouble in Samoa* (1892).

4. 'Jack', the New Zealand pony bought from Moors for £10 in 1890, bore his eight-stone rider faithfully on his frequent rides through the bush and villages. 'He reigned alone in Stevenson's affection' (Balfour, *Life*, II, 121).

5. In the South Seas, Louis's utter disregard of orthodox dress enabled him to appear as beachcomber with buccaneer accessories, or in whites for formal occasions. In Tahiti one witness praised him for only wearing what was useful and necessary. His mother wrote in some amusement: 'he has *at last* found someone who appreciates his taste in dress'; she added that since his usual wear was a pyjama suit, badly shaped and '*dreadfully* unbecoming', this was no example for anyone' (*From Saranac to the Marquesas and Beyond*, 1903).

Writings as Pure as Possible

SYDNEY PRESS

(1) from *Sydney Morning Herald*, 14 Feb 1890, 4; (2) from *Illustrated Sydney News*, 6 March 1890, 11. Samoa was a powder keg politically, and Louis's concern at the situation is apparent here, along with frank professions of his literary tastes. Leaving the recently acquired Vailima property, Fanny and Louis sailed on the *Lübeck* in February 1890 for Australia, putting up at the Victoria Hotel, Sydney. The morning after his arrival, his name 'blazed across the front page of every newspaper'. Fan mail, reporters seeking interviews, literary and church organisations wanting lectures, autograph hunters galore, are reported (Field, *This Life*, 242–3). Their plans were to reunite with the Strongs and then make a trip to Britain. But sickness forced a change of plans and once again drove the Stevensons to sea; they shipped on the *Janet Nicholl* during April to August to the Gilberts, Marshalls and other islands. They sailed from island to island recording impressions, and Louis's health rallied as it always did at sea. Back in Sydney in August, though, Louis fell ill once more. It was the decisive moment: they turned towards Samoa for good.

(1) Our representative found Mr Stevenson but newly arrived at his hotel, and in all that state of 'demènagement' which settling down in a strange city involves.[1] Samoa, as the place from which he has just arrived, was naturally first alluded to. 'Yes,' said Mr Stevenson, 'the islands are beautiful, so beautiful, in fact, that I have decided to make a home for myself there. You see it is very difficult to purchase land in any of the South Sea Islands, but I have been fortunate enough to get a place which suits me in Samoa.'

'But do you consider that the affairs of the island are sufficiently settled to justify you in settling there?'

'That's as it may be,' said Mr Stevenson. 'I shall have to take my chance. Malietoa who has been elected king, does not really possess supreme power, and has only control over about two-thirds of the islands. The chiefs in the north and south refuse to recognise his authority, and really there can be no such thing as a king in Samoa. The appointment of a vice-king is merely an idea of the consuls, whose jealousies have resulted in so much trouble to the islanders. Naturally the German interest is preponderant there, as the firm of Goddefroy owns large estates, out of which it is endeavouring to make a profit – I am afraid in vain. The king can after all only be the head chief, and, to take a comparison from Europe, occupy the same position towards the other chiefs as the Emperor of Germany does towards the Prince of Monaco. He can advise, and, if necessary, bring pressure to bear, but he cannot really rule. Still I trust that in course of time the affairs of the islands will become settled, and at any rate I am going to make a home there.'[2]

'I suppose', said our representative, 'that you will utilise your experience in the South Seas in your next work of fiction? By the by, did you visit Treasure Island?'

Mr Stevenson smiled humorously. 'Treasure Island,' he said, 'is not in the Pacific. In fact, I only wish myself that I knew where it was. When I wrote the book I was careful to give no indication as to its whereabouts, for fear that there might be an undue rush towards it. However, it is generally supposed to be in the West Indies. But to be serious. My next work of fiction will be called "The Wrecker", and will deal with the career of a wreck in the Pacific.'[3]

'Can a wreck have a career?'

'Certainly, this one has. The scene is laid on the South Pacific Coast, where the vessel is lost, and the wreck is subsequently sold at auction at San Francisco. There are various bidders, and one man shows such an intense desire to become possessed of the vessel that other people begin to think there is something in it. A smart Yankee and his friend, who play leading parts in the story, accordingly bid against the other man, and eventually become possessed of the wreck at a fabulous price. After buying the vessel they find that there is nothing about it to recompense their outlay, and this is where the mystery comes in. Eventually, of course, they discover the reason for the great value placed on her.'

'How?'

'Well, that's just where it is,' said Mr Stevenson. 'Wild horses wouldn't drag any more out of me at present.'

'And where do the love episodes come in?'

'Oh, there are not any,' replied Mr Stevenson, smiling. 'In fact,' he added confidentially, 'I am afraid that I have not been altogether successful with my heroines in the past and intend to avoid any mistakes of this kind in the future. Wait till you read the book and you will know all about it. I am also engaged in a more serious work, which will deal historically with the events of recent years in Samoa and the other islands of the South Seas.[4] Mr Osbourne, who is with me now, is collaborating in this work.'

'I suppose that that is in order to secure the American copyright?'

'Well, no,' replied Mr Stevenson, 'that is hardly the *raison d'être* of our collaboration, although the result is certainly attained by it. I have lost a great deal of money through the piracy of my works in America, and should consider it quite fair to use any means to defeat the lower class of American publishers, who calmly appropriate one's works as soon as they are issued. But in justice to my American publishers, Messrs Scribner and Co., I may say that they have always treated me most fairly, and even now I receive a considerable sum annually from them. They, of course, obtain the proof-sheets of my work, and this gives them a day or two start of the pirates. But how little advantage this is, may be judged from the fact that, within a week after the issue of 'Kidnapped', there were no less than 25 editions being sold throughout America, at prices varying from 10 to 25 cents. All this naturally has a demoralising effect on the American national literature, and no one prays for international copyright more than the American author himself. It is impossible for him to compete against the cheap pirated editions of English works, and publishers cannot therefore afford to pay sufficient for native work.'

Then Mr Stevenson, in response to a query from our representative, branched off into a dissertation on modern fiction generally. 'I have not', he said, 'yet read the article on "Candour in Fiction", in the *New Review*, to which you allude; but I gather that it deals with a phase of the question which I hardly care to touch. I do not in my own works like to trench on dangerous ground, and prefer to have my writings as pure as possible. For instance, I would not like to think that anyone read a novel of mine on account of its pruriency, although at the same time I do not approve of the English prudery of the present day. This false sentiment, after all, is hardly a century old, and we have only to turn to the works of Richardson and Fielding to assure ourselves of this. Their novels, which are now considered almost indecent, were looked upon as quite proper and fit for general reading when they were written. I fancy that we shall in time change all this, and that the people will eventually revert to the plain speaking habits of their ancestors.'

'But do you not consider that the modern realistic author, such as Zola or George Moore with his "plain speaking", aids in attaining this end?'[5]

'No, certainly not, for he gives us an entirely unreal and false picture of life, picking out merely the blemishes of our modern civilisation, and exaggerating them as if they were really expressions of the average type. Zola, I consider, is a victim of sexual insanity. The influence of this mania is prominent throughout all his works, and he thus produces scenes and characters which have no actual existence. I may say,' said Mr Stevenson, growing excited and pacing up and down the room, 'that familiar as I am with the French life, I have never seen anything to justify the brutality painted by Zola. In "Le Rêve" [1888] we get the key to the whole position, for there the author paints himself as the artist, who is the principal character in the book.'

'Then, taking realistic literature as a whole, on which side do you consider the balance lies – for good or for evil?'

'For evil decidedly. Your average bourgeois-English shopkeeper gets hold of a work of Zola's and rubs his hands delightedly. "Ha, ha," he cries, "here is something really indecent at last. Never thought they would have allowed anything like this to be published." And he gloats over it,' said Mr Stevenson sadly. 'All he sees is the indecency, and the fine lesson in humanity, or the warning against the continuance of social inequality, which the author intended to convey, is entirely lost.'

On the question of Australian literature Mr Stevenson candidly confessed that he was not well informed, and he therefore wisely refrained from expressing any opinion. 'I intend,' he said, 'to read Marcus Clark's "Natural Life", which I have heard highly spoken of, and when I have time I am going to study your poetry.[6] With regard to his tour through Australia, Mr Stevenson is vague, with the pleasant uncertainty of a man who is not compelled to go anywhere, or to do anything in particular. He's just going to look round and perhaps spend five or six months here, during which period no doubt he will pick up enough knowledge of Australian character and *mise en scène* to form the basis of another novel. Then in November he will return to Samoa, and so on to England, which he hopes to reach in the summer time. Meanwhile he is in good health, and enjoying his travels.

(2) He isn't in the least like what you expected; people never are. You had visions of a tall and dignified man of science, *à la* Jekyll with a laboratory air about him; of an uncanny dwarf whose hand-shake made you 'creep' *à la* Hyde; of a dashing outlaw with the fascinations of the Evil One, *à la* Master of Ballantrae; or perchance of a De Quincey, full of morbid fancies; a Coleridge with a frenzied eye; and barring the fascination you come upon none of these things. The delicate refined man who is now among us – presumably 'taking notes' – is chiefly characterised by a total absence of self-consciousness or conventional stiffness. He has never acquired the roar of the literary lion, and he treats that leonine appendage, 'the interviewer', with the weary courtesy due to licensed bores. After all, what is popularity to this quiet, pale man, whose long hair and facial type suggest a musical artist, whose soft brown eyes have that mesmeric quality which is the invariable attribute of your genuine *conteur*? Does he owe the public any gratitude because, forsooth, his writings fascinate it? The public can't help itself; he has the power, it is the 'subject' lying at his mercy. What need has he to talk to the public about himself? But because the wide-spread race of interviewers exists, thrives, and fattens – a lying race, seeking, like their historical father, whom they may devour – Mr Stevenson has wisely submitted to interviews innumerable, lest, if he refused, a worse thing should befall him. . . .

When asked why he is so indefatigable, instead of annihilating you with the pressure of inspiration, he answers with naive simplicity that he has two expensive indulgences – ill-health and love of travel – and that he is a poor man. Poverty is a relative term, and most of us are apt to be somewhat in love with it, as understood by Mr Stevenson, i.e., taking the shape of a roving life with a sympathetic life companion who shares your intellectual pursuits, and with an imagination which procures you constant mental pabulum from your surroundings. Whether some new and thrilling tale is to be dredged up from 'our beautiful harbour' remains to be seen; but we shall be sorely disappointed if out of his projected residence in Samoa Mr Stevenson does not evolve some romantic South Sea dreamings for our benefit.

NOTES

1. At the Victoria Hotel Belle Strong found her step-father furiously demanding of the desk clerk why he had been given a poky room on the fourth floor. He promptly checked out and moved into a suite at the Oxford Hotel nearby.
2. With increasing trade rivalry among the three powers and indigenous discontents and national pride the political situation was volatile, and Stevenson (some thought unwisely) threw himself into the conflict. Malietoa was no favorite of his, as a figure manipulated by the Germans. He supported the chief Mataafa, a Catholic, which complicated matters further. Becoming embroiled in politics, Louis felt deeply for the Samoan people, writing letters to *The Times*, thereby embarrassing the local British power and risking deportation. Hostilities broke out, and at one time Vailima looked to be in danger. But Mataafa was defeated and deported. See *Our Samoan Adventure*, 208–26; Mackay, 406–7, 432–3.
3. Inspiration for the mystery came from a story picked up in Honolulu when some shipwrecked sailors from the *Wandering Minstrel* arrived with tales of a rogue cargo. Of interest to Stevensonians is the series of locations associated with the novelist's past life, including Scotland, Paris, eastern United States, San Francisco and other venues.
4. *A Footnote to History: Eight Years of Trouble in Samoa* (1892).
5. 'Candour in Fiction', *New Review*, 11, (Jan–June 1890) 6–21, essays by Walter Besant, Mrs Elizabeth Lynn Linton and Thomas Hardy, discussing issues of truth and moral purpose in fiction in the face of modern naturalism and its practitioners, notably Zola, Moore and Gissing. Like James, Stevenson came to respect Zola more than this interview suggests.
6. Marcus Clarke (1846–81) published *His Natural Life* in the *Australian Journal*, March 1870–June 1872; thought by some to be the greatest Australian novel of the century.

Queer Birds – Mighty Queer Ones Too

HENRY ADAMS

From *Henry Adams and his Friends, A Collection of his Unpublished Letters*, ed. Harold Dean Cater (1947) 201–2, 234–6, 238–9; and *Letters of Henry Adams (1858–1891)*, ed. Worthington Chauncey Ford (1930) 426, 446–7, 450–3. Henry (Brooks) Adams (1838–1918) taught history at Harvard from 1870 to 1877, editing the *North American Review* for most of this period; he wrote *The History of the United States during the Administration of Thomas Jefferson and James Madison*, 9 vols (1889–91); travels in the Pacific resulted in *Memoirs of Marau Taaroa, Last Queen of Tahiti* (1893). Vailima was in its first stage of development when he arrived. Bush was being cleared and freed of stumps, tracks opened up and areas fenced, especially for Fanny's precious garden. But already Louis was proud of his purchase. He wrote to E. L. Burlingame from the *Janet Nicholl* on 13 July 1890: 'The ancestral acres run to upwards of three hundred; they enjoy the ministrations of five streams, whence the name' (*Letters*, II, 190). In time a second wing would be added to the house, to make two continuous blocks, each of two storeys with ample verandahs, spanned by corrugated iron roofing, which rang like pistol shots during storms. Materials had to be transported uphill over difficult terrain. What Adams saw was primitive backwoods life from which his fastidious taste recoiled. Louis, however, was in seventh heaven. Again to Burlingame he wrote in December 1890: 'I am a mere farmer: my talk, which would scarce interest you on Broadway, is all of fuafua and tuitui, and black boys, and planting and weeding, and axes and cutlasses; my hands are covered with blisters and full of thorns ... Life goes on in enchantment' (*Letters*, II, 212). What is interesting from the correspondence is that, despite his obvious delight in trashing the Stevensons in their Samoan kingdom, Adams over a period came to wonder at Louis's strength of character.

[to John Hay (1838–1905) one time private secretary to President Lincoln, 16 Oct 1890]   We rode about four or five miles up the hills and struck a clearing covered with burned stumps with a very improvised house in the middle and a distant sea-view over the forest below.[1] There Stevenson and his wife were perched – like queer birds – mighty queer ones too. Stevenson has cut some of his hair; if he had not, I think he would have been positively alarming. He seems never to rest, but perches like a parrot on every available projection, jumping from one to another, and talking incessantly. The parrot was very dirty and ill-clothed as we saw him, being perhaps caught unawares, and the female was in rather worse trim than the male. I was not prepared for so much eccentricity in this particular, and could see no obvious excuse for it. Stevenson has bought, I am told, four hundred acres of land at ten dollars an acre, and is about to begin building. As his land is largely mountain, and wholly impenetrable forest, I think that two hundred acres would have been enough, and the balance might have been profitably invested in soap.... Stevenson claims to be very well, and has not the slightest intention of dying, but his emaciation is a marvel, and his weakness is such that, if not supplemented by a sufficient diet of self-esteem, I think he would drop, as it were, all standing. Meanwhile he goes through fatigues, deprivations and squalor enough to kill a dozen robust Samoan chiefs, not to mention his wife, who is a wild Apache.

[to John Hay, 4 Jan 1891] My dyspepsia here is greatly modified by a counter-diet of mangoes. Anyway it is due to the hothouse atmosphere of the tropics, where the slightest physical effort wastes itself in perspiration. Stevenson is the only man whose energy resists the atmosphere, and Stevenson owes it to his want of flesh to perspire with. La Farge usually announces his arrival in one of the happy phrases which are La Farge's exclusive property: 'Here comes the *aïku* [*aitu*]!' An aïku is a Samoan ghost, spirit, or demon in the Greek sense. The islands swarm with aïku, sometimes friendly, as of dead parents of children; sometimes hostile, as of tempters; occasionally verging on flashes or symbols like the rainbow, or certain rocks; but at bottom simply uncanny. This is the note of Stevenson, although to us he has been human, not to say genial. He comes to pass half the day with us. He gives us letters to Tahiti and the Marquesas. His talk is lively, agreeable, and almost quiet. Yet in spite of this, he is an aïku, and whenever we catch him unprepared, we feel that he has no real body, but only eyes, hair and bones. His strength or energy is phenomenal; he has done in these seas ten times what would have done me for life; he enjoys hardships that none but an aïku could face, and he is killing his poor wife, who, though another aïku of great promise, is yet unable to keep him from sucking her blood.

[to Elizabeth Cameron, 8 Nov 1890] Stevenson returned our call the other day, and passed several hours with us. He was cleaner, and his wife was not with him, for which reasons perhaps he seemed less like W– E–. He talked very well, as usual, but said nothing that stuck very hard. He will tell his experiences in the form of Travels, and I was rather surprised to find that his range of study included pretty much everything: geology, sociology, laws, politics and ethnology. We like him, but he would be, I think an impossible companion. His face has a certain beauty, especially the eyes, but it is the beauty of disease. He is a strange compound of callousness and susceptibility, and his susceptibility is sometimes more amusing than his callousness. We were highly delighted with one trait which he showed in absolute unconsciousness of its simplicity. The standard of domestic morality here is not what is commonly regarded as rigid. Most of the traders and residents have native wives, to whom they are married after the native custom: that is, during pleasure. A clerk in the employ of an American trader named Moors was discovered in too close relation with the native wife of a lawyer named Carruthers. The offence was condoned once, and this lenity seemed very proper to Stevenson, who declared that he had no difficulty in forgiving his wife once, but not a second time. Recently the scandal was renewed, and caused great tribulation. Stevenson was deeply outraged, and declared that he would no longer dine with Moors for fear of meeting the clerk. Moors, who has had various wives to say nothing of incidental feminine resources, was also scandalized, and dismissed the clerk, though the clerk was indispensable to his business.... The unfortunate clerk is the victim of outraged Samoan morality, and is to be sent back to San Francisco where the standard is, I presume, less exalted. This part of Stevenson's talk was altogether the most humorous, and as grotesque as the New Arabian Nights; but Stevenson was not in the least conscious of our entertainment.[2]

[to Elizabeth Cameron, 27 Nov 1890] We have seen much of Stevenson these last few days, and I must say no more in ridicule, for he has been extremely obliging, and given me very valuable letters of introduction to Tahiti and the Marquesas. He has amused and interested us, too, and greatly by his conversation. Last evening he came at five o'clock and brought his wife to dine with us. Their arrival was characteristic. He appeared first, looking like an insane stork, very warm and very restless. I was not present, and the reception fell on little Mrs Parker, who is as delicate and fragile as Stevenson, but as quiet and gentle as a flower. Presently Mrs Stevenson in a reddish cotton nightgown, staggered up the steps, and sank into a chair, gasping and unable to speak. Stevenson hurried to explain that she was overcome by the heat and the walk. Might she lie down? Mrs Parker sacrificed her own bed, and gave her some cognac. Stevenson says that his wife has some disease, I know not what, of a paralytic nature, and suffers greatly from its attacks. I know only that when I arrived soon afterwards, I found her on the piazza chatting with Mrs Parker, and apparently as well and stalwart as any other Apache squaw.

His sufferings here as a farmer are his latest fund for humor, and he described, with bounds of gesticulation, how he had just bought two huge farm horses, and stabled them in a native house near his; and how at midnight, in a deluge of rain and a gale of wind he had heard unearthly howls from the stable, and had ventured out with a lantern. As he approached, by the glimmer of the light, he became aware of two phantom excrescences protruding from the stable roof. These were his horses' heads, which, after eating off the roof of the house, were wildly tossing in the storm, while the legs and bodies were inconceivably mixed up, inside. . . .

Enough of Stevenson. His stories are not for me to tell, and towards eleven o'clock, we summoned our boat crew, and sent him back by water, in the moonlight to Apia. We may never see him again, for he talks of going to Auckland next week, and some day I suppose we too shall go away somewhere.[3] Our parting last night, on the beach, in the Samoan moonlight, was appropriate, and my last distinct vision of his wife was her archaic figure in the arms of my coxswain, trying to get her legs – or feet – over the side of my boat.

[to Elizabeth Cameron, 15 Dec 1890] My object is only to find out what they have done; so I listened with gravity to Mata-afa, who labored on, until at length Stevenson dropped in, and we turned to discussing the latest appearance of a certain interesting spirit or female enchantress who recently killed a young chief, in whose father's house we stayed at Vao-vai. I thought then that we were rather an interesting company, as the world goes. Mata-afa may fairly rank as one of the heroic figures of our times.[4] Stevenson is a person sufficiently known to fame; and La Farge will probably not be less well known a hundred years hence than now. The group struck me as rather a peculiar one, considering that we were a good many thousand miles from places where people usually hunt lions, and I felt encouraged to think that even here I was not in an atmosphere of hopeless mental stagnation. Stevenson stayed to dine with us, and was quite on his manners, but as usual had to borrow Sewall's clothes.[5] La Farge and I promised to come up to his place next morning (Sunday), and to send our breakfast before us. I cannot conceive why they should ever be without food in the house, but apparently their normal condition is foodless, and they not only consented but advised my making sure of my own breakfast. Stevenson himself seems to eat little or nothing, and lives on cheap French *vin ordinaire* when he can get it. I do not know how this régime affects his complaint, for I do not know what his complaint is. I supposed it to be phthisis, or tubercular consumption; but am assured here that his lungs are not affected.... We found Stevenson and his wife just as they had appeared at our first call, except that Mrs Stevenson did not think herself obliged to put on slippers, and her nightgown costume had apparently not been washed since our visit. Stevenson himself wore still a brown knit woollen sock on one foot, and a greyish purple sock on the other, much wanting in heels, so that I speculated half my time whether it was the same old socks, or the corresponding alternates, and concluded that he must have worn them ever since we first saw him. They were evidently his slippers for home wear. He wore also, doubtless out of deference to us, a pair of trousers, and a thin flannel shirt; but, by way of protest, he rolled up the sleeves above his shoulders, displaying a pair of the thinnest white arms I ever beheld, which he brandished in the air habitually as though he wanted to throw them away.... Both La Farge and I came round to a sort of liking for Mrs Stevenson, who is more human than her husband. Stevenson is an *a-itu* – uncanny.[6] His fragility passes description, but his endurance passes his fragility. I cannot conceive how such a bundle of bones, unable to work on his writing without often taking to his bed as his working place, should have gone through the months of exposure, confinement and bad nourishment which he has enjoyed. Their travels have broken his wife up; she is a victim to rheumatism which is becoming paralysis, and, I suspect, to dyspepsia; she says that their voyages have caused it; but Stevenson gloats over discomforts and thinks that every traveller should sail for months in small cutters rancid with cocoa-nut oil and mouldy with constant rain, and should live on coral atolls with nothing but cocoa-nuts and poisonous fish to eat.[7]

[to John Hay, 20 Jan 1891] Go to Tahiti I must, and yet if you knew the disgust we have for another ocean voyage, you would feel our heroic qualities. Stevenson absolutely loves dirty vessels and suffocating cabins filled with mildew and cockroaches; he has gone off to Sydney chiefly, I think, to get some more seadirt on, the land-dirt having become monotonous. By the bye, for our eternal souls' sake, don't repeat what I say of the Stevensons, for he has been extremely and voluntarily obliging to us. I have none but the friendliest feelings for him, and would not for the world annoy him by illnatured remarks; yet he is dirty. On that Samoan soil I feel no fear of contradiction, though some of contact. A man who likes cruising on steamers and copra-schooners in the South Seas, must be able to stand more than becomes a clean man.

NOTES

1. His companions were Harold Marsh Sewall (1860–1924), Consul-General at Samoa, minister to Hawaii (1897), and the artist John La Farge (1835–1910). Louis accompanied Sewall on a three-week tour of Tutuila in Eastern Samoa.
2. An illuminating account of domestic morality and the impact of the *aholes* (white intruders) upon the Samoan people, and the hypocrisies inherent in colonial attitudes, about which Louis grew increasingly irritated.
3. Stevenson went to Sydney in Jan 1891 to bring his mother back to Samoa. Hearing how conditions were at this stage of development, Maggie prudently departed for relatives in New Zealand.
4. Adams agreed with Stevenson's estimate of Mataafa, one of three Samoan chiefs involved in the power struggles among British, German and American interests for control of the islands. Rumours spread that Louis was helping to arm Mataafa's forces, although in fact he was doing little more than giving sympathetic ear to native grievances and cursing the great powers: 'We sit and pipe upon a volcano, which is being stoked by bland, incompetent amateurs', he wrote to Baxter the following year (quoted in Balfour, *Life*, II, 139).
5. Writing to Henry James two weeks later, Louis said he had not been able to return the clothes – 'as soon as the wash comes in, I plump straight into the American consul's shirt or trousers!' (*Letters*, II, 214).
6. Vailima was thought to be haunted by 'aitu', the demon ghosts of both sexes which played such a part in Samoan culture. On one occasion during the clearing of high bush, a Samoan worker rushed back to the house crying that he had been molested by an 'aitu'. The spirit world is brilliantly conveyed in 'The Beach of Falesá' (1892).
7. Amidst the preponderance of unsympathetic portrayals of Fanny in recent years, it is interesting to interpret the underlying messages here concerning the toll Louis's needs must have taken on his wife's health. Furnas is still worth attention in this regard (see *Voyage*, 253–9).

The Misspent Sunday

W. E. CLARKE

From 'Robert Louis Stevenson in Samoa', *Yale Review*, X (Jan 1921) 275–96. The Reverend William Edward Clarke (1854–1922) was the London Missionary Society's representative in Samoa. About as knowledgeable a mentor as Louis could have hoped to meet, Clarke knew the people and their customs well, and took the new arrival around schools and communities on the island. A simple, devout man, Clarke had to keep Stevenson up to the mark where Sunday worship was concerned. For his part Stevenson, the one-time agnostic, probably benefited from Clarke's practical Christianity. Louis wrote of Clarke: 'A man ... I esteem and like to the sole of his boots. I prefer him to anyone in Samoa, and to most people in the world' (quoted in Field, *This Life*, 332). When Louis lay dying, Clarke was at his side. He accompanied the cortège to the burial place on Mount Vaea and recited Louis's own prayer at the interment, part of which reads:

> Bless to us our extraordinary mercies; if the day come when these must be taken, have us play the man under affliction. Be with our friends; be with ourselves. Go with each of us to rest; if any awake, temper to them the dark hours of watching; and when the day returns, return to us, our sun and comforter, and call us up with morning faces and with morning hearts – eager to labour – eager to be happy, if happiness shall be our portion – and if the day be marked for sorrow, strong to endure it.

My recollection of Stevenson dates from the day of his first arrival in Samoa. I remember it well. A gorgeous tropical morning; the sun relentless; the trade wind sweeping across the bay; the white surf leaping over the reef in clouds of glistening silver; the two giant palms which mark the approach to the mission compound arching and creaking in the gale, their plumes crackling like the rattle of musketry. A little vessel was fluttering into port; it skimmed swiftly across the bay, and presently dropped anchor amid the small flotilla lying at rest.

An hour later, making my way along the 'Beach' – the sandy track on the sea front with its long, straggling line of stores and saloons – I met a little group of three European strangers, two men and a woman. The latter wore a loose native gown, a brilliant plaid shawl across her shoulders, a Gilbertese straw hat, its crown encircled with strings of shells, a necklace of scarlet berries; across her shoulders was strung a mandolin. I noticed that her hair was jet-black, her face browned and burnt by the sun. She wore large crescent gold earrings, and her bare feet were encased in white canvas shoes. The central figure of the group was a tall gaunt man in shirt sleeves, with a brown velvet coat flung over one shoulder, a white broad-peaked yachting cap, white flannel trousers, once clean, a cigarette in his mouth, and a camera dangling on its strap in one hand. He turned on me a pair of singularly arresting and penetrating eyes as he passed. A younger man walked by his side, clad in a striped pyjama suit, the undress uniform of most European traders in those seas, a broad-brimmed, slough straw hat, dark blue sun spectacles; he carried a banjo in one hand, a concertina in the other. They had evidently just landed from the little schooner now lying placidly at anchor, and my first impression was that probably they were a party of vaudeville artists *en route* to Australia or the States, compelled by their poverty to take the cheap conveyance of a trading vessel, and exploring ashore while the vessel was detained in port. . . .

One evening as we were sitting together on the veranda, the conversation turned on the strange fascination that the unusual and horrible has for most of us in fiction. Stevenson remarked that he himself enjoyed it, and that when he took an excursion into the region of the dreadful, Edgar Allan Poe had a grim fascination for him. I replied that I had recently read a modern story, 'The Strange Case of Dr Jekyll and Mr Hyde', which had so enthralled me by its psychological insight and fearsome climax that I had sat up reading through the night, unable to leave it till the finish. 'By the way,' I remarked, 'it was written by a namesake of yours; have you read it?' 'Yes,' he said, 'I have not only read it, but I wrote it before I read it, and dreamed it before I wrote it.' Thus I learned for the first time that my new friend was a well-known and distinguished figure in the world of literature. . . .

There is a little English church at Apia in which a service is held on Sunday evenings, after the native services are concluded, and R.L.S. and his mother regularly attended it. There was a curiously composite assembly. A sprinkling of refined and educated men, the consuls, officers from the warships, a few government officials, a number of the men of the 'Beach' – rough in exterior, but men who had graduated in the school of travel and experience – a residuum of half-castes and illiterates who could receive truth only in its simplest form. Amongst this motley crowd sat R.L.S. and his mother, the latter's fine, intellectual face alight with eager devoutness; R.L.S. reverent in attitude, tender to his mother, fraternal to myself.

Stevenson and his mother usually spent the week-end at the mission house to avoid the long ride in the heavy night damp after the heated atmosphere of the church, but if the night were exceptionally fine, with a good moon, she rode back to Vailima with her son. It was pleasant to see the attention of R.L.S. to his mother, and her passionate devotion to him; and as we listened to the conversation of this gracious lady it was easy to divine from whom he received the heritage of brilliant fancy and quaint thought which made him great. The friendship, inspiration, and sympathy I received in the delightful intercourse of those week-end visits are some of my most precious memories.

While thinking of the strong vein of deep religion which underlay the nature of this gay, witty, and vivacious life, I recall a visit to Samoa of Dr James Chalmers, the veteran pioneer missionary who was murdered by the natives in New Guinea, and who was affectionately known as 'Tamate' throughout the South Pacific. Chalmers was a man of infinite charm and humor, and a man whose daily life was one of peril, Papua at that time being saturated with cannibalism and savagery. He had come to Samoa to recruit native missionary volunteers for that dangerous service and was a guest at my house. R.L.S. was charmed with him and took up his abode with us during the whole month 'Tamate' was in Samoa. On Chalmers's departure R.L.S. wrote him a letter, a phrase of which is most illuminating: 'Oh Tamate, if I had met you when I was a boy and a bachelor how different my life would have been.'[1]

It will give some indication of the interest R.L.S. manifested in the religious life of the natives of Samoa when I mention that on two occasions he addressed the students of the pastors' training institution at Malua, and that for some months he taught a class of half-caste children in the Sunday School of the European church at Apia.

He was also much interested in a little monthly magazine printed in the vernacular, called the 'Sulu' (Torch), which enjoys a large circulation among the natives, and on one occasion he expressed a desire to contribute something to its pages. Needless to say, the offer was eagerly accepted, and he gave us the manuscript of the story of 'The Bottle Imp'. The story was duly translated into Samoan, was published as a serial in the pages of the 'Sulu', and was read with delight in hundreds of thatched Samoan houses before it appeared to gratify the army of more critical readers in Europe and America. It was the first excursion of the Samoans into the region of fiction, and, the scene being laid in Hawaii in a local coloring much like their own, it was difficult at first for them to realize that the characters were the creation of fancy and not veritable men and women.[2]

Stevenson thoroughly appreciated the peculiar difficulty of religious work among the cosmopolitan white population of Apia, and rarely offered suggestions, and never any criticism. He was, however, generous with his purse, and he never refused his personal service when it was asked. Remembering the frailty of his health, and the strenuous and meticulous labor he expended in his study, I was chary of asking his services.[3] I remember two occasions on which he made a public appearance. One was a lecture on the Marquesas, which he gave on behalf of the church funds; the other was a reading at an entertainment for some charitable object, at which he read the chapter on the hurricane from 'A Footnote to History', not then published. R.L.S. was not very successful as a lecturer. There was a crowded house, and a full treasury, but he was consumed with nervousness, and so obviously ill at ease that we all suffered with him....

I recall another time when Stevenson organized a paper-chase on horseback for a Sunday's amusement and, with a large company of young officers from the men-of-war in the harbor and the clerks and others connected with the German Plantation Company, careered with much vociferous noise through the native villages at the hour of worshp, to the great indignation and discomfort of the Samoan pastors. I believe that he persuaded himself at the moment that he was acting rightly, influenced by the sincere feeling that it was better for these young men to be so employed than in their usual Sabbath occupations, but also fully aware that it would be displeasing to us. R.L.S. did not turn up at the mission house on Monday, but the next day he sent an invitation to my wife and me to dine at Vailima. I declined, pleading my work, but really feeling too angry with him; my wife, however, went. When asked, she frankly said that I had not come because I had too much affection for him to quarrel, and I was feeling too sore to ignore the matter if we met. R.L.S. attempted an argument to justify himself, but my wife refused a discussion, exclaiming: 'I have no doubt you can easily silence me in argument, but I am astonished that you attempt any justification. You know quite well that you did wrong. What would Samoa be like without a Sabbath? And have you no thought of the effect of your conduct upon the natives, who regard you as a Christian man, and as our friend, and do you, moreover, think you have set a dignified example to the young Englishmen and Germans, many of them only just freed from the restraints of home?'

R.L.S. stood tugging at his moustache during this fusillade, a group of German officers on the veranda near him looking on wonderingly. After musing in silence for some minutes, he turned round and, holding out his hand, exclaimed: 'Forgive me, Mrs Clarke, you are quite right, and I was altogether wrong. I regret it with all my heart.' 'Well,' said my wife, looking significantly across at the Germans, 'you must prove your contrition.' R.L.S. consented and, advancing towards them, remarked that he had just been expressing his regret for the part they took in the paperchase on Sunday, assuring her, on their behalf and his own, that they would not again be guilty of such misconduct. 'I am sure,' he added, 'that you feel with me that we were altogether wrong, and setting an extremely bad example to all the "Beach".' At this moment one of the young English naval officers rode up and my wife remarked, 'There is your second opportunity, you owe it to your own countrymen.' 'Ah!' replied he, 'now you ask me something much harder, but I'll do it'; and, greeting the young officer, he went on to say with that charm of manner so entirely his own: 'I was just expressing to these gentlemen my contrition and regret that we should have allowed ourselves to forget our principles as we did last Sunday; we all did wrong and I have been apologizing to Mrs Clarke for the pain we must have caused our missionary friends. I am sure that I express the feelings of us all when I assure her we shall not so transgress again.' To make such an avowal in a place like Apia, where the Sabbath was systematically disregarded by most of the white population, required plenty of moral courage. News travels quickly along the 'Beach'. Before night it was known in every German household, and in the wardroom of every gunboat in the bay, that R.L.S. had openly expressed his penitence for the misspent Sunday.

NOTES

1. The Reverend Dr James Chalmers (1841–1901), explorer and missionary, noted for his unorthodox methods. He was one of Stevenson's heroes (along with General Gordon): 'a man I admire for his virtues, love for his faults' (*Letters*, II, 220). According to one witness, Clarke invited Louis to meet Chalmers at the Apia Mission House in 1890 and the two 'Celtic spirits sparked and soared', until at one point Chalmers demonstrated a highland fling on the missionary verandah (Caldwell, *Last Witness*, 155). At Goaribari Island, in April 1901, Chalmers and a fellow missionary were knocked on the head, killed and eaten.

2. 'The Bottle Imp' was published in the *New York Herald* in four instalments, Feb–March 1891 (*Island Nights' Entertainments*, 1893). It tells of a genie's powers of making dreams come true, but with the prospect of damnation to the last owner of its bottle prison. For Samoans it explained the story-teller's wealth and occasioned requests from visitors to see the bottle itself. Translation into Samoan was undertaken by the Reverend Arthur E. Claxton; the story ran in seven instalments May–Dec 1891 in *O Le Sulu Samoa* (Torch), the magazine of the London Missionary Society (Swearingen, 144).

3. Immersing himself in local life, Stevenson acquired some proficiency in the Samoan language. His tutor, the Reverend Samuel James Whitmee (1838–1907), was delighted by his pupil's perseverance, noting that on one occasion, having missed 'class', he excused himself by saying that he felt 'like an empty bag' after having just finished a novel: *Catriona* ('Tusitala, a new reminiscence of R.L.S.', *Outward Bound*, Feb 1922, 355–60).

The Soul of a Peasant

FANNY STEVENSON

From Fanny and Robert Louis Stevenson, *Our Samoan Adventure*, ed. Charles Neider (1955) 25–6, 31, 37–8, 107, 137, 221. This work splices excerpts from Louis's *Vailima Letters* with Fanny's Samoa diaries of 1890 to 1893. Fanny is at last in the foreground, and deserves it. In dry, matter-of-fact terms (for she had none of Louis's felicities of style), she shows the daily routine of Vailima life with which she was so deeply involved. At 50 she ran a large household efficiently in a climate of earthquakes, hurricanes and rainstorms that set the house swaying and groaning. She gardened with ferocious zeal, while Louis pursued his writing and politics. Her journal is full of details from the natural world of tropical island life: plagues of mosquitoes, burnished beetles, swarming bees, wild pigs, tree frogs, cows trampling her precious vegetables and mysterious night creatures slaughtering the chickens. She coped with servants and their awful injuries amidst the gathering threats of war, reacting bravely when violence broke out on their very doorstep. Her mother-in-law had to be pacified if prayers were scamped, and Joe Strong, her son-in-law, added to her trials, and in turn upset Belle. Small wonder Fanny's own health at last gave way. Many of her problems arose from low self-esteem, which emerges poignantly from the editor's restoration of crucial passages previously deleted from the text, some of which are reproduced here.

[from Diary, 14 Oct 1890]   After Mr Moors and Mr Willis were gone, Louis volunteered to show me the banana patch, carrying a knife with him to clear the path.[1] These explorations on one's own estate are most exciting. For a little way we followed a pretty open path that had been cleared by Louis, but by and by it began to close up and become treacherously boggy under foot. Several times we were ankle deep in mud and water and Louis had to slash down the lianas and tall vegetation that obstructed our way. Before very long Louis cried out, 'Behold your banana patch!'

There it was, sure enough, a great number of sturdy thick-set young trees, many with bunches of fruit hanging above the strange purple flower of the plant, choked with a rank undergrowth and set with their roots in sluggishly running water. Here and there the gigantic leaves of the great taro spread out, dark shining green. It was too much for Louis, who fell to clearing on the spot, while I went on to the end of the plantation. Once or twice I was nearly stuck in the bog, but managed to drag myself from the ooze by clutching to a strong plant....

[23 Oct 1890]   Louis says that I have the soul of a peasant, not so much that I love working in the earth and with the earth, but because I like to know that it is my own earth that I am delving in. Had I the soul of an artist, the stupidity of possessions would have no power over me. He may be right. I would as soon think of renting a child to love as a piece of land. When I plant a seed or a root, I plant a bit of my heart with it and do not feel that I have finished when I have had my exercise and amusement.[2] But I do feel not so far removed from God when the tender leaves put forth and I know that in a manner I am a creator. My heart melts over a bed of young peas, and a blossom on my rose tree is like a poem written by my son. After I had made a perfect garden and it had been sold and bought several times I beheld it ploughed up, the vines torn down, my trees cut for firewood, the flowers uprooted – planted in potatoes. I could not have felt worse had I seen my favourite riding horse, hock-kneed and ruined, dragging the plough. After all, I believe we present our home the best of it: we possess something deep and strong and never the evanescent sports of the artist. I love the earth not only when she is beautiful but when she is called ugly. I cannot play with her and love her. My things, my house have favoured me, and I cannot loosen the strings that bind us without something breaking. . . .

[5 Nov 1890] My garden looks quite like a real garden under Lafaele[3] and a very handsome Samoan. It also looks something like a graveyard, the beds being made about the size and shape of graves. Lafaele asks every time I go to the garden if I am *surely* going to plant cabbages. Unless I plant cabbages he will feel that his time has been wasted and he betrayed. Consequently, I am forced to plant cabbages. I have found a great many lemon trees in full bearing in the further hedge, amongst citron and limes. One day, bent on a voyage of discovery, I lost myself in the bush. To be lost in a tropical bush is a very alarming thing. The vegetation is so dense that there are no shadows, and the whereabouts of the sun are an unsolvable mystery. And yet the terror has an element of pleasure in it, difficult to explain. Had I not feared that Louis would be alarmed at my absence I should have consciously gone deeper into the wood. As it was, I trusted to my instinct, which always betrays me in a town but seldom if ever in the bush, and in a short time found myself in the edge of the clearing.

I am feeling very depressed, but my vanity, like a newly felled tree, lies prone and bleeding. Louis tells me that I am not an artist but a born, natural peasant. I have often thought *that* the happiest life and not one for criticism. I feel most embittered when I am assured that I am really what I had wished to be. Of course, I meant a peasant without aspirations. Perhaps if I had known in time I should have had none of it! I have been brooding on my feelings and holding my head before the glass and now I am ashamed. Louis assures me that the peasant class is a most interesting one, and he admires it hugely. . . .

[23 Sep 1891] There is a big row on hand concerning – prayer! It seems that Lafaele had to be with the wounded horse at prayer time and Joe, having scalded his right hand very badly, took Austin away to help him with the fowls.[4] All this work *must* be done before the sun gets too hot, and it could not be helped. Unfortunately Belle was caught prowling like a cat, with no ostensible – and I fear no real – business on hand, and then there was an explosion. Mrs S considers that she has received a personal insult from them all, and when Austin came to her for his lessons he was sent flying.

A fight about prayers is really enough to bring a cynical smile to the lips of a bishop. Mrs S says she will not be left to pray with only servants. I am afraid that distinction is not made in other quarters. I see again she dislikes the life here which we find so enchanting and is disappointed and soured that she is not able to persuade us to throw it all up and go to the colonies. We have given the colonies a fair trial and they mean death to Louis, whereas this is life and reasonable health. . . .

[25 Dec 1891] When Lloyd and I were coming down to Apia we forded the river at the plantation (Hufnagel's) and made a different route.[5] As we were crossing a broad open common, Lloyd cried out to me, 'Look at the bird!' Just in front of us, on a low white stump, sat a large white owl. As we came quite close to it, it slowly turned round its head and gazed steadily at us for some moments with big, solemn, questioning eyes. It was very like an aitu. Perhaps it was one. I told this tale to Louis, which reminded him to tell me of a creature he had met in his study. It was one of those enormous salmon-coloured moths whose hearts, or something in their inside, beats against your hand when you hold them, so loudly that you can hear them. Louis cannot bear the sight of them because they are marked like a skeleton. I suppose they are a variety of the death's head moth. The wretched thing was determined to burn itself at the lamp.

I am long past trying to save the ordinary moth from its usual fate, but a moth as big as a hummingbird we can none of us bear to see going to such a terrible fate. When the little moths are scorched, it is easy enough to kill them, but it would be a brave man who could put his foot on a salmon death's head. This moth of Louis's evaded him continually and at last dropped to the floor, apparently under the table. Louis got down on his knees to look for him and to his surprise discovered that the table seemed to be on fire. He could see a beautiful glowing point, which on further examination turned out to the insect's *eye*! . . .

[20 July 1893]   I wish I were able to write a little tale that I might save some money of my own. I know that people speak of my [about eight words missing]. I don't mind that so much, for there is such a blessing and pleasure in sharing anything in the [about six words missing]. All the money I have earned [about eight words missing] away to other people. Of the last I got twenty-five dollars out of a hundred and fifty, which I sent to my dying brother-in-law. I wonder what would become of a man, and to what he would degenerate, if his life was that of a woman's: to get the 'run of her teeth' and presents of her clothes, and supposed to be always under bonds of the deepest gratitude for any further sums. I would work very hard to earn a couple of pounds a month, and I could easily earn much more, but there is my position as Louis's wife, therefore I cannot. Louis comes in and proposes to send [about two words missing] which is rather awkward: both about the German boy and the above, which looks like begging for money, which idea would shame me beyond measure.[6]

NOTES

1. Alex Willis, a carpenter involved with the Vailima construction work. Willis had married Laulii, a Samoan of great charm and a favourite with Louis. Her reminiscences, dictated to her husband, resulted in a book, *The Story of Laulii* (1889).
2. Fanny took her horticulture seriously, studying all the books she could lay hands on, taking cuttings, experimenting, and consulting experts at Kew, Brisbane, Honolulu and Florida. This heartfelt passage was deleted from the original text at Monterey State Historical Monument.
3. Lafaele (Raphael), a favourite in the Vailima household.
4. Another deleted passage from the diary. Austin Strong (1881–1952), Belle's son, joined the Vailima household when he was ten. He was sent to school in Monterey in 1892, returning home for holidays in Samoa. After a period as a landscape architect, he turned to play-writing, in which he enjoyed popular success with over ten Broadway shows, among them *Seventh Heaven* (1922) which ran for 704 performances and was made into a film. Among his other successes were *The Toymaker of Nuremburg* (1907), *A Good Little Devil* (1913) and *Three Wise Fools* (1918).
5. Captain Hufnagel, German manager of the Vailele plantation, who supplied Fanny with trees and roses.
6. This revealing passage was also deleted from the diary.

A Feast at Vailima

MARIE FRASER

From *In Stevenson's Samoa* (1895) 27–9, 32, 163–9. Marie Fraser was an English actress who played Nora in Ibsen's *A Doll's House* at Edinburgh in November 1890 and again at a London theatre in January 1891. Late the following year she visited Samoa with her mother. They took a cottage near Vailima, and soon Marie was scrounging material for a book. Aunt Maggie describes an occasion when Lloyd took the actress to the banana patch and seemed to get lost in the bush (*Letters from Samoa 1891–1895*, 253). Louis, too, liked the 'pretty blonde and ... graceful horsewoman' (Mackay, 411) and, when a hurricane threatened, persuaded her to stay at Vailima. She shopped with Louis and Belle at Moors' store and joined the Christmas festivities. Fanny loathed her, and made no reference to her visit in her three-year diary. Marie Fraser published some of the material here in *Cornhill*, XXXI (July 1894) 27–33, and in *English Illustrated Magazine*, XI (1893–4), 768–75.

Mr Stevenson and his family received their friends on the verandah, generally barefooted, always bareheaded, and clad in loose garments suitable to the climate. A number of happy, guileless-looking retainers, clad in Stuart tartan lava-lavas, the Vailima livery, grouped themselves about, suitably filling in a picturesque background. These were the 'house boys', all characters, and all good Samoans. There were a host of 'outdoor boys', too, who worked on the plantations and looked after the horses and cows. They became visible from time to time, especially in the evening, when Mrs Stevenson's son and daughter and I used to play guitar, mandoline, and banjo. This fascinated the natives, and they appeared in twos and threes out of the darkness till there was quite a crowd sitting on the verandah keeping time to the music; and they always took care to encourage us with the most outrageous flattery, of which they thoroughly appreciated the humour.

On the 13th of November a *fête* was held at Vailima to celebrate the birthday of the poet and novelist, and it was characteristic of the host that the gathering consisted almost entirely of natives, very few white people being present.[1] It had been a raging storm of wind and rain all day, but towards evening the rain ceased and the wind fell; nevertheless, it was fortunate that we had been invited to remain all night, as the road was reduced to a deplorable condition. After a hearty welcome from Mr and Mrs Stevenson, who were surrounded by native chiefs, their wives, &c., and a drink of kava, we were carried away to be suitably decorated for the feast.[2] Ropes of many-coloured, sweet-smelling flowers were twisted round our necks and waists, and wreaths placed on our heads. Everyone was decked out in like manner – our host wearing his wreath of jessamine with grace and distinction, as if to the manner born....

When everyone had thoroughly enjoyed the island fare, a few appropriate speeches were made. A chief who sat at the foot of the – well, the board, after proposing the health of 'Tusitala' (the writer of tales), who replied in a few kindly words to his island friends, commenced the function of sending round the kava. *He* would make no mistake about the order in which it should be served. The large kava bowl was placed before him, and taking a small bowl of polished cocoa-nut, he filled it with kava, while he chanted in a loud voice to whom it was to be taken. It was to 'Tusitala', who clapped his hands while the servitor took it to him. Before drinking he held up the basin, and looking towards his guests said, 'Ia manuia!' (Here's to you!); to which everyone answered, 'Soi fua!' (May you live long!). Next it was passed to Mrs Louis Stevenson, the same formula of 'Ia manuia!' and 'Soi fua!' always being repeated; then to Mrs Stevenson, our host's mother, a clever, delightful old Scotch lady, who heartily toasted all present. Soon the chief shouted in Samoan it was for the 'New great lady', and the cup was taken to my friend. Then he ordered the kava to be carried to 'Matalanumoana', and while we speculated as to who that could be, it was brought smilingly to me. On inquiring what that meant, it was translated as 'The fair young stranger with blue eyes from over the seas', and to the end of our sojourn in Samoa that name stuck to me, the smallest children rolling it out....

When he had finished a book he would sometimes rest from his writing for a short time. Then a new romance would begin to piece itself together in his mind, till it took tangible shape, and then, by five in the morning his lamp would be lit and his pen flying over the paper, while he lay propped up by pillows on a narrow bed in a little room which looked out on the mountains.

He would continue without intermission, sometimes till twelve o'clock; but generally he would stop at eleven for tiffin, and rarely returned to his writing again during the day; but next morning he would be at it again by five. Sometimes he dictated, and then he would walk about, dictating with great rapidity, and seldom having to correct anything afterwards.

The library at Vailima was a beautiful room opening off the second verandah, and the walls lined with books, arms and pictures.[3] 'But I can't write in that room,' said our host; 'it's all so *suitable* for a literary man – drives every idea out of my head. Sometimes I go in to look up something, but I generally seize the book and rush off with it to my den.' So we crossed the flying bridge from one verandah to another, and entered his little workroom, with its bare floor and varnished walls. 'This,' he continued, curling himself up on a mat in the corner, 'is the sort of place I can write in – where nothing looks like literature. A deal kitchen table and a small bed are all I require; chairs are an unnecessary luxury; a mat flung on the ground is all one wants.' And from where we sat could be seen the snow-white tropic birds soaring over Vaea, the summit of which he always spoke of as his last resting-place on earth. While we were talking the whole place shook and vibrated with earthquake shocks; and, as Tusitala remarked, 'It is not so much what happens as what one waits for!' . . .

It was strange that, with his poetic mind and fastidious love of tone and colour, he had almost no ear for music. In the evening we used to sit on the verandah, or lounge in hammocks slung from the supports of the second verandah, and three of us used to play guitar, mandoline and banjo. We could make the most discordant sounds, or play our instruments horribly out of tune, the humid atmosphere rendering them independent of each other in a very short time – it never disturbed Louis Stevenson; he would placidly continue his conversation with his wife or mother (the latter a delightful old Scotch lady), or any visitor who happened to be staying at Vailima, and while he talked he would thoughtfully stroke the backs of Maud and Henry with his lithe feet and long toes. Animals loved him, and those two house cats always tried to lie within reach of his sympathetic touch.

It was a lonely life as far as white people were concerned, but the most favoured guests were his own brown neighbours. Sometimes a superficial globe-trotter, or some British or American acquaintance, would arrive at Apia by the San Francisco mail packet, and would ride up to Vailima to make a brief call on the Stevensons. They received a hearty welcome from Mrs Stevenson. Sometimes Louis would be visible, but just as often he did not appear; if he was busy on a new book he never allowed visitors to interfere with his writing. Occasionally, however, a friend who had been cruising on board some trading schooner would land at Upolu; then, indeed, the novelist was interested in his guest. He would listen with avidity to the accounts of the gales he had encountered, or the characters who had been traded with, his black eyes blazing with excitement over any adventures and sparkling with enjoyment at any quaint tales. He revelled in those South Sea yarns, and when the clouds descended on Vailima, and a fire was kindled in the only fireplace in the island, we would sit round the 'tongafitie,' as the natives called it, and he would pour out his wonderful experiences while sailing for months among the islands, specially luxuriating in the yarns of mingled gore and profanity.[4] But he was so simple in his interests, any tale of humanity or animal life pleased him; nothing seemed to bore him. . . .

Tusitala told me of a certain white lady on whom he called, and he observed that the native girls in her house were wearing made dresses. On commenting on the matter to her, she answered, 'Yes, they are all clothed; no woman shall come into my presence who shows any part of her body!' 'Well,' continued Louis Stevenson, 'I just blazed at her. "Woman!" I thundered, "is your mind so base that you cannot see and admire what is beautiful in the form God Almighty has created? Do you not understand that their own dress is right for the climate and their simple way of living? and do you not see that the first thing you do on landing on this beautiful island is to pollute their minds and sully their modest thoughts?"'

NOTES

1. Louis's forty-second birthday (1892).
2. Kava, the root of a kind of pepper plant, grated or chewed and steeped in water, was usually drunk ceremonially and involved a precise ritual in presentation.
3. Referring to another visit to the library towards the end of 1892, she saw chairs, tables and floor littered with books in great piles, which Louis blamed on his cousin, Graham Balfour: 'he sometimes had diffi-

culty in finding things... But it's much better to leave them alone – things are more easily found when they are lying about' (*English Illustrated Magazine*, XI, (1893–4) 773).

4. Here the writer's imagination runs away with her. One of Louis's grandiose additions to the house – the fireplaces – seldom if ever blazed, at least according to Moors, but R.L.S. insisted that 'a fireplace makes a house home-like' (Moors, *With Stevenson*, 43). But the baronial hall nonetheless glittered with lights everywhere and braziers burning to keep the mosquitoes away.

Patriarchal Relations

VARIOUS

(1) from W. H. Triggs, 'Mr R. L. Stevenson as a Samoan Chief', *Cassell's Family Magazine*, 21 (1895) 183–7. An able and reliable journalist, William Henry Triggs asked Louis to check his copy before publication, so the facts are authentic. His account gives due regard to the unusual loyalty the Samoan servants felt for their master, and shows plainly how much the laird mentality manifested itself in this final phase. As one biographer succinctly put it: 'He liked to be chief of his clan' (Calder, 283); (2) from 'A Chat with Robert Louis Stevenson', *Today*, 1 (2 Dec 1893) 7–8. The interview is unsigned, but the editor, Jerome K. Jerome (1859–1927), author of *Three Men in a Boat* (1889), indicates 'a San Francisco journalist'. The perspective here dwells on more personal aspects of the Stevensons at Vailima.

(1) In the first instance, Mr R. L. Stevenson chose Apia, Samoa, as his place of residence because it suited his health, which has always been very delicate. He clings to it as a home because it is unconventional and free, and accords with his love for the untamed and romantic. If you question him on the subject, he will tell you that, as regards health, Honolulu suited him equally well; the Alps probably better: the very reason that would make most literary men avoid Samoa caused the author of 'Treasure Island' to select it.[1]

'I chose Samoa instead of Honolulu, for instance,' he informed the present writer, 'for the simple and eminently satisfactory reason that it is less civilised. Can you not conceive that it is awful fun?'

To the nineteenth-century Philistine fresh from the luxury and excitement of a bustling civilisation, this is at first a hard saying.

When we have seen Mr Stevenson at home, however, entering into the simple joys and sorrows of the interesting natives among whom he has cast his lot, living for the world's benefit, and yet himself keeping apart from its feverish allurements, we begin to understand the secret of his content.

Mr Stevenson's house is removed even from such semblance of nineteenth-century civilisation as is to be found in Apia, the little capital of Samoa. It lies about three or four miles from the beach of Apia up towards the hills. The first part of the road is civilised macadam. You turn up past the Tivoli Hotel, through plantations of cocoanut trees, interspersed with bananas, candlenut trees, bread-fruit trees, and other tropical productions.

You pass a few houses on the way, but not many – the suburban residences, no doubt, of traders and officials living in Apia.

From the gardens come brilliant flashes of colour from tropical flowers, all the more striking as they gleam upon you suddenly from the sombre depths of the plantation. Presently you come to a road that is not a road at all, and to bush that is only now being cleared in patches. English readers will best understand the position when I state that all the wood to build Mr Stevenson's house was carried about a third of the way on men's shoulders, and that all the stores and parcels are brought by pack-saddle. This important work is admirably performed by Donald and Edie, two old Auckland tramcar horses, a most excellent selection, the biggest and handsomest horses in the island. The Sydney Civil Service Co-operative Society – the popular writer's universal provider – have accurately gauged the tonnage of these faithful animals, and pack accordingly. They make their way through the forest, with its tall trees, lianas, wild pineapples, etc., wearing quite an air of importance, and, needless to say, their arrival is always an important event in the household.

When Mr Stevenson bought his land, the price was thought extravagant. He gave £1 an acre for about 300 acres, and there are other 73 acres in dispute. Nobody, however, could buy land so cheaply now. He has spent at least £2 000 on the residence. It is a large two-story house, with a verandah and balcony running round; and taking it altogether, it is by far the largest and finest house I saw in and around Apia.[2]

The owner is also gradually improving the estate by felling trees, opening up views, and cultivating the land. It is known as Vai

Lima, which means 'Five Waters' in Samoan, and indicates the number of streams which flow by the spot....

Mr Stevenson, of course, is mainly engaged with his literary work. As regards the household, he may be described as playing the part of veiled prophet in general. He rarely appears upon the scene unless some of the 'boys' have misbehaved. The reader must not imagine that these are frequent occasions, or that the misdemeanours are serious. 'The boys,' as Mr Stevenson told me, 'are awfully good, on the whole. They are more like a set of well-behaved young ladies. They are a perfectly honest people; nothing of value has ever been taken from our house, where doors and windows are always wide open; and upon one occasion, when white ants attacked the silver chest, the whole of my family plate lay spread upon the floor of the hall for two days unguarded.' The hall, it may be added, is on the ground floor, while the family all sleep upstairs....

If the visitor arrives at Vai Lima at about five o'clock he will very likely find Mr Osbourne and Mrs Strong playing lawn tennis with some of the boys who take it à *tour de rôle*, and sometimes go on with the game by themselves after the 'bosses' go in to dinner. Not always 'bosses' with regard to the game, be it understood, for some of the Samoans are capital players. At night you hear the Samoans singing in their houses, shouting with laughter, and speechifying.

At Mr Stevenson's last birthday feast there were great doings, one or two of which, as related by the author, illustrate the feeling of 'the boys.'

'You must know,' he said, 'that every chief who respects himself in Samoa must have an officer called a *Tulafale* – usually Englished "speaking man." It is a part, and perhaps the most momentous, of this officer's attributions to cry out the names at the *ava* drinking. This is done in a peculiar howl or song very difficult to acquire, and, I may say, to understand. He must also be fairly well versed in the true science of Samoan names, as no chief above a certain rank is ever "called" under his own name. He has another, an *ava* name for the purpose. Well, I had no *Tulafale*, and Mr Osbourne held a competition, in which three or four of our boys howled against each other. The judgment of Apollo fell upon one boy, who was instantly a foot taller.

'I am sorry to make such confession of my disrespectability, but I must continue. I had not only no *Tulafale* – I had no *ava* name. I was called plain, bald *"Tusitala,"* or *"Ona,"* which is only a sobriquet at the best.[3] On this coming to the knowledge of a high chief who was present, he paid me the graceful attention of giving me one of his own, and I was hurriedly warned before the event that I must look out and recognise the new name, Au-Mai-Taua-Ma-Le-Manuvao. The feast was laid on the floor of the hall – fifty feet by about eight of solid provisions. Fifteen pigs cooked whole, underground; two hundred pounds of beef, ditto of pork, two hundred pineapples, over four hundred head of taro, together with fish, chickens, Samoan prepared dishes, shrimps, oranges, sugar-cane, bananas, biscuit and tinned salmon in proportion. The biscuit and tinned salmon, though not exactly to *our* taste, are a favourite luxury of the Samoans. By night – and we sat down at four p.m. – there was nothing left beyond a few oranges and a single bunch of bananas. This is not to say, of course, that it was all eaten – the Samoans are comparatively dainty at a feast; but so soon as we rose the arduous and difficult task of dividing what remained between the different guests was at once entered into, and the retainers of our guests, white and Samoan, departed, laden, to the sea. The wretched giver of a feast thus wakens on the morrow with a clean house. But it is not all loss. All gifts or favours in Samoa are to be repaid in kind and in a proportion, and to my feast nobody had come empty-handed. It was rather strange to look out next morning and see my courtyard alive with cocks, hens, and chickens.'

(2) We met on the broad verandah of his island home, far back in the hills of Upolu, the land of the Southern Cross and the sacred hen.

There was a dim suspicion of a smile in the depths of his big black eyes as he extended his hand – a long, thin, cool, patrician hand, which fluttered for a moment in the palm of my large, moist paw. Then he withdrew a step, and eyed me with the air of a man who could read the thoughts of another better than he could express them himself. I started in to explain that I was not going to misrepresent nor garble the statements of earth's greatest living novelist.

'That's all right,' he said, laughing. 'Don't make matters worse. We know all about it. Come in and see what there is to be seen, and ask us all sorts of questions. Then run riot with your pen, and when the paper comes I'll read the article, damn till the air is blue, and everything will be all right.'

While extremely cordial in his manner, the novelist talked guardedly and was careful not to commit himself on any vital point. He steered wide of politics and all other matters pertaining to the situation in the islands.

He sat directly in front of me, viewing the ceiling in a retrospective manner and holding a home-made cigarette in his right hand. On a table within easy reach stood a can of tobacco, from which he rolled a fresh smoke as soon as the old one gave out. His attire consisted simply of a tight-fitting, sleeveless undershirt, cut decollette, and which set off his sparsely settled figure in startling relief. A pair of black trousers rolled up half way to the knees completed the toilet of this eccentric genius of the South Seas. His feet were bare, and while talking he rested his right foot across his left knee. It was a symmetrical foot, long and slender and beautifully arched, and as he talked he toyed among his toes with his disengaged hand. Somehow, it occurred to me while noticing these peculiarities that any man who would describe Robert Louis Stevenson as half clad when he was fully two-thirds covered was taking a mean advantage of the author's hospitality.

In stature Stevenson is a little above the medium, but woefully thin and pale. His face is gaunt and haggard, and wears an expression of continual weariness. In fact, he is ill most of the time, but is uniformly good-natured in spite of his afflictions. Callers are numerous at the big house in the hills, dropping in at all hours of the day and on all kinds of business, but the novelist is always ready to meet these social obligations.

We talked on various topics subject to interruptions, some of them of a startling nature. Mr Stevenson was preparing for a trip to Honolulu, and the house was in a state of turmoil incident to packing trunks and bags. Mrs Stevenson sat on the floor at one end of the table enjoying a cigarette of her own manufacture and packing shells in a cigar box for a friend in Honolulu.

'Louis, have you got a string?'

He hastily replied, 'No, dear; but I'll hunt for one.'

With that he hastened upstairs in search of twine, while his wife adroitly turned the conversation into the interviewing channel.

She dwelt at length on their outrageous mendacity, and cited one instance where a story had been published to the effect that Mr Stevenson once invited a gentleman in Samoa up to lunch, but advised him to bring a can of corned beef, if he expected anything to eat. During this interesting recital the novelist returned with a string, and, to the horror of the good lady, corroborated the tale.

'It was this way,' he explained. 'At that time, the butcher in Apia had not fully established his business. There was no regular killing day, and unless a person happened to be on hand at the slaughter no meat could be had. Sir Baden-Powell, travelling in the islands, was invited to the house, and I jocularly told him to bring some meat if he hoped to eat meat with us.[4] The yarn made the rounds minus the explanation, and gave rise to the rumour that we were starving to death. But we can stand it,' he added, with a laugh.

I asked him about his latest book, 'The Ebb Tide', which is now running in *To-Day*.[5]

'It isn't a book,' he said, 'and it's a brutal, brutal story about three first-class dead beats. It is a sea story, and a horrible one at that,' continued the author, stroking his chin, and smiling in anticipation of the shudders soon to convulse our readers.

'There are three of the dead beats,' he went on, 'two Englishmen and an American sea captain. They are all at Tahiti together, when a ship comes in with small-pox on board. Her skipper deserts, but the American captain is prevailed upon to take command, and the two Englishmen go with him. Oh, it's a brutal affair from beginning to end,' declared its author, indulging in a slight shudder himself.

Then we chatted over his work and his way of doing it.

He arises at six o'clock in the morning, eats breakfast shortly after, and works till noon. At two o'clock in the afternoon he takes up his pen again, and labours diligently till five o'clock. Sometimes he works too hard, and nervous prostration follows. It is then he seeks rest and recreation in a sea voyage, generally to Sydney and back, and the journey does him good. He was in the middle of a graphic description of the agonies endured while pausing in a passage of fiction, and turning his burning eyes to the ceiling in search of a reluctant word, when a scream from Mrs Stevenson on the back porch again interrupted the interview. We rushed out and found a robust Samoan seated on the verandah, and holding a bleeding foot in the air, with the lady fluttering about in a most distressing state of agitation.

It seems she had sent the man, who was her favourite gardener, into the brush to cut down a couple of young cinnamon trees. He somehow missed the trees, but managed to damage his foot. The novelist and his wife immediately set to work on the victim of chance with tender solicitude, and in the midst of this scene of lint and bandages I brought my visit to a close.

NOTES

1. The interview took place in Auckland in 1893. One reason Hawaii had been rejected as a permanent residence was that even with mean temperatures in the seventies it was not warm enough, and Stevenson detested Honolulu.

2. Actually 314 $1/2$ at about £1 per acre. Additions and developments made a total investment up to £4 000 (some $20,000), part of which came from sale of Skerryvore, nominally Fanny's (Furnas, 362-3). The estate was a constant financial burden as the Stevensons grew more obsessed with Vailima, for which upkeep alone cost some £1 500 annually. A second two-storey block was added, and furniture shipped from Heriot Row and Skerryvore. The staff grew to 19 servants (McLynn, 396-8). Comparisons with Scott's Abbotsford were unavoidable, as Louis was well aware.

3. Stevenson acquired several soubriquets. In the Marquesas, as the apparent owner of the *Casco*, he became 'Ona'. In Tahiti he exchanged names with the chief, Ori a Ori, and became Teriitera. In the Gilberts he was Kaupoi. The name by which he became best known is discussed in a reminiscence by the Reverend S. J. Whitmee, who explained that the Samoan version of his name would have given it six syllables, 'Setevinisoni'. Therefore it became 'tusi', to write, and 'tala', a story or stories (Masson, *I Can Remember*, 233). According to Balfour, the Reverend James Edward Newell (1852-1910) was the first to introduce Louis as 'Tusitala' to students at a training college in Malua run by the London Missionary Society (LMS), but Furnas credits a neighbouring chief Suemanu (*Voyage*, 385) (*Life*, II, 85). Newell, an authority on Samoan affairs, edited the LMS publication *O le Sulu O Samoa*.

4. (Henry) Warrington (Smyth) Baden Powell (1847-1921), served in the Royal Navy in various parts of the world and practised as a barrister in Admiralty, Wreck and Northern Circuit Courts. He first became known to Louis for articles on canoeing in Scandinavia published in *Cornhill* in 1870.

5. Begun by Lloyd in Honolulu in spring, 1889, it was much worked over in stages by R.L.S. and completed by June, 1893. Serialisation in 13 weekly instalments in *Today*, 11 Nov 1893-3 Feb 1894, was followed by book publication in Sep 1894.

Working Away Every Morning Like Steam-engines

ISOBEL FIELD

From Isobel Field and Lloyd Osbourne, *Memories of Vailima* (1902) 8–16, 41–53, 81, 96–103. Hostility towards her step-father had long since evaporated (the reconciliation is described in her later book, *This Life I've Loved*, 251–2) and Belle became an invaluable amanuensis. Towards the end of 1892 she began keeping a journal, which allegedly recorded substantial amounts of Louis's sayings and conversations, and eventually filled two volumes. As evidence of his fondness, she notes that while in Sydney in March 1893, Louis gave her mother and herself topaz rings (his birthstone) accompanied by verses:

> These rings, O my beloved pair,
> For me on your brown fingers wear:
> Each a perpetual caress,
> To tell you of my tenderness. (31–2).

Divorced from her feckless husband, Joe Strong, she immersed herself in Vailima life, learning the Samoan language and customs, and acquiring the name 'Teuila'.

[from her journal, late 1892] I have been writing to Louis's dictation the story of 'Anne de St Ives', a young Frenchman in the time of Napoleon.[1] Some days we have worked from eight o'clock until four, and that is not counting the hours Louis writes and makes notes in the early morning by lamp-light. He dictates with great earnestness, and when particularly interested unconsciously acts the parts of his characters. When he came to the description of the supper Anne has with Flora and Ronald, he bowed as he dictated the hero's speeches and twirled his moustache. When he described the interview between the old lady and the drover, he spoke in a high voice for the one, and a deep growl for the other, and all in broad Scotch even to 'coma' (comma).

When Louis was writing 'Ballantrae' my mother said he once came into her room to look in the glass, as he wished to describe a certain haughty, disagreeable expression of his hero's. He told her he actually expected to see the master's clean-shaven face and powdered head, and was quite disconcerted at beholding only his own reflection.

I was sitting by Louis's bedside with a book, this evening, when he asked me to read aloud. 'Don't go back,' he said; 'start in just where you are.' As it happened, I was reading 'The Merry Men'; he laughed a little when he recognized his own words. I went on and finished the story. 'Well,' he said, 'it is not cheerful; it is distinctly not cheerful!'

'In these stories,' I asked, 'do you preach a moral?'

'O not mine,' he said. 'What I want to give, what I try for, is God's moral!'

'Could you not give "God's moral," in a pretty story?' I asked.

'It is a very difficult thing to know,' he said; 'it is a thing I have often thought over – the problem of what to do with one's talents.' He said he thought his own gift lay in the grim and terrible – that some writers touch the heart, he clutched at the throat. I said I thought 'Providence and the Guitar' a very pretty story, full of sweetness and the milk of human kindness.

'But it is not so sweet as 'Markheim' is grim. There I feel myself strong.'[2]

'At least,' I said, 'you have no mannerisms.'

He took the book out of my hand and read 'it was a wonderful clear night of stars'. 'Oh,' he said, 'how many, many times I have written "a wonderful clear night of stars!"'

But I maintained that this, in itself, was a good sentence and presented a picture to the mind. 'It is the mannerisms of the author who can't say "says he" and "says she" that I object to; whose characters hiss, and thunder, and ejaculate and syllable – '

'Oh my dear,' he said, 'deal gently with me – I once *fluted*!'

[16 Jan 1893] Oh poor *Anne*! Louis has been laid up with threatenings of a hemorrhage and is not allowed to speak. It is a cruel blow just when we were getting on so well with *Anne*. When I went in to his bedside this morning he wrote on a slate, 'Allow me to introduce you to Mr Dumbley!' He was leaning against a bed-rest to which he called my attention. It was the one Sir Percy Shelley gave him; my mother had taken all the upholstery out as being too warm for this climate, putting in a back of woven cocoanut sinnet, which is very neat and pretty, and comfortable besides. He cannot speak nor lean forward to write, for fear of starting a hemorrhage, and yet he does not look ill at all. He is tanned a good brown, has a high colour and very bright eyes. In illness he is never pale; as he lies back against the rest in his blue and white Japanese kimono, with a wide red sash, so fresh and bright, looking at you with such a pleasant smiling face, it is hard to realize he is in great danger.

He has a slate by his side and writes nonsense on it. 'I'm a rose-garden invalid wreathed in weak smiles.' To a visitor who asked 'how are you!' he wrote: 'Mr. Dumbley is no better and be hanged to him!'

To pass the time I showed him how to make a, b, and c, on the hands, and we were getting some entertainment out of it when suddenly the brilliant idea struck us both to dictate *Anne* in the deaf and dumb alphabet. It was slow work, and I often made mistakes, but we got on pretty well to the extent of five pages.[3]

In the afternoon Aolele [Fanny] entertained him by playing patience on a table drawn to the bed. For his amusement she learned a game from a book, and he is always pleased and interested to see it played, making signs when she goes wrong and pointing at cards for her to take up.

We are only allowed in to him one at a time, when we all try to be entertaining and recount cheerful adventures of the household. Aolele is very successful at this, but she leaves her smile at the bedroom-door; indeed we are all terribly anxious.

[20 April 1893] I was pottering about my room this morning when Louis came in with the remark that he was a gibbering idiot. I have seen him in this mood before, when he pulls out hairpins, tangles up his mother's knitting, and interferes in whatever his women-kind are engaged upon. So I gave him employment in tidying a drawer all the morning – talking the wildest nonsense all the time, and he was babbling on when Sosimo came in to tell us lunch was ready; his very reverential, respectful manner brought the Idiot Boy to his feet at once, and we all went off laughing to lunch.[4]

[31 May 1893] I asked Louis, in the course of a conversation this evening, how he defined the word literature.

'It is capable of explanation, I think,' he said; 'when you see words used to the best purpose – no waste, going tight around a subject. Also they must be true. My stories are not the truth, but I try to make my characters act as they would act in life. No detail is too small to study for truth. Lloyd and I spent five days weighing money and making calculations for the treasure found in "The Wrecker'."

I asked him why Charles Reade was not a stylist, though his writing answered to the description.[5]

'You are right,' Louis said; 'he is a good writer, and I take off my hat to him with respect. And yet it was in continuity that he failed. In the "Ebb Tide", that is now under way, we started on a high key, and oh, haven't we regretted it! If I wanted to say "he kicked his leg and he winked his eye", it would be perfectly flat if I wrote it so. I must pile the colours on to bring it up to the key. Yet I am wrong to liken literature to painting. It is more like music – which is time; painting is space. In music you wind in and out, but always keep in the key; that is, you carry the hearer to the end without letting him drop by the way. It winds around and keeps on. So must words wind around. Organised and packed in a mass, as it were, tight with words. Not too short – phrases rather – no word to spare.

'There are two kinds of style, the plastic, such as I have just described; the other, the simple placing of words together for harmony. The words should come off the tongue like honey. I began so as a young man; I had a pretty talent that way, I must confess.'

[30 June 1894] We miss Louis so terribly, even for a few days, that now we all rejoice to be together again. There are just seven of us: Aunt Maggie and her son Louis, Aolele and her son Lloyd, myself and my son Austin, and Palema, as the natives call Louis's cousin, Graham Balfour.[6]

Our furniture has come all the way from Scotland: thirty-seven cases, some of them fifteen feet square, weighing in all seventy-two tons. The boxes were brought up on the bullock-carts of the German firm by scores of Solomon Island black-boys, in a most exciting and noisy procession.

Mr Moore, chaplain of HMS *Curaçoa*, came up in his spotless white clothes to help us unpack, returning to his ship in the evening the picture of a chimney sweep – or, as Louis said, 'black but comely'.

[9 July 1894] We have been very gay. Lloyd, Louis, and I went to the officers' ball on the 3d, and on the 4th, two *Curaçoa* marines appeared on the veranda. 'Me and my messmates,' one of them said, 'invites Mr and Mrs Stevenson, Mrs Strong, Mr Osbourne and Mr Balfour to a sailors' ball in the same 'hall as last night, not forgetting young Goskin.' We accepted with pleasure, and I went, escorted by Louis and Austin. The ball was a great success; everybody was there. Louis said, as he looked on at officers and sailors dancing in the same set, harmony and good-fellowship on all sides, 'The *Curaçoa* revives my faith in human nature!'

[27 Aug 1894] To-day we were in the middle of the chapter about the claret-coloured chaise, when we were interrupted by the arrival of eight chiefs. They proved to be the liberated political prisoners that we had been interested in for so long, whose freedom from jail they owe to Louis. Louis entertained them in the smoking-room; we all sat on the floor in a semicircle and had *kava* made. Their speeches were very beautiful, and full of genuine gratitude as they went back over the history of every kindness that Louis had done for them. In proof of their gratitude they offered to make a road, sixty feet wide, connecting us with the highway across the island. The offer touched and surprised Louis very much, and though he tried to refuse, they overruled every objection. He said if they made the road he would like to name it 'The Road of the Grateful Hearts', but they said no, it would be called 'The Road of the Loving Heart,' in the singular, and they asked me to copy out a paper they had written with that name, and all their titles attached, to be painted on a board and put up at the cross-roads.[7]

[24 Sept 1894] Louis and I have been writing, working away every morning like steam-engines on *Hermiston*. Louis got a set-back with *Anne*, and he has put it aside for awhile. He worried terribly over it, but could not make it run smoothly. He read it aloud one evening and Lloyd criticized the love-scene, so Louis threw the whole thing over for a time. Fortunately he picked up *Hermiston* all right, and is in better spirits at once. He has always been wonderfully clear and sustained in his dictation, but he generally made notes in the early morning, which he elaborated as he read them aloud. In *Hermiston* he had hardly more than a line or two of notes to keep him on the track, but he never falters for a word, giving me the sentences, with capital letters and all the stops, as clearly and steadily as though he were reading from an unseen book. He walks up and down the room as I write, and his voice is so beautiful and the story so interesting that I forget to rest; when we are interrupted by the lunch-bell, I am sometimes quite cramped, and Louis thumps me on the back in imitation of a Samoan *lomi-lomi* (massage) and apologizes. The story is all the more thrilling as he says he has taken me for young Kirsty.

We had such an interesting time today, looking over old fashion-books for the heroine's clothes. Her dress is grey, to which I suggested the addition of a pink kerchief; this afternoon Louis came into my room to announce that in her evening walk Kirsty would wear pink silk stockings to match her kerchief; he said he could use the incident very artfully to develop her character. 'Belle,' he said, 'I see it all so clearly! The story unfolds itself before me to the last detail – there is nothing left in doubt. I never felt so before in anything I ever wrote. It will be my best work; I feel myself so sure in every word!'

[30 Nov 1894] A few days ago three sailors of HMS *Wallaroo* came up and asked for a drink of water. We gave them seats on the veranda and offered them some cool beer after their long, hot walk. When Louis came down to talk to them he was not long in discovering that they were all three Scotch; they had made for Vailima, 'like homing pigeons', on their first day of leave. When they were going away I gave them an opportunity to return by asking for a pattern of a sailor jacket.[8]

Yesterday we were sitting on the little front veranda by Louis's work-room, pegging away at *Hermiston* like one o'clock. I hardly drew breath, but flew over the paper; Louis thinks it is good himself, so we were in a very cheerful humour; we heard a babble of voices at the gate and recognized our sailors. Louis gave up with the utmost good-nature, and came down to talk with them....

He took them over the house and showed them the busts and statues, the Burmah gods, the curiosities from the island, the big picture of Skerryvore lighthouse, built by his grandfather on the coast of Scotland; the treasured bit of Gordon's handwriting, from Khartoum, in Arabic letters on a cigarette paper, framed, for safety, between two pieces of glass; and the library, where the Scotchmen gathered about an old edition of Burns, with a portrait. Louis gave a volume of *Underwoods*, with an inscription, to Grant, the one who hailed from Edinburgh, and the man carried it carefully wrapped in his handkerchief. As they went away, waving their sailor hats and keeping step, Louis leaned over the railing of the veranda and said, looking after them with a smile, 'How I love a blue-jacket! What a pity we can't invite them to our dinner tonight; they would be so entertaining!'

NOTES

1. *St Ives* was first published in *Pall Mall Magazine*, Nov 1896–Nov 1897. It was written at the height of the Samoan war and when Louis was in poor physical condition. With 30 chapters done, he set it aside for the more compelling *Weir of Hermiston*. Belle noted him saying of *Weir* that he saw it unfolding to the end: 'It will be the best thing I have ever done' (*This Life*, 274).

2. 'Providence and the Guitar', first published in *London*, 2–23 Nov 1878 (*New Arabian Nights*, 1882); 'Markheim', *Unwin's Annual*, Dec 1885 (*The Merry Men and Other Tales*, 1887).

3. Belle had learned 'a sort of deaf-and-dumb alphabet' in school, for secret communication with other girls. Quickly mastering the sign language, Louis dictated 15 pages of *St Ives* (*This Life*, 273–4).

4. Sosimo, devoted member of the household, kept vigil at Louis's deathbed prior to the burial on 4 Dec 1894.

5. Charles Reade (1814–80), novelist and dramatist, best known for *It Is Never Too Late to Mend* (1856) and *The Cloister and the Hearth* (1861).

6. Since no equivalents existed for Mr, Mrs or Miss, special Samoan names avoided the embarrassment of staff using Christian names as they would normally have done. Hence Fanny was Aolele or more formally Tamaitai (meaning high-born lady); Lloyd was Loya, and Belle, Tuila (M. Stevenson, *Letters from Samoa*, 97).

7. Defying the authorities in Nov 1893, the Stevensons took gifts of tobacco and kava to Mataafa's minor chiefs imprisoned in Apia. The political prisoners returned the favour with a feast in the courtyard of the jail. After their release they made the road linking the island public road with Vailima. It was completed in Oct 1894 and named 'The Road of the Loving Heart'.

8. Regular visits of crew members continued until the *Curaçoa* was relieved by the *Wallaroo*. Before it sailed for England the Stevensons entertained 15 sailors to a farewell party on 11 Nov 1894.

Barley-sugar Effigy of a Real Man

W.E. HENLEY

From 'R.L.S.', *Pall Mall Magazine*, XXV, (Dec 1901) 505–14. William Ernest Henley (1849–1903), poet, critic, dramatist and editor; for several years editor of the *National Observer* (formerly *Scots Observer*), which featured notable writers of the day including Hardy, Kipling, Barrie, Wells, Yeats and Stevenson; editor of the monthly *New Review* (1894–8); he also published several volumes of verse, as well as editing the works of Burns, Byron and others. Leslie Stephen brought Louis to Edinburgh Infirmary in 1875 to meet Henley, then undergoing hideous treatment after losing lost one foot to a tuberculous disease. Stevenson marvelled at his fortitude and vitality, depicting him as Burly in 'Talk and Talkers' and dedicating *Virginibus Puerisque* to him. Much of Henley's rambunctious nature went into Long John Silver. Their collaboration in four plays was a failure and a source of resentment for Henley, exacerbated by intense dislike of Fanny; he was, notes one biographer, in a sense, in love with Louis (Calder, 95). Deeply embittered by life and 'the fell clutch of circumstance', Henley exploded with pent up jealousy on seeing Balfour's biography, and helped to launch attacks on the Stevenson myth. At least one voice for the prosecution has its place in a volume of reminiscences.

For me there were two Stevensons: the Stevenson who went to America in '87; and the Stevenson who never came back. The first I knew, and loved; the other I lost touch with, and, though I admired him, did not greatly esteem. My relation to him was that of a man with a grievance; and for that reasons, perhaps – that reason and others – I am by no means disposed to take all Mr Balfour says for gospel, nor willing to forget, on the showing of what is after all an official statement, the knowledge gained in an absolute intimacy of give-and-take which lasted for thirteen years, and includes so many of the circumstances of those thirteen years that, as I believe, none living now can pretend to speak of them with any such authority as mine.[1] This, however, is not to say that Mr Balfour's view of his famous cousin is not warranted to the letter, so far as he saw and knew. I mean no more than that the Stevenson he knew was not the Stevenson who came to me (that good angel, Mr Leslie Stephen, aiding) in the old Edinburgh Infirmary; nor the Stevenson I nursed in secret, hard by the old Bristo Port, till he could make shift to paddle the *Arethusa;* nor the Stevenson who stayed with me at Acton after selling Modestine, nor even the Stevenson who booked a steerage berth to New York, and thence trained it 'across the plains', and ended for the time being as a married man and a Silverado squatter; though I confess that in this last avatar the Stevenson of Mr Balfour's dream had begun, however faintly and vaguely, to adumbrate himself, and might have been looked for as a certainty by persons less affectionate and uninquiring than those by whom he was then approached. Mr Balfour does me the honour of quoting the sonnet into which I crammed my impressions of my companion and friend; and, since he has done so, I may as well own that 'the Shorter Catechist' of the last verse was an afterthought. In those days he was in abeyance, to say the least; and if, even then, *il allait poindre à l'horizon* (as the composition, in secret and as if ashamed, of *Lay Morals* persuades me to believe he did), I, at any rate, was too short-sighted to suspect his whereabouts. When I realised it, I completed my sonnet; but this was not till years had come and gone, and the Shorter Catechist, already detested by more than one, was fully revealed to me.

I will say at once that I do not love the Shorter Catechist, in anybody, and that I loved him less in Stevenson than anywhere that I have ever found him. He is too selfish and too self-righteous a beast for me. He makes ideals for himself with a resolute regard for his own salvation; but he is all-too apt to damn the rest of the world for declining to live up to them, and he is all-too ready to make a lapse of his own the occasion for a rule of conduct for himself and the lasting pretext for a highly moral deliverance to such backsliding Erastians as, having memories and a certain concern for facts, would like him to wear his rue with a difference. At bottom Stevenson was an excellent fellow. But he was of his essence what the French call *personnel*. He was, that is, incessantly and passionately interested in Stevenson. He could not be in the same room with a mirror but he must invite its confidences every time he passed it; to him there was nothing obvious in time and eternity, and the smallest of his discoveries, his most trivial apprehensions, were all by way of being revelations, and as revelations must be thrust upon the world; he was never so much in earnest, never so well pleased (this were he happy or wretched), never so irresistible, as when he wrote about himself. Withal, if he wanted a thing, he went after it with an entire contempt for consequences.... But in the South Seas the mask got set, the 'lines' became a little stereotyped. Plainly the Shorter Catechist was what was wanted. And here we are: with Stevenson's later letters and Mr Graham Balfour's estimate.

'Tis as that of an angel clean from heaven, and I for my part flatly refuse to recognise it. Not, if I can help it, shall this faultless, or very nearly faultless, monster go down to after years as the Lewis I knew, and loved, and laboured with and for, with all my heart and strength and understanding. In days to come I may write as much as can be told of him. 'Till those days come, this protest must suffice. If it convey the impression that I take a view of Stevenson which is my own, and which declines to be concerned with this Seraph in Chocolate, this barley-sugar effigy of a real man; that the best and the most interesting part of Stevenson's life will never get written – even by me; and that the Shorter Catechist of Vailima, however brilliant and distinguished as a writer of stories, however authorised and acceptable as an artist in morals, is not my old, riotous, intrepid, scornful Stevenson at all – suffice it will....

I have said nothing of Stevenson the artist in this garrulous and egotistic pronouncement on his official *Life*; for the very simple reason that I have nothing to say. To tell the truth, his books are none of mine: I mean, that if I want reading, I do not go for it to the *Edinburgh Edition*. I am not interested in remarks about morals; in and out of letters I have lived a full and varied life, and my opinions are my own. So, if I crave the enchantment of romance, I ask it of bigger men than he, and of bigger books than his: of *Esmond* (say) and *Great Expectations*, of *Redgauntlet* and *Old Mortality*, of *La Reine Margot* and *Bragelonne*, of *David Copperfield* and *A Tale of Two Cities*: while, if good writing and some other things be in my appetite, are there not always Hazlitt and Lamb – to say nothing of that 'globe of miraculous continents' which is known to us as Shakespeare? There is his style, you will say; and it is a fact that it is rare, and in the last times better, because much simpler, than in the first. But after all, his style is so perfectly achieved that the achievement gets obvious: and when achievement gets obvious, is it not by way of becoming uninteresting? And is there not something to be said for the person who wrote that Stevenson always reminded him of a young man dressed the best he ever saw for the Burlington Arcade? Stevenson's work in letters does not now take me much, and I decline to enter on the question of its immortality; since that, despite what any can say, will get itself settled, soon or late, for all time. No; when I care to think of Stevenson it is not of 'R.L.S.': R.L.S. 'the renowned, the accomplished, Executing his difficult solo': but of the 'Lewis' that I knew, and loved, and wrought for, and worked with for so long. The successful man of letters does not greatly interest me: I read his careful prayers, and pass on, with the certainty that, well as they read, they were not written for print; I learn of his nameless prodigalities – and recall some instances of conduct in another vein. I remember, rather, the unmarried and irresponsible Lewis: the friend, the comrade, the *charmeur*. Truly, that last word, French as it is, is the only one that is worthy of him. I shall ever remember him as that. The impression of his writings disappears; the impression of himself and his talk is ever a possession. He had, as I have said elsewhere, all the gifts (he and his cousin, he and Bob) that qualify the talker's temperament: – 'As voice and eye and laugh, look and gesture, humour and fantasy, audacity and agility of mind, a lively and most impudent invention, a copious vocabulary, a right gift of foolery, a just inevitable sense of right and wrong' (this though I've blamed him for a tendency to monologue, and a trick of depending too much on his temperament). And I take leave to repeat what I've said elsewhere, that those who know him only by his books – (I think our Fleeming Jenkin, were he alive, would back me here) – know but the poorest of him. Forasmuch as he was primarily a talker, his printed works, like those of others after his kind, are but a sop for posterity: 'A last dying speech and confession (as it were) to show that not for nothing were they held rare fellows in their day.'

A last word. I have everywhere read that we must praise him now and always for that, being a stricken man, he would live out his life.[2] Are we not all stricken men, and do we not all do that? And why, because he wrote better than any one, should he have praise and fame for doing that which many a poor, consumptive sempstress does: cheerfully, faithfully, with no eloquent appeals to God, nor so much as a paragraph in the evening paper? That a man writes well at death's door is sure no reason for making him a hero; for, after all, there is as much virtue in making a shirt, or finishing a gross of match-boxes, in the very act of mortality, as there is in polishing a verse, or completing a chapter in a novel. As much, I say; but is there not an immense deal more? In the one case, the sufferer does the thing he loves best in life. In the other, well – who that has not made shirts, or finished match-boxes, shall speak? Stevenson, for all his vocalisings, was a brave man, with a fine, buoyant spirit; and he took the mystery of life and time and death as seemed best to him. But we are mortals all; and, so far as I have seen, there are few of us but strive to keep a decent face for the Arch-Discomforter. There is no wonder that Stevenson wrote his best in the shadow of the Shade; for writing his best was very life to him. Why, then, all this crawling astonishment – this voluble admiration? If it meant anything, it would mean that we have forgotten how to live, and that none of us is prepared to die; and that were an outrage on the innumerable unstoried martyrdoms of humanity. Let this be said of him, once for all: 'He was a good man, good at many things, and now this also he has attained to, to be at rest.' That covers Sophocles and Shakespeare, Marlborough and Bonaparte. Let it serve for Stevenson; and, for ourselves, let us live and die uninsulted, as we lived and died before his books began to sell and his personality was a marketable thing.[3]

NOTES

1. The intimate relations lasted until Fanny came on the scene and their departure for New York in 1887. A full blown row erupted the following year when a short story 'The Nixie' appeared in *Scribner's*, March 1888, credited to Fanny van de Grift Stevenson, plagiarised to Henley's eyes from work by Katherine de Mattos. He wrote maliciously a letter marked private, which appalled Louis and produced almost suicidal despair. Modern biography inclines to blame Katherine for fanning the flames, but there is little doubt that Henley behaved badly. The state of Louis's mind can be gauged from his letters (*Baxter Letters*, 188–228). He cannot leave the subject alone: 'The bottom wish of my heart is that I had died at Hyères: the happy part of my life ended there', he writes, 12 April 1888 from Saranac (208). 'O, Henley's letter! I cannot rise from it... This business has been my headstone; I will never be reconciled to life' (22 May, 224). Escape to sea aboard the *Casco* was his deliverance.

2. Perhaps the unkindest cut of all; ironically they were so alike in surmounting physical adversity and not whining about it. Henley's well-known lines equally stand for Stevenson:

> In the fell clutch of circumstance,
> I have not winced nor cried aloud:
> Under the bludgeonings of chance
> My head is bloody, but unbowed.
> ('Invictus', 1875)

3. Henley's diatribe provoked counterblasts from Lang in the *Morning Post*, 16 Dec. 1901, and in several periodicals. See, for example, 'The Candid Friend', and 'Not as the Bookmen', *Academy*, LXI (23 Nov 1901), 487–8; (30 Nov 1901), 512–13.

Whatever He Did He Did with His Whole Heart

GRAHAM BALFOUR

From *The Life of Robert Louis Stevenson*, 2 vols (1901) II, 160–86. Sir Thomas Graham Balfour (1858–1929) could have pursued a literary career, but chose instead to serve British education; he was admitted to the Bar (1885), Director of Education for Staffordshire (1903–26), member of the Board of Education (1926–9); his *Educational Systems of Great Britain and Ireland* (1898) became a standard work. He was knighted in 1917. Balfour travelled widely throughout the world, joining the Vailima household (1891) and living with the Stevensons intermittently until the novelist's death. It seems appropriate to counter Henley's view of the 'Seraph in Chocolate' and 'barley-sugar effigy', even if that criticism is not entirely without foundation.

R.L.S.

Thin-legged, thin-chested, slight unspeakably,
Neat-footed and weak-fingered: in his face –
Lean, large-boned, curved of beak, and touched with grace,
Bold-lipped, rich-tinted, mutable as the sea,
The brown eyes radiant with vivacity –
There shines a brilliant and romantic grace,
A spirit intense and rare, with trace on trace
Of passion, impudence, and energy.

> Valiant in velvet, light in ragged luck,
> Most vain, most generous, sternly critical,
> Buffoon and poet, lover and sensualist:
> A deal of Ariel, just a streak of Puck,
> Much Antony, of Hamlet most of all,
> And something of the Shorter-Catechist.
>
> (W. E. Henley)

Of Stevenson's personal aspect and bodily powers it may be fitting here to make mention. Of his appearance the best portraits and photographs give a fair idea, if each be considered as the rendering of only one expression.... the eyes were the most striking feature of the face; they were of the deepest brown in colour, set extraordinarily wide apart. At most times they had a shy, quick glance that was most attractive, but when he was moved to anger or any fierce emotion, they seemed literally to blaze and glow with a fiery light. His hair was fair and even yellow in colour until he was five-and-twenty; after that it rapidly deepened, and in later years was quite dark, but of course without any touch of black. When he reached the tropics, and the fear of taking cold was to some extent removed, he wore it short once more, to his own great satisfaction and comfort. His complexion was brown and always high, even in the confinement of the sick-room; the only phrase for it is the 'rich-hued' used by Mr Henley in the spirited and vivid lines he has kindly permitted me to quote.

In height he was about five feet ten, slender in figure, and thin to the last degree. In all his movements he was most graceful: every gesture was full of an unconscious beauty, and his restless and supple gait has been well compared to the pacing to and fro of some wild forest animal. To this unusual and most un-English grace it was principally due that he was often taken for a foreigner.... In France he was sometimes taken for a Frenchman from some other province; he has recorded his imprisonment as a German spy; and at a later date he wrote, 'I have found out what is wrong with me – I look like a Pole.'

This difficulty, of course, was not smoothed by the clothes he used to wear, which often in early days were extremely unconventional, and of which he then took so little notice that at times they were even ragged.[1] In cool climates he often used a velveteen smoking-jacket; in undress at Vailima he wore flannels or pyjamas, with sometimes a light Japanese kimono for dressing-gown. On public occasions in Samoa he used the white drill that constitutes full dress in the tropics, with perhaps light breeches and boots if he had been riding.

Considering his fragility, his muscular strength was considerable, and his constitution clearly had great powers of resistance. Perhaps what helped him as much as anything was the faculty he had under ordinary circumstances of going to sleep at a moment's notice. Thus, if he anticipated fatigue in the evening, he would take a quarter of an hour's sound sleep in the course of the afternoon.

His speech was distinctly marked with a Scottish intonation, that seemed to every one both pleasing and appropriate, and this, when he chose, he could broaden to the widest limits of the vernacular. His voice was always of a surprising strength and resonance, even when phthisis had laid its hand most heavily upon him. It was the one gift he really possessed for the stage, and in reading aloud he was unsurpassed. In his full rich tones there was a sympathetic quality that seemed to play directly on the heart-strings like the notes of a violin....

His hearing was singularly acute, although the appreciation of the exact pitch of musical notes was wanting. But between delicate shades of pronunciation he could discriminate with great precision. I can give an instance in point. The vowels in Polynesian languages are pronounced as in Italian, and the diphthongs retain the sounds of the separate vowels, more or less slurred together. Thus it can be understood that the difference between *ae* and *ai* at the end of a word in rapid conversation is of the very slightest, and in Samoa they are practically indistinguishable. In the Marquesas Stevenson was able to separate them. At Vailima one day we were making trial of these and other subtleties of sound; in almost every case his ear was exactly correct. Nothing more shook his admiration for Herman Melville than that writer's inability to approximate to the native names of the Marquesas and Tahiti, and in his own delicate hearing lay perhaps the root of his devotion to style....

Over and above all there was the talk of the man himself, in which the alternations were even more rapid and more striking.[2] Wit, humour, and pathos; the romantic, the tragic, the picturesque; stern judgment, wise counsel, wild fooling, all fell into their natural places, followed each other in rapid and easy succession, and made a marvellous whole, not the least of the wonder being the congruity and spontaneity which gave to it the just effect of being a perfectly natural utterance. . . .

Taken together with the kindliness of his nature it also, to a great extent, explains his extraordinary gift of sympathy. He seemed to divine from his own experience how other people felt, and how best they might be encouraged or consoled. I doubt if any one ever remained for long in his company either reticent or ill at ease. Mr Gosse reminds us of Stevenson's talks at Sydney with a man formerly engaged in the 'blackbirding' trade, who was with great difficulty induced to speak of his experiences.[3] 'He was very shy at first,' said Stevenson, 'and it was not till I told him of a good many of my escapades that I could get him to thaw, and then he poured it all out. I have always found *that* the best way of getting people to be confidential.' We have seen with what success he approached the natives in this manner; in like fashion, no doubt, he inquired of Highlanders about the Appin murder.

But even where he had some set purpose in view, his talk seemed to be a natural and purely spontaneous outpouring of himself. It never seemed to me to be vanity – if it were, it was the most genial that ever existed – but rather a reference to instances within his own knowledge to illustrate the point in hand. He never monopolised the conversation, however eager he might be, but was faithful to his preference for talk which is in its nature a debate; 'the amicable counter-assertion of personality', and 'the Protean quality which is in man' enabled him, without ceasing to be himself, to meet the temper of his company. . . .

But the supreme instance of diverse elements in him was patience and its opposite. Never have I heard of any one in whom these contradictories were both shown in so high a degree. His endurance in illness and in work we have seen: no pain was too great to bear, no malady too long: he never murmured until it was over. No task was too irksome, no revision too exacting – laboriously, and like an eager apprentice he went through with it to the end.

But on the other hand, when impatience came to the surface, it blazed up like the anger of a man who had never known a check. It was generally caused by some breach of faith or act of dishonesty or unjustifiable delay. The only time I know of its being displayed in public was in a Paris restaurant, where Stevenson had ordered a change of wine, and the very bottle he had rejected was brought back to him with a different label. There was a sudden explosion of wrath; the bottle was violently broken; in an instant the restaurant was emptied, and – so much for long-suffering – the proprietor and his staff were devoting the whole of their attention and art to appease and reconcile the angry man....

There was this about him, that he was the only man I have ever known who possessed charm in a high degree, whose character did not suffer from the possession. The gift comes naturally to women, and they are at their best in its exercise. But a man requires to be of a very sound fibre before he can be entirely himself and keep his heart single, if he carries about with him a talisman to obtain from all men and all women the object of his heart's desire. Both gifts Stevenson possessed, not only the magic but also the strength of character to which it was safely intrusted.

But who shall bring back that charm? Who shall unfold its secret? He was all that I have said: he was inexhaustible, he was brilliant, he was romantic, he was fiery, he was tender, he was brave, he was kind. With all this there went something more. He always liked the people he was with, and found the best and brightest that was in them; he entered into all the thoughts and moods of his companions, and led them along pleasant ways, or raised them to a courage and a gaiety like his own. If criticism or reminiscence has yielded any further elucidation of his spell, I do not know: it defies my analysis, nor have I ever heard it explained.

There linger on the lips of men a few names that bring to us, as it were, a breeze blowing off the shores of youth. Most of those who have borne them were taken from the world before early promise could be fulfilled, and so they rank in our regard by virtue of their possibilities alone. Stevenson is among the fewer still who bear the award both of promise and of achievement, and is happier yet in this: besides admiration and hope, he has raised within the hearts of his readers a personal feeling towards himself which is nothing less deep than love.

NOTES

1. See *An Inland Voyage* (1878), dedicated to Sir Walter Simpson, an account of their travel by canoe through rivers and canals of northeastern France during 1876. At Chatillon-sur-Loing, on the last leg of the journey, the two were separated, and Louis, without identity papers, was arrested on suspicion of spying. See 'An Epilogue to "An Inland Voyage"', *Across the Plains* (1892).

2. Balfour draws attention to Colvin's remarks on the play of word, look and gesture: '*Divers et ondoyant*, in the words of Montaigne, beyond other men, he seemed to contain within himself a whole troop of singularly assorted characters – the poet and artist, the moralist and preacher, the humourist and jester, the man of great heart and tender conscience, the man of eager appetite and curiosity, the Bohemian, impatient of restraints and shams, the adventurer and lover of travel and action' (*Letters*, I, xxix). From such eulogy stemmed many accusations of hagiography.

3. 'Blackbirding' was widely practised by unscrupulous traders. It involved importing abducted labour, chiefly from the Solomon islands, to work the cocoa and pineapple plantations. The British turned a blind eye to the activity, but vociferously blamed German landowners for the practice.

Called Home

MARGARET STEVENSON

From *Letters from Samoa, 1891–95*, ed. Marie Clothilde Balfour (1906) 313–28. The indomitable Aunt Maggie showed her mettle in this and her preceding account of travels, *From Saranac to the Marquesas and Beyond* (1903), and no one fails to respond to the courage and determination she showed after her husband's death in May 1887. Then aged 58, she abandoned her comfortable Edinburgh life and voyaged with her son, first to the United States and then on his Pacific journeys. Margaret Stevenson is quite remarkable, whether surviving mountainous seas in the South Pacific or grappling with the rigours of plantation life. She retained a sense of humour and unflinching determination to make each day count. Her watchword, according to her editor, fitted her son's prayer:

> Give us to awake with smiles;
> Give us to labour smiling.

The Samoa letters give a spirited picture of Vailima life and fully display her loyalty to Fanny as well as to her son. In photographs of the Stevenson family, one is always drawn to the primly upright Victorian lady in her freshly starched white widow's cap. After Louis's death she returned to Edinburgh and lived with her sister, Jane Whyte Balfour, until she died from pneumonia in 1897 at the age of 68. The night before she died she is said to have started from her bed saying: 'There is Louis; I must go' (Simpson, *Originals*, 21). To conclude, as well as to begin this book with her recollections, seems only appropriate.

[4 Dec 1894] How am I to tell you the terrible news that my beloved son was suddenly called home last evening. At six o'clock he was well, hungry for dinner, and helping Fanny to make a Mayonnaise sauce; when suddenly he put both hands to his head and said, 'Oh, what a pain!' and then added, 'Do I look strange?' Fanny said no, not wishing to alarm him, and helped him into the hall, where she put him into the nearest easy-chair. She called for us to come, and I was there in a minute; but he was unconscious before I reached his side, and remained so for two hours, till at ten minutes past 8 p.m. all was over.[1]

Lloyd went for help at once, and got two doctors wonderfully quickly – one from the *Wallaroo* and the other, Dr F—, from Apia; but we had already done all that was possible, and they could suggest nothing more. Before the end came we brought a bed into the hall, and he was lifted on to it. When all was over his boys gathered about him, and the chiefs from Tanugamanono arrived with fine mats which they laid over the bed; it was very touching when they came in bowing, and saying 'Talofa, Tusitala'; and then, after kissing him and sitting a while in silence, they bowed again, and saying 'Tofa, Tusitala', went out. After that our Roman Catholic boys asked if they might 'make a church,' and they chanted prayers and hymns for a long time, very sweetly.... We had sent for Mr C—, who stayed with us till all was over, and made the necessary arrangements for us; Louis wished to be buried on the top of Vaea Mountain, and before six this morning forty men arrived with axes to cut a path up and dig the grave. Some of Mataafa's chiefs came this morning; one wept bitterly, saying, 'Mataafa is gone, and Tusitala is gone, and we have none left.' ...

[9 Dec 1894] Life seems to have stood still with us since Tuesday, and none of us can do anything but think over our loss, which only grows greater as we begin dimly to realise it. No one, at least, was ever more universally mourned than my beloved son.... The ascent to the top of Vaea Mountain was a very difficult matter, and many of the men found it more than they could manage. The coffin left half an hour before the invited guests, as the labour of climbing with it was so great; but there were many relays of loving Samoan hands ready to carry their dear Tusitala to his last home amongst them, and they took the utmost pains to bear him shoulder high, and as steadily and reverently as possible. Behind them came the few near and good friends that we had invited to be present; and when they reached the top of the mountain they found the coffin laid beside the grave, and covered with the flag that used to fly over us in those happy days upon the *Casco*. . . .

Mr C— read portions of the Church of England burial-service, and also a prayer written by Louis himself, which he had read at family worship only the night before his death; and Mr N— gave an address in Samoan, which made all who understood it weep; and prayed also in the same language, that Louis loved so well.[2] . . . When they returned to the house I talked for a while to Mr N—, and he told me that when he was here more than a year ago Louis told him of his great desire to be buried on the top of Vaea, and showed him where his new study was to be built, with a window from which he could see the place. I wonder if it suggested to him the upliftedness of death.

It was a terribly tiring day, but perhaps it was good for us that we had no time to ourselves. Many Samoan ladies came to bring us flowers and show their sympathy, and they sat on the verandah for several hours. As soon as the boys returned we gave them tea, but we were thankful when it was all over. You see we had had no food ourselves. No one had had time or inclination for eating from midday on Monday, our usual lunch, till Tuesday morning; and even then we could scarcely take enough to help us through with all that had to be done. I am thankful to know that we got through it somehow. And I am glad, too, to feel how cheerful and happy he was to the very last; he bore the signs of it still about him, and looked so sweet and peaceful, with his face so full of life, and far less thin, it seemed to me, than I had ever seen it.

I must tell you a very strange thing that occurred just before his death. For a day or two Fanny had been telling us that she knew – that she *felt* – something dreadful was going to happen to some one we cared for; as she put it, to one of our friends. On Monday she was very low about it, and upset, and dear Lou tried hard to cheer her. He read aloud to her the chapter of his book that he had just finished, played a game or two of patience to induce her to look on, and I fancy it was as much for her sake as his own that the Mayonnaise sauce was begun upon. And, strangely enough, both of them had agreed that it could not be to either of *them* that the dreadful thing was to happen! Thus far, and no further, can our intuitions, our second sight, go....

I have had so many letters from our friends here, and especially from the missionaries; Mr C—, indeed, has been like a son to me during these sad days. And we are not alone in our grief. Sosimo, Lou's special boy, is quite inconsolable; he keeps Tusitala's room in exquisite order, and when Fanny and I were there this morning, we were touched to find two glasses filled with beautiful fresh white flowers on the table beside his bed. And the Apia people were deeply disappointed when they found that the funeral was not to be in the little cemetery there; they say that every man, woman, and child in the place would have attended it. But he seems nearer to us on Vaea. Did I tell you that we had a tree cut down on the mountain, so that now we can see his last resting-place quite distinctly from the verandah; Fanny would have to have a Scottish cairn errected on the spot, and I am sure our Samoans would be eager to take their share in it.[3] ...

[16 Dec 1894]   Another Sunday without my child; his leaving us was so swift and sudden, that I seem only now to begin to realise that I shall see him on earth no more.... Yesterday we had another sad scene to go through, the paying-off of the outside boys; their last work had been to make a better road to the top of the mountain, and it was finished yesterday....

Of the outside boys we have only kept our old friend Lafaële, who takes care of the cows and pigs, Leuello, Fanny's boy, who works in the garden, and a Tongan who has only one eye, and is delicate as well. Some time ago Lloyd suggested to Louis that as he was of little use, he had better be sent away; but Louis replied that he had no home to go to, and there was every chance of his becoming altogether blind, and that as long as *he* was at Vailima, the Tongan should have a home there too. Now we feel that he is a precious legacy to us, and the poor boy's look of relief when he found that he was to be allowed to stay on was good to see. But it was nice to find that Talolo had told this boy Tuli that if he had to go, he should have a home in his, Talolo's, family....

[13 Jan 1895]   We have got many letters and newspapers from New Zealand and Australia, and I am grieved to find that you did not receive the telegrams we sent you till after the news was published in the papers. I do hope you were not long kept in suspense; the wire was to be despatched immediately on arrival at San Francisco, but they warned us that press despatches would be sent through first.[4]

I don't think I told you of a remark made by the doctor of the *Wallaroo* that haunts me constantly. We were watching round dear Lou, Fanny and I were rubbing his arms with brandy, and his shirt-sleeves were pushed up, and showed their thinness; some one made a remark about his writing, and Dr. A— said, 'How can anybody write books with arms like these?'

I turned round indignantly and burst out with, 'He has written *all* his books with arms like these!'

I don't think I was ever before so terribly impressed with the greatness of the struggle that my beloved child had made against his bad health. He has written at the rate of a volume a year for the last twenty years, in spite of weakness which most people would have looked on as an excuse for confirmed invalidism; and he has lived, too, and loved his life in spite of it all. Do you remember how years ago, when some one was comforting him by saying that the Balfours always got stronger as they grew older, he replied, 'Yes; but just as I begin to outgrow the Balfour delicacy, the Nemesis of the short-lived Stevensons will come in and finish me off!' That has been at the back of my mind all these years, and you see it has come true. I wonder if it would have been better to let him start in the *John Williams*, as he proposed, and get a complete rest. But there is no use in asking oneself such questions; it seemed so unwise then, and who could foresee what was to happen?

Lafaële told us that when he was on his way to milk the cows a very short time before Louis was struck down, he saw him throw open the Venetian shutters of his window, and gaze up at the top of Vaea Mountain; when he noticed Lafaële he waved his hand, and called *talofa* to him quite cheerily.

NOTES

1. Lloyd Osbourne suggests that he had cried out 'My head – oh, my head', *Portrait*, 143–55. The two doctors were the local general practitioner, Dr Barnhard Funk, and Dr Anderson, surgeon from HMS *Wallaroo*. Both concurred that a cerebral haemorrhage had occurred.

2. The two clergymen referred to in the excerpt were the Reverend Newell and Louis's particular friend, the Reverend Clarke.

3. A bronze plaque at the site bears Louis's 'Requiem':

Under the wide and starry sky,
Dig the grave and let me lie.
Glad did I live and gladly die,
And I laid me down with a will.

This be the verse you grave for me:
Here he lies where he longed to be,
Home is the sailor, home from sea,
And the hunter home from the hill.

Fanny died in Santa Barbara, California, in February 1914 at the age of 73. Her ashes were brought back to Mount Vaea to be interred beside her husband. Her plaque has the verses 'Teacher, tender comrade, wife' from his poem 'To my Wife' in *Songs of Travel*.

4. Among the hundreds of letters, Henry James's was a particularly fine tribute and condolence to the widow: 'He lighted up one whole side of the globe, and was in himself a whole province of one's imagination. We are smaller fry and meaner people without him... And, with all the sad allowances in his rich full life, he had the best of it – the thick of the fray, the loudest of the music, the freshest and finest of himself' (quoted in Sanchez, *Life*, 222–5).

Suggestions for Further Reading

Biographical materials are very numerous. Some of the most helpful articles and essays may be traced through references in the text. Longer studies include the following:

A. St J. Adcock (ed.), *Robert Louis Stevenson: His Work and His Personality* (1924); H. B. Baildon, *Robert Louis Stevenson* (1901); Sir Graham Balfour, *The Life of Robert Louis Stevenson*, 2 vols (1901); Ian Bell, *Robert Louis Stevenson: Dreams of Exile* (1992); Adelaide A. Boodle, *Robert Louis Stevenson and his Sine Qua Non: Flashlights from Skerryvore* (New York, 1926); Jenni Calder, *RLS: A Life Study* (1980); Jenni Calder (ed.), *The Robert Louis Stevenson Companion* (Edinburgh, 1980); Elsie Noble Caldwell, *Last Witness for Robert Louis Stevenson* (Norman, Oklahoma, 1960); G. K. Chesterton, *Robert Louis Stevenson* (1927); Stephen Chalmers, *The Penny Piper of Saranac: An Episode in Stevenson's Life* (Boston, Mass., 1916); Sidney Colvin, *Memories and Notes of Persons and Places, 1852–1912* (1921); Sidney Colvin, *The Letters of Robert Louis Stevenson to his Family and Friends*, 2 vols (1900); David Daiches, *Robert Louis Stevenson and His World* (1973); De Lancey Ferguson and Marshall Waingrow (eds), *R.L.S.: Stevenson's Letters to Charles Baxter* (1956); Isobel Field and Lloyd Osbourne, *Memories of Vailima* (New York, 1902); Isobel Field, *This Life I've Loved* (1937); Barry Menikoff, *Robert Louis Stevenson and the Beach of Falesá* (Edinburgh, 1984); Marie Fraser, *In Stevenson's Samoa* (1895); J. C. Furnas, *Voyage to Windward: The Life of Robert Louis Stevenson* (New York, 1951); Sir Edmund Gosse, *Critical Kit-Kats* (1896); Charles J. Guthrie, *Robert Louis Stevenson: Some Personal Recollections* (Edinburgh, 1924); J. A. Hammerton, *Stevensoniana* (Edinburgh, 1910); J. R. Hammond, *A Robert Louis Stevenson Companion* (1984); James Pope Hennessy, *Robert Louis Stevenson* (1974); Anne Roller Issler, *Happier for His Presence: San Francisco and Robert Louis Stevenson* (Stanford, Cal., 1949); Arthur Johnstone, *Recollections of Robert Louis Stevenson in the Pacific* (1905); Alanna Knight, *Robert Louis Stevenson in the South Seas* (Edinburgh, 1986); Alanna Knight, *Robert Louis Stevenson Treasury* (1985); William G. Lockett, *Robert Louis Stevenson at Davos* (1934); Will H. Low, *A Chronicle of Friendships, 1873–1900* (New York, 1908); Sister Martha Mary MacGaw, *Stevenson in Hawaii* (Honolulu, 1950); Margaret MacKay, *The Violent Friend: The Story of Mrs Robert Louis Stevenson* (New York, 1968); Rosaline O. Masson, *I Can Remember Robert Louis Stevenson* (1922); Rosaline O. Masson, *Robert Louis Stevenson* (1914); Rosaline O. Masson, *The Life of Robert Louis Stevenson* (1923); Frank McLynn, *Robert Louis Stevenson, A Biography* (1993); H. J. Moors, *With Stevenson in Samoa* (Boston, Mass., 1910); Lloyd Osbourne, *An Intimate*

Portrait of Robert Louis Stevenson (New York, 1924); Nellie Vandegrift Sanchez, *The Life of Robert Louis Stevenson* (1920); Eve Blantyre Simpson, *Robert Louis Stevenson* (Edinburgh, 1906); Eve Blantyre Simpson, *Robert Louis Stevenson's Edinburgh Days* (1898); Eve Blantyre Simpson, *The Robert Louis Stevenson Originals* (1912); Janet Adam Smith (ed.), *Henry James and Robert Louis Stevenson* (1948); J. A. Steuart, *Robert Louis Stevenson, Man and Writer*, 2 vols (1924); Fanny and Robert Louis Stevenson, *Our Samoan Adventure* (New York, 1955); Margaret I. Balfour Stevenson, *Letters from Samoa: 1891–1895* (1906); Margaret I. Balfour Stevenson, *From Saranac to the Marquesas and Beyond* (1903); Margaret I. Balfour Stevenson, *Stevenson's Baby Book* (San Francisco, 1922); Roger G. Swearingen, *The Prose Writings of Robert Louis Stevenson: A Guide* (Hamden, Conn., 1980).

Index

Adams, Henry, xx, 157–63
Ah-Fu, 141, 143, 144
Aitu (Samoan spirits), xxv, 159, 161, 162, 163n, 172
Archer, William and Charles, 104–10, 124, 142

Baden-Powell, Sir H. W., 183, 184n
Baildon, H. B., 20–4
Baker, Shirley, xxvi
Bakers of Saranac, 124, 128
Balfour, 'Cramond' Lewis, 45–8
Balfour, Revd David (uncle), 3, 7
Balfour, Graham, xix, xxii, xxixn; Balfour lineage, 1; Louis's name, 10n; Louis's politics, 30, 163n; 61n, Belle's attachment to, 67, 115, 118n; penny-whistle, 133n, 177–8n, 184n; his Samoan name, 188, 189; Henley's disagreement with biography, 192–4, 197–202
Balfour, Jane (Whyte), xx, 7, 13, 14n, 29–30, 202
Balfour, Dr John, 38, 39
Balfour, Lewis, 1, 7, 14n, 39
Balfour, Marie and Dr Craig, 14–20
Ballantyne, R. M., 5n
Balzac, H., 34, 78, 80n
Barrie, J. M., xxi, 7, 10n, 122n, 192
Baxter, Charles (and *Letters*), xv, xxviii, 5n; Louis on his name, 10n; Louis gives up engineering, 31n; 34; business agent, 38n; 53, 76, 84n, 104n, 125, 147n; Louis on Samoan politics, 163; Louis on break with Henley, 196n
Bell, Ian, xiii, 88n, 115, 129

Benson, E. F., 69, 72n
Bisset, Revd Archibald, 28, 31n
Black, Margaret, xx, 38–42
Blaikie, W. B., 5n
Bloomer, Hiram, 105, 110
Boodle, Adelaide, xvi, xviii, xix, 100–4
Bookman, xxii, 85
Bough, Samuel, 56n
Box Hill, 85
Bridges, Robert, 66
Brookfield, Charles, 57n, 134n
Burlingame, E. L., 122, 127n, 158
Burns, Robert, 31n, 43, 190, 192

Calder, Jenni, xxixn, 76n, 96, 143n, 178, 192
Carlyle, Thomas, 49–50, 52n
Carruthers, R. H., 151n, 160
Chalmers, Revd James, 166, 169n
Chalmers, Stephen, 128–34
Chambers's Journal, 15, 32
Chesterton, G. K., xv, xxii
Clarke, Marcus, 155, 157n
Clarke, William Edward, 164–9, 204, 205, 206n
Colvin, Sidney, xvi, xvii, xviii, xx; Louis at Colvin's house, xxi, 65–6; xxiv, xxvi, 10n, 12; editor of Edinburgh edition and letters, 14n, 53–5, 55, 56, 58, 59; first meets Louis, 62–5; 107, 110n, 114n, 128n; eulogy, 202n
Cornhill Magazine, xx, 32, 45, 84n, 92n, 96, 138n, 174, 184n
Cunningham, Alison ('Cummy'), Louis's nurse, xvii, xxx, 1, 2, 3, 10–14, 27n

Damien, Father, 144
de Mattos, Katharine, 142n, 196n
de Quincey, Florence, 25, 27n
de Quincey, Thomas, 25, 92, 156

Dew Smith, A. G., 99
Dickens, Charles, 53, 79, 132
Disraeli, Benjamin, 49
Don Quixote, 62, 132

Eaton, Charlotte, xix, 134–8
Edinburgh University Magazine, 43, 44n
Edinburgh University, xii, xxx, 10, 24–5, 27, 28, 30, 38n, 39, 42n, 42–3, 49, 51n, 57, 104
Eliot, George, 109

Fairchild, Charles, 122
Fergusson, Robert, 31n
Ferrier, James Walter, xv, 43, 44n
Fowles, John, xiii, xxixn
Fraser, Sir Andrew, 50, 52n
Fraser, Marie, 174–8
Furnas, J. C., xiii, xxixn, 76n, 143n, 147, 163n, 184n

Gilder, Jeannette L., xviii, 118–22
Gordon, Alice, 85–8
Gosse, Edmund, xix, xxii, xxiv, 10n, 52–7, 68, 69, 75, 200
Guthrie, Lord (Charles), xix, xx, 10–14, 49–52

Hamerton, Philip, xxiii, xxixn
Hamley, Sir Edward, 98, 100n
Hammerton, J. A., xxii, 31n, 92, 118n
Hardy, Thomas, 142, 157n
Harrison, Birge, xviii, 76–80
Hawthorne, Nathaniel, xxi, 84n, 87n
Henderson's School, 4, 47, 48n
Henley, W. E., xxiv, xxx, 27n, 45n, 53, 57n, 68, 87n, 92, 107, 122; collaboration in playwriting, 24n, 108, 110n; business manager, 38n; poem to Louis, 48–9n, 197; editor, 84n; break with Louis, 142n; hostile criticism of Louis, 192–7
Hennessy, James Pope, 114n
Hume, David, 25, 29

Hyde, Revd Dr, 144

James, Henry, xvi, xvii, xx, xxiv, 68, 106, 110n; initially wary of Louis, 61n; Louis leaves England, 134; Louis on joys of travel, 138, 157n, 163n; tributes to Louis, vi, 207n
Japp, Alexander, xviii, xx, xxixn, 10n, 92–6, 149
Jenkin, Fleeming, xx, xxx, 26, 27, 32, 35, 37, 38n, 51n, 107, 108, 117n, 195
Jenkin, Anne (Mrs F.), 26, 27n, 32, 35, 37, 117n
Jerome, Jerome K., 178
Jersey, Lady, xxii
Jex-Blake, Sophia, 42

Kalakaua, 'King', 144, 147n
Kelland, Philip, 43, 44n
Knight, Alanna, xxi, xxiii, 57, 67

Lafaele (Raphael), 171, 173n
La Farge, John, 159, 161, 162, 163n
Lang, Andrew, xviii, xx, xxi, xxii, xxiii, 49, 57–61, 61n, 62, 142
Lawrence, D. H., xv
Lisle, George, 45–9
Low, Will, 68, 70, 72–6, 107, 110n, 121, 122, 127n, 134
Lowe, Charles, 42–5
Lysaght, Sidney, xxi

MacCallum, T. M., 143–7
Macmillan's Magazine, 27, 61n, 76n
Malieto, 'King', 152, 157n
Masson, Flora, xvi, xviii, xxixn, 32–8
Masson, Rosaline, xxii, 5n, 27n, 27–31, 31n, 39, 56n, 105, 115, 184n
Mataafa, 'King', 14n, 157n, 161, 162, 163n, 191n
McClure, S. S., 122–8
McLynn, Frank, 85, 88n, 128n, 129, 147, 184n

Menikoff, Barry, xxv, xxix*n*
Meredith, George, xvi, 85–7, 87*n*, 88*n*, 109, 113, 142
Moore, George, 155, 157*n*
Moors, H. J., xviii, xxvi, 147–51, 160, 170, 178*n*

Neider, Charles, 128, 169
Newell, Revd James, 184*n*

Odyssey, xiv
Oliphant, Mrs (Margaret), 109, 110*n*
O'Meara, Frank, 67, 68, 70, 71, 72*n*
Osbourne, Isobel (Belle), xix, xxii, xxv, 81, 140, 142, 152, 157, 170, 174, 180; amanuensis, xxvii, 185–91; studies art, 67–72, 91*n*
Osbourne, Lloyd, xviii, xxii, xxv, xxx, xxxi, 67, 68, 70, 71, 72, 80*n*, 121, 127*n*, 132, 134, 138, 140, 143, 146, 148, 165, 172, 180, 189, 191*n*; first meets Louis, 81–4; printing press productions, 94–5; war games, 100*n*; writing of *Jekyll and Hyde*, 115–18; collaborations with Louis, 127*n*, 141, 145, 154, 184*n*; at Louis's death, 203, 205, 206
Osbourne, Katharine, xxii
Osbourne, Samuel, xxiv, 81, 92
Otis, A. H. Captain, xx, xxiii, 138

Pall Mall Gazette, 100*n*, 109, 191*n*, 192
Palmer, W. L., 70, 72*n*
Payn, James, xvi, xxii
Pears, Sir Edmund Radcliffe, 138–43
Pinero, Sir Arthur Wing, 105, 117*n*
Poe, Edgar Allan, 59, 79, 165

Reade, Charles, 188, 191*n*
Reid, Denny, 143–7
Reid, Thomas Mayne, 5*n*

Robinson, Theodore, 76, 77
Roch, Valentine, 100, 104*n*, 138
Rodin, Auguste, 107
Ruedi, Karl, 96, 122

Said, Edward, xiv, xxix*n*
Saint-Gaudens, Augustus, 72, 118, 119, 123, 127*n*, 134
Samoan politics, xxv, xxvi, xxxi, 142*n*, 147, 152–3, 157*n*, 163*n*, 191*n*
Samoan social life, xxv–xxvi, 160, 175, 178, 180–1
Sanchez, Nellie, xxii, 117*n*, 128*n*, 207*n*
Sargent, John Singer, xix, 107, 110*n*
Scott, Dr Thomas Bodley, 115
Scott, Sir Walter, 20*n*, 50, 51, 78, 79, 184*n*
Scribner, Charles, 125, 154
Scribner's Magazine, 20*n*, 45, 117*n*, 118*n*, 122, 127*n*, 138, 141, 142*n*, 196*n*
Seed, William, xii, xiii, xvi, xxix*n*
Sellar, E. M., 23–7
Sellar, William Young, 24–5
Sewall, Harold, 161, 163*n*
Sharp, William, 111–14
Shelley, Lady and Sir Percy, xix, 106, 110*n*, 114, 114*n*, 186
Simpson, Eve Blantyre, xix, xx, xxii, 6–10, 38*n*, 49, 114
Simpson, Sir Walter, xv, xxx, 6, 14*n*, 33, 38*n*, 45*n*, 53, 68, 70, 71, 201
Simpson, Sir James Young, 6
Sitwell, Mrs Frances (*later* Colvin), xii, xvii, 37*n*, 64, 66, 67*n*
Stephen, Leslie, xx, 55, 61*n*, 84*n*, 192, 193
Stevenson, Alan, 6, 10*n*, 25, 26, 27*n*, 110*n*
Stevenson, David, 3, 5*n*
Stevenson, Fanny (Frances Vandegrift Osbourne), wife of RLS: appearance, personality and manner, xxiv, 53, 67*n*, 70, 80, 88*n*, 96,

101, 102, 104n, 106, 110n, 114n, 126–7, 128, 139–40, 146, 147, 151n, 162, 165, 169, 177, 182–4, 191n, 192; loyalty and courage, xxiv–xxv, 94, 96n, 128n, 147n, 169–70, 183–4; unhappy first marriage, xxiv, xxx, 81, 91n; art training, 67, 91–2; meets Louis, 69, 80, 82; nurses Louis, 100n, 187, 203; own artistic yearnings, xxiv, 171, 173; gardening, xxiv, xxvii, 158, 169–71, 173n; writings, 142–3n, 196n; 'Critic on the Hearth', 115–16, 117–18n, 124; ill health and death, 16, 162, 163n, 207n

Stevenson, Margaret Isabella, mother of RLS: appearance, personality and manner, 7, 8, 11, 23, 26, 33–5, 140, 143n; writings, xxii; faith, xxvi, 172, 166, 204; devotion to husband, xvii, 25; closeness to Louis, xv, 1–4, 6, 13, 16, 29, 31n, 36, 42, 85, 141, 151n; journeys to America, xxx, 72, 122, 134, 202; in the South Seas, xxxi, 138, 172, 175, 202–7

Stevenson, R. A. M. (Bob), youthful escapades with Louis, xv, 38n, 41–2; childhood games, 3, 5n, 10n; family, 27n, 57n; artist, 59, 67, 68, 70, 71, 72, 73, 75, 77, 80n, 81, 82; witty conversation, 77–8, 122, 195

Stevenson, Robert, xxixn, 7

STEVENSON, ROBERT LOUIS
Life (*see also under 'Letters'*):
summary of events in, xxx–xxxi
ancestry, xxixn, 1, 7, 8, 10n
birth, early childhood, 1–5, 5n, 7, 10–24
nicknames, 1–4, 9, 11, 14n, 16 , 184n; 'Velvet Coat', xv, 48n;

'Tusitala', xxiii, 6, 9, 11, 12, 53, 175, 176, 177, 181, 184n, 203, 205
schooling, 4–7, 21–4
loss of faith, xii, xv, 67n
university, 28, 30, 39–40, 43–4, 47, 49–51; Speculative Society, xix, 10, 50, 51, 52n
homes, Edinburgh: xv, xvi, no. 8 Howard Place, xxx, 2, 5n, 25; Inverleith Terrace, 4, 5n; no. 17 Heriot Row, xii, xxvi, 4, 5n, 17, 18, 23, 26, 33, 39, 184n; Princes Street, xvi, xx, 41–2; Colinton, 1, 4, 7, 8, 14, 14n; North Berwick coast, xviii, 15, 19, 20n; 'Skerryvore', Bournemouth, xvi, xxiv, xxv, xxvi, xxx, 27n, 59, 88, 100–7, 133n, 184n; 'Vailima', Apia, Samoa, xxii, xxiv, xxv, xxvi, xxvii, xxx, 67, 81, 149–50, 152, 157, 158–63, 163n, 165, 167, 169–73, 174–7, 178–91, 197, 198, 199, 202–6
travels: Barbizon, xii, 74, 75, 124, 134; Davos, xxiii, xxv, xxx, 59, 93–4, 95, 95n, 96–9, 99–100n, 108; Fontainebleau, 78; Gilbert Islands, xxx, xxxi; Grez-sur-Loing, xii, xxx, 67–72, 74, 75, 76–80, 81, 83, 84n, 91–2n, 126–7; Hawaii (Honolulu), xvi, xx, xxiv, xxv, xxx, 134, 138–42, 143, 144, 157n, 173n, 178, 184n; Hyères, France, xxiii, xxiv, xxv, xxx, 104n, 196; Manasquan, N. J., xix; Monterey, xviii, xxx, 88, 91n, 173n; Navigators' Islands (Samoa), xiii; New York, xxiii, 118; Paris, 70–1, 72, 74, 200–1; Polynesia, 138; Samoa, xvi, xvii, xviii, xxi, xxx, 16, 59, 90, 133, 137, 138n, 143, 146, 147–51, 158–91; San Francisco, xvi, xxiii, 6, 67, 81,

88, 91, 128n, 134, 206; Saranac Lake, 122, 128–33; Silverado, xxiv, xxx, 92n, 93, 94, 193; Sydney, xxxi, 149, 152–7, 163n, 183, 185; Tahiti, xiv, 138
health, xiv, xvii, xviii, xxi, xxiii, 2–5, 58, 59, 63, 74, 76, 90, 91n, 95n, 96–8, 100n, 104n, 105–6, 110n, 119, 123, 133, 133n, 138, 148, 149, 152, 158, 162, 186–7, 200
law study, xv, 51
engineering, 30, 31n, 53–4, 56n
arrival in California, 88
Savile Club, xxx, 54–5, 56n, 59, 62, 73
financial security, 122, 125, 127n
first meets Fanny, 69, 70, 80, 82
success with *Treasure Island*, 92, 96n
final years, xxv–vi, 174–91, 202–6
arrival in Samoa, 146; purchase of Vailima, 158
'Road of the Loving Heart', 12, 13, 14n, 189, 191n, 205
Mount Vaea, xxv, 147, 164, 176, 203, 205, 206, 207n
death, xxvii, xxxi, 57, 202–7
Appearance, character, habits:
affectation, xix, 26, 29, 65, 97, 195
art of conversation, xx, 33, 40, 44, 54, 57n, 77, 86, 88, 101, 119, 150, 159, 160–1, 199
clothing, xx, xxi, 29, 34, 41–2, 46, 56, 57n, 58, 64–5, 74, 81, 83, 84, 93, 100, 101, 106, 111–12, 113, 119, 121, 127n, 133, 150, 151, 151n, 162, 165, 174, 182, 187, 195, 198–9
constitution and energy, ix, xviii, xxiii, 54–5, 62–3, 66, 74, 93, 158–9, 198–9
eyes, xviii, 19, 25, 31n, 34, 73, 93, 112, 120, 121, 123, 149

father–son relations, xv, xviii, 8–9, 24n, 33–4, 38n, 48n, 67n, 91n, 127n, 134n
grace and manners, xix, 26, 43, 97, 101, 121, 135, 139, 144, 150, 194
hair, xviii, 25, 53, 63, 65, 74, 81, 88, 93, 106, 112, 133, 158
height, weight, xviii, 19, 22, 31n, 34, 53, 58, 62, 66n, 90, 92, 111, 159, 182, 198
optimism and fortitude, 24n, 148–9, 182
personality, 16, 23, 24n, 27–30, 39–41, 44, 60, 75, 79, 89, 113–14, 119, 126, 193–6, 199–201, 202n
portraits, sculpture, xix, 72, 107, 118, 119, 120, 123, 127n
smoking, xix, xxi, 93, 105, 108, 119, 121, 122n, 127n, 130, 135, 139, 150, 165, 182
temper, xix, 116, 148, 200–1
voice, 113, 132, 134n, 135, 199
Interests, opinions, etc.:
acting, reading aloud, xx, 3, 5n, 17, 20n, 35–7, 38n, 95, 108, 117n, 132, 140, 150
art collection, 106–7
canoeing, sailing, 4–6, 68, 201n
religion, 25, 31n, 48, 48n, 67n, 89, 126, 166–8, 193–4, 198, 202, 204
library at Vailima, 176, 190
music, 108, 130, 133n, 141–2, 176
politics, 30, 49–50, 52n, 152–3, 157n, 163
ships and sea, 6; 'Casco', xiv, xvi, xx, xxiv, xxx, 92n, 104n, 126, 134, 138, 141, 147n, 196; 'The Equator', xxx, 138, 143–7; 'The Janet Nicholl' xxxi, 151n, 152, 158; 'Ludgate Hill', xvi, 72, 122; 'Pharos', 18, 20n
skating, 32, 37n, 124
war games, 98, 100n, 120

Literary concerns:
active vocabulary, 102–4, 186–8
'crawlers', 59
dreams, 115, 117*n*, 137–8
heroes and heroines, 87
moral concerns, 154–5, 157*n*, 186, 193–4
plays, 23, 108, 110*n*
printing-press productions, 94–5, 108
realism and romance, xxii–iii, 126, 132, 136, 155
study and research, 78–9, 86, 87*n*
work methods, 117, 175–6, 183, 185, 190, 191*n*, 206
Works mentioned in the text:
Novels:
Black Arrow, The, 123, 124
Catriona, xxxi, 1, 87, 88*n*, 169*n*
Dr Jekyll and Mr Hyde, xvii, xxii, xxx, 24*n*, 59, 66*n*, 90, 110*n*, 112, 115–18, 123, 127*n*, 136, 137, 140, 143, 156, 165
Ebb-Tide, The, xxxi, 81, 183, 184*n*, 188
Kidnapped, xxx, 1, 56*n*, 110*n*, 123, 124, 127*n*, 154
Master of Ballantrae, The, xvii, xxx, 127*n*, 129, 141, 156, 185
Prince Otto, 110*n*
St Ives, 48*n*, 124, 185–91
Treasure Island, xvi, xxx, 5*n*, 44, 86, 90, 91, 92, 94, 95*n*, 96*n*, 96, 107, 115–17, 123, 127*n*, 153, 178, 192
Weir of Hermiston, xiv, xxvi–xxvii, xxxi, 8, 57, 80, 189–90, 191*n*
Wrecker, The, 59–60, 72, 81, 88, 122, 138, 143*n*, 143, 145, 153
Wrong Box, The, xxx, 81, 124, 127*n*, 141
Short-story collections
Island Nights' Entertainments, xxxi
Merry Men and Other Tales, 84*n*, 110*n*, 191*n*
More New Arabian Nights: The Dynamiter, 110*n*, 142*n*
New Arabian Nights, 77, 191*n*
Short stories:
'Beach of Falesá, The', 143, 163*n*
'Body-Snatcher, The', 95*n*
'Bottle Imp, The', 167, 169*n*
'Convicts, The', 24*n*
'Count's Secret, The', 24*n*
'Lodging for the Night, A', xxx
'Markheim', 186, 187*n*
'Merry Men, The', 56*n*, 95*n*, 138, 186
'Misadventures of John Nicholson, The', 23, 24*n*
'Providence and the Guitar', 71, 72*n*, 191*n*
'Suicide Club, The', 77, 84*n*
'Thrawn Janet', 59, 95*n*, 105
'Will o' the Mill', 83, 84*n*, 137, 138*n*
Plays:
Beau Austin, 108
Deacon Brodie, xxx, 23, 24*n*, 108
Poems:
Child's Garden of Verses, A, xvii, xxx, 2, 14*n*, 20*n*, 47, 89, 105, 110, 110*n*
Songs of Travel, xiv, 80
Underwoods, xv, 20*n*, 96, 106, 108, 109, 110*n*, 191
Travel:
Across the Plains, xxii, xxx, 15, 20*n*, 56*n*, 80*n*, 117*n*, 118*n*, 210*n*
Amateur Emigrant, The, xv, 91
Inland Voyage, An, xxii, xxx, 38*n*, 55, 84*n*, 125, 201*n*
Silverado Squatters, The, 88, 91*n*, 93, 96
South Seas, The: A Record of Three Cruises (In the South Seas), xxii, 126, 128*n*, 138
Travels with a Donkey in the Cévennes, xxii, xxx, 125
Biography:
Records of a Family of Engineers, 10*n*
Letters:
Letters of Robert Louis Stevenson

to His Family and Friends, ed. Sidney Colvin, 2 vols (1900), 14*n*, 24*n*, 38*n*, 42*n*, 45*n*, 62, 66*n*, 110*n*, 122, 134, 138, 149, 158, 169, 202*n*
Vailima Letters, xxii, xxvi, 77, 169
Collections of essays:
Familiar Studies of Men and Books, 10*n*, 51
Memories and Portraits, 5*n*, 6, 10*n*, 15, 20*n*, 24*n*, 44*n*, 45, 49*n*, 52*n*, 52, 56*n*, 57*n*, 87*n*
Virginibus Puerisque, 5*n*, 52*n*, 61*n*, 76*n*, 96, 192
Essays and belles-lettres:
'Beggars', 129
'Books which have Influenced Me', 134*n*
'Chapter on Dreams, A', 117*n*, 129, 138*n*
'Child's Play', 5*n*
'College Magazine, A', 52*n*, 87*n*
'Education of an Engineer, The', 56*n*
'Fontainebleau', 80*n*
'Footnote to History, A', xxxi, 157
'Foreigner at Home, The', 49*n*
'Gentlemen', 129
'Henry David Thoreau', 92
'Lantern Bearers, The', 15, 129
'Memoirs of an Islet', 45, 56*n*
'Ordered South', 58, 61*n*, 65, 75, 76*n*
'Pentland Rising, The', 61*n*
'Roads', xxx, 61*n*
'Some College Memories', 24*n*, 52*n*
'Talk and Talkers', 38*n*, 52, 57*n*, 100*n*, 192
'Virginibus Puerisque', 86
Miscellaneous:
'Blue Scalper, The', 95
'Hair Trunk, The', *or* 'The Ideal Commonwealth', xiii
'Inn of Aberhuern, The', 41–2, 42*n*
'Juvenilia', 129
'Moral Emblems', 95

'New Form of Intermittent Light for Lighthouses, A', 30
'Outlaws of Tunstall Forest, The', 126
'Requiem', xiv, 207*n*
'Scott's Voyage in the Lighthouse Yacht', 20*n*
'Travelling Companion, The', 118*n*
Stevenson, Thomas (father of RLS):
engineer, xii, xiv, xxix*n*, 5*n*, 27, 31*n*; faith, xv, 13, 67*n*; relations with Louis, xv, xviii, 1, 8–10, 30, 31*n*, 33–4, 127*n*; generosity towards Louis and Fanny, 61, 100, 122; *Treasure Island*, 95–6*n*
Stoddard, Charles Warren, xviii, 88–92
Strong, Austin, 67, 172, 173*n*, 188, 189
Swearingen, Roger, 61*n*, 118*n*, 127*n*
Sydney Press, 152–7, 162
Symonds, John Addington, 61*n*, 66*n*, 93, 96, 100*n*

Taylor, Sir Henry and Una (daughter), 107, 110*n*, 114*n*
Tennyson, Alfred Lord, xiii
Thompson, D'Arcy Wentworth (Class Club), 30, 31*n*
Thompson, Robert (day school), 20, 21, 23*n*
Thoreau, Henry David, 89, 92, 105
Triggs, William Henry, 178–81
Trollope, Anthony, 110*n*, 117, 118*n*
Trudeau, Dr Edward, 122*n*, 128–32, 133*n*

Vallings, Harold, xxiii, 96–100
van Rensselaer, M. G., xix, 118–22

Whitman, Walt, xxi
Williams, Virgil and Dora, 91, 92
Wordsworth, William, xxi

Zola, Emile, 155, 157*n*

The manufacturer's authorised representative in the EU is Springer Nature Customer Service Centre GmbH, Europaplatz 3, 69115 Heidelberg, Germany. If you have any concerns regarding our products, please contact ProductSafety@springernature.com

Printed and bound by CPI Group (UK) Ltd, Croydon, CR0 4YY
23/03/2026
02076673-0012